MR. MASTERS

T L SWAN

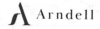 Arndell

Arndell

Keeperton Australia acknowledges that Aboriginal and Torres Strait Islander people are the Traditional Custodians and the first storytellers on the lands of which we live and work. We pay our respects to Elders past, present and emerging. We recognise their continuous connection to Country, water, skies and communities and honour more than 60,000 years of storytelling, culture and art.

Originally self published in 2018 by T L Swan
Copyright © 2024 by T L Swan ®

First Published by Arndell, an imprint of Keeperton
1527 New Hampshire Ave. NW
Washington, D.C. 20036

Paperback ISBN: 9781923232006

Library of Congress Control Number: 2024936530

Printed in the United States of America

Sydney | Washington D.C. | London
www.keeperton.com

ALSO BY T L SWAN

Standalone Books

The Bonus

Our Way

Play Along

Kingston Lane Series

My Temptation

The Miles High Club Series

The Stopover

The Takeover

The Casanova

The Do-over

Miles Ever After

The Mr. Series

Mr. Masters

Mr. Spencer

Mr. Garcia

Mr. Prescott (Coming 2025)

The Italian Series

The Italian

Ferrara

Valentino (To be released)

SUGGESTED READING ORDER

The Mr. Series books can all be read as standalone books.
However, for the best reading experience, we suggest the following
reading order:

Mr. Masters
Mr. Spencer
Mr. Garcia
Mr. Prescott (Coming 2025)

ACKNOWLEDGMENTS

There are not enough words to express my
gratitude for this life that I get to live.
To be able to write books for a living is a dream come true.
But not just any books, I get to write exactly
what I want to, the stories that I love.

To my wonderful team,
Kellie, Christine, Alina, Keeley and Abbey.
Thank you for everything that you do for me,
you are so talented and so appreciated.
You keep me sane.

To my fabulous beta readers, you make me so much better. Vicki,
Am, Rachel, Nicole, Lisa K, Lisa D and Nadia.

To my home girls in the Swan Squad, I feel like I can do anything
with you girls in my corner.
Thanks for making me laugh every day.

My beautiful Mum who reads everything I write and gives me
never-ending support. I love you Mum, thank you xo

My beloved husband and three beautiful kids, thanks for putting
up with my workaholic ways.

And to you, the best most supportive reader family
in the entire world.

Thank you for everything, you have changed my life.

All my love,
Tee xoxo

GRATITUDE

The quality of being thankful; readiness to show appreciation for, and to return kindness.

DEDICATION

I would like to dedicate this book to the alphabet.
For those twenty-six letters have changed my life.

Within those twenty-six letters,
I found myself and live my dream.

Next time you say the alphabet remember its power.

I do every day.

PROLOGUE

Julian

ALINA MASTERS
1984 – 2013
Wife and beloved mother.
In God's hands we trust.

Grief. The Grim Reaper of life.

Stealer of joy, hope and purpose.

Some days are bearable. Other days I can hardly breathe, and I suffocate in a world of regret where good reason has no sense.

I never know when those days will hit, only that when I wake, my chest feels constricted and I need to run. I need to be anywhere but here, dealing with this life.

My life.

Our life.

Until *you* left.

The sound of a distant lawnmower brings me back to the present, and I glance over at the cemetery's caretaker. He's concentrating as he weaves between the tombstones, careful not to clip or damage one as he passes. It's dusk, and the mist is rolling in for the night.

I come here often to think, to try and feel.

I can't talk to anyone. I can't express my true feelings. I want to know why.

Why did you do this to us?

I clench my jaw as I stare at my late wife's tombstone. We could have had it all...but we didn't.

I lean down and brush the dust away from her name and rearrange the pink lilies that I have just placed in the vase. I touch her face on the small oval photo. She stares back at me, void of emotion.

Stepping back, I drop my hands in the pockets of my black overcoat.

I could stand here and stare at this headstone all day—sometimes I do—but I turn and walk to the car without looking back.

My Porsche.

Sure, I have money and two kids that love me. I'm at the top of my professional field, working as a judge. I have all the tools *to be* happy, but I'm not.

I'm barely surviving, holding on by a thread. Playing the façade to the world.

Dying inside.

Half an hour later, I arrive at Madison's—my therapist.

I always leave here relaxed.

I don't have to talk, I don't have to think, I don't have to feel. I walk through the front doors on autopilot.

"Good afternoon, Mr. Smith." Hayley the receptionist smiles. "Your room is waiting, sir."

"Thank you." I frown, feeling like I need something more today. Something to take this edginess off.

A distraction.

"I'll have someone extra today, Hayley."

"Of course, sir. Who would you like?"

I frown and take a moment to get it right. "Hmm. Hannah."

"So, Hannah and Belinda?"

"Yes."

"No problem, sir. Make yourself comfortable and they will be right up."

I take the lift to the exclusive penthouse. Once there, I make myself a scotch and stare out the smoked glass window overlooking London.

I hear the door click behind me and I turn towards the sound. Hannah and Belinda stand before me, smiling.

Belinda has long blonde hair, while Hannah is a brunette.

There's no denying they're both young and beautiful. "Hello, Mr. Smith," they say in unison

I sip my scotch as my eyes drink them in. "Where would you like us, sir?"

I unbuckle my belt. "On your knees."

1

Brielle

CUSTOMS IS RIDICULOUSLY SLOW, and a man has been pulled into the office up ahead. It all looks very suspicious from my position at the back of the line. "What do you think he did?" I whisper as I crane my neck to spy on the commotion up ahead.

"I don't know, something stupid, probably," Emerson replies. We shuffle towards the desk as the line moves a little quicker.

We've just arrived in London to begin our yearlong working holiday. I'm going to work for a judge as a nanny, while Emerson, my best friend, is working for an art auctioneer. I'm terrified, yet excited.

"I wish we had come a week earlier so we could have spent some time together," Emerson says.

"Yeah, I know, but she needed me to start this week because she's going away next week. I need to learn the kids' routine."

"Who leaves their kids alone for three days with a complete stranger?" Em frowns in disgust.

I shrug. "My new boss, apparently."

"Well, at least I can come and stay with you next week. That's a bonus."

My position is residential, so my accommodation is secure. However, poor Emerson will be living with two strangers. She's freaking out over it.

"Yeah, but I'm sneaking you in," I say. "I don't want it to look like we're partying or anything."

I look around the airport. It's busy, bustling, and I already feel so alive. Emerson and I are more than just young travellers.

Emerson is trying to find her purpose and I'm running from a destructive past, one that involves me being in love with an adultering prick.

I loved him. He just didn't love me. Not enough, anyway.

If he had, he would have kept it in his pants, and I wouldn't be at Heathrow Airport feeling like I'm about to throw up.

I look down at myself and smooth the wrinkles from my dress. "She's picking me up. Do I look okay?"

Emerson looks me up and down, smiling broadly. "You look exactly how a twenty-five-year-old nanny from Australia should."

I bite my bottom lip to stop myself from smiling stupidly. That was a good answer.

"So, what's your boss's name?" she asks.

I rustle around in my bag for my phone and scroll through the emails until I get to the one from the nanny agency. "Mrs. Julian Masters."

Emerson nods. "And what's her story again? I know you've told me before, but I've forgotten."

"She's a Supreme Court judge, widowed five years ago."

"What happened to the husband?"

"I don't know, but apparently she's quite wealthy." I shrug. "Two kids, well-behaved."

"Sounds good."

"I hope so. I hope they like me."

"They will." We move forward in the line. "We are definitely going out on the weekend, though, yes?"

"Yes." I nod. "What are you going to do until then?"

Emerson shrugs. "Look around. I start work on Monday and

6

it's Thursday today." She frowns as she watches me. "Are you sure you can go out on the weekends?"

"Yes," I snap, exasperated. "I told you a thousand times, we're going out on Saturday night."

Emerson nods nervously. I think she may be more nervous than I am, but at least I'm acting brave. "Did you get your phone sorted?" I ask.

"No, not yet. I'll find a phone shop tomorrow so I can call you."

"Okay."

We are called to the front of the line, and finally, half an hour later, we walk into the arrival lounge of Heathrow International Airport.

"Do you see our names?" Emerson whispers as we both look around.

"No."

"Shit, no one is here to pick us up. Typical." She begins to panic.

"Relax, they will be here," I mutter.

"What do we do if no one turns up?"

I raise my eyebrow as I consider the possibility. "Well, I don't know about you, but I'm going to lose my shit."

Emerson looks over my shoulder. "Oh, look, there's your name. She must have sent a driver."

I turn to see a tall, broad man in a navy suit holding a sign with the name Brielle Johnston on it. I force a smile and wave meekly as I feel my anxiety rise like a tidal wave in my stomach.

He walks over and smiles at me. "Brielle?"

His voice is deep and commanding. "Yes, that's me," I breathe.

He holds out his hand to shake mine. "Julian Masters."

What?

My eyes widen.

A man?

He raises his eyebrows.

"Um, so, I'm... I'm Brielle," I stammer as I push my hand out.

"And this is my friend, Emerson, who I'm travelling with." He takes my hand in his and my heart races.

A trace of a smile crosses his face before he covers it. "Nice to meet you." He turns to Emerson and shakes her hand. "How do you do?"

My eyes flash to Emerson, who is clearly loving this shit. She grins brightly. "Hello."

"I thought you were a woman," I whisper.

His brows furrow. "Last time I checked, I was all man." His eyes hold mine.

Why did I just say that out loud? Oh my God, stop talking.

This is so awkward.

I want to go home. This is a bad idea.

"I'll wait over here." He gestures to the corner before marching off in that direction. My horrified eyes meet Emerson's, and she giggles, so I punch her hard in the arm.

"Oh my fuck, he's a fucking man," I whisper angrily.

"I can see that." She smirks, her eyes fixed on him.

"Excuse me, Mr. Masters?" I call after him.

He turns. "Yes."

We both wither under his glare. "We...we are just going to use the bathroom," I stammer nervously.

With one curt nod, he gestures to the right. We look up and see the sign. I grab Emerson by the arm and drag her into the bathroom. "I'm not working with a stuffy old man!" I shriek as we burst through the door.

"It will be okay. How did this happen?"

I take out my phone and scroll through the emails quickly. I knew it. "It says woman. I knew it said woman."

"He's not that old," she calls out from her cubicle. "I would prefer to work for a man than a woman, to be honest."

"You know what, Emerson? This is a shit idea. How the hell did I let you talk me into this?"

She smiles as she exits the cubicle and washes her hands. "It doesn't matter. You'll hardly see him anyway, and you're not

8

working weekends when he's home." She's clearly trying to calm me. "Stop with the carry on."

Stop the carry on.

Steam feels like it's shooting from my ears. "I'm going to kill you. I'm going to fucking kill you."

Emerson bites her lip to stifle her smile. "Listen, just stay with him until we find you something else. I will get my phone sorted tomorrow and we can start looking elsewhere for another job," she reassures me. "At least someone picked you up. Nobody cares about me at all."

I put my head into my hands as I try to calm my breathing. "This is a disaster, Em," I whisper. Suddenly, every fear I had about travelling is coming true. I feel completely out of my comfort zone.

"It's going to be one week...tops."

My scared eyes lift to hold hers, and I nod. "Okay?" She smiles as she pulls me into a hug.

"Okay." I glance back in the mirror, fix my hair, and straighten my dress. I'm completely rattled.

We walk back out and take our place next to Mr. Masters. He's in his late thirties, immaculately dressed, and kind of attractive. His hair is dark with a sprinkle of grey.

"Did you have a good flight?" he asks as he looks down at me.

"Yes, thanks," I push out. Oh, that sounded so forced. "Thank you for picking us up," I add meekly.

He nods with no fuss.

Emerson smiles at the floor as she tries to hide her smile. That bitch is loving this shit.

"Emerson?" a male voice calls. We all turn to see a blond man, and Emerson's face falls. Ha! Now it's my turn to laugh.

"Hello, I'm Mark." He kisses her on the cheek and then turns to me. "You must be Brielle?"

"Yes." I smile then turn to Mr. Masters. "And this is..." I pause because I don't know how to introduce him.

"Julian Masters," he finishes for me, adding in a strong handshake.

Emerson and I fake smile at each other. Oh dear God, help me.

Emerson stands and talks with Mark and Mr. Masters, while I stand in uncomfortable silence.

"The car is this way." He gestures to the right.

I nod nervously. Oh God, don't leave me with him. This is terrifying.

"Nice to meet you, Emerson and Mark." He shakes their hands.

"Likewise. Please look after my friend," Emerson whispers as her eyes flicker to mine.

Mr. Masters nods, smiles, and then pulls my luggage behind him as he walks to the car. Emerson pulls me into an embrace. "This is shit," I whisper into her hair.

"It will be fine. He's probably really nice."

"He doesn't look nice," I whisper.

"Yeah, I agree. He looks like a tool," Mark adds as he watches him disappear through the crowd.

Emerson throws her new friend a dirty look, and I smirk. I think her friend is more annoying than mine, but anyway... "Mark, look after my friend, please?"

He beats his chest like a gorilla. "Oh, I intend to."

Emerson's eyes meet mine. She subtly shakes her head and I bite my bottom lip to hide my smile. This guy is a dick. We both look over to see Mr. Masters looking back impatiently. "I better go," I whisper.

"You have my apartment details if you need me?"

"I'll probably turn up in an hour. Tell your roommates I'm coming in case I need a key."

She laughs and waves me off, and I go to Mr. Masters. He sees me coming and then starts to walk again.

God, can he not even wait for me? So rude.

He walks out of the building into the VIP parking section. I follow him in complete silence.

Any notion that I was going to become friends with my new boss has been thrown out the window. I think he hates me already.

Just wait until he finds out that I lied on my resume and I have no fucking idea what I'm doing. Nerves flutter in my stomach at the thought.

We get to a large, swanky, black SUV, and he clicks it open to put my suitcase in the trunk. He opens the back door for me to get in. "Thank you." I smile awkwardly as I slide into the seat. He wants me to sit in the back when the front seat is empty.

This man is odd.

He slides into the front seat and eventually pulls out into the traffic. All I can do is clutch my handbag in my lap.

Should I say something? Try and make conversation? What will I say?

"Do you live far from here?" I ask.

"Twenty minutes," he replies, his tone clipped.

Oh...is that it? Okay, shut up now. He doesn't want a conversation. For ten long minutes, we sit in silence.

"You can drive this car when you have the children, or we have a small minivan. The choice is yours."

"Oh, okay." I pause for a moment. "Is this your car?"

"No." He turns onto a street and into a driveway with huge sand- stone gates. "I drive a Porsche," he replies casually.

"Oh."

The driveway goes on and on and on. I look around at the perfectly kept grounds and rolling green hills. With every metre we pass, I feel my heart beat just that bit faster.

As if it isn't bad enough that I can't do the whole nanny thing... I really can't do the rich thing. I have no idea what to do with polite company. I don't even know what fork to use at dinner. I've gotten myself into a right mess here.

The house comes into focus and the blood drains from my face. It's not a house, not even close. It's a mansion, white and sandstone with a castle kind of feel to it, with six garages to the left.

He pulls into the large circular driveway, stopping under the awning.

"Your house is beautiful," I whisper.

He nods as his eyes stay fixed out front. "We are fortunate."

He gets out of the car and opens my door for me. I climb out as I grip my handbag with white-knuckle force. My eyes rise to the luxurious building in front of me.

This is an insane amount of money.

He retrieves my suitcase and wheels it around to the side of the building. "Your entrance is around to the side," he says. I follow him up a path until we get to a door, which he opens and lets me walk through. There is a foyer and a living area in front of me.

"The kitchen is this way." He points to the kitchen. "And your bedroom is in the back left corner."

I nod and walk past him, into the apartment.

He stands at the door but doesn't come in. "The bathroom is to the right," he continues.

Why isn't he coming in here? "Okay, thanks," I reply.

"Order any groceries you want on the family shopping order and..." He pauses, as if collecting his thoughts. "If there is anything else you need, please talk to me first."

I frown. "First?"

He shrugs. "I don't want to be told about a problem for the first time when reading a resignation letter."

"Oh." Did that happen before? "Of course," I mutter.

"If you would like to come and meet the children..." He gestures to a hallway.

"Yes, please." Oh God, here we go. I follow him out into a corridor with glass walls that looks out onto the main house, which is about four metres away. A garden sits between the two buildings, creating an atrium, and I smile as I look up in wonder. There is a large window in the main house that looks into the kitchen. I can see beyond that into the living area from the corridor, where a young girl and small boy are watching television together. We continue to the end of the glass corridor where there is a staircase with six steps leading up to the main house.

I blow out a breath, and I follow Mr. Masters up the stairs. "Children, come and meet your new nanny."

The little boy jumps down and rushes over to me, clearly excited, while the girl just looks up and rolls her eyes. I smile to myself, remembering what it's like to be a typical teenager.

"Hello, I'm Samuel." The little boy smiles as he wraps his arms around my legs. He has dark hair, is wearing glasses, and he's so damn cute.

"Hello, Samuel." I smile.

"This is Willow," he introduces.

I smile at the teenage girl. "Hello." She folds her arms across her chest defiantly.

"Hi," she grumbles.

Mr. Masters holds her gaze for a moment, saying so much with just one look.

Willow eventually holds her hand out for me to shake. "I'm Willow."

I smile as my eyes flash up to Mr. Masters. He can keep her under control with just a simple glare.

Samuel runs back to the lounge, grabs something, and then comes straight back.

I see a flash. Click, click. What the hell?

He has a small instant Polaroid camera. He watches my face appear on the piece of paper in front of him before he looks back up at me. "You're pretty." He smiles. "I'm putting this on the fridge." He carefully pins it to the fridge with a magnet.

Mr. Masters seems to become flustered for some reason. "Bedtime for you two," he instructs, and they both complain. He turns his attention back to me. "Your kitchen is stocked with groceries, and I'm sure you're tired."

I fake a smile. Oh, I'm being dismissed. "Yes, of course." I go to walk back down to my apartment, and then turn back to him. "What time do I start tomorrow?"

His eyes hold mine. "When you hear Samuel wake up."

"Yes, of course." My eyes search his as I wait for him to say some- thing else, but it doesn't come. "Good night, then." I smile awkwardly.

"Good night."

"Bye, Brielle." Samuel smiles and Willow ignores me, walking away and up the stairs.

I walk back down into my apartment and close the door behind me. Then I flop onto the bed and stare up at the ceiling.

What have I done?

It's midnight and I'm thirsty, but I have looked everywhere and I still cannot find a glass. There's no other option; I'm going to have to sneak up into the main house to find one. I'm wearing my silky white nightdress, but I'm sure they are all in bed.

Sneaking out into the darkened corridor, I can see into the lit-up house.

I suddenly catch sight of Mr. Masters sitting in the armchair, reading a book. He has a glass of red wine in his hand. I stand in the dark, unable to tear my eyes away. There's something about him that fascinates me, but I don't quite know what it is.

He stands abruptly, and I push myself back against the wall. Can he see me here in the dark?

Shit.

My eyes follow him as he walks into the kitchen. The only thing he's wearing is his navy-blue boxer shorts. His dark hair has messy, loose waves on top. His chest is broad, his body is...

My heart begins to beat faster. What am I doing? I shouldn't be standing here in the dark, watching him like a creep, but for some reason I can't make myself look away.

He goes to stand by the kitchen counter. His back is to me as he pours himself another glass of red. He lifts it to his lips slowly and my eyes run over his body.

I push myself against the wall harder.

He walks over to the fridge and takes off the photo of me. What?

He leans his ass on the counter as he studies it. What is he doing?

I feel like I can't breathe.

He slowly puts his hand down the front of his boxer shorts, and then he seems to stroke himself a few times.

My eyes widen. What the fuck?

He puts his glass of wine on the counter and turns the main light off, leaving only a lamp to light the room.

With my picture in his hand, he disappears up the hall. What the hell was that?

I think Mr. Masters just went up to his bedroom to jerk off to my photo.

Oh.

My.

God.

Knock, knock.

My eyes are closed, but I frown and try to ignore the noise. I hear it again. Tap, tap.

What is that? I roll towards the door and I see it slowly begin to open.

My eyes widen, and I sit up quickly.

Mr. Masters comes into view. "I'm so sorry to bother you, Miss Brielle," he whispers. He smells like he's freshly showered, and he's wearing an immaculate suit. "I'm looking for Samuel." His gaze roams down to my breasts hanging loosely in my nightdress, and then he snaps his eyes back up to my face, as if he's horrified at what he just did.

"Where is he?" I frown. "Is he missing?"

"There he is," he whispers as he gestures to the lounger.

I look over to see Samuel curled up with his teddy in the diluted light of the room. My mouth falls open. "Oh no, what's wrong?" I whisper. Did he need me and I slept through the whole thing?

"Nothing," Mr. Masters murmurs as he picks Samuel up and rests his son's head on his strong shoulder. "He's a sleepwalker.

Sorry to disturb you. I've got this now." He leaves the room with his small son safely asleep in his arms. The door gently clicks closed behind them.

I lie back down and stare at the ceiling in the silence. That poor little boy. He came in here to see me and I didn't even wake up. I was probably snoring, for fuck's sake.

What if he was scared? Oh, I feel like shit now.

I blow out a deep breath, lift myself up to sit on the edge of the bed, and I put my head into my hands.

I need to up my game. If I'm in charge of looking after this kid, I can't have him wandering around at night on his own.

Is he that lonely that he was looking for company from me—a complete stranger?

Unexplained sadness rolls over me, and I suddenly feel like the weight of the world is on my shoulders. I look around my room for a moment as I think.

Eventually, I get up and go to the bathroom, and then walk to the window to pull the heavy drapes back. It's just getting light, and a white mist hangs over the paddocks.

Something catches my eye, and I look out to see Mr. Masters walking out to the garage.

Wearing a dark suit and carrying a briefcase, he disappears, and moments later I see his Porsche pull out and disappear up the driveway. I watch on as the garage door slowly closes behind him.

He's gone to work for the day.

What the hell?

His son was just found asleep on my lounger and he just plops him back into his own bed and leaves for the day. Who does that? Well, screw this, I'm going to go and check on him. He's probably upstairs crying, scared out of his brain. Stupid men. Why don't they have an inch of fucking empathy for anyone but themselves?

He's eight, for Christ's sake!

I walk up into the main house. The lamp is still on in the living room, and I can smell the eggs that Mr. Masters cooked himself for breakfast. I look around, and then go up the grand staircase.

Honestly, what the hell have I got myself into here? I'm in some stupid rich twat's house, worried about his child, who he clearly doesn't give a fuck about.

I storm up the stairs, taking two at a time. I get to the top and the change of scenery suddenly makes me feel nervous. It's luxurious up here. The corridor is wide, and the cream carpet feels lush beneath my feet. A huge mirror hangs in the hall on the wall. I catch a glimpse of myself and cringe.

God, no wonder he was looking at my boobs. They are hanging out everywhere, and my hair is wild. I readjust my nightgown over my breasts and continue up the hall.

I pass a living area that seems to be for the children, with big comfy loungers inside it. I pass a bedroom, and then I get to a door that is closed. I open it carefully and allow myself to peer in. Willow is fast asleep, still scowling, though. I smirk and slowly shut her door to continue down the hall.

Eventually, I get to a door that is slightly ajar. I peer around it and see Samuel sound asleep, tucked in nice and tight. I walk into his room and sit on the side of the bed. He's wearing bright blue and green dinosaur pyjamas, and his little glasses are on his side table, beside his lamp. I find myself smiling as I watch him. Unable to help it, I put my hand out and push the dark hair from his forehead.

His bedroom is neat and tidy, filled with expensive furniture. It kind of looks like you would imagine a child's bedroom being set out in a perfect family movie. There's a bookcase, a desk, a wing-back chair in the corner, and a toy box. The window has a bench seat running underneath it, and there are a few books sitting in a pile on the cushion, as if Samuel reads there a lot. Everything in this house is the absolute best of the best. Just how much money does Mr. Masters have?

I glance over to the armchair in the corner to his school clothes all laid out for him. Everything is there, folded neatly, right down to his socks and shiny, polished shoes. His school bag is packed, too.

I stand and walk over to look at his things. Mr. Masters must do this before he goes to bed. What must it be like to bring children up alone?

My mind goes to his wife and how much she is missing out on. Samuel is so young. With one last look at Samuel, I creep out of the room and head back down the hall, until something catches my eye.

A light is on in the ensuite bathroom of the main bedroom. That must be Mr. Master's bedroom.

I look left and then right; nobody is awake. I wonder what his room is like, and I can't stop myself from tiptoeing closer to inspect it.

Wow.

The bed is clearly king-size, and the room is grand, decorated in all different shades of coffee, complimented with dark antique furniture. A huge, expensive, gold and magenta embroidered rug sits on the floor beneath the bed. The light in the wardrobe is on. I peer inside and see business shirts all lined up neatly in a row. Super neatly, actually.

I'm going to have to make sure I keep my room tidy or he'll think I'm a pig.

I smirk because I am one, according to his standards of living.

I turn to see his bed has already been made, and my eyes linger over the velvet quilt and lush pillows there. Did he really touch himself in there last night as he thought of me, or am I completely delusional? I glance around for the photo of me, but I don't see it. He must have taken it back downstairs.

An unexpected thrill runs through me. I may return the favour tonight in my own bed.

I walk into the bathroom. It's all black, grey, and very modern. Once again, I notice that everything is very neat. There is a large mirror, and I can see that a slender cabinet sits behind it. I push the mirror and the door pops open. My eyes roam over the shelves. You can tell a lot about people by their bathroom cabinet.

Deodorant. Razors. Talcum powder. Condoms.

I wonder how long ago his wife died. Does he have a new girlfriend?

It wouldn't surprise me. He is kind of hot, in an old way. I see a bottle of aftershave and I pick it up, removing the lid before I lift it up to my nose.

Heaven in a bottle.

I inhale deeply again, and Mr. Master's face suddenly appears in the mirror behind me.

"What the hell do you think you're doing?" he growls.

2

Brielle

I SPIN AROUND, filled with horror. "I-I... I'm so sorry," I splutter. "I was checking on Samuel, and I—" I pause as I try to think of a justified reason for me being in here, doing this.

He narrows his eyes, anger oozing from him as he waits.

"I walked past your room and I could smell something nice. I've been wanting to buy my father some new cologne and—" I'm talking way too fast to sound like I'm telling the truth.

He folds his arms over his chest, clearly not believing this bull-shit story for a single moment.

"And I wanted to know what cologne it was so I could buy it for my father."

He raises his eyebrow in question. "You think I smell like your father?"

I shake my head. "No. You smell way better than him." My eyes widen. Did I just say that out loud?

Amusement crosses his face before his eyes drop to my night-dress. "I came back home to retrieve my phone, which I acciden-tally left on charge." He gestures to his side table and I see his damn phone on charge. "And I find you"—he holds out both his hands toward my body—"in a state of undress, standing in my bedroom, smelling my cologne."

I wrinkle my nose and scrunch up my face. "It sounds kind of weird when you say it like that."

He looks at me, deadpan. "It is weird."

I fake a smile and hand him the bottle of cologne. "You should maybe take it as a compliment. Not very many men smell nice enough for me to be so curious. It's actually one of the biggest mistakes a man can make—"

"Enough!" he cuts me off. "This is an invasion of my privacy."

I nod. "I can see why you would think that." I swallow the lump of sand in my throat. Oh fucking hell, get me out of here. This is mortifying. I readjust my nightdress to try and cover my breasts. "It wasn't intended to be creepy."

He lifts his chin in defiance. "We'll talk about this tonight when I have more time." I collect air in my cheeks and nod.

"Now, if you don't mind, will you please go and put some damn clothes on?" he snaps.

"Yes, sir," I whisper. "I'm sorry." I drop my eyes to the floor.

"I need to go to work." He gestures towards the door with his hand. I exhale heavily and start walking.

"Miss Brielle?"

I spin back to him.

"The children go to bed at 8:30 p.m. sharp. I would like a meeting with you then."

"Of course." I hesitate, and then, unable to help it, I blurt out my thoughts, "Are you going to fire me, Mr. Masters?"

His eyebrows rise, and he pauses for a moment. "Let's take the day to reassess?"

My eyes hold his for a moment. "Yes, of course. Have a nice day," I mutter as I leave the room. I feel the heat from his stare on my back as I walk away.

I rush down the stairs as fast as I can, back into the safety of my room. I close the door behind me, lean on it, and shut my eyes. I've done a lot of stupid things in my life, but I think that really takes the cake.

I drop to the bed and put my head into my hands as my heart hammers in my chest. What kind of fool gets caught in her new boss's bedroom, in her pyjamas, sniffing his aftershave on her first day of work? Of course he would forget his stupid phone on that exact day, wouldn't he?

Now, if you don't mind, will you please go and put some damn clothes on.

His words run through my mind and I cringe. My thoughts are interrupted as I hear a car door slam outside. I go to the window and peer through the sheer curtain, watching on as Mr. Masters gets into his flashy black car before it slowly disappears down the driveway.

Day one got off to a great start. What the hell am I doing?

I'm on the other side of the world, pretending to be a super nanny. Who was I kidding? I don't know the first damn thing about looking after children and minding my own business. I do know that I don't want to have a meeting with him tonight.

What's he going to say?

I remember the lame excuse I gave him about my father, and I cringe, filled with embarrassment. Oh, I can't face him, it's just too mortifying.

My mind goes to Emerson. I can't stand the thought of letting her down. If I don't have a job, then I can't afford to stay in England on our working holiday, and we're both so excited for this adventure.

I stare at the carpet for a moment as I try to think of a solution.

If I just try to work as hard as I can so that I don't get fired, I'll be okay. As soon as I can find another job, I will, and then I'll give my notice and leave. Emerson is tied here to her position for twelve months. I really need to make this work for her.

Just suck it up, princess.

Well, I did come to England for an adventure, and I suppose

wearing a skimpy nightdress and getting caught in my boss's bedroom could qualify as such.

It could be worse; he could have caught me masturbating to his photo.

A stupid smile crosses my face. Did he do what I thought he did, though? Did he really take my photo upstairs and get himself off last night, while picturing me, or am I just having some kind of boss fantasy?

I shrug to myself. It doesn't matter either way, and I don't care if he smells stupid hot. He's too old for me. I just have to look after the kids and do my job. Yes, I can do this.

I feel my determination return.

Right, so what's my plan of attack for today?

Get dressed, go back to the main house, and be the best damn nanny I can be until I find another job. Yes.

I go to the bathroom and stare at my reflection in the mirror. Despite my determination, my face is dejected and sad. It kind of feels weird living with people that aren't my family, and I imagine it will take me some time to adjust. I swallow the lump in my throat.

It will be okay. Just try really hard and it will be okay.

An hour later, I'm sitting at the kitchen table, rolling my fingers. I've finished two cups of coffee and I'm already buzzing.

Am I supposed to wake these kids up? I glance at my watch to see it's 7:15 a.m.

What time do they have to be at school?

I stand and begin to pace back and forth. I don't know what in hell I'm doing here. Mr. Masters hasn't left any instructions or anything.

The phone on the wall in the kitchen begins to ring, and I look around, confused. Should I answer it?

Ring, ring. Ring, ring.

I bite my thumbnail and stare at it as it vibrates on the wall. I peer into the living room, and then up the stairs.

Ring, ring.

If I don't answer it, who will? I'm the only adult home, so... I tentatively pick up the phone. "Hello." I frown.

"Hello, Miss Brielle." The voice is stern and commanding, and I feel my stomach flutter.

It's him.

"Oh, hello, Mr. Masters."

"Is everything all right?" he asks. "I've been emailing you, but you haven't responded."

Emailing me?

I shrug, because I really don't know what I'm supposed to be doing. "Of course, everything is fine."

"Are the children dressed? Have they had breakfast?"

I frown harder. "Erm..."

"If you're having any problems, you do have all of the information on the list on the fridge."

Oh shit, there is a list? I walk over and take the piece of paper from the fridge.

6:30 a.m. - Wake children and prepare their breakfast.

My eyes widen and I glance at my watch. It's now 7:25 a.m. Shit.

"The children are upstairs." Which is not technically a lie because they are upstairs.

"You have to leave in ten minutes or they'll be late," he says.

"Late?"

"Yes, late. Willow starts school at 8:00 a.m., and it's a half-hour drive from our house."

My eyebrows rise. Oh crap. "Of course, Mr. Masters. I have to go now, though, so we can leave in time."

"Janine will be there at 9:00 a.m." He says it casually, like I should already know all about this.

"Janine?" My eyes widen. Who the hell is Janine?

24

Honestly, did I listen to anything that came out of that perfect mouth of his last night?

"She's the cleaner and our cook. She cleans the house today and then normally comes back around 4:00 p.m. each day to prepare the night's meal."

"Yes, okay," I snap, because I really need to get off the phone and wake these children up as a matter of urgency. "I'll see you tonight, then?" I ask.

He pauses on the other end of the line. "You sound in a rush to get off the phone. Talk to me for a moment. It sounds like you have everything under control."

Jesus Christ, I don't have time for this shit. "Definitely in full control, just not a big phone talker," I add.

"I see." He pauses, and I can almost hear him smirking on the other end of the phone. "Don't forget our meeting tonight, either."

"Julian, I really need to go."

"Goodbye, Miss Brielle. Stay out of trouble."

I roll my eyes. "Yes, I will. Goodbye." I hang up and run to the stairs, taking them two at a time. Fucking hell. Willow is likely to give me a black eye when I wake her up this late.

The list. Why didn't I remember the list? It seems like a lifetime ago that he told me about it. So much has happened since then. What with all the wanking and sniffing aftershave we've both been doing.

I get to the top of the stairs and run down to Samuel's room. I open the door to see that he's still sleeping soundly.

"Sam," I whisper. "Sam, wake up, baby." I rub his little head and he frowns with his eyes still closed. "Sammy, wake up. We're running a little late this morning." He rolls on his side to face me. His hair is tousled and his face is so sleepy. He is the epitome of cute, and I can't help but smile down at him. "I love your pyjamas. I wish I had some like that."

He rubs his eyes. "You have to get them from Grandma, these are my birthday pyjamas."

"Oh, I see." I grin. "Go to the bathroom and wash your face. Do

I need to help you dress?" I ask. He puts his little arms up for a cuddle, and I feel myself melt. I hold him for a second.

"No." He hops out of bed. "I can do it myself. I'm big, you know?"

"Okay, good. I'll go and wake up Willow while you wash."

I leave him to go to the bathroom, and I make my way down to Willow's room, where I tentatively open the door. She's lying in her bed with her back to me. "Willow, you need to wake up. We're running late."

She ignores me. Great, I'm going to have to go in. "Willow?" I repeat.

She rolls over and looks at me with no emotion. "What?"

I force myself to fake a smile. "I didn't realize that I was meant to wake you up earlier."

She puts the phone back to her ear. "Yeah. She's finally decided to turn up." She listens for a moment and then passes the phone to me. "He wants to talk to you."

I frown as I stare at the phone in her outstretched hand. "Who is it?" I ask.

She smirks sarcastically and climbs out of bed before she disappears into her bathroom, shutting the door hard behind her.

"Miss Brielle?" Mr. Masters snaps, pulling me from my thoughts.

My eyes widen in horror and I put the phone to my ear. What's he on, fucking speed dial? "Yes?" I reply meekly.

"I thought the children were up and dressed already?"

"Me too." I cringe. "Weird, huh?"

"You're just waking them up now?"

I scratch my head. I can't believe I'm getting caught on my second lie this morning.

This whole day is already one huge monumental fuckup. It's a conspiracy.

"They are going to be late for school," he growls. "Why didn't you wake them up earlier?"

"Why didn't you tell me I had to? This is new to me, you

know. I can't be expected to remember all this shit," I whisper angrily. "I didn't know about the list, okay? And you should have called, emailed me, or whatever the hell you were meant to do, earlier."

He stays silent on the other end of the phone, and I scrunch up my face. Oh God, just shut up, Brielle.

I'm totally blowing this job.

He stays silent for a moment longer before he speaks. "I'm putting this down to jet lag, Miss Brielle. Take the children to school and go back to bed yourself before you make any more"— he pauses—"bad judgements."

I roll my eyes and feel my cheeks heat with embarrassment. "Yes, sir."

He stays on the line, an awkward silence hangs between us. "I'll see you tonight." I sigh.

The line clicks as he hangs up without another word.

Willow appears out of the bathroom and glares at me. "Get out of my room. Thanks a lot. I'm going to be late." She sneers.

I stare at her, and suddenly, I'm feeling so overwhelmed that I don't think I can take it. My eyes fill with tears. This isn't how I imagined my exciting new job to be. I drop my head and leave her room quickly so she doesn't see my tears.

Screw this.

I want to go home.

Julian

I end the call and pinch the bridge of my nose.

Here we go again. Another catastrophe of a nanny, and this one seemed so promising according to her resume.

"Morning, Your Honor." Marcy smiles as she walks in and holds out my morning coffee.

"Thank you," I mouth as I take it from her. I won the jackpot seven years ago when I hired her as my personal assistant. Best thing in this damn courthouse.

"How did the new nanny go?" she asks as she slides into her seat at her desk and sips her coffee.

I roll my eyes. "Don't ask. Nightmare." I sigh as I pick up my phone. "I'm calling the agency now and requesting someone else." I wait on as the call goes through.

I get a vision of Brielle in her white silk nightdress in my bedroom this morning. It wasn't light, and yet I could see her every curve, the way it hung over her hard nipples. Her caramel skin with her Australian tan. Her big brown eyes and red lips that looked like they belonged around me...

I close my eyes and inhale deeply.

Fuck me, if she isn't every man's wet dream, I don't know who is.

I drag my hand down my face. I need to get out more. Drinking red wine and jerking off to a photo of my children's nanny is unacceptable Thursday-night behavior.

I clench my jaw as I feel myself harden at the thought of her, and uneasiness sweeps over me. She's the nanny.

Cut it out.

The sooner I get her out of my house, the better. "Hello, Andersons Agency," the receptionist answers.

"Hello, this is Julian Masters."

"Oh, hello, Mr. Masters. How can I help you, sir?"

"My new nanny arrived yesterday."

"Yes." I hear her flick through some papers. "Brielle Johnston."

I purse my lips. "I don't think it's going to work out. Can you arrange some interviews for me to find someone else, please?"

She hesitates for a moment. "But—"

"No buts. I'm not happy. I would prefer someone else."

"Mr. Masters, Brielle is over here on a working visa. If she doesn't have another job to go to, she will have to go back to Australia immediately."

I frown. "What?"

"When you signed her au pair contract, you agreed to sponsor

28

her for her visit to the United Kingdom for a twelve-month period."

"I did no such thing. I signed an employment contract for a nanny."

"Yes, you did, sir. The employment contract is the working visa contract for an au pair, which is different to a nanny. It's in section 6a. I have the paperwork."

I pause for a moment, and Marcy frowns as she listens on. Our eyes meet and I shake my head in disgust. How the hell did I miss that? "Her visa isn't my problem. I want a new nanny as soon as possible."

"That's really disappointing, sir. We really feel that Brielle will work out if you just give her a chance."

"No. Arrange other interviews."

"Leonie, my manager, isn't here right now. Can I get her to call you when she gets in?"

I exhale heavily. "Fine. I'll be available after five."

"Thank you, Mr. Masters." She hangs up.

I sit back in my chair and roll my pen on my desk as I think.

"What's wrong with her? Are the children safe?" Marcy frowns.

"Yes, of course the children are safe."

"What? Does she seem rough or something?"

"Quite the opposite." I stand and remove my suit jacket, placing my judge's cape over my clothes. I slowly fasten the buttons down the front. "She's just young and not the right woman for the job, that's all. Willow and her have a personality clash."

Marcy watches me for a moment. "I hope I'm not talking out of turn, sir, but Willow has a personality clash with everyone."

My eyes meet hers and I exhale heavily. "I know. Even me, lately." With a heavy heart, I pick up my pile of court documents and make my way into the courtroom with Marcy following close behind.

"All rise," the secretary calls.

The courtroom stands, and I nod and walk in to take my place at the front of the room. I look around at the full courtroom, with the jury sitting to my left. My eyes roam to the man in front of me, accused of both rape and murder. Contempt fills my every pore. He's been in my court before, although we didn't have enough evidence to charge him. I hope today's result is somewhat better.

"You may be seated."

Brielle

I stand at the front door with the keys in my hand as I wait for Willow so I can take them both to school. Samuel is ready, waiting with his backpack on his back. I look up at the stairs. I want to scream out hurry the hell up, but I don't want to upset her.

She seems troubled, and for some reason, I don't think it's just because of me. Eventually, she comes into view and starts walking down the stairs. Her dark hair is in two braids, and she's wearing a snooty-looking grey tunic uniform. Her skirt hangs below her knees with big box pleats, her legs covered in thick grey tights and finished off with black school shoes. She's pretty, in a scowly kind of way.

I smile. "You look nice."

She rolls her eyes in disgust.

"Come on, let's go. I hope I can drive this van."

"Van?" Willow frowns. "We're not going in the van."

I stare at her for a moment. "Why not?"

"Because it's embarrassing. Like I want to be seen in that crap car."

"Oh, please," I snap. "Stop being such a snob." Her eyes meet mine, and I internally kick myself. Did I really just say that out loud?

"A snob?" she repeats, as if shocked at my audacity.

"What I meant is, I don't want to crash your dad's fancy SUV. So when you are with me, we are taking the van."

"Well, I won't be seen dead going anywhere with you." She sneers. "I'm not into hanging out with dumb bimbos. Just fuck off and go back to the hole you came from."

I inhale sharply, and we stare at each other—a silent standoff.

Samuel takes my hand, and I can't help but think it's a silent apology for his sister's rudeness. Something snaps inside of me, annoyed that she would put him in a position to hear that and feel so uncomfortable. What a selfish little bitch.

I smile down at him and hand over the keys. "Go out the front, baby, and open the car for me, will you?"

He snatches them and runs out the door. Willow lifts her chin defiantly.

I raise my eyebrow. "Let us get one thing straight here, dear Willow." I sneer.

She puts her hand on her hip in disgust.

"I'm here to look after Samuel, and I really don't care whether you like me or not—"

"I don't," she cuts me off.

I smile sarcastically. "Is that what your game is? Be an evil little bitch until the nanny runs away? Do you try and make their life a living hell, Willow?"

She narrows her eyes.

"Does Daddy come to your rescue?" I whisper in a baby voice.

"Fuck you." She sneers. "Stay out of my fucking way."

"Oh, I'm in your way, and don't fucking speak to me like that in front of Samuel again. I don't give a fuck if you don't like me, but you will not upset him. Do you hear me?"

Her eyebrows rise in surprise.

"He is only a little boy, and having a witch of a sister is not helping him one little bit. I don't want you to hold your tongue for me, but for God's sake, hold it for him."

She glares at me.

"Now get inside the damn van," I growl.

She takes off outside in a huff, and I close my eyes as fury pumps through my blood.

Great. This day just keeps getting better and better.

. . .

"So, just up here," Sam directs me as I pull into the circular school drop-off bay.

Sam is in the front seat and Willow is in the back. She wouldn't get in the front with me.

I peer out at the fancy school in front of me. It looks like Hogwarts from Harry Potter or something. "Wow," I whisper. "This is swish."

Willow climbs out of the car and slams the door.

I open my window. "Have a nice day, dear," I call out.

She flips me the bird as she walks away, and I giggle and look down at Samuel. He bites his bottom lip to hold back his smile.

"Well, she's clearly not a morning person, is she?" I widen my eyes at him.

He shakes his head and fidgets with his hands on his lap. "Where is your school, buddy?" I ask.

"We go up here and turn left."

He directs me again as I drive, and ten minutes later we get to his school. I pull up out the front. I dip my head and look around at the empty playground. "Where is everyone?" I ask.

"Oh." His little face falls. "They don't get here yet. They don't come until right on the bell."

"What do you do until your friends get here?"

He shrugs. "I just sit in the playground near my classroom."

"By yourself?" I frown.

He shrugs again.

"What time do you get to school each day?" I ask.

"About 7:50 a.m."

"What time does your bell go?"

"9:15."

"So you just sit here in the cold every morning, all by yourself?"

He nods.

I stare at him for a moment and shake my head before I pull back out into the traffic.

"What are you doing?" he asks.

"We're going for hot chocolate. You don't sit in the cold alone on my watch." I reach over and squeeze his little thigh, and he smiles broadly. "We might even have chocolate cake." I tickle him, and he laughs, wriggling to get away from me. "Don't tell your dad we had cake for breakfast, will you?"

He shakes his head with a big goofy smile on his face, and then he takes my hand in his on his lap.

This kid has got me already.

I get back home at about 9:45 a.m. I got completely lost and had to use the Maps app on my phone to find the damn house. When I walk inside, I can hear a vacuum running upstairs. The cleaner is clearly here. What was her name again? Damn it, I need to sleep. This jet lag is kicking my butt. I glance into the office near the staircase, and I tentatively walk up the stairs and down the hall. The cleaner is in Willow's room, and I open the door to introduce myself.

An elderly lady is inside vacuuming, wearing a light blue uniform and looking every bit the part of the housemaid. She looks up and smiles broadly. "Hello."

"Hi." I smile, grateful to see a friendly face.

She turns the vacuum off and shakes my hand. "I'm Janine. You must be the new nanny?"

I nod nervously. "Yes. I'm Brielle, but call me Brelly."

She smiles as she looks me up and down. She has this warm, safe feel about her. "How's it going?"

I roll my eyes and flop onto the bed. "Really bad."

She chuckles as she picks up a feather duster and begins to dust the dresser. "Why is that?"

I blow out a defeated breath. "Willow hates me, Mr. Masters is only tolerating me, and I just can't seem to do anything right."

Her eyes hold mine and she smiles softly. "Finally."

I frown. "Finally?"

"Finally, an honest nanny."

My face falls. "They all leave, don't they?"

She nods.

"Because of Willow?" I ask.

"Among other things." She dusts for a moment as she thinks. "They are a lovely family, dear, just a little dysfunctional."

"Does Willow hate everyone?"

"Yes."

"How long have you been with them?"

"Five years. I came to work for them the week after Alina died."

"Alina?"

"The children's mother."

"Oh." I stay silent, thinking carefully about what to say next. "I think Mr. Masters is going to fire me tonight."

"Why?"

"I got caught in his room this morning. I was smelling his after-shave, and then I forgot to wake the kids up and lied about it, and then I had a raving row with Willow and dropped the F-bomb on her."

Janine bursts out laughing. "Oh my...you are honest."

I roll my eyes. "Yeah. It's my biggest fault."

Her eyes dance with delight. "Fault? I think it's a virtue." She dusts a little more. "One that is not shown around here often, unfortunately."

I scowl. "What do you mean?"

She shrugs as she continues to clean. "It's really none of my business, dear."

I watch her for a while. "But if I'm going to try and make this work, any information you have could be helpful. I don't want to fail."

She bends down and cleans the skirting board, her back to me. "Well, for what it's worth, here's my take on it."

I listen intently.

"Mr. Masters has a broken heart, and Willow reminds him of his late wife. They hardly speak unless she is getting disciplined for something, and Samuel overcompensates their lack of relation-

34

ship with too much sweetness to make up for his sister's cold front."

My face falls. "Mr. Masters shuts her out?" I whisper.

"That, and she won't let him in now. She won't let anyone in. The damage has been done. You'll soon know that she's very difficult to get along with."

Oh, that poor girl. Sadness fills me. She's still only a baby. Suddenly, I feel guilty for being horrible to her this morning. No wonder she's snarky, and what an asshole he must be for shutting his only daughter out after her mother died.

I blow out a deflated breath and flop back on the bed. Jeez, it's like a bad Nicholas Sparks movie.

Janine continues to clean around me. "How did their mother die?" I ask.

"Car accident."

"How was he after she died?"

"Who, Mr. Masters?"

I nod. "Quiet."

I frown. "Is he always quiet?"

She shrugs. "He is with me. He holds a very powerful position at work, and I think it's very taxing on him. When I first started, just after she died, I searched for Alina on Facebook. There were a lot of shots of the two of them out on the town together. She was beautiful."

My eyebrows rise as I listen.

"But her page was shut down not long after."

"Hmm." All this information and I have no idea what to do with it. Janine continues to clean, and I feel guilty for lounging here, just watching her work. "Do you want some help?" I ask. "Can I do anything?"

She smiles warmly. "No, dear, but why don't you go and have a lie down. I'm sure you must still be jet-lagged."

"Yeah, I am. Dead tired, to be honest." I hop up and make my way to the door, glancing back over my shoulder. "It was lovely meeting you."

She smiles warmly. "You, too, dear. Sweet dreams."

I make my way down to my room, set my alarm, and climb into bed. I pull my big, heavy quilt over me, and then I try to imagine I am home.

Julian

I walk into Rodger's bar at around 4:00 p.m. to meet with Sebastian and Spencer—something we all do at least once a week. We've been best friends since we were ten years old. I don't see them as much as I would like to, but they keep me sane when I need them.

"Hey, Jules." Seb smiles.

"Hey. Where's Spence?"

"At the bar."

I glance over, falling onto a stool, and see Spencer deep in discussion with a woman at the bar.

"How's your week been?" Seb asks.

"Yeah, pretty good. Yours?"

He curls his lip. "This new building is giving me a fucking headache." He shrugs. "I'll get it right eventually."

Sebastian is an architect and Spencer owns a steel company and designs skyscrapers. They both do very well for themselves.

Spence arrives back at the table with our three beers in hand. "Hey, Masters, what's up?" He holds a beer out for me too as he sits down.

"Not much." I sip my beer. "My new nanny started."

"What's she like?" Seb asks.

"Fucking hot." I sigh.

The boys both exchange a look and smile before they turn their attention back to me. "Seriously?" Spence asks. "How hot?"

"Like, I'm fucking hard in my pants every single time she's in the room hot," I answer dryly.

"Have you shagged her?" Spence asks.

I wince as I sip my beer. "You don't shag the nanny, Spence."

36

"Why not?" He shrugs, raising his brows. "I would."

Seb smirks and Spencer's eyes widen all at once. "Oh hell, I didn't tell you about Marie."

Seb and I sip our beers as we listen.

"Okay, so you know how I've been seeing that flight attendant, Marie?"

"Yeah."

"I started going around to her apartment a bit more, and it turns out she's got this female flatmate called Ricky."

"Oh God, don't tell me." I smile to myself. Spencer is the worst player I know. He can't keep it in his pants for longer than five minutes.

Spencer smiles and winks. "Ricky's fucking hot." He shakes his head, as if the memory of this Ricky is making his mind foggy. "Like...stupid hot."

Seb and I roll our eyes at each other.

We already know where this story is going.

"The other night, I was in bed with Marie, completely naked. She's on top of me, and the bedroom lamp is still on..." He pauses to take a quick drink.

"Then all of a sudden, the door opens, and in walks Ricky, wearing nothing. Nude." Seb and I glance at each other, both of us wearing a frown.

"She asks if she can join us in bed."

"Where the fuck do you find these women?" Seb asks, indignant.

"I know, right?" I chuckle. "What did Marie say?"

He smirks and holds his hands out as he explains the story. "Marie asks me if I mind if her flatmate joins us. Apparently, Ricky hasn't had sex in a while, and Marie hates knowing her friend is lonely."

I sit forward, my face creased with confusion. "Wait, so are those two fucking each other when you're not there?"

Spence shrugs. "Fuck knows." He sips his beer. "All I know is the next minute, I've got Marie riding my cock and Ricky sitting on my face."

Seb and I laugh at the lucky son of a bitch.

Spence holds his hands out. "It's like a fucking Tuesday, and there I am getting double pumped without any warning. I hadn't even had a drink."

I throw my head back and laugh louder.

"I fucked both of them, and then I'm dozing off in between them when Marie falls asleep first."

"What happened?" I ask.

"Well, Ricky gets under the blankets and just starts giving me the best fucking head I've ever had in my life."

Seb slaps his forehead, unable to believe Spencer's luck. Spencer's eyes widen. "But I don't know what to do, right? Marie is asleep next to us."

"But you just fucked Ricky in front of Marie?"

"I know." He shrugs. "But I had her permission that time. It felt weird with her asleep. I'm lying there getting head, doing a risk assessment in my mind of what Marie will do if she wakes up."

Seb throws his head back and roars with laughter, holding his arm up to the waitress for another round of beers. "Only fucking you."

"Then Ricky asks me to take it to her room, which meant us not waking Marie."

"Did you go?" Seb frowns.

"Yeah, and on the way there she goes to her handbag and gives me a blue pill out of a bottle."

My eyes widen. "She gave you a Viagra?"

He nods, and Seb and I hoot with laughter. "What the fuck, man?" Seb cries. "What fucking chick carries Viagra around in her purse?"

Spencer shrugs. "I don't know, but I took the blue pill. My dick turned into a rocket cock, and I turned into a porn star, fucking her for six hours straight." He holds his hands up. "Hands down, the best sex I've ever had. She is fucking insane, so hot. I fucked her every which way."

I hold my glass up and wink. "To Viagra," I toast. They smile and lift their glasses to tap against mine. "We should maybe try this shit," I mutter to Seb, and he chuckles in response.

"Then I crawl back to Marie's bed just as the sun is coming up. I have to go to work in, like, two hours, and I have a huge meeting with new investors at 9:00 a.m." His eyes widen. "I can hardly fucking walk. My balls are blue and bruised."

"What happened next?" Seb dares himself to ask. "Marie wakes up." Seb shakes his head. "Why doesn't this shit ever happen to me?"

"Right?" I chuckle. "I want my new nanny to do this to me."

Seb points at me. "You should totally tap that. How hot would that be, sneaking into her room at night?"

I nod as I sip my beer, my cock tingling at the thought. "God, I wish."

Spence continues his story. "So, there I am, trying to die in peace and get in two hours of sleep, cock throbbing in pain, when Marie decides to start sucking my dick, wanting more action."

"She didn't know where it'd been all night," I say.

Seb winces. "Oh, I hate to think."

I shiver at the thought.

"What did you do?" Seb frowns.

"I had to do what any self-respecting boyfriend would do."

I laugh sarcastically. "Like you would know what a self-respecting boyfriend is supposed to do."

He turns to me, annoyed. "Oh, and you would?" I smile and wink as I sip my beer.

"Anyway, there I am, knowing damn well I have to fuck Marie now. I swear, I'm nearly crying."

Seb and I burst out laughing, and Seb slaps the table. "Fuck me, man, this is the best story ever."

Spence's eyes widen. "It isn't over yet. Let me tell you, that

Viagra kicked back in and I regained my superhuman strength again, but I can't come."

We both lean forward, waiting to hear how this ends.

"I'm fucking and fucking and fucking, and I can't come." He sips his beer. "My dick has literally got no skin left on it, burning like a motherfucker. Now I really am almost crying."

Seb and I are laughing out loud as we imagine our stupid friend fucking with a sore dick.

"What did you do?" Seb gasps for air, trying to regain control. "I did what I had to do."

I frown. "What's that?"

"I faked it."

"You faked it?" I gasp.

He nods and sips his drink. "Yep."

The table falls silent. None of us has ever faked it before. I wouldn't know how to.

"Then Marie calls me today. She says the other night was fun and could we do it again tonight. She wants Ricky to join us too."

We all lean closer to him, waiting to hear his response. "I told her I was out of town."

Seb's face twists in disgust.

"Why would you do that?" I frown.

"Because I have no skin left on my fucking dick, man. I need a skin graft. It is literally grazed like a third-degree burn." He shakes his head and we all burst out laughing. "If I wasn't circumcised already, I would have been after that."

I wince. "Who is this chick with the iron snatch?"

Seb chuckles. "My new drug dealer."

Brielle

It's 9:30 p.m., and the walk up the hall towards the main house feels long. I've been watching from my darkened spot in the glass hallway for the last fifteen minutes. Mr. Masters is still in his suit, obviously unable to relax until this meeting is over.

Not a good sign.

I walk up the six stairs and around the corridor until I come into his view. He's in the kitchen, filling his thick glass tumbler with ice.

"Hello." I smile meekly.

He turns to face me. "Hello." He gestures to the stool at the island bench. "Please, sit down."

I slink into the chair and watch as he pours scotch over his ice, and then takes a seat opposite me.

He rolls his lips and takes a sip. "Miss Brielle," he sighs.

"Brelly," I correct.

He raises his eyebrows. "No offence, but I'm not calling you Brelly. You're not an umbrella."

I bite my bottom lip to stifle my smile. I feel like I am in the principal's office, about to be expelled from school. He's wearing an expensive navy suit with a white shirt. His dark hair is longer on the top, with a curl running through it, and he has the squarest jaw I think I've ever seen. His eyes are big and brown, and...he really is very good-looking.

"I don't think this is going to work out," he says calmly, slicing my thoughts in two.

"What?" I whisper.

He gives a subtle shake of his head. "I'm sorry, I just—"

"Is this about this morning?" I interrupt.

"Brielle, I deal with liars and thieves all day at work. I don't have the energy to have someone living under my roof who I don't trust."

"You-you can trust me," I stammer. "I'm the most honest person you could ever meet. Too honest, in fact. Ask anybody."

He sips his drink, and his cold eyes hold mine.

"Ask me anything. Ask me anything right now and I will tell you the whole truth, I promise."

He lifts his chin. "All right then, what did you say to Willow this morning?"

My face falls. Oh, he had to ask that, didn't he?

I swallow the lump in my throat. That little snitch. If I wasn't already getting fired, I definitely am now.

"I think it went something like..." I readjust my position in my seat, and he raises an eyebrow, waiting. My heart begins to beat fast. "I asked her if that was what her game was? To be an evil little bitch until the nannies run away. And then I asked her if she tries and makes their lives a living hell."

He narrows his eyes.

"And then I asked her if her daddy comes to her rescue every time."

He glares at me and bites his bottom lip, as if he's stopping himself from snapping or yelling.

I cringe openly. "And then she said something along the lines of 'fuck you, stay out of my fucking way.' So I warned her not to fucking speak to me like that in front of Samuel ever again. I don't give a fuck if she doesn't like me, but I will not put up with her upsetting him." I shrug. "Give or take a few insults."

He tips his head and drains his glass, clearly disgusted.

My heart begins to hammer so hard, I feel like I can literally hear the blood pumping in my ears.

His eyes hold mine. "And what gives you the right to speak to my daughter like that?"

"I don't have that right, and I'm sorry, it won't happen again. She just got me so mad speaking to me like that in front of Samuel. He needs to be protected from her venom. He's just a baby, and I know she's troubled, but I needed her to know that it's not okay and I won't be putting up with it."

He blows all the air from his cheeks and pours another scotch, glancing up mid pour, as if realizing he's being rude by not offering me one. He tilts the bottle my way.

"Yes, please," I say, grateful for the offer—I'll try anything to calm my nerves. This is harrowing.

He fills my glass with ice and then pours me a scotch. Hell, where's the mixer? Do I drink this straight?

He passes it over. "Thank you." I take a sip and feel the heat go down and slowly warm my oesophagus. "Hmm." I lift the glass and inspect the golden fluid. "This is...strong."

A trace of a smile crosses his face as he sits back at his stool.

He watches me intently, and then finally responds. "Willow is a lot to handle, I know that."

"I was a nightmare, too, at that age. I can handle her."

"I have no doubt." He purses his lips. "But this isn't about Willow."

I frown. "Then what is it about?"

"It's about you being in my bedroom and looking through my things this morning."

I gulp my drink down and nearly choke. This stuff is like rocket fuel. I cough loudly, clearing my throat. "Oh, that." I wince around the fire in my throat. Sweet Jesus, am I drinking petrol here?

"Yes, that," he answers. "Please explain what you were doing in my bedroom."

I glance at the door. Run...just fucking run.

I swallow the sand in my throat. "I went to check on Samuel because I was worried about him sleepwalking again and I thought you had left for the day." I frown as I try to make this story sound reasonable. "On the way back to my room, I saw your door was open and I just..."

He watches me as he takes a sip of his drink.

"I wanted to see what your bedroom looked like." He raises a brow.

I offer a half smile and try to sweeten the story as much as I can. "I walked in, looked around, and then I saw your bathroom cabinet was slightly ajar." I shrug. "You can find out so much about a person by their bathroom cabinet, you know?" I take another big gulp of my rocket fuel.

Holy hell, this is strong shit. I half cough, my oesophagus burned beyond belief.

I get a vision of myself falling off the stool, drunk, and I shiver in horror.

Great, a hopeless nanny who can't hold her liquor—this story just keeps getting better and better by the minute.

He lifts his chin once more, in defiance, and the energy between us begins to change. His questions somehow turn into a silent dare for me to tell the truth, and he watches me intently. "What did you find out about me, Brielle?"

I swallow the lump in my throat. "You're very neat," I whisper nervously.

He doesn't react.

"I really like your cologne." A trace of a smile crosses his face, and it gives me the confidence to keep going.

"And...you're...sexually active."

His eyes darken, and the air suddenly crackles between us.

He takes a slow, steady sip of his scotch, and I watch closely as his tongue darts out to lick his bottom lip. I feel my insides clench.

Huh?

He leans forward in his chair. "What are you doing here, Brielle?" he whispers. The electricity between us has stolen my ability to think straight.

"Drinking the strongest alcohol known to man?" I offer.

He smiles sexily and releases a low chuckle. "I meant, why did you come to England?"

I bite my bottom lip. "To get away from my ex-boyfriend. We broke up last year and I needed a change...to move on."

His eyes drop to my lips. "And how long has it been since you've been with a man?"

I frown, but without putting my brain-to-mouth filter on, I whis- per, "Too long. Way too long."

3

_____

Brielle

OUR EYES ARE LOCKED, and when his tongue swipes over his lips again, my breath catches.

"How long has it been since you've been with someone?" I ask. What the hell is in this drink? Truth serum?

He smiles sarcastically. "My sexual behavior isn't up for discussion tonight."

My eyebrows rise in surprise. "But mine is?"

"I was merely doing a character analysis."

I smile against my glass. "As am I."

His eyes dance with mischief as he watches me. "You're right, you are refreshingly honest, Miss Brielle."

I smile.

"If not a little forward," he adds.

"I could say the same for you, but I don't see how when I was last with a man has anything to do with my character."

"It gives me an insight into the kind of life you live."

I think on it for a moment. "Well, if that's the case, I'm sorry to report that I live the most boring life imaginable, because I haven't thought about a man or been with a man for over twelve months."

"I see," he murmurs, seemingly impressed with my answer.

"Mr. Masters, I know I may be a busybody, but I can assure you that I am not here to steal your things or fight with your daughter. I'm here to do a great job for you for twelve months, and hopefully find myself in the process."

He narrows his eyes and sits back in his seat. "And how do you plan on doing that?"

I sip my drink as I contemplate my answer. "I'm going to see the country, learn about its history, and spend my weekends with Emerson." I shrug. "You never know, I may meet a man and have some fun while I'm here, too."

"And exactly what does that entail?" he asks, bemused.

This man is so intelligent that I have no idea if he's genuinely interested in the answer to these questions, or if he's really just being condescending.

"I'm not sure. All I know is that if I really knew what I needed, I would have gone out and found it at home."

His eyes hold mine.

What the hell is he thinking?

"Hmm." He hesitates for a moment. "Tell me about your visa."

I exhale heavily and sip my rocket fuel. It's so strong, the fumes go up my nose and I have another coughing fit. "How do you drink this?" I splutter as I pound my chest with a closed fist.

"Takes the edge off." He smirks.

"Off what?" I continue to cough. "What edge is this sharp?" I wince.

He chuckles, a deep velvety sound that seeps into my bone marrow, and I feel my heart flutter.

He's just so...

He arches an eyebrow, and I realize that he's waiting for my answer. "Oh, the visa?" He raises his glass impatiently. God, he really does think I'm dense. "Will you please stop that?" I snap.

"Stop what?"

"The condescending looks and quips."

A trace of a smile crosses his face. "My apologies."

I drain the rest of my glass and hold it out for a top-up. I have no idea what I'm doing here, but sweetening him up while drinking scotch seems to be a perfect plan.

He refills my glass, and then I sip my drink, simply watching him for a moment. "Do you always do this?"

"Do I always drink scotch with my nannies and get reprimanded for answering their questions? No."

"So, you're a scotch nanny virgin?"

This time it's him who chokes on his drink as he laughs. "Most definitely. A nanny virgin, anyway. Not so much a scotch virgin."

I smile broadly. For some reason, I like that answer. "See? We're getting along fine now. This is all going to work out."

"This is not working out. This is a pleasant distraction."

My face falls. "Oh."

His brows furrow. "Please don't take this personally, but you're just not what I expected, Brielle."

"What did you expect?"

He shrugs. "Someone older, experienced, more professional."

I think for a moment. "The ad didn't request any of that."

He sips his scotch and rolls his eyes. "My mother put the ad in with the agency."

"Your mother?" I frown.

He smirks around his glass. "You seem surprised."

"Well, I didn't take you as a mummy's boy."

He laughs that velvety laugh again, and I feel it deep in the pit of my stomach. "Not by any means. But she is concerned about Willow, and she wanted to take care of this placement and for us to try something different."

I smile goofily. "Well...I am different."

"That you are."

"Just give me another chance, please?" I plead. "We got off on the wrong foot, sure, but I promise you I will turn this around."

His eyes hold mine.

"If in three weeks you're still not happy, I'll get another job in a bar or something, but please don't get me deported before I have a chance to find another job. I've been saving for this trip for twelve months."

He watches me. "Please..."

He inhales sharply. "Fine, you have twenty-one days. But next time I fire you, don't beg me to stay."

I shake my head. "I won't."

"Because next time I won't be pushed over so easily."

I nod. "Fine, but you have to promise not to give me this truth serum again." I hold up my glass of scotch.

"Truth serum?"

"I'm quite sure if you asked me anything right now, I would have no choice but to give it to you straight."

His eyes dance in delight. "Ask me anything," he whispers darkly.

"What?" I frown.

"Go on. What do you want to know about me?" He raises a single brow. "Off the record, of course."

I bite my bottom lip to bite back my goofy smile. I like this game. "Okay." I pause for a moment as I think. "Do you like your women wholesome and pure, or dirty and slutty?"

Satisfaction flashes across his face, and I realize that I just played straight into his hands. He used the truth serum tactic to see what I really wanted to know: his taste in women.

Shit, I need to up my game if I'm going to keep up with this master manipulator.

He sips his scotch, and the air swirls between us. "I like the first to act like the latter...but only for me."

I swallow the lump in my throat. God, good answer. What would he be like in bed with all this dominant power? "Oh," I mumble. I get a vision of him naked, and suddenly, I can't think of an intelligent reply.

Think... Think...

Say something intelligent.

"Wholesome sluts must be hard to find these days," is all I manage to come up with.

He throws his head back and laughs deeply. I find myself smiling like an idiot. Then his face falls serious. "Go to bed, Miss Brielle, before this game of truth or dare turns sour."

I drain my glass and stand. "Yes, of course. Thank you, Mr. Masters. I really do appreciate you giving me another chance. You will never find me in your bedroom again."

He licks his bottom lip as he watches me intently. Sitting on the stool, in his suit with his just-fucked hair, he looks nothing short of dreamy.

Electricity zaps between us, and we stare at each other for an extended moment.

Abort mission. He's old...er... he's your boss, and you are obviously intoxicated.

Truth serum may also be code for fuck serum.

I stand abruptly. "Thank you, I'll leave you in peace. Enjoy your night, sir."

Without looking back, I scurry to my bedroom. Once inside, I lean on the back of the closed door.

My heart is pounding in my chest Thank God my job is safe.

I have twenty-one days left to secure it. Don't blow this, Brielle.

I wake to a thudding sound outside. My room is still somewhat dark, although the sun is trying to rise outside.

Bump. Bump. Bump.

What is that noise? I remain still for a while longer, until I hear it again.

Bump.

Bump.

Bump.

I get up and go to the window. Willow is down below, dressed in a bright blue and white sports uniform. She's kicking a ball into some nets. Oh, she plays soccer. I wonder why she's up practicing so early. Maybe she plays this time every week? It's Saturday. I'm going to go and investigate.

I pull on my robe and make my way up into the house. Mr. Masters is sitting at the table, reading the paper, and Samuel is eating his porridge.

"Brelly," Samuel squeals as he jumps down from his chair to hug me.

"Hello, cutie pie." I smile as I hug him back. My eyes eventually rise to glance at Mr. Masters, and I feel my cheeks heat in embarrassment. I can't believe I asked him what type of woman he likes. What was I thinking?

Mental note: don't drink straight scotch ever again. Hardened criminals don't even drink that shit. No wonder my head is pounding. Suddenly, I feel underdressed and over daggy. I run my fingers through my rat's nest hair as Mr. Masters appears to study me. "What are you guys doing up and dressed so early?" I ask.

"Willow plays soccer this morning," he replies.

"What time will we leave?"

Mr. Masters' face falls. "You don't work weekends, Brielle. That isn't necessary."

"I know." I take Samuel's hand in mine. "I'd like to come and support Willow, if that's okay."

He frowns, just as Willow walks through the door with her ball tucked under her arm.

"Willow, give me a minute and I'll just get dressed," I say. "I'll be five minutes, tops."

She scowls. "What for?"

"I want to come and watch you play soccer."

"What? You're not coming, and it's football. Stay at home and paint your nails or something."

"Willow," Mr. Masters chastises. "Where are your manners?"

I raise an eyebrow. "To be honest, football isn't my thing, but coffee vans and sunlight are, so I would like to come."

She glares at me, and I smile sarcastically, my eyes wide and waiting. "Besides, my nails are already painted." I hold my hand up and wiggle my fingers. Willow rolls her eyes in disgust.

"Come on, Sammy, you can help me find some clothes." I smile at the cute little boy holding my hand.

"Please don't call him Sammy," Mr. Masters interrupts. "His name is Samuel. Sammy is a seal's name."

"Oh." I frown down at Samuel. "Is Sammy the Seal a thing?" I think for a moment. "I don't know about that. I've never heard of a seal called Sammy."

"That's because even seals don't like the name Sammy," Mr. Masters says flatly.

Samuel swings my hand in his and I smile down at him. "What would you like me to call you?" I ask.

He glances at his father nervously before he brings his attention back to me. "I like it when you call me Sammy," he whispers.

My eyes rise to meet Mr. Masters', and I raise my eyebrow sarcastically.

Willow folds her arms over her chest in disgust. "Didn't you hear what Dad said? He doesn't like it."

"Then I won't call your father Sammy," I reply. "Easily fixed."

Mr. Masters drops his head, resigned, and I turn my attention to Willow. "What would you like me to call you?" I ask sweetly.

She narrows her eyes in contempt. "Stupid." She sneers.

"Willow," Mr. Masters growls. "Cut. It. Out. Immediately."

I smile. "Now, I know for certain your dad wouldn't like me calling you stupid, but if you insist, I'll call you Queen B."

She rolls her eyes. "Fucking unbelievable," she mutters under her breath.

"When you two are quite finished," Mr. Masters snaps, interrupting our quarrel. "Willow, mind your language and show Miss Brielle some respect."

"But I don't want her to come to football." She pouts.

"Too bad." I smile. "I'll be five minutes. Come on, Sammy, let's go find me some clothes."

. . .

The walk across the fields to the soccer game is awkward for two reasons. Firstly, Willow hasn't talked to me at all since we left the house, and I feel I may have made a mistake pushing my way here. Secondly, the mothers that are now staring right at me. Holy hell on a broomstick. Every millionaire mummy in the world must be here, looking like they've just stepped out of a photo shoot, yet all eyes are now fixed firmly on me. The women are literally pausing their conversations to stare at me. Mr. Masters must be the topic of a lot of conversation around here. And why wouldn't he be? They probably all want to bang him.

I really didn't think this through very well, and I most definitely didn't think about my outfit. I'm wearing tight denim jeans, a white T-shirt, with a large army green jacket over the top. My long, dark hair is pulled into a high ponytail, and I have white runners on, with gold Ray-Ban aviator sunglasses framing my face. I must look eighteen at most.

Mr. Masters and Willow are walking in front of Sammy and me, the two of us holding hands. We walk past at least twenty people standing on the sidelines, and I can almost hear the whispers of judgement as we pass.

"Did your other nannies ever come to watch, Willow?" I ask Sammy.

"Nope."

"Has your father ever brought someone else to a soccer game?"

"Like who?" Sammy frowns.

"Like, one of his lady friends, perhaps?"

He shrugs. "Dad doesn't have lady friends, just man friends."

"He's never had a lady friend?" I ask, surprised.

Sammy shakes his head. "Nope."

"Oh."

Willow waves to her friends before she runs off to the dressing shed.

Mr. Masters chooses a spot and puts down three fold-up chairs. "Here, Miss Brielle." He gestures to my chair.

"Thank you." I smile before I fall into it awkwardly. I really should have stayed home. I'm feeling very uncomfortable.

"Dad, do you want to kick?" Sam asks as he throws the spare soccer ball to his father.

"Sure thing." He takes Sam over to the other field, where they begin to kick the ball to each other. I watch on, and if I were a nice person, I would tell you I am watching Samuel playing happily with his father. But, because I'm a dirty pervert, I can openly admit that I'm watching Mr. Masters and nobody else.

He's wearing a cream cable-knit jumper with light, tight jeans that fit snug in all the right places. His dark hair has a bit of a curl to it from the moisture in the early-morning air.

Sam kicks a high ball, and Mr. Masters laughs as he tries to reach it.

He has a beautiful laugh and such straight teeth.

I can't help but wonder when his last girlfriend was.

He must have a girlfriend now. Men who look like that, with his charisma and brains, are never single. He obviously just hasn't introduced her to the children yet.

Good for him. I hope she's fucking his brains out. God, I know I would be if I was her.

Wait, where did that come from? Since when have I ever found thirty-nine-year-old men attractive? Not that I've ever really known one.

It's okay to think he's attractive. He is attractive. It doesn't mean that I want to fuck him, although one does have to wonder what he would be like in bed.

I bet he's well-endowed. My eyes drop to his jeans as I investigate my theory.

"I'm sorry, we haven't met?" a snooty female voice interrupts. I glance up to see an attractive blonde lady standing over me, and I quickly stand from my seat.

"Hello. I'm Brielle." I hold out my hand and she shakes it in hers.

"I'm Rebecca." She smiles.

"Hi, Rebecca." I smile awkwardly.

She frowns, clearly concentrating as she studies my face. "Have we met before?"

"No." I pause as my eyes seek out Mr. Masters on the other field, completely oblivious. "I'm Mr. Masters new au pair. I'm from Australia."

Her eyebrows rise in surprise. "Oh, really?" She turns to look at Mr. Masters. "How...lovely." She hesitates. "I currently have an au pair living with me, but she's from Italy. Her name is Maria."

"Really?" I smile.

"Yes. You two will have to meet. She's around your age, I'd say, and she's been with me for six months now."

"That would be fantastic, thank you." Maybe I could get some survival tips off this girl. This could work out well.

"She's not here today. Maria doesn't work weekends." She catches Mr. Masters' eye and waves sexily, and he waves back as he kicks the ball. "I'll go get my chair and sit with you guys."

"Okay." I smile. "Do you need any help?"

"No, I'm fine, dear," she replies as she walks off.

She seems surprisingly nice. I sit and look around for a moment, spotting Willow near the sheds. A group of three girls from the other team are around her, and I can tell by Willow's body language that they are not her friends. She seems uncomfortable.

One of them hits the ball out of Willow's hand. What? Are they messing around?

I watch them and unease fills me. I look around, but nobody else seems to be noticing this exchange. Maybe they are her friends and I'm just imagining things.

Mr. Masters comes and takes a seat next to me just as I sit down, while Sam keeps kicking with another boy.

"Who are those girls talking to Willow?" I ask him. He narrows his eyes, trying to focus.

"Do you wear glasses?" I ask as I watch him.

"I don't need glasses," he huffs.

"Then why are you squinting?"

"Because my eyes aren't bionic." Jeez. Touchy.

"I think they go to her school, yes. One of them used to be a good friend of Willow's, but she hasn't been around for years now."

"Oh," I reply, distracted as I turn my attention back to the girls. Willow's teammates come out of the sheds, and one of the girls says something to the three girls that were talking to Willow, and then one of them snaps back. Nope, definitely not friends. That is a hostile exchange.

The coaches come out and the teams line up to run onto the field.

Rebecca arrives back, struggling with her chair before she sets it up next to Mr. Masters. He rolls his lips, as if he's unimpressed. "Hello, Rebecca," he offers.

"Hi, Julian, how are you?" She leans over and kisses him on the cheek. I have to bite my bottom lip to hide my smile. I keep my eyes on the field in front of me.

I think Rebecca is a bit sweet on Mr. Masters. The whistle blows and the game begins.

"Willow is playing centre forward?" I whisper to him.

"Yes." He frowns, turning to me. "You know football?"

"I know most things," I whisper back as I keep my eyes on the game.

"I seriously doubt that."

"Julian, I called you this week about the fundraiser. Did you get my message?" Rebecca asks in a high-pitched voice, trying too hard to sound casual.

He hesitates. "No, I didn't, sorry."

"I wanted to see if you would like to go to the fundraiser together. We could carpool. I can drive so you can have a few drinks."

"Erm..." He hesitates again, and I bite the inside of my cheek to stop myself from smiling as I stare at the game.

"I'm sorry, I already have a date for that night. Some other time, perhaps?"

55

Awkward.

"Oh," she sighs, dejected. "I didn't realize you were seeing anyone."

"It's new," he says quietly.

I smile on the inside. I'm happy he isn't interested in going on a date with Rebecca. She's just too 'blah' for someone like him.

They fall into an uncomfortable silence until I can't take the awkwardness of it anymore.

"I'm going to go and get a coffee." I stand.

"I'll show you where to go." Mr. Masters immediately gets up too.

I smile at him knowingly, and he widens his eyes, silently asking for me to rescue him.

"Okay, lead the way." I hold my hand out.

He looks down, and his good manners prevail. "Would you like a cup of coffee, Rebecca?"

"Yes, please, darling. Just white."

"No sugar?"

"I'm sweet enough." She winks and gives a sexy little shrug of her shoulder.

Oh, she's creepy weird. Unable to help it, I release a little giggle.

Mr. Masters frowns and walks towards the coffee van, leaving me to fall beside him.

"Do you really have a date on that night?" I ask.

He fakes a shiver. "No, but I have a new incentive to find one now."

I laugh out loud. "I think she seems nice."

"Then you should date her."

"Julian," a brunette lady in her early forties calls. "Where have you been hiding, darling?" She waves and smiles before she comes over and kisses him on both cheeks. She holds his biceps and inspects him from head to toe. "I swear, Julian, you get yummier every time I see you."

"Flattery will get you everywhere." He laughs, and it's that deep, velvety laugh of his that tells me he genuinely likes this lady. "Nadia, please meet Brielle, my new nanny," he introduces.

She looks me up and down too. "Hello." But her offered smile is fake.

"Hello," I reply timidly.

Jesus, this place is like Tinder on crack.

They begin to make conversation, but I feel like a third wheel. "I'll leave you two to it." I smile. "Nice to meet you, Nadia."

"Likewise, Brielle. See you next time."

I make my way over to the coffee van and stand in line to order. I watch Mr. Masters escape one woman only to be accosted by another, again and again.

He's like a rock star around here.

I make it back to my seat and continue watching the game, until eventually he returns and falls back into his chair beside me.

"You sure are definitely popular around here," I whisper.

He seems embarrassed. "Unwanted attention, I can assure you." He looks around. "Where's Rebecca? I have her coffee."

"Oh, she's over there organizing another date for the charity auction."

He rolls his eyes. "No doubt."

My phone rings, the name Emerson lighting up my screen. "Hey, babe." I smile.

"Hi!" she squeals, and I hold the phone away from my ear and giggle. Mr. Masters frowns.

"We still on for tonight?" I ask.

Mr. Masters keeps his eyes on the game and pretends not to listen, but I know he can hear everything.

"Yep. Wear something sexy. The Canadian boys are coming."

"Really?" I glance at my boss as I speak to Emerson. "Have you spoken to them?" I reply as I lower my voice. We met two Canadian backpackers on the flight on the way over. We did mention going out with them tonight, but this is the first I've heard of it since.

"Yes. Oh my God, and the gorgeous one is really into you." I

57

bite my lip to stifle my smile, and I push the phone so close to my head, it feels like it nearly becomes embedded in my skull. I know how childish we sound, and for some reason, I don't want Mr. Masters hearing this.

"We'll see," I reply, trying to act casual.

"See you at eight at my house. Wear your sexiest dress."

I feel my nerves flutter. "Okay, see you then." I hang up and sip my coffee awkwardly. Mr. Masters stares at the soccer game, and for some reason I feel like I should offer an explanation.

"I'm a little nervous about going out tonight."

His unimpressed eyes turn to me. "Why?"

I swallow the lump in my throat. "Strange country, new people."

He raises an eyebrow and seems amused. I turn and continue to watch the game. It's weird. I go from feeling comfortable around him one minute, to feeling like a stupid child in the next.

"You did come here to find yourself, Brielle. I assume you will start that particular project tonight," he says flatly.

Are you for real?

He's openly sarcastic about the fact that I'm going out with the backpackers tonight. Is he unaware that, for the last two hours, I have watched every woman around this godforsaken field try to bang him as if he's the king of England?

I sip my coffee, remaining silent. Screw this.

I am going to have sex tonight. I'm going to have wild, uninhibited sex with a young Canadian—one who doesn't make me feel like I'm an errant teenager.

One who doesn't have a brain or a cute curl through his hair. Somebody whose name isn't Mr. Fucking Masters.

4

Brielle

I HOLD THE TISSUE FLAT, press the soft white parchment to my lips then roll them together as I look at my reflection in the mirror. My hair is full and curled just on the ends. My makeup is smoky sexy, and my lips are now a glossy gold.

I turn to look at my behind, and I feel my nerves flutter in my stomach.

I'm wearing a fitted, strapless cream dress, with high-heeled gold stilettos, plus a small gold clutch giving me something to cling to. I look good. I know I look good. Sexy and fun was my aim, and I think I nailed the brief.

Tonight's the night.

For twelve months, Emerson and I planned our trip to London, convincing ourselves that we were going to be new people. People who have fun and live by the seat of their pants. Not that we didn't do that back home, but we were definitely in a rut. I didn't want to go out in fear that I would run into my ex and one of his bimbos. Emerson didn't want to go out in case we saw her ex with someone else. Our social lives were completely dependent on other people, and I hate that we let that happen.

I hate that I unconsciously let my stupid ex determine what I did. Maybe I wasn't ready to move on, and that was just my excuse to keep my heart safe. I've been asked on dates—many times, actually—but nobody ever caught my interest, and I know it would have been a letdown and I'd have come home feeling flat. Declining dates was a better option than suffering disappointment.

So, Emerson and I would watch movies and eat takeout at each other's houses to save money for our trip. We both moved home with our parents a year ago when our relationships fell apart, and that, in itself, was a challenge.

Neither of us had lived at home since we were twenty, but we didn't want to commit to a new lease or anything until we came home from this trip. It was like our lives were on hold until we lived through this experience. And this is it...now we're here.

But the bravery I was sure I would have has suddenly disappeared.

The Canadian boys we met on the plane were nice. One of them was gorgeous, and we had an instant spark.

Is tonight the night, though? He leaves for Greece tomorrow. This is our one and only night together, and then I'll probably never see him again. Not that I'm complaining. He isn't the kind of man I can see myself ending up with long-term, but one night of passion might not be such a bad thing. Will I really have sex with a stranger? I haven't had sex in twelve months, and God, has that particular drought been hard. Harder than hard. I never realized how much I needed sex until I couldn't have it.

I feel a wave of nausea run through my stomach. I know it's just nerves, but staying home and spying on Mr. Masters while eating ice cream seems so much more appealing right now.

Ah, Mr. Masters—the man who makes my stomach flutter, whose voice makes me imagine things that I shouldn't be imagining.

I need to call a cab. I'll have to ask him who I call because I have no idea. With one quick look in the mirror, I make my way up into the main house.

Mr. Masters has been snappy with me all day, and I'm not really sure why. We seemed to get along well after our nanny scotch the other night, but today, after he heard me on the phone talking about tonight, we are back to square one.

Sam is sprawled on the living room floor, and Mr. Masters is sitting in his wingback chair, reading his book. Willow is sitting at the kitchen table, doing an assignment.

"Oh my God," Sammy yells. "You look so beautiful."

I hold my clutch in my hands with white-knuckle force, and I swallow the lump in my throat. Mr. Masters' eyes rise over the top of the book, and he gives me the once-over.

"Do you know what cab company I call, please?" I ask.

He smiles warmly. "You look lovely, Miss Brielle."

A stupid smile crosses my face as I squeeze my handbag so tight, I might break it. "Really?"

"Really." His eyes hold mine.

I glance over to Willow, who is watching me. "Do you like my dress, Will?" I ask.

She shrugs and goes back to her assignment.

Sammy jumps up from his place on the floor and circles me. "You look like a movie star." He gasps. "Like a gold and glittery Barbie."

Mr. Masters chuckles, and I feel the heat of it warm my blood. "You have a beautiful laugh," I say without thinking.

A scowl creases his forehead, and he stops laughing immediately. "I'll have my driver pick you up."

I frown too. "I don't want to bother you." I twist my hands in front of me. "I'll just catch a cab, honestly."

"Don't be daft." He picks up his phone.

"But how much does your driver charge?" I ask. "I'm on a budget."

His eyes rise to meet mine, he shakes his head, and then holds a finger up. "Hello. This is Julian Masters. Can you come and pick a guest up from my estate, please?"

I bite my bottom lip as I listen. How much does a damn private driver cost? Shit.

He nods. "I see, that's fine, although I will need you to pick her up later tonight too."

Oh no. I shake my head. "No, I'm staying at Emerson's," I mouth.

He frowns and looks down at the floor to avoid my gaze. "She will call you when she is ready to come home." He listens for a moment, and then smiles. "Yes, please, and I would like Frank to pick her up—"

"Mr. Masters," I interrupt. "I'm not coming home tonight."

He puts his hand over the phone. "Yes, you are."

"No, I'm not," I whisper.

"Yes. You. Are." He looks away and continues listening. "Yes, and charge her fare to my account, please."

I huff and put my hands on my hips. Of all the nerve. It's the weekend.

A trace of amusement crosses his face as he speaks. "Thank you. She'll see you then."

What the hell?

I glance up to Willow, who is smirking to herself. "This isn't funny, Will," I call to her, and she smiles down at her paper.

Finally, Julian's eyes rise to mine.

"Mr. Masters. I'm not coming home tonight. I'm staying at Emerson's."

"I'm sorry, Miss Brielle, I need you here in the morning, as I'm playing golf. Some other time, perhaps?"

My face falls. "But... I had plans tonight."

His eyes hold mine and he raises a sarcastic brow. "Change them." He gets up and grabs his keys. "Come on."

"Come on where?" I sigh. Damn it. Emerson's going to be pissed because she really wanted me to stay over at her new house. She's called me five times today already.

"I'll drive you into town...unless you'd prefer to walk?"

I smile and put my thumb out playfully. "I could always hitch a ride."

"Looking like that, you wouldn't last long."

"Looking like what?"

He looks me up and down and frowns. "Like a gold and glittery Barbie."

I smile. Oh, he's being cute now. "It is a strain being this beautiful, you know." I bat my eyelashes playfully and put my hands on my hips, wiggling my behind.

"Oh God," I hear Willow moan, and Sammy giggles in the background.

Mr. Masters smirks. "I have no doubt. Now get in the car before I throw you in the trunk."

I bite my bottom lip and smile at his playful return. Has his mood switched because I am no longer staying out?

Interesting.

"I'll be back in twenty minutes," he tells the children.

I smile at his fancy accent. He sounds like British royalty or something. I've never known anyone who talks as snootily as he does.

"Okay," the kids reply, going back to what they were doing.

I follow him as he walks down the front steps and out to the garage. The roller door goes up slowly and the Porsche lights beep as it unlocks.

My eyes widen in excitement. "Are we taking the pimp car?"

His face falls. "The pimp car?" He slinks into the lowered seat.

I bounce in beside him. "Yes, you know... I would expect the mafia or something to own this car." I look around. Wow! This really is a pimp car. It's compact, sporty, sexy...not at all something I would have imagined he would drive.

He rolls his eyes and looks through the rearview mirror to reverse the car out of the garage. "Or perhaps just a man who has studied at university for twelve years," he replies dryly.

"That, too," I giggle. "Although a pimp car does sound way more exciting."

He smirks, and we make our way down the driveway. I don't know if it's the excitement of going out in London for the first time, my sexy dress, or the fact that a gorgeous older man is driving me out in a Porsche, but I feel excited, alive, and I can hardly wipe the stupid smile from my face.

We pull out onto the open road and drive for a while, until I look over at him. "Show me."

He raises a brow. "Show you what?"

"What this baby can do."

I see excitement dance in his eyes, and it isn't long before he accepts my dare.

Without emotion, he changes gears and floors it. The engine roars like a tiger, and I am thrown back into my seat as the car takes off like a rocket.

I squeal with excitement, and he laughs at my reaction, and then moments later he slows the car back to what feels like a snail's pace now. We're back to the speed limit.

I smile broadly as I stare through the windscreen, my heart pumping hard as adrenaline courses through my veins.

His eyes flash to me.

"This car is a fucking turn-on," I whisper as I rub the dashboard. "I hope you do that on all your first dates with women. That, dear sir, is a legitimate deal closer."

He throws his head back and laughs freely. "I don't need a car to close my deals, Miss Brielle."

I smile as butterflies dance in my stomach, my eyes lingering on his handsome face. I bet he doesn't. A tiny part of me wonders what it would be like to go on a date with him—to get that deal sealed. He's so controlled and powerful, but I just saw a tiny glimmer of his naughty side.

Fucking hot is an understatement.

We pull into town, and for some reason, I don't really want to get out of the car now. I want to drive around at high speed in this pimp car with Mr. Masters.

The car roars into the parking spot, and he turns to me. "The restaurant is just across the road."

I look up and see the packed, trendy restaurant, and I know Emerson is inside. She's already texted me three times since I left. "Thanks." I smile.

His hand is resting on the steering wheel. "Have a great night. Be safe."

I stay seated in the car, and he looks over and raises an impatient eyebrow.

Oh shit! Get out, you idiot.

I climb out of the car and lean in through the window. "I'm glad the cab company couldn't bring me. That was way more fun."

He smiles sexily and revs the engine.

I laugh and shake my head. "See you in the morning." The car pulls out and roars up the street as I watch on. Wow, that was unexpected. Who knew?

I walk into the crowded restaurant to see Emerson waving from her table at the back. I laugh and almost run to meet her. "Oh God, it's so good to see you." I smile into her hair, hugging her tight. It feels like so much has happened since I saw her last.

"Look at us being all hot and grown up in London."

"I know." I giggle as I fall into my seat opposite her. "Can you believe we are actually here?"

"Yes." She smiles broadly as a waiter comes over with two margaritas and puts them in front of us.

I hunch my shoulders together. "Are we drinking cocktails?"

"Why not? It's our opening night. Screw it."

I pick up my drink and take a sip. Heaven in a glass. "Ah, that's the stuff." I eye my glass suspiciously. "How much are these babies?"

"More than we can afford, but who cares?" She holds her drink up and we clink our glasses together. "To London." She smiles proudly.

"To London." I giggle.

"Tell me everything." She widens her eyes.

I shake my head and hold up my hand. "You wouldn't believe the three days I've had."

"Try me."

"Well, Mr. Masters picks me up, and you saw what he was like..."

"Cranky. Has he gotten any better?"

I shrug. "I don't know, but get this... I think he jacked off to my photo."

Emerson spits out her drink and nearly chokes. "What the fuck?" She then goes into a full-on coughing fit as she tries to deal with margarita up her nose.

"He showed me to my room and wouldn't come in, and then later that night, when I was spying on him—"

She scowls hard. "Wait, what? You were spying on him?" she interrupts.

I put my hands over my face. "Long story, but he's kind of hot."

"He's old, Brell."

"He's thirty-eight...or nine. I'm not actually sure, to be honest," I reply dryly.

"Either one is still old."

I roll my eyes. "Anyway, I was spying on him and I saw him take my photo off the fridge. Then he put his hands down his boxer shorts and played with himself."

Emerson's eyes widen, and her mouth falls open.

"Then he took the photo and went upstairs to his bedroom."

"Fuck off."

"I've still got it." I giggle, and we clink our glasses together.

We smile at each other as we sip our drinks. This is so much fun.

"Oh my God, tell me about Mark."

She twists her lips. "He's okay, I suppose."

66

I wince. "Just okay?"

"He's a bit of a dick, to be honest." She thinks on it for a moment. "I've met a few dicks this week, come to think of it."

For some reason I get the giggles and hold my glass up in a cheers symbol. "Well, I got fired. Beat that."

Emerson chokes again. "What?" She begins to drain her glass, and I throw my head back and laugh. "What the hell, Brell?"

I shake my head. "The first morning I'm working, the little boy, Samuel, comes into my room sleepwalking. Mr. Masters then came into my room to get him."

She frowns as she listens. "What are the kids like?"

"Sammy is eight and beautiful."

"That's the boy?"

"Yes, and the girl, Willow, is sixteen, and she's a witch."

"We were all witches at sixteen."

"Exactly," I reply. "She'll warm up to me." I sip my drink. "Anyway, after Mr. Masters leaves for work, I go upstairs to check on Sammy. He was fine and asleep, so I'm walking back to my room and I walk past Mr. Masters' room, and I think to myself... I wonder what his room is like, you know?"

"Of course, good question. Anybody would want to know that."

"So I go in, and I'm looking around, and then I open his bathroom cabinet."

She lifts her glass at me. "You can tell a lot about a person from their bathroom cabinet."

"Exactly." I point at her.

"What did you find out?"

I sip my drink. "That he smells fucking good and he has a lot of sex."

She giggles.

"Next minute, he's behind me, growling and raging with anger when I look up to see his reflection in the mirror, "What the hell do you think you're doing?"

Her eyes widen. "He came home?"

"Yes. In some kind of bust-a-move, backdoor attack."

"Oh no."

We burst out laughing.

"Then I got caught lying about waking the kids up already when they were still in bed. After that, Willow and I had a stand-up row and told each other to fuck off on the way to school."

She puts her hands over her mouth in horror.

"And then he and I drank some freaky truth serum while he fired me."

She downs her drink again. "Are you for real? Did this shit really happen?"

"I swear."

"But I talked him round, and now I have nineteen days to prove myself before he fires me again."

She looks at me, speechless.

"But...it turns out he's a scotch nanny virgin, and he is kind of hot, in a rich-old-guy way. So I'm going to try and be good so I can stay there. I think I can actually do it."

Emerson holds her hand up. "You've completely lost me. What the hell is a scotch nanny virgin?"

"He's never drunk scotch with his nanny before."

She frowns.

"And we played this mindfuck of a game where he dared me to ask him anything."

She bites her fingernail as she listens, fascinated. "And?"

"And I asked him how he liked his women."

"You did what?" she shrieks as she puts her hands over her eyes again. "Oh God, you really are going to get fired. Do you have to be so damn honest all the time?"

"Yeah, but I wanted to know the answer."

She laughs. "So do I. What did he say?"

"He said he likes his women to be pure and wholesome with a side of dirty and slutty...but only for him."

She bites her bottom lip as her eyes hold mine. "That's kind of hot."

"I know, right?"

We both sip our drinks as we think. "Oh." She smiles. "I met a pig."

"You met a pig, as in oink oink pig?" I giggle.

"When I bought my ring."

"Oh, show me your ring."

She holds out her hand and shows me a gorgeous emerald ring. "I love it, I'm so glad you got it."

"Me too. But get this... I'm trying the ring on, when suddenly, this arrogant twat makes an offer on it."

"What do you mean?"

"I had the ring on my finger and this weird, rude guy starts bidding for it."

"While you were still looking at it?"

"Yep."

"You're joking?"

"Nope. So then I had to buy it just so he couldn't." She smiles as she looks down at her hand and wiggles her fingers. "Sucked in, Mr. Twinkle."

"Twinkle?" I frown.

She rolls her eyes. "He calls himself Star."

I laugh and put my hand over my mouth. "Are you for real?"

"Yes." She frowns as she thinks. "It was weird, you know... I felt like I knew him somehow."

"Did you?"

"No. We've never met. He was Irish, had a beautiful accent. Shame he was such a pig."

We both laugh.

"Can I take your order, ladies?" the waiter asks.

"What are we having?" I ask her.

She opens the menu and smiles broadly. "Whatever the hell we want."

Three hours later, we walk into Club Alto, the two of us holding hands. I can hardly contain my excitement. We just got a call from the Canadian boys we met on the plane. They said they were near the bar, so we head over to it. We look around for a while, and Emerson lines up at the bar to get our drinks. I spot one of the guys through the crowd, and he waves back, instantly making his way over.

"Hello." He smiles sexily.

"Hi." But before I can say anything else, he takes me in his arms and plants a soft, prolonged kiss on my lips. I feel my feet lift off the floor.

Oh shit. It's like that, is it?

He looks down at me darkly and licks his lips. "I've been waiting to do that all week."

"You have?" I smile.

He kisses me again, and this time his tongue slides into my mouth and I feel my arousal begin to roll in.

"I have," he whispers. His hand drops down to my behind, and he gives it a firm squeeze. "Have you thought about me?"

This night is taking an exciting turn. "Not really." I smile. "But I am now."

Julian

Buzz, buzz.

Buzz, buzz. Buzz, buzz.

I frown and roll over to grab my phone—the one currently dancing on my side table. I pick it up and see the blurred name of Miss Brielle light up the screen.

I glance at the clock. It's 4:00 a.m.

Great. She's obviously staying out and calling to let me know. "Yes?" I snap on answering.

"Ohhhhhhh," she slurs.

"What are you doing?" God, she's blind drunk. I can hear it in her voice.

"Well..." She pauses. "Can you please put Julian on the phone, Mr. Masters?"

"Miss Brielle, it's 4:00 a.m. and I'm not in the mood for your games. What do you want?"

"I've told you. I need to speak to Julian, my housemate, and not Mr. Masters, my boss."

I lie back and inhale sharply. "Why do you need Julian?"

"Because I only have nineteen days left to prove that I'm a good nanny and I really don't want to wake Mr. Masters up." She hesitates. "I want to speak to Julian, please."

"Miss Brielle, enough of the games."

"Please," she begs. "Put Julian on the phone."

I roll my eyes and exhale heavily. "Speaking."

"Oh my God, Julian, my key is not working and I'm locked out of the house."

I close my eyes. "What? Where are you?"

"I'm at the front door."

"Why isn't your key working?"

"I don't know, but can you come open the door before Mr. Masters wakes up? I'm on a good behavior bond, you know."

I smirk, stupid fool. "Fine. But I'm telling him in the morning."

"Whatever. Just don't tell him now, and please hurry up."

I climb out of bed and make my way downstairs to open the front door. The front light is on, but she's not there. I look around. Where is she? "Miss Brielle?"

"Boo!" She springs out from around the corner, and I jump. "What the hell?" I cry. Her hair is dishevelled and her makeup worn off. She has her gold heels in her hand, and to be honest, she looks even better than she did when she left.

She laughs out loud and points at me. "Ha-ha, got you." She looks down at me and stumbles back as her pointer finger drops to my stomach. "Ohhhh, your abs are out," she slurs. "This is an added bonus."

I look at her, deadpan.

She points at my boxer shorts. "I didn't know you were coming down in your cutie patootie pyjamas."

"Jesus Christ," I mutter under my breath. "How much have you had to drink?"

"Way too much. I just nearly had a nap in the front garden." She nods and then does an over-exaggerated hiccup. "True story."

"Come in," I sigh.

She links her arm through mine and tiptoes beside me.

I smirk at her overfamiliarity. "How was your night?" I ask.

"Oh God, my night," she whispers. "You wouldn't believe what happened."

"Try me," I whisper as we walk through the kitchen.

"Oh." Her face suddenly gets excited. "We need to drink truth serum for this story."

I raise my eyebrows. "Miss Brielle, I am not drinking scotch with you at 4:00 a.m." My eyes drop down her hot body. "Not with you in this state."

"Okay, good. You watch me drink it, then. I need a snack anyway."

She pushes me down onto a stool at the counter. "Sit there and I'll make us food."

"I'm not hungry."

She smiles sexily and leans over the bench toward me. My eyes drop to her large breasts that are ready to break free from her tight dress.

"All men say they're not hungry, but they always eat the house down when it's offered."

I don't know if it's the fact that she's wearing next to nothing, or the image I get of me eating every last drop of her, but I inhale sharply as I feel my cock begin to swell.

Cut it out.

"Miss Brielle," I reply.

"Yes, Julian."

Something about the way she says my name like that makes me smile. I suppose it couldn't hurt to stay with her while she eats something. "Make it quick."

"What do you want to eat?" she asks innocently.

I get an image of myself kissing her inner thigh as she lies back over the kitchen counter, but I snap myself out of the daydream quickly. "I'm really not hungry."

She begins to open and close doors. "Where is the truth serum?"

I point to the cupboard, and she smiles and leans over to get it. My eyes drop to her behind. That dress leaves nothing to the imagination.

Tanned muscular thighs.

This isn't a good situation to be in...at all.

Go. To. Bed.

She grabs two thick tumbler glasses, fills them with ice, and then places them on the counter in front of us. She pours the scotch into the first and I put my hand over the top of the second glass. "Not for me," I mutter.

She lifts the glass and sips it, licking her lips. "I think scotch nanny virgin may be my new favorite thing."

"It's just called scotch. The nanny virgin thing is irrelevant."

She grins. "Or is it?"

The air zaps between us, and she holds my gaze, as if daring me to say something.

Don't get into this with her. Go upstairs and go to sleep.

I can't help myself. I have to ask. "Why would a nanny virgin be anything but irrelevant?"

She sips her drink and licks her lips again. I feel my cock contract.

Fuck.

Go. To. Bed.

She leans forward, resting on her elbows on the other side of the counter, and my eyes drop to her large, perfect tits. "I like the fact that you haven't let your other nannies drink scotch with you." She smiles innocently.

I get a vision of drinking scotch from her navel. Cut it out.

"I'm going to bed, Miss Brielle." I stand.

"No. No. No." She shakes her head and grabs my shoulders,

pushing me back onto my stool. "We just need some music. I'll make us some toast and then I'll go to bed, I promise." She looks through the cupboard. "Do you have any Vegemite?"

"I don't want Vegemite on toast."

"You'll get what you're given." She smiles cheekily.

Our eyes lock, and I feel electricity zap through the air between us.

Okay, what the fuck? Is she trying to turn me on right now?

Because it's working.

She'll get what she's fucking given in a minute.

She picks up her phone and flicks through to Spotify. She hits play and a dance tune rings out, giving her an excuse to dance. "You like this song?"

"I don't know it."

"*Sexy Bitch* by David Guetta."

She starts to dance freely, not trying to be cool at all, and her hips move to the rhythm as she turns to look in the fridge. With her back to me, my eyes stay firmly on her ass as it sways to the beat. The words ring out.

I hold my breath as I watch her.

Fitting song. "*Sexy Bitch*" should be her anthem. The song continues and she really gets into it, picking up her glass and giggling as she dances. She spills her drink down her forearm, and then she puts her arm up and slowly licks it off.

I clench as I feel it all the way to the tip of my cock.

Jesus Christ. I pick up the scotch and pour myself a glass too quickly. It sloshes over the side. How much seduction can a man take before he fucks his nanny on his kitchen floor?

I sip my drink as my eyes rake her in. She's laughing freely as she dances.

The warmth of the liquor heats my throat, but it's nothing like the fire that's starting down below.

Stop dancing like that, baby, or you will wake Mr. Masters... and he doesn't treat naughty girls like you so well.

She looks down and notices my drink. "Oh, you're drinking

now." She smiles as she bounces to the beat. "Can we play truth or dare?"

I lick my bottom lip. "If you like." This is dangerous territory, but I can't make myself go to bed. At least...not alone.

"You go first." She beams.

I sip my scotch as I think of my first question. "How did your night go with the man you met on the plane?"

She curls her lip. "Started out okay." She shrugs. "We kissed."

"How was it?"

Her eyes drop to my lips and she licks her own. My cock clenches in approval.

"The kiss?" she asks.

I nod.

"The kiss was okay, I guess."

I can't help myself and I have to ask. "You went home with him?"

This is so inappropriate.

She shakes her head. "No." She shrugs. "He asked me to have a threesome with him and his friend."

I raise an eyebrow. "Who on Earth would want to share you?" Our eyes lock.

She leans over the counter onto her elbows, our faces only inches apart.

"Did you come home because you were angry with him for asking you for a threesome?" I ask.

"No. I came home because when I was kissing him, I was thinking of somebody else."

"Who?"

"I think you know.

5

Julian

A TRACE of a smile crosses my face. "I have no idea who you would be thinking about."

She sits down on her stool and tips her glass at me. "If you were out on a date tonight..." She rearranges herself and pulls her dress down. "Who would you be thinking about?"

I raise my eyebrows. Where is she going with this? "I would be thinking about the person I was on a date with."

She narrows her eyes, questioning me. "Really?"

I bite my bottom lip to stop myself from smiling. "And why are you surprised that I give my full attention to my dates?"

She rests her hand under her chin and smiles up at me playfully. "I don't know," she breathes dreamily. "I just am." Our eyes linger on each other's just a little too long. She's soft, beautiful and playful, and I know if I stay here, I'm going to do something that I'll regret later. Something that entails her being naked and bent over the kitchen counter, while I fuck her hard from behind. I would hitch her right leg up to rest on the counter to give me better access.

I get a vision of her bent over, naked and wet. Open...wide open.

Her big, beautiful tits would be free for me to look at.

She hasn't had sex for twelve months. Imagine how tight she is. Cut. It. The. Fuck. Out!

I shake my head and clear my throat, disgusted where my thoughts are going. "Miss Brielle." I stand abruptly, hoping that she doesn't see the tent in the front of my shorts. "I'm going to bed."

She jumps up and grabs my hand. "Come on, let's dance. The night is young."

"Go to bed!" I demand.

"Oh...but I'll fall down the stairs and break my leg." She pulls a whiney face. "I'm too tired to walk all that way. Can't I sleep here on this stool?"

"No. You cannot." I grab her hand. "In bed, now, please." I lead her through the house and down the hall to her bedroom. My heart begins to beat faster and faster with every step closer to her door.

"Julian," she purrs playfully from behind me.

"Mr. Masters to you," I snap. This is way too familiar for my liking.

Her hand is small and deliciously soft, just how I imagine her body to be.

For fuck's sake, rein it in.

"Mr. Masters," she repeats in a gruff voice, mimicking me.

I open her bedroom door and am greeted with her scent. Sweet-smelling perfume fills my nostrils, and I start to hear my heartbeat pump in my ears as my arousal begins to take over.

Get out of here.

Get out of here now!

My cock is now at full length and dripping. Her scent is all around me and I just need to fuck her.

I throw her on the bed, and she laughs freely as she falls back onto the mattress. Her eyes hold mine as she giggles playfully, her arms up above her head and her long dark hair splayed across her pillow.

"So bossy, Mr. Masters," she whispers.

I clench my hands into fists as I stand over her. "You have no idea," I whisper. God, she looks fucking edible.

Leave...

My heart is racing.

I hesitate as I take a moment to control my voice. "Goodnight, Miss Brielle."

"Goodnight, Mr. Masters," she breathes sexily.

I leave the room and practically run up the stairs. I tear open the bathroom cabinet and take out the baby oil.

A man's got to do what a man's got to do.

Brielle

Pound, pound, pound.

Oh God, my head.

What the fuck happened last night?

I frown as I try to focus around my room, and then down at myself. I'm still in the clothes I wore out last night.

I feel so sick. What the hell was I thinking, drinking all those cocktails?

I can hardly remember anything since I got in the car to come home.

That's weird. I was fine when I left the club.

I get up, go to the bathroom, and then take a look at myself in the mirror. My hair is wild. My hot, smoky makeup from last night now looks like a half-dead racoon. I look like roadkill.

Oh, dear God, my breath.

I squeeze toothpaste on my toothbrush and begin to brush my teeth while I feel sorry for myself, staring at my reflection. And now I have to babysit today while Mr. Masters plays golf.

A fleeting image of myself dancing in the kitchen crosses my mind.

Wait, when was that? Did I?

I close my eyes as I try to remember what happened last night. Was he already awake? Did I wake him up?

Oh no. Fuck.

I spit out the toothpaste with force and quickly wash my face.

Then I run into the bedroom and start climbing out of my dress.

Oh my God. Oh my fucking God. What did I do? What did I do?

I nearly rip the dress as I tear it down, throwing my dressing gown over my underwear before I run out into the hall. I race up the stairs into the main house and find Willow sitting at the breakfast table, eating her porridge.

"H-hi, Willow," I stammer.

She looks up and frowns. "What happened to you?"

"Good question," I mutter as I look around the house in a panic. "Where's your father?"

"He's just about to go golfing. I think he's in the garage."

I bite my bottom lip. "Okay, thanks. I need to see him about something." I run out and down the back steps to the garage. I find Mr. Masters in there, cleaning his golf clubs with a rag and what looks like a bottle of oil. He's looking down and concentrating on the task at hand.

"Good morning." I smile. Please let this all be a figment of my warped imagination.

His eyes flicker up to me, and then back to his golf clubs. Shit. He's pissed.

I twist my fingers together as I watch him, not knowing what to say.

"Is everything okay?" I whisper.

His cold eyes rise to meet mine. "No, everything is not all right," he says coldly.

My eyes widen. "What's wrong?"

"You can't be that obtuse, Miss Brielle."

My heart starts to beat faster.

He goes back to cleaning his golf clubs. "Did I wake you last night?" I whisper.

His furious eyes rise to meet mine. "Among other things."

I scratch my head in confusion. "What does that mean?"

"It means your sexual advances are superfluous." He sneers.

My eyes widen in horror. What the fuck? "S-sexual advances?" I stammer. "Why...what? What do you mean, sir?"

He slams the golf clubs down on the ground with a thud. "You know exactly what I mean."

I wring my hands together in front of me. "I'm so sorry, Mr. Masters, but I don't even remember getting home last night. Please tell me what happened."

He shakes his head in disgust, opens his car, and walks around the side of it. I run after him like a puppy. "What happened? What did I do?" I plead.

Oh God. What did I do?

He throws his clubs into the trunk and slams it shut. "And this incongruous behavior is unacceptable," he growls.

"I don't understand."

"This..." He gestures to my dressing gown. "This has got to stop."

"What has?"

"You walking around my house in a state of undress. Coming home in the middle of the night and dancing half naked in my kitchen, while being all flirty and suggestive." He steps closer to me and narrows his eyes. "I can assure you, Miss Brielle, that I am not the kind of man who has sexual relations with his staff."

My face falls.

"What?" I whisper. "I don't know what you're talking about. What happened last night?"

"You arrived home, called me, and when I came downstairs, you got all excited when you saw me in my..."—he air quotes to accentuate his point—"*cutie patootie pyjamas*."

My eyes widen. Oh fuck. I didn't call his pyjamas cutie patootie.

Surely not?

They are anything but cutie patootie. They are smoking hot. "Then you proceeded to dry hump my refrigerator, all while wearing next to nothing."

I swallow the lump in my throat. This just keeps getting worse. Kill me now.

"You practically went down on a glass of scotch before you started licking your arm in some kind of porn display, and then you insisted on talking about me being a nanny virgin."

My hands go over my mouth in disbelief. "I came on to you?" I whisper.

He gets into his car, slams the door shut, and winds down the window. "Your impropriety is alarming and will not be tolerated in this house under any watch."

I drop my head in shame. "Yes, sir."

"Now, if it isn't too much trouble, Miss Brielle...do your job and go look after my children. If you are uninterested in performing the position you applied for, go find something else, because I can assure you that the position of being a hooker, on your back, in my bed, is unavailable."

My eyes fill with tears.

He starts the car and I step back, out of his way. I quickly swipe a tear from my eye as it tries to escape, but he doesn't miss it, and he hesitates as he watches me, as if he's going to say something more.

Finally, without another hurtful word, he chooses to leave.

I stand alone in the garage and look around at the spotless space as I hear his sports car roar down the driveway. My heart is racing, and my face is hot, flushed with embarrassment.

A heavy sense of regret sits in the pit of my stomach. I'm so ashamed.

I'm a prude; I don't come on to people. I get annoyed and disgusted when people come on to me.

And he's my boss.

I put my hands on top of my head as the tears burst through the dam and roll down my face. What must he think of me?

Fuck, this is the worst hangover ever.

I'm slumped on my bed half an hour later, completely defeated.

This job is harder than I thought, but I never imagined that my sense of character would be under scrutiny.

Why the hell didn't I just stay over at Emerson's last night? None of this would have happened. It's a complete disaster, and to be honest, one that I don't think I can work through. That's if he even wanted me to.

I'm mortified at my behavior and I want to run to him and tell him he's got it all wrong, but who am I kidding? He saw it with his own eyes, and he wouldn't just make this stuff up for fun on a Sunday morning.

His disappointed voice echoes in my mind. *You were dry humping my refrigerator.*

Oh, the horror.

I pinch the bridge of my nose in disgust. I'm going to leave. He thinks I'm a skanky ho. Why wouldn't he? I am. I can't believe I acted that way. I have no idea what came over me. What in the world would possess me to come home and start dirty dancing in the kitchen?

I dry humped his fridge.

That's it—the decision has been taken out of my hands. I have to leave. I want Emerson to come over and get me tonight. I can't pack up all my stuff and do this alone, so I dial her number.

"Oh, hell, I'm dying over here," she answers roughly.

"Yeah, well, you and me both. Great idea drinking cocktails, Einstein. I need you to come over here tonight and help me move my stuff. I'm resigning."

She sighs. "What now? I'm too ill for dramatics today."

"Apparently, I dry humped Mr. Masters' fucking refrigerator

82

last night when I got home, and I was dancing around like a hooker and coming on to him. The worst part is that I can't even remember it."

"What?"

"You heard me. I had a slut brain snap and—" I throw my hands in the air in exasperation. "I don't know what the hell was going through my thick head."

She lets out a shocked chuckle. "Are you joking?"

"I wish."

"Oh God." She pauses for a moment. "What the hell did you do?"

I close my eyes, because it's mortifying to say it out loud. "I told him his pyjamas were cutie patootie pyjamas."

She bursts out laughing. "What? Cutie patootie? Who says cutie patootie?"

I find myself smiling. She's right, this really is unbelievable. "And then I dry humped his fridge and started licking scotch off my fingers or something. After that, I came on to him."

"Jesus. You must be hanging for it." She thinks for a moment. "Did you have sex?"

I cringe. "No, idiot! He hates me."

"Oh, bullshit. He was probably loving every minute of it. There isn't a man alive who could watch you dry hump a fridge and not get aroused."

"You're not helping!"

"Did you ask him to have sex?"

I scowl and wrinkle my nose. What if I did? "I can't stay here. I'm so embarrassed, you have no idea."

"Well, what did he say to you?"

"He told me off using all these intelligent words I hardly understood, and then he said that I should stick to the position I applied for because the hooker position in his bed, on my back, isn't available."

She stays silent.

"Are you still there?" I snap.

"Yeah, the hooker-in-his-bed bit threw me. That's kind of a hot thing to say, you know? Do you reckon he has hookers in his bed for real?"

"No!" I shriek. "He's probably fucking gay. Get me out of here!"

"Calm down. We'll find you another job. Just hang in there for another week or two. Anyway, doesn't he go away this week?"

"Yeah, on Wednesday."

"Well then, you won't even see him."

"I wish I went home with those two guys last night. I bet I would feel like less of a slut than I do now." I sigh.

"If you did go home with those two guys last night, they would have taken turns fucking your ass all night, and we would be in emergency right now getting it sewn back together."

I wince at the thought. "Oh God. Can you imagine?"

"Just suck it up for a few weeks until we find you another job. Take the kids out today, do something fun and outdoorsy so that he doesn't think you are staying at home, nursing a hangover."

"Yeah, that's a good idea." I wonder where I could take them.

"Look, he's been drunk before, surely. Nobody is that perfect."

"I honestly doubt it. He stays home and studies his thesaurus."

She giggles. "Just behave yourself until we find you another job."

I roll my eyes. "Fine." I shake my head. "But if you ever buy me another cocktail, I'm tipping it over your head."

She laughs, and I hang up.

I sit for a moment as I process her words, knowing she's right. I can't fuck this whole thing up until I get another job.

Which brings me to my next problem: the kids. I march up into the house with renewed determination, and I find them both on the sofa, lazing like sloths with their phones in their faces. "Let's go out for the day."

"Pass." Willow sighs without looking up.

I lift my chin to stare at the ceiling, and I suck in a breath. Please, God, give me the strength to deal with her today. I don't want to add a murder to my list of misdemeanor.

"It's a beautiful day, so we're going outdoors. You can pick the activity," I announce.

Sammy frowns as he thinks. "We could play golf like Dad does?"

"Hmm. I don't think your father would appreciate us annoying him."

"No, Dad has gone far away to play golf. He told me so. We could just play at the country club down the road."

"We don't have any golf clubs. What else could we do?" I say.

"We have golf clubs. We can use Dad's old ones that are in the garage," Sam replies.

Hmm, I don't feel like driving around. Unless...

I glance over at the phone constantly attached to Willow's palm. "Willow, you could drive the golf buggy."

Her eyes lift to mine. "Really? You would let me drive?"

"Of course, why not?"

She sits up, her excitement stirring.

"I could make us a picnic, we could play some music on our phones, and we could enjoy an afternoon out in the sun."

Willow bites her bottom lip. She can't show me she's excited; that would go against her game plan. "I suppose I could do that... for Sam, I mean," she eventually agrees. For Sam. Obviously.

I smile and place my hands on my hips. "Well, we just have to wait for a few hours." I can't tell them we have to wait until the alcohol has left my system. "But once we're ready, we'll go and have fun."

"Woohoo!" Sammy squeals as he punches the air.

I frown. "What do you wear to play golf in London?"

"Collared shirts," Willow replies as she takes off upstairs. I smile. You know, I think they are actually excited.

This could be fun.

Julian

I hit the ball off the tee and we watch it fly down the fairway. "How's your dick?" I ask Spence.

He rolls his eyes as he stands next to me, holding his golf bag. "Recovered. I'm going back tonight." He looks down the fairway. "I had to psych myself up." He chews the gum in his mouth as he concentrates on his hit. He lines up and smacks the ball high into the air.

I glance at Seb and raise a brow before I look back at Spence. "Fuck off. Who the hell has to psych themselves up to fuck two beautiful, kinky women?" I mock as I drag my second ball over to the tee with the back of my club.

He raises his eyebrows at me and tilts his head. "How's that hot nanny of yours, anyway?" He chews his gum, waiting.

I blow out a breath. "Trouble. She nearly got herself fucked on my kitchen floor last night."

They both grin, flashing their teeth. "What happened?" Seb asks.

"Came home drunk and horny, waking me up."

Seb's eyebrows rise. "And?"

"And nothing." I take my hit, and we watch the ball fly into the air. "She's too young. It's a no go."

Seb lines his ball up. "How old?"

"Twenty-five."

"That's a perfect age. She's old enough to know how to fuck, loose enough to fuck hard, but tight enough to drive you wild."

I roll my eyes. "Yeah, well, she would drive me fucking wild. I already know that. I'm telling you, I've never been so attracted to someone in my life." I get into the golf buggy. "I have to grit my teeth the whole time I'm talking to her so I don't get a raging boner."

They smile as we drive down the fairway. "You should just do it."

I shake my head. "I can't. My kids seem to like her. I have to behave." I sigh.

"Fuck the kids." Spence sighs. "This is all about you. The kids don't pay her fucking wage, do they?" We pull up at the green. "Get your money's worth, I say." He smiles cheekily, popping his gum.

"You just worry about that iron snatch that's going to rip your cock off tonight." I smirk as I take out my club. "Leave my nanny to me."

Brielle

Three hours later, we drive into the swanky-looking golf club, and I pull into a parking space.

The sun is out, the birds are chirping, and the day is perfect. This place is very posh indeed. Rolling green hills stretch out as far as the eye can see. There are groups of distinguished-looking people—all being very conservative and quiet—playing golf together.

We sit in the car for a moment as we look around. "God, these people look so bored, don't they?" I say.

"Truth," Willow agrees as she looks around.

"Can we please go in?" Sammy pleads. "You promised."

I exhale. "Yes, we're here now. Let's do this." I climb out of the car and look down at myself. I'm wearing my navy pants and a white cotton shirt. My hair is in a high ponytail, and I have my gold aviator sunglasses on. I look like I don't belong here, but the kids follow me anyway as we go into the reception area. A good-looking young man and a beautiful girl are standing behind the counter. They look to be around Willow's age. The young man glances at Willow and then does a double take. She instantly drops her head and bites her bottom lip.

She's kind of cute when she gets shy. Shy is a lot more appealing on her than evil.

The beautiful girl smiles warmly. "Hello, can I help you?"

"Yes. We would like to play golf, please?"

Her gaze turns to Willow. "Okay." She smiles at her, and Willow drops her head...again. Oh, she really is shy.

We need to work on this.

"Can we please hire a golf cart too?" I ask.

"Sure." She takes a photocopy of my license and hands over the keys as I pay.

"There are a few rules that you need to adhere to."

"Such as?" More damn rules.

The handsome young man interrupts the girl as she speaks. "We ask that you don't cut in front of other players, stay out of the bunkers, and treat the greens with respect."

"Of course." I glance over to see Willow is twisting her hands in front of her. This boy is obviously affecting her. How cute.

"This is our first time, but if we like it, we will be coming back to learn properly," I add.

"Oh." The young girl turns to Willow. "There are lessons for girls on Wednesday afternoons at 5:00 if you're interested?"

Willow smiles awkwardly.

Oh jeez. She's never getting a boyfriend at this rate.

"Your golf buggy is the one parked to the right. Take it easy if you've never driven one before."

I take the keys from the boy's hand. "Thanks, we will keep that in mind." I grin at the kids. "Let's go hit some balls."

We walk out, get the clubs from the car, and then we put them into the back of the golf buggy. "You sit in the back, Sammy, and I will drive until they can't see us. After that, you can drive, Will."

"Okay." She bounces her shoulders with excitement.

We all get in and I start the cart. I raise my eyebrows to the kids, and Sammy laughs out loud. "Yes. We are driving."

I pull out onto the path, and we begin to drive under the stretch of large green trees. We pass a bunch of golfers and I wave, giving a little toot, toot of our horn.

Willow smiles and shakes her head. I think she's finally getting to like my goofiness a smidge, even if she doesn't know it yet. "So, where do we go?" I ask.

"I don't know," Sammy calls from the back.

"Was there a map in those papers she gave us, Will?" Willow flicks through the papers.

I glance over at her. "The staff here are quite attractive, don't you think, Will?"

She smirks and rolls her eyes.

We drive for a bit longer and I see a drink cart. "Oh, we need some roadies," I say as I pull over.

"Roadies?" Will asks.

"Yes, you know...drinks to take on the road. You call them roadies."

"Oh."

I hand Sam some money. "Can you go and get us three cans of Coke, Sammy, please, and some crisps and chocolate."

He holds the money in his hand and looks at me. "What?" I ask.

"We aren't allowed to drink Coke."

"Says who?"

"Dad."

I roll my eyes. "Well, I'm not going to tell him. Are you?" He smiles cheekily and goes to the cart.

"God, don't tell your father I'm letting you drive this golf buggy. He will have a conniption."

"What's new, that's all he does."

I watch her for a moment as she looks out over the green. Her dark hair is in two plaits. She's wearing a black cap, and she has her usual grungy-style clothing on. Her skin is porcelain clear and she has the prettiest eyes. She's actually very attractive underneath all her witch wear. Poor kid. She has this straight-laced father, and I'm pretty sure all of her nannies have been as boring as batshit.

Has she ever had someone in her life to have fun with?

Sammy returns, jumping in the back, and we crack open our cans of Coke. I hold mine up in the air.

"Cheers. A Coca-Cola toast."

They both put their cans up to mine.

"To crazy fun on the golf course today." I widen my eyes. "With no rules."

Sammy laughs, and I see excitement dancing in Willow's eyes as we hit our cans together.

"Anyone know where the first hole is?" I ask as I pull out onto the path.

Willow points to the left. "Up over the hill."

I grin mischievously. "Hold on, everybody."

I floor it and we go flying. Sammy squeals in delight, and even Willow cracks a smile. "Let's show these boring golfers how it's done." I drive like a maniac, and as soon as we are out of the club-house's view, I start to zigzag. The kids both laugh out loud as I try to tip them out.

"We need some tunes." I glance over at Will. "Can you get my phone and hit Spotify, please."

She frowns and swipes through the options on the screen. Hmm, I think for a moment. "I think this day calls for Kanye."

Willow raises her eyebrow. "Kanye?"

"Yeah. Kanye. Hit the Kanye West playlist."

"Who's Kanye West?" she asks.

"Are you kidding me?"

She shakes her head. "Nope."

"Oh God, do you live under a rock? Don't answer that. He's a rapper. I like his old stuff better than his new."

We arrive at the first hole. I park and we all climb out. The tee off is on a hill, and the golf green is way, way down below. I put my hands on my hips as I look into the distance.

Willow takes a golf club and ball out, and then she hands them to me.

"I'm supposed to hit this tiny ball into that tiny hole all the way down there?" I point to the green.

"Yep."

Sammy and Willow stand beside me with their hands on their hips as we contemplate how we can complete this impossible task.

I lean over, place the ball down, and then wiggle my behind. "White ball in the sand pocket," I announce.

"Oh God," Willow moans.

I take a swing and completely miss the ball, which causes them both to laugh. I take another, and another, until finally I connect with the ball and it goes scooting across the ground.

I hit the club on the ground. "I'm completely shit at this."

"It's true, you are," Sammy chuckles.

"Your turn, Will," I say.

She lines it up and takes a swing, missing the ball completely.

"You're shit too." I laugh.

She smiles as she concentrates on hitting it again. This time she connects with the ball and it sails high in the air.

"Wow!" Sammy shouts.

"Yeah, baby!" I call. "Have you ever done this before?"

She shakes her head. "No."

"Holy crap. You could be the next Tiger Woods or something."

"Who's Tiger Woods?"

I roll my eyes. "You need to read tabloid gossip more, girl-friend." She smiles proudly as her ball bounces way down the green. "Maybe you should do those golf lessons, Will? I can bring you."

She shrugs and we watch as Sammy takes his turn. He, too, starts off by missing terribly, but finally, he beats my shot.

"You drive now, Will."

"Really?"

"Yeah, why not?" I shrug. "Can't hurt." I watch her get behind the steering wheel and I direct her on what to do. When we take off slowly, she laughs out loud.

"Look at me! I'm driving." She laughs.

I giggle and hit my playlist. The song "*Gold Digger*" rings out. I turn it up so it's loud.

"You're not just driving, baby, you're driving to '*Gold Digger*.' I laugh. "This is our aim. Today we are learning all the words to '*Gold Digger*' and '*Black Skinhead*.'"

She turns to me in disbelief. "You want us to learn rap songs, while we play golf?"

I dance as I mouth the words to her. "Sure do." I put my hand over to the backseat. "Hit me with some chocolate, Sammy. I need sustenance."

"Yeah!" he yells, full of excitement. "This is the best day ever!"

It's 4:00 p.m. and we have laughed our way around every hole.

Kanye has been blaring out, and we now know most of the words. Willow has been speeding and trying her best to hit every pothole on the paths. Sammy is beaming with happiness. Come to think of it, so am I.

We got told off twice by boring golfers who told us to turn our music down, which we did for approximately seven minutes each time.

We overtook some slow golfers and missed a hole completely.

We stopped at the shop and bought lunch, because I didn't feel like eating the shitty jam sandwiches I made for us.

It has been a perfect day.

We have just finished the last hole, and Willow won the game. "I'll have to drive back to reception, Will, so they don't see you."

She pulls the car over and I jump into the driver's seat. I slowly drive us back down the hill towards reception.

"I've had a really great day." I smile at the kids. "Thank you. That was the most fun I have had in ages."

"Me too!" Sammy calls from the back. Willow smiles.

I point at her. "Ha-ha, I got you smiling. Admit it. You had fun," I tease, and she rolls her eyes.

We drive down the hill slowly, with our music now off, when Sam calls out to me from the back. "Is that Dad?"

"What? Where?" I gasp.

"Over there, behind the tree."

I look over and see a man in a navy polo shirt who kind of looks like him. He's taking a shot with his club.

"Shit, is that him, Will?"

She sits up and narrows her eyes as she studies the man in the distance.

"Look out!" Sammy yells from the back seat.

I snap my attention back to the path to see Mr. Masters standing directly in front of the cart. I swerve, trying my best to avoid him, but it's too late, and I hit him full force, running him over.

The cart bounces twice as he goes under the wheel. I screech to a stop.

Holy. Fucking. Hell.

6

***

Brielle

WE ALL JUMP out of the cart, running to where Mr. Masters is sprawled on the ground. "Oh my God, Mr. Masters. Are-are you all right?" I stammer as I drop to the ground beside him.

"I'm fine." He groans, slowly trying to push himself up. "Why weren't you looking where you were going?"

"Why did you jump in front of the buggy?" I hit back.

"I was trying to get your attention." He stands and dusts the dirt from his shirt.

Stupid man. Who runs out in front of a moving vehicle? I could have killed him.

"Dad." Sam hugs him.

"It was an accident, Dad," Willow mutters. "Brielle didn't mean it." Her nervous gaze flashes to me. "Did you?"

I shake my head. "No, no, I didn't. I'm so sorry. Are you okay?" I ask. I cannot believe I actually ran him over. "We need to take you to the hospital."

"I'm not hurt." He steps out and winces when his foot tries to take his weight for the first time.

My eyes widen. "You are hurt. Where did I hit you?"

"You just ran over my foot, but it's fine." He seems embarrassed, or perhaps just furious. Who can tell with this man?

A golf cart approaches us with two men riding in it. As they get closer, I can see that they're all splitting their sides, laughing. The cart comes to a slow halt beside us. "Masters, funniest thing I've ever seen. I wish I'd filmed it." One man laughs as he holds his stomach.

Mr. Masters looks at his friends. "Hilarious," he mutters dryly. He tries to walk again and winces as his foot takes his weight.

I grab his arm to support him. "Please stay off it until we see a doctor."

"I'm going to go home with these guys." He digs around his pockets and hands one of his friends his set of keys. "Can somebody bring my car home, please?"

I glance up at the children, who are both deathly silent. They watch on in shock.

Great, this is just great. We were having such a fun day, too. Honestly, I have never had so many things go wrong for me in one week in my entire life.

London is trying to bring me undone. Day by day my mistakes are getting bigger and bigger.

Mr. Masters waves his friends off and turns back to me.

I swallow the lump in my throat. "Let's get you to a doctor." I sigh.

He nods, and Willow takes one arm, helping him as he limps back to the car. I return the buggy and climb into the driver's seat. I glance over to see him sitting in the passenger seat, glaring out the front window.

I grip the steering wheel and drop my head. "I'm so sorry," I say again.

Regret swirls around in me. "Sorry" seems to be the only word that I ever say to him. That's it now. I know that's it. And I'm okay with it being over. Some things just aren't meant to be.

"You didn't mean it," Willow interrupts from the back seat. "It was an accident, Dad."

Mr. Master's jaw clenches as he looks out through the front windscreen. His anger is palpable.

"Tell Brielle you know it's not her fault," Willow demands.

"I said it was fine," Mr. Masters growls. "I would like to go home now."

The car falls silent, and I start the car. I pull out of the parking lot and onto the road. "Can we go to the hospital and get some x-rays, please?"

"It's not broken," he says flatly.

"Fine." I sigh. I turn onto the road that takes us home. "Have it your way."

It's 9:00 p.m. and I am washing the last of the dishes. Due to the fact that Mr. Masters is laid up on the lounge with an icepack on his foot, I cooked Italian for dinner, and I know I surprised everyone with my culinary skills. One thing I can do well is cook. They all devoured every last mouthful, and the kids even asked Mr. Masters if I can be the new cook from now on.

The silence is now deafening, though. He hasn't said a word to me all afternoon other than to say that his foot is fine. I've cooked and chatted and helped the children with their homework, all while he stayed solemn and stared at the television. I feel sorry for these kids. He's miserable. He makes everyone around him miserable. Willow was right today: he doesn't communicate at all other than to tell people off. It's like he gets off on the power of reprimanding people around him. I know I deserved a spray about last night, but this is another level of coldness, and it's grossly unfair when he knows I feel so bad about hitting him earlier. To be honest, I don't even want him to talk to me now. My dream of having a boss that I can be friends with is long gone.

He's not the kind of person I would want to be friends with. He has a mean streak. I may have made a string of errors since I started, but the way he is treating me is making me feel very uncomfortable.

The kids eventually say goodnight to us both and head up to their beds.

I finish cleaning the kitchen and my stomach churns. I've never lived in a house where I haven't felt welcome before. I don't like it — not one little bit.

He makes me feel inadequate. Just because I'm not a judge, it does not make me stupid. But he loves to insinuate that that's exactly what I am, making me feel inferior.

I fluff around in the kitchen for fifteen minutes as I psych myself up for this conversation.

Just do it.

"Mr. Masters, can I speak to you for a moment, please?" I ask.

His eyes rise to mine. "Of course." He gestures to the sofa beside him. "Take a seat."

I sit down, and my nervous eyes hold his. "I'm sorry about today, sir."

He nods once.

"In fact, I'm sorry for everything, and I'm sorry I wasted your time when I applied for this job."

His face remains emotionless.

"I would like to give you my three weeks' notice."

His eyebrows rise, eyes full of surprise. "You're resigning?"

"I think it's for the best."

"Why?"

"Isn't it obvious why?"

"Not to me."

I stare at him for a moment. What is he playing at?

"I asked you when you started to let me know if there was a problem before you resigned. If it's the children..." he says.

"It's not the children. The children are angels." A frown crosses my face. "Wait, what are you talking about? There has been nothing but problems since I arrived," I splutter.

"It's only been four days."

"You fired me on the first day!"

"Because you were looking through my private things."

97

I drop my head. "I know, and I don't blame you for being upset about that. Look, you said I had eighteen days to find another job, and I just wanted to let you know that I will be doing just that."

He stares at me for a moment. "Is this about last night?"

Regret hits me like a freight train. "Yes," I exhale heavily. "I'm mortified that I came on to you. It's not who I am, and every time I look at you, I feel nothing but embarrassment."

He watches me.

"I am not easy in any shape or form." He frowns.

"But..." I pause. "You really do make me feel inadequate."

His face falls. "Of what?"

"Of this position. It's like you look down on me all the time for being playful."

His eyes search mine, and I feel like he wants to say something, but he doesn't.

"It's just..." I shrug. "For the first time in a long time...I feel cheap and stupid."

His eyes drop to the floor and he clenches his jaw.

I swallow the lump in my throat. I know I have to say this even though he won't want to hear it. "Can I speak out of turn for a moment, please, sir?"

"You have since you started. No point in asking my permission now," he replies flatly.

"Willow needs you."

He swallows the lump in his throat, our eyes locked.

"I'm worried she's going to become depressed...if she isn't already."

"Willow is fine."

"No. She's not. You need to wake up and deal with the fact that you have a teenage girl with some serious problems."

He sits up, suddenly defensive. "In four days you have worked out that my daughter has problems?"

"No." I stand, because obviously this conversation was a mistake. "In four days, I have been a witness to everything you don't say. Not once have you talked to her unless it's been to repri-mand her. I feel sad for her."

He watches me intently, and I have no idea what he's thinking. Maybe I've crossed the line by saying this, but I really feel it needed to be said.

He doesn't respond.

"Anyway, I'll work until the end of the month." I smile sadly. "Thank you for the opportunity. I'll give the position my all until I leave. I know you're away this week. The children will be cared for as if they were my own until I leave."

He clenches his jaw and stands abruptly. "You said you would tell me if there was a problem with the children before you resigned."

I frown and stare up at him. Did he just hear anything that came out of my mouth?

"It's not the children. The children are perfect." His frown gets deeper as I pause to take a breath. "I've told you, I don't like the way you make me feel."

For some stupid reason, my eyes fill with tears. I'm tired and I'm emotional. Hell, it's been a tough afternoon. I just feel so vulnerable being here in this situation. "I'm so sorry I ran over you today. I'm so sorry about last night. Please forgive me," I push out through tears.

He drops his chin to his chest.

"Goodnight, Mr. Masters," I whisper, and then I turn and walk to my room.

Half an hour later, I'm in bed, facing the wall. The television is on but I'm not watching it. I think back to before I arrived in London and how excited I was at the prospect of this position. It was so different from my other job. I honestly thought 'how hard could it be'?

Not everyone was born to be a nanny.

I'm annoyed at myself for resigning out of shame, but I can't feel like a cheap whore every time I look at my boss. I don't know what the hell came over me last night, and every time I think of our conversation in the garage this morning, I cringe. I hate that I'm attracted to him.

Knock, knock.

I frown. "Come in."

Mr. Masters walks in, his eyes finding mine across the room. "Can I talk to you for a minute, please?" he asks quietly.

I nod.

He clenches his hands together in front of him as he stands at the end of the bed.

"Take a seat."

He looks around, realizing he doesn't have any other option but to sit down on the side of the bed.

"What is it?" I ask.

"About last night."

I scrunch my eyes shut. "I don't want to talk about last night. I'm so embarrassed about it."

"Don't be."

My eyes open, and he watches me intently.

"I have to ask you a question. Why did you call me Julian last night?"

I frown and scratch the top of my head. I shrug. "I guess I was hoping we could be friends."

"You want to be friends with me?"

I shake my head. "No." I think for a second. "I want to be friends with the fun guy who drove me into town in his Porsche. I wanted to be friends with Julian."

He fiddles with the blanket as he listens.

I smile sadly. "I had built up in my head that I was coming to work for a woman, that I could support her for twelve months, and that we could form a friendship."

"You were disappointed when you found it was me?"

"No." I exhale heavily. "I just think that maybe last night I was too familiar, expecting a friendship that wasn't there."

"I wasn't offended. I was tempted," he whispers.

I frown. "W-what do you mean?"

He swallows what seems like a lead ball in his throat. "I was tempted to be Julian...for just one night."

The air between us changes. What?

"I was never..." My voice trails off. "I'm not that kind of girl. You didn't need to be tempted. I can assure you that nothing would have happened."

He drops his head. "I can see that. I didn't mean to make you feel cheap this morning. That was never my intention."

We stay silent for a moment.

"I told you off this morning because I was embarrassed."

"You?" I whisper. "Why on Earth would you be embarrassed?"

"Because I'm a lot older than you and I... I hold a position of power by being your boss."

I roll my eyes. "I just want a friend to talk to sometimes. It's lonely living in a strange country by myself. Emerson lives in another house and I only see her once a week. I don't want to jump your bones. I honestly don't. I promise," I whisper.

He smirks at my honesty. I feel like I said the right thing. He suddenly seems at ease.

"Why are you like this?" I ask.

"Like what?"

"Cranky all the time."

He smiles softly. "I don't know. It's just who I am."

"It must get lonely."

His eyes search mine, and I feel a power change between us, as if it's a palpable thing. Suddenly, I see him for what he really is: a very misunderstood man sitting on the side of my bed.

He's broken.

"I don't want you to leave," he says.

I frown. "But..."

"You are the first person Willow has ever defended to me."

"What?"

"I saw you today, I was watching as the three of you drove around like maniacs with music playing."

I get a vision of what we must have looked like from a distance. "God," I mutter.

"You seemed so carefree."

I stay silent.

"It's the happiest I have seen them in a very long time."

I tear up. Not for me but for him. What must it feel like to never see your own children happy?

"My children have had nine nannies in two years." He bites his bottom lip. "Although your nannying technique is very"—he raises his eyebrows—"unorthodox."

I smirk.

"I do have to admit you seem to be getting through to Willow like nobody else ever has."

"She's just misunderstood," I tell him calmly. "She's a good kid."

He frowns as his eyes search mine, seeming shocked that those words just left my lips. "Don't go," he says. "We can try and work this out."

"But I can't be this straight-laced nanny you want me to be. I'm not used to this job. It's a world away from what I do back home."

"What do you do back home?"

"I'm an engineer." His face falls.

"What?" He shakes his head in disbelief. "You are an engineer?"

I smile. "Why do you seem so shocked?"

"Because I thought you were…" His voice trails off.

"Just a ditzy nanny?" I ask.

He presses his lips together tightly.

"Far from it. I wanted a job that was completely different to what I was doing at home. I love kids, and I thought this would be the perfect job for me, but I just don't want to feel like I'm doing something wrong all the time. You know?"

He offers me a half smile. "You do seem to do a lot of nanny things wrong, even you have to admit."

I giggle. "God, I know. I'm a train wreck."

"I'll tell you what. Going forward, when you call me Julian, I'll know that you just want a friend and you are not being flirty with me. I'll know to turn my Mr. Masters boss hat off."

I smile. "But how will I know when you need a friend?"

"I can assure you I won't need a friend."

"Everyone needs a friend sometimes."

His lips curl into a sexy smile. "Not me."

Our eyes are locked, and I feel like there is another part of this conversation I'm missing.

He shakes his head. "An engineer?"

I laugh. "Yes, an engineer. Why do you seem so shocked?"

"Because I am. Where do you work?"

"A company called Biotech. I design machines, although I want to get into mining when I go home."

He studies my face. "Not many people shock me, Miss Brielle."

"I seem to be good at giving you nanny shocks."

He smirks. "That you do. Running me over in a golf cart is a highlight though."

I laugh, and his eyes twinkle with a special something. "What would you call me? I mean, if we were friends?" I ask.

He bites his bottom lip. "Bree."

A warm, soft feeling runs over my body. "Nobody has ever called me Bree," I whisper.

"That's not true, I just did."

I smile softly.

"So, do we have a deal? You won't leave? We can try and work this out?" His hopeful eyes hold mine.

I nod. "I guess."

He stands and looks around, as if he suddenly wants to run.

"Why do you hate being in this room so much?" I frown. "The day you showed me this room, you wouldn't even walk in."

He shrugs. "I don't know. It feels very personal being in your space. Makes me uncomfortable."

"You're weird." I smile. "Goodnight, Mr. Masters."

He grins, clearly happy he got me to stay. "Goodnight, Miss Brielle."

He hobbles on his sore foot, and then stops at the doorway, turning back. "Please don't ever run me over again."

"If you don't stand in front of my golf buggy again, I won't."

He shakes his head in amusement and leaves my room, and I smile at the back of the closed door.

Well, that was unexpected.

I wait at the bottom of the stairs. "Come on, guys, we have to go or we will be late."

The sun is shining brightly, and I slept well last night for the first time since I arrived. I'm feeling a bit better after Mr. Masters came to talk to me last night. Maybe this will work out after all. Sammy bounces down the stairs in his school uniform, passing me his school bag when he reaches the bottom step. "Willow, come on!" I call.

"Don't rush me," she growls as she comes down the stairs. She stomps down past us with her school bag slung over her shoulder. Sammy and I exchange looks.

Hmm, she's in a mood this morning. I get into the car and she sits in the backseat, glaring out the window with her arms folded over her chest. I glance at her in the rearview mirror.

What is her problem? She was fine yesterday. God, teenagers. "What's on today, guys?" I ask.

"I have library, and then we have sport after lunch," Sammy answers.

"I put your lunches in your bags. Your dad left them in the fridge after he made them last night," I say.

"I'm not eating it." Willow scowls. "I hate what he packs me. It tastes like shit."

I bite my lip to stop my smile. Good to know it's not just me she hates today.

We get to her school and I pull the car over. Willow climbs out without a word. I wind the window down and call out, "Have a nice day, dear."

She flips me the bird and keeps walking, making me giggle.

Sammy smiles and grabs my hand, grateful that she doesn't get a rise out of me.

"Are we going to go and have our coffee and hot chocolate now, little man?"

He nods with a beaming smile. "Yep."

I pull out into the traffic. "I think I'm the luckiest nanny in the whole world to get to have hot chocolate with you every morning."

His cute little face lights up, and I feel my heart constrict. No shit. I really am the luckiest nanny in the whole world.

"Spill the beans," I say to Emerson.

It's Monday night and we are at Willow's soccer. It's dark and cold. Huge lights light up the fields. Sammy is kicking a ball with some little kids on the fields next to us. Emerson has come with me so we can catch up and talk about Mark, the guy who picked her up from the airport. She worked for an art dealer back in Australia and had to email Mark's company about some art that had to be shipped over. They got talking and started a friendship. She was convinced he was the one. He ended up getting her a job so that we could do this working-holiday thing. I'm not sure we would be here if it wasn't for his hounding.

"God, I don't know." She sighs. "There just seems to be no spark."

"What do you mean?"

"He doesn't have 'the thing', you know. He's short, and to be honest, he kind of annoys me."

I giggle as I sip my coffee. We're sitting in the car as we watch Willow train.

We watch the cold mist appear in front of everyone's mouths when they speak.

"This place is fucking freezing," she mutters into her coffee.

"I know, right? Witches' tits cold."

I glance over and see Mr. Masters walking across the field. He's wearing his navy suit and a long, dark overcoat. His hair is short, and his jawline strong.

I feel a flutter in my stomach. Something seems to have changed for me with him. Now, I seem to be thinking about him all the time.

When he talks to me, I have to concentrate on not watching his big red lips.

It's distracting. He really is gorgeous.

"Mr. Masters is here." I smile. "Back in a second." I jump out of the car and make my way over to him.

"Well, hello, Miss Brielle." He has this Cheshire cat kind of grin on tonight.

"Hello." I go up on my toes as I speak.

"How was your day?" he asks. His tongue darts out to lick his bottom lip, and I feel my stomach clench.

"It was great. How was yours?"

He smirks. "Good. Run over any poor, unsuspecting golfers today?"

I giggle as I run my hand through my ponytail. "No, I save my specialized driving skills for you." I look down. "How's your foot?"

"Barely attached," he replies dryly.

"I can cut it off if you like? Save you a hospital visit."

He chuckles. "Scarily, I have no idea if you're joking or not."

We both laugh. Willow looks up, and he gives her a wave. She waves back.

"I didn't know you were coming tonight," I say.

"I thought I'd make the effort." His eyes hold mine and I smile.

This has to do with my dig at him the other night. "You go away on Wednesday, right?" I ask.

"Yes, first thing. Are you sure you're going to be okay?"

"We'll be fine."

"Janine is going to do extra hours too. She's there to help you at any time. She and her husband can come and stay at the house if you want them to."

"We'll be fine," I repeat. I point to the car with my thumb. "Emerson came with us tonight. She's sitting in the car."

He dips his head and smiles. He waves at her and she waves right back. "I should let you get back to her," he says.

"Okay."

"I'm going to sit on the other side of the field. I'll see you at home?"

The air between us is buzzing like it's electricity. Where is this coming from?

"Sure."

Our eyes linger a little too long on each other's until I force myself to look away. "See you at home."

I turn, walk back to the car, hop in, and slam the door. My heart is beating in my chest.

"Are you fucking kidding me?" Emerson snaps.

"What?"

"You flirt with each other?"

"No. What do you mean?"

"He just checked out your ass as you walked away." My eyes widen, my excitement soaring.

"Really?"

She rolls her eyes. "He's fucking old, Brell."

I smile as I watch him walk across the fields away from us. "He's not that old. He's thirty-nine."

"That's old."

"You do have to admit, he is pretty hot for an old guy." I smile.

She smirks as she watches him. "I suppose in an old rich guy kind of way...he is."

. . .

I'm sitting at the table and helping Willow with her homework. She has an assignment due tomorrow and is freaking out.

Mr. Masters is in his office. I can hear him on the phone, talking to someone. He's been on and off his phone all night.

"I need my compass." Willow sighs.

"Where is it?"

"In my desk drawer."

"I'll get it." I walk out to the foyer and take the bottom step. I can hear Mr. Masters speaking on the phone.

"They are about to go up," he says.

He listens for a moment. "Buy five hundred now."

I stop on the second step so I can eavesdrop. He listens for a moment. "I'm considering putting a million on."

What the fuck is he talking about?

"Okay, yes." He pauses. "I'll transfer five hundred thousand now. It's a sure thing. I'll double it in a month."

Holy shit!

Mr. Masters plays the stock market. That's where this money comes from.

I trudge up the stairs, feeling very incompetent indeed.

It takes money to make money.

Hence why I have none.

7

Brielle

KNOCK, knock.

I glance up. "Come in."

Mr. Masters puts his head around the door. "Nightcap, Bree?"

I smile. Bree. He called me Bree.

"Erm." I scratch my head, glance back at my book, and then back at him. God, I'm at a really good part of my book, and they are just about to get it on.

"If you would rather read your book, don't worry about it," he snaps quietly.

"Look at you, getting all annoyed." I smile.

"I'm not annoyed."

I hold my fingers up and pinch the air. "Little bit?"

He looks at me, deadpan. "Nightcap or not?"

"Yes. That would be lovely, thanks." He turns and walks back to the kitchen, and I follow him. My stomach does a nervous jitterbug dance as I take a seat at the kitchen counter.

He pours us a glass of red wine each, handing me mine.

We clink glasses and I smile. "I can't stay long. One glass only."

He raises a brow. "Are you brushing me off for your book?"

"Completely. Don't be offended. I would brush Superman off for this book."

He smiles and takes a seat opposite me. We sit in silence for a moment, neither of us sure what to say.

"Where are you going on your trip tomorrow?" I ask.

"Kent."

"Ah." I sip my wine, and then eye it in the crystal glass. "Hmm, this is delicious."

"I have good taste."

"Obviously." I wink. "You hired me."

"Sight unseen." He smirks.

I giggle. "Kent is where Dover Castle is."

"Yes. Have you been?" he asks, seeming surprised that I know this.

"No, but I want to. It's on my to-do list while I'm here. Its history fascinates me."

"Why is that?"

"The archbishop was slaughtered there in front of his altar by King Henry's Household Knights."

A frown crosses his face. "History buff, are you?"

I smile. "Perhaps. It was one of the reasons that Emerson and I wanted to come here. We love old buildings and history."

He sips his drink and licks the red wine from his bottom lip. "There are lots of old things in the United Kingdom." He raises his eyebrow suggestively as if to imply that he is one of those old things.

He's just so...

"Do you travel much for work?" I ask as I try and remain casual. No drooling at the table, fool.

"Not really." He sips his wine. "I'm guest speaking at a conference."

"Wow." I smile. "Impressive."

He smiles shyly and drops his head. "Hardly. I'm speaking on the effects of prison on drug addicts."

"Oh, that sounds heavy."

He nods. "Could say that."

We stay silent for a moment as the air buzzes between us, and if I'm not mistaken, he seems a little nervous too...or maybe that's just because I'm nervous enough for the both of us.

"What have you got on this weekend? Anything fun?" I ask.

He exhales. "No. Not yet. You?"

"I'm going out with Emerson on Saturday night." I sip my wine and lift my glass to him. "And you needn't worry, I won't be coming back here to embarrass myself again."

He rolls his eyes. "Why do you keep bringing that up?"

"Because it's beyond mortifying. I'm having it put on my tombstone." I put my hand up in a rainbow shape. "Here lies Brielle, champion refrigerator humper."

He chuckles, and I close my eyes, faking a shiver.

"Are you going out with your Canadian friend again?" he asks, suddenly falling serious.

I cringe. "God, no. That guy is a douche, and so not my type."

His sexy eyes hold mine. "You have a type?"

My stomach flutters.

You... You're my type.

"Everyone has a type...don't they?" I smile shyly.

He shrugs. "I don't know."

"Do you have a type?" I ask.

He refills our glasses as he contemplates my question. Jeez, slow down. These drinks are going down way too easily. We don't want a repeat fridge-humping performance.

He purses his lips as he contemplates my question. "I guess the women I've dated lately do fall into somewhat of a type."

"You're dating?" I ask, acting surprised. Thankfully, he has no idea about my spying activities this week.

His eyes dance with delight...or mischief. I really can't tell.

"I date." He smiles against his glass. "I'm not that old. I'm not dead...yet."

I bite my bottom lip to hide my goofy smile. "I never said you were old."

"You seem surprised that I date." He raises his eyebrow, and this time I know it's from curiosity.

"Not surprised." I wobble my head from side to side. "Okay, maybe a little. I thought you would have a steady girlfriend."

It's him that fakes a shiver this time. "I have no desire to have a steady girlfriend."

"A wife, then?" I laugh.

"Oh, hell, don't wish that on me."

We both laugh, and our eyes linger on each other's face a little too long.

This is getting a bit weird. I am seriously attracted to him. "No girlfriend. No wife. What do you have?" I ask.

His dark eyes hold mine. "Friends with benefits."

My heart begins to thump hard in my chest. "What benefits?" I whisper.

He smiles sexily and sips his drink, giving me his best 'come fuck me' look. "Sexual satisfaction."

I swallow the lump in my throat as I imagine him naked.

I really need to have sex. He could say the word "milk" and I would find it stupid hot.

"I should get back to my book," I whisper.

He nods and rolls his lips, as if stopping himself from speaking.

"Thanks for the chat, Julian."

His sexy eyes hold mine. "You're most welcome, Bree."

My breath hitches.

There is something about the way he says Bree that is just so... perfect. "Can I help you with anything before you go?" I ask.

His eyes darken. "Like what?"

"Um." I get a vision of me on top of him, naked in my bed, and I feel myself get wet instantly.

Okay, get back to your room, you dirty ho.

"Your itinerary or something," I splutter, distracted by my wayward thoughts.

He smiles, as if knowing exactly where my thoughts were. "My itinerary is sorted, but thank you anyway."

I stand and wash my glass up before I turn back to him. "Have a great trip."

"I will. I'll call you each day to check on the children."

Our eyes lock once more, and my stomach dances with excitement that he will be calling me.

Just for the children, stupid, I remind myself.

I smile bashfully, embarrassed that he makes me feel like a giddy young girl.

I don't remember any man ever making me feel like this. Is there something more going on here, or just wishful thinking on my behalf?

"Goodnight, Mr. Masters."

He stands, and suddenly we are brought face to face, only millimeters apart. "Julian," he corrects me.

My heart skips a beat at our close proximity, and I look up into his sexy eyes.

The power emanating from his body is palpable. He'd be so fucking dominant in bed. "Julian," I whisper.

His eyes drop to my lips.

Oh God, is he going to kiss me? Do it. Do it.

After a moment, he seems to remember where he is, and he takes a purposeful step backwards, nodding like a gentleman. "Goodnight, Bree."

"What book do you want to read, Sammy?" I ask as I look over to his bookshelves. It's 8:30 p.m. and I am sitting on the end of his bed while he dries himself after his bath. Mr. Masters left early this morning, and we haven't heard from him all day. Janine left about an hour ago after cooking dinner.

"I don't know, do we have to read? Can't we do something else for a change?" he asks as he pulls on his striped flannelette pyjamas.

"Why, what do you want to do?"

He shrugs. "Watch YouTube or something."

"We don't learn much from YouTube, Sam."

"That's not true," Willow calls from her room. "Everything I know, I learnt from YouTube."

"Is that where you learnt to eavesdrop?" I call.

"Funny," she calls back.

I throw Sammy a wink. "I know, right? I'm hilarious. And I learnt it on YouTube," I shout.

"Oh God," I hear her mutter.

I think for a moment. What is something we could watch together, the three of us?

"I know. We could watch cat videos," I say.

Sam frowns. "What for?"

"Haven't you ever watched cat videos on YouTube?" I ask, shocked.

"No."

"Will, have you?" I call, knowing that she's eavesdropping.

"Nobody does that except losers," she hits back.

I giggle. "Lucky I'm a loser, then."

I open up Sam's computer at his desk and I log into YouTube, searching for cat bloopers.

Sam and I take a seat at the desk and we both wait.

A toddler is walking down a driveway when a cat jumps out and crash tackles him. He falls spectacularly into the garden, and we both laugh. A printer is printing out paper in an office and a cat comes in, attacking the printer with both paws as the paper comes out, and we both laugh out loud again. A cat gets stuck in a cereal box and goes ballistic. A cat slips on the edge of the bath and falls in.

Stupid, stupid cats, doing every possible thing wrong.

It isn't long before Willow appears at the door, lurking and wanting to see what's so funny.

Naughty cat after naughty cat, we watch on as they jump scare, attack dogs, fall off things, and generally act like me—super goofy —and we are all hysterical with laughter. This is the funniest thing

I have seen in ages, and it just keeps on getting funnier. We are splitting our sides in laughter.

My phone rings in my pocket and I fish it out. The name Mr. Masters lights up the screen.

"Hello," I answer, trying to act serious.

"Hello, Miss Brielle," his velvety voice purrs through the phone.

My heart skips a beat at the sound of his beautiful voice. "Hi," I breathe.

"Is everything all right?" he asks.

I see a cat fall into a pool after attacking its owner and I giggle. "Everything is great. Everything okay with you?" I ask.

"Yes, all good here. How are the children?"

A video of a cat chasing a bear comes on the screen, and the children hoot with laughter. I can't help but chuckle too.

"What's going on?" he asks. "Where are you?"

"We're watching cat bloopers on YouTube."

"Cat bloopers? It's 9:00 p.m. Bedtime was half an hour ago."

A man sleeping on a sofa comes on the screen, and a cat jumps up and attacks his dick. He jumps in fright and falls off the couch in shock. The three of us all burst out laughing.

"What's so funny?" he snaps.

"The cat just attacked the man's dick." I laugh. "He fell off the lounge." I can hardly speak from laughing.

"What the hell? Put the children on the phone." I hand the phone to Sammy.

"Hello, Dad," he says, his eyes glued to the screen.

"Hello, Samuel. Is everything okay?"

"The cat attacked the man's privates," he blurts out.

"Stop watching such rubbish," I hear Mr. Masters say.

A cat jumps off the kitchen bench and falls into the rubbish bin. It tips over and scares the dog, and we all burst out laughing again. Sammy can't speak for laughing.

"The cat fell in the bin," he screams in excitement.

"Good grief," Mr. Masters groans. "Put your sister on the phone." Sam passes the phone to Willow.

"Hello, Dad." She smiles.

"Is everything okay, Will?"

A cat falls into a fish tank and we erupt again.

She laughs out loud. "Yes, Dad, everything is fine. I have to go." She hands the phone back to me.

"Can we get a cat?" I ask.

"Definitely not. I don't think it's at all humorous that a cat attacks a man's dick while he sleeps."

I burst out laughing again. "I'm so training it to do that to you."

"Jesus Christ, Brielle."

"All is good here, no need to worry." I smile.

"Miss Brielle," he sighs. "Please put the children to bed now. Enough with the stupid cats."

I roll my eyes to the kids, and they both grin back at me. "Okay, fun cop. Roger that. Say goodbye to Dad, kids," I call.

"Goodbye, Dad," the kids cry in unison, just as a cat jumps on a dog's back. The dog takes off at full speed while the cat hangs on to its back for dear life. The kids all squeal again, and I hang up just before I burst out laughing.

We are so getting a cat.

It's Thursday afternoon, and Sam and I are waiting for Willow outside her school. I have a surprise for her and I'm excited to share.

She walks up and gets into the car. "Hi." I smile.

"Hey," she mutters as she does her seatbelt up.

I pull out into the traffic, and my eyes flicker to her in the rearview mirror.

"I have a surprise for you."

"Don't tell me. You're really a YouTube cat and not really a nanny?" she offers sarcastically.

"Meow," I tease.

"Oh God." She winces. "Please, stop."

I smile as I drive, and Sammy giggles. "I have two surprises for you, actually."

"Yeah? What're they?" She sighs, uninterested.

"I thought you two could help me cook tonight."

She frowns. "What for?"

"I gave Janine the night off."

"Why?"

"So I could teach you how to make pasta."

She screws up her face. "Is that my surprise? Sounds more like a punishment."

"Well, I thought you could learn how to make fresh pasta, and then on Sunday night you could make dinner for your father, all by yourself."

I watch her in the mirror as her eyes rise to meet mine, her interest sparked.

"Your father loved that pasta so much the other night, and imagine how surprised he will be if you know how to make it yourself."

She bites her bottom lip as she contemplates the idea. "What's the second surprise?"

"I enrolled us both in golf lessons."

"What?" she shrieks. "I'm not doing golf lessons with you. You're so embarrassing." She stays silent for a moment. "Probably run over somebody or something," she mutters under her breath.

I smile because I knew she was going to say that. "Okay, I won't come, but you start Friday." I was never really enrolled anyway.

She twists her lips as she looks out the window, and I know that, even though she will never admit it, she's kind of happy about it.

I grip the steering wheel and pretend to drive really fast. "Let's get home and get our cooking on, baby," I say in a French accent.

She rolls her eyes in disgust. "Oh God, make it stop."

. . .

"You see this?" I bring my ball of dough back to me and then forward again. "You knead it across the bench."

The children concentrate as they watch me, both of them kneading their dough.

Willow's is sticking to the counter. "You need some more flour," I tell her.

She dips her hand in the jar and puts the minuscule amount onto the counter.

"Not like that," I say. "Get a whole handful. Get into it, woman. There isn't a flour shortage."

I dig my hand into the jar and grab a big handful of flour and throw it across the counter. A little falls on the floor.

"You're getting it everywhere," she snaps.

I smile, pick my hand up, and I blow a little puff of flour into the air.

"Stop it," she snaps as she concentrates on her dough.

Sammy's dough begins to stick, so Willow grabs a huge handful and throws it across the counter, watching as it goes all over me.

My mouth falls open in surprise as I look down at myself. She smiles goofily. "Oops."

"Do that again and I'm going to crack an egg over your head." I smirk as I continue to knead.

Her eyes dance with delight, and she puts her hand into the jar, throws a handful of flour across the counter, and watches as it goes all over me again.

"Right, that's it." I pick up an egg and Sammy squeals.

"You wouldn't." She gasps.

"Oh... I think I would." I crack it over her head and it drips down her face.

"Ahh!" she screeches. "I can't believe you just did that."

"Believe it, sister."

She picks up an egg and pelts it at me, smashing it straight into my chest.

"No," Sammy yells excitedly, and we both turn to him. "Get him," I say.

"Ohhhh!" Sammy squeals, but before he can run, Willow cracks an egg over his head. Then she picks up a handful of flour and throws it at me, and it sticks to the egg and covers the floor.

"That's it," I cry. "It's war." I pick up another egg and pull my arm back to hurl it at her.

Ding dong.

We all freeze on the spot and turn towards the sound of the doorbell. "Who's that?" I whisper.

Sammy jumps down and runs to the window to look out. "Grandma!"

"What?" "Grandma's here."

"Shit," Willow cries.

"Oh no." I bounce on the spot in a panic and the doorbell rings again right before the front door opens. Shit, we left it unlocked.

"Hello?" their grandma calls.

The three of us go into overdrive as we quickly try to wipe up the flour from the floor, but Grandma appears before we can dispose of the evidence.

Her face falls as she walks into the room.

"Why...?" Her voice trails off as she looks around. "What on Earth is going on here?"

I look around at the mess. "We're cooking." I wince.

She's a very stylish and attractive woman, in her late fifties or early sixties at the most. She's wearing a tight black woolen dress and low black heels. Her hair is styled in a perfect blonde bob, and she is wearing a coral-color lipstick to compliment her outfit.

She has money. It's blatantly obvious.

The shock on her face is priceless, and I bite my bottom lip nervously. "I'm Brielle," I tell her with a smile. I put my hand out but realize it's covered in flour and dough. "I would shake your hand, but..." I show her my palm.

"I'm Frances." She frowns and then turns her attention to the children. "Hello, dears. I thought I would come and check on you, what with your father being away."

The children both smile cheekily.

She looks around and picks a piece of eggshell out of Sammy's hair.

Oh hell, what must this look like? We all have eggs smashed over our heads and chests, and I am completely white-faced from the flour.

"This is most unexpected," she mutters, almost to herself.

"We're cooking," Willow offers as an excuse. "And..." She pauses as she tries to think of a reason. "The eggs slipped out of our hands."

"Slippery little suckers," Sammy adds.

I laugh because that story is just ridiculous. "I'm sorry, but you've caught us in the middle of a good old-fashioned food fight."

Frances smiles awkwardly. "So I see." She looks me up and down. "So, you're Miss Brielle?"

"Yes." I smile as I dust some flour from my shirt. "Nice to meet you."

Her eyes dance with delight. "Julian said you were very different. Now I see why."

I laugh and shake my head. "Oh, kids, haven't I had a dreadful first week? I've made every mistake possible."

The kids both nod with enthusiasm.

"She even ran Dad over in a golf cart," Sammy blurts out.

"Dear God." She puts her hand to her chest. "Is he okay?"

"He's fine," Willow answers. "He sulked all night over it."

Frances laughs, and I get the feeling that I'm going to like this woman.

"We're practicing making fresh pasta so that Willow can cook dinner for her father on Sunday night," I say.

"Really?" She looks between the two of us, impressed.

"You should come over," I say. "The more, the merrier. Willow is a fantastic cook."

"I haven't cooked anything yet," Willow interrupts.

"I know, but you're going to be a fantastic cook when I finish with you."

Frances beams. "Thank you for the invitation. I'd be delighted."

She looks back at the door. "Don't let me hold up your fun. I'll get going."

We all follow her and she turns back. "What time is dinner on Sunday night, Will?"

Willow looks to me for guidance.

"What time, pumpkin?" I whisper. "You pick."

"About six?" Willow shrugs.

Frances smiles and rubs her arm. "Lovely, see you at six, darling." She walks out the door and calls over her shoulder, "Have fun. I wouldn't want to be the one cleaning that floor."

We all scowl at the thought of having to do it ourselves. "Let's just clean up first and we can start again." I sigh.

With a roll of their eyes, they both follow me back to the battle zone.

This place is trashed.

It's now 11:00 p.m. and I'm back in bed, reading. The room is dark, lit only by my bedside lamp. I didn't hear from Mr. Masters today, but I know he called the children. I heard him on the phone to Willow earlier. Part of me is a little disappointed he didn't call me. God knows why. I blow out a deep breath and shuffle around on the bed, annoyed at myself.

I turn the page a little too aggressively and continue reading.

My phone dances across my side table, the name Mr. Masters lighting up the screen.

My heart instantly races.

It's him.

Act casual, I remind myself.

"Hello?"

"Hello, Bree," he purrs.

Bree, holy shit!

This is a personal call.

I bite back my smile. "Hi."

It sounds like he's in a bar or something; there's lots of background noise.

"So...I hear you met my mother."

God, she called him.

"Yes." I scrunch my eyes shut. "She seems nice." I wince. Hell.

He stays silent.

"What did she say about me?" I ask.

He hesitates for a moment. "Let's just say that you have added another member to your ever-growing fan club."

I smile goofily. Another? Does that mean he's in that club too? "Is everything all right?" I ask. "Did you call to check on the children?"

He chuckles, and I can tell he's been drinking. "I called to check on my naughty nanny."

My stomach flips at the tone of his voice. "Your nanny is well." I frown. "Although from the tone of your voice, I have no idea if you are being facetious or salacious," I whisper.

He laughs a deep belly laugh and I feel it heat my blood as the sound rolls over me.

I smile.

"Let's just say it's a lot of one and a little of the other," he replies. Trust him to give me a conundrum for an answer.

"How well?" he asks sexily. "How well is my nanny?"

I swallow the lump in my throat. "As well as can be expected when the man of the house is away."

He inhales sharply. I hear it catching in his throat. What the hell am I doing? This is a dangerous game I'm playing.

"Where are you?" I ask.

"At a bar."

"Who with?"

"Not you."

My heart stops. What the actual fuck is going on here? "Are you flirting with me, Julian?" I smirk.

"Would it bother you if I was?"

My heart begins to hammer, and the background noise begins to fade, as if he's moved somewhere quieter. "No, it wouldn't." I pause for a moment. "Just the opposite, actually."

I can almost see his smile on the other end of the phone. "I wish we didn't meet under the circumstances we did."

"Why?" I whisper."

"Because I'm attracted to you," he breathes roughly.

My heart is hammering hard, and I scrunch my eyes shut to focus on his breaths. Holy shit, is this happening?

"It's a two-way street," I confess.

"I'm not after a relationship," he whispers through a heavy breath, and my sex clenches to the sound of his deep, commanding voice.

"Neither am I."

"What are you looking for?"

"Some of that satisfaction you told me about." I bite my bottom lip and cringe at myself. Did I just say that out loud?

He inhales sharply, neither one of us speaking for a moment or two.

"I can't mix business and pleasure in my house," he eventually says.

"If it doesn't happen in this house, I'm not your employee. I'm just a woman," I whisper. Okay, where did that come from? Who am I?

He hisses with approval, and I know he liked that answer. "That's something to think about," he whispers.

God, I'm so fucking aroused by this man, it isn't even funny.

"Are you in bed?"

"Yes."

"Touch yourself."

My eyes widen. What the...?

"Put that pretty little hand in that beautiful cunt and tell me what you feel."

Holy fuck. Holy fucking fuck. He's dirty.

I slide my hand between my legs and swipe through my flesh. "I'm wet," I breathe.

"Swollen?" I can hear the arousal in his voice.

"Yes," I rasp.

"Fuck."

This is insane, and so damn hot.

A commotion happens in the background and some men begin to talk loudly to him. "I've got to go," he grinds out, clearly annoyed. "We will finish this conversation later."

I nod. Damn it. "Okay."

"Goodnight, my naughty nanny."

I smile, hang up, and stare blankly at the wall. Did that just happen?

Sammy and I sit in the car as we wait for Willow to come out from her golf lessons. This seems to be the only activity that she really gets excited about attending. She even wore lip gloss today, and if my suspicions are right, the boy in the office might be in her sights.

I hope he is. He's so cute.

She walks out with the girl and the boy from the office, and she stands and talks to them for a moment. I can't help but smile as I watch them.

Willow is twirling her long hair between her fingers. I'm no body language expert, but even I can see that she's interested.

How sweet. This is what she needs—a high school romance. She waves goodbye and bounds towards the car, slamming the door shut once she's inside.

She grins over at me and my heart melts.

I put my hand on her thigh. "What a beautiful smile that is."

She glances out the front windscreen, looking very pleased

with herself, and I pull out of the parking lot, unable to stop myself from smiling the whole way home.

Her being happy makes me happy.

It's 1:00 a.m. and I'm in bed, reading again. I'm wearing my silky black spaghetti-strap nightgown. I hop up and go into the main house and check the doors again. Mr. Masters comes home tomorrow. I've been so busy with the children since he's been away. I already checked the doors earlier, but because I'm on my own with his children, I always double-check the deadlocks so that Sammy can't escape if he happens to sleepwalk. It's my worst fear to wake up in the morning and he is gone. He hasn't had another episode since that first time. Apparently, he only does it when there is a change in his home environment. Me arriving set him off. He seems to be settled now, though. I glance over at the stairs. The poor little guy had a bad dream a couple of hours ago. I might just go check on him one more time before I go to bed for the night.

I walk up the stairs in the dimly lit house, treading lightly down the hall. I slowly open the door and check on Willow first. She's fast asleep, so I close the door behind me. I walk down to Sammy's room and open the door, grateful to see he's sleeping like a baby. The sound of his peaceful breathing makes me smile. This child has got me wrapped around his finger so tight, even his breathing makes me melt now. I turn around to go back downstairs when I hear a noise in Mr. Masters' bedroom. I stop dead in my tracks.

What the hell was that?

Shit. I'm frozen in place as I listen, but I can definitely hear some rustling.

Oh my God, is someone in his room? Are we being robbed?

My heart begins to beat furiously. What do I do?

I slowly walk over to his room, peering inside, where I see his bathroom light is on and the door is ajar.

Someone is in the bathroom.

I tiptoe over to his bathroom door and peer inside.

Oh dear God.

Mr. Masters is in there, and he's naked, with his hard dick in his hand as he strokes himself.

He's lost in the moment, looking down at himself. Watching his cock.

Holy fucking wet dream.

My lips part in awe. I can see every muscle in his shoulders and back in the mirror behind him as he strokes hard. His stomach muscles contract with every jerk of his hand.

He gets harder and harder, and his mouth hangs slack as he concentrates.

The man is so fucking hot.

My body instantly starts to hum with arousal, and I feel myself get a rush of moisture below.

He spreads his legs wide and leans back against the side of the basin as he really starts to let himself have it.

His pubic hair is dark and well-kept, his cock huge, and I'm in fucking heaven watching this forbidden show.

I just want to drop to my knees in front of him and take the job off of his hands...literally.

His strokes get harder, faster, and I feel as though I'm going to come too.

I can feel how aroused he is, feel how good his cock would feel if it were inside me. He lets out a deep moan as he lets his head fall back, and I find myself holding my breath.

What are you doing? Leave! Leave now before he sees you. His eyes flash up, and he falters as he sees me.

Our eyes lock, but something happens, and as if knowing how much I need to see this, he slowly strokes himself again.

I swallow the lump in my throat. Fuck, yeah.

I begin to pant.

He starts again with long strokes, and I can hardly keep myself standing up.

This is ridiculous, but I can't make myself leave.

He gets harder and harder, and my mouth hangs open as I watch his dick with anticipation. His dark eyes are locked on mine when he shudders and comes in a rush up onto his stomach.

The moan he lets out echoes all around me, and I begin to pant as I struggle for air. His semen is thick and white—perfect—and as an added bonus, he watches my reaction as he smears it across his stomach and chest.

I have no words.

What the fuck? What the actual fuck?

With my chest rising and falling, my eyes meet his again, and I watch as satisfaction crosses his face. "Good evening, Miss Brielle," he whispers sexily as he continues to rub his semen in, his stomach glistening. I feel my insides clench. "We meet in my bathroom once again."

My eyes widen. I don't know what to say. What can possibly explain what I just saw?

What I just did... What he just did. So I turn and I run.

8

Brielle

I SIT at the café's table with a cup of coffee in my hands, and I stare through the window at the people on the streets as they casually wander to and fro.

How the fuck did I get myself in this situation?

I watched my boss jack off, and then I ran away like a scared little girl after I'd been flirting with him and asking for satisfaction.

It's just embarrassing. But in my defense, that dick looked very angry, and I'm not quite sure I could have handled it anyway.

I get a vision of his face as he ejaculated, and my insides clench in appreciation. He's so hot, it's just ridiculous.

God, imagine fucking him.

I get tingles to my toes and wiggle on my chair to try and relieve the pressure between my legs. I've been dripping wet since 1:00 a.m. this morning.

What I wouldn't give to see what he's got to offer.

My email pings and I pick up my phone, smiling when I see the name.

From: Mr. Masters

To: Miss Brielle
Miss Brielle
It seems that there was a privacy breach in the master bedroom
last night. As an employee of mine, I would like to give you the
opportunity to explain your behavior.
Yours Sincerely,
Mr. Masters

What the hell do I say to that?

I put my hand over my mouth as I stare out the window and think. Okay, I'm just going to take the personal versus business line of thinking.

I shrug, hit reply, and smirk as I begin to type.

From: Miss Brielle
To: Mr. Masters
Mr. Masters,
I apologize for my alter ego, Bree, and her misdemeanor. She
wasn't working at the time and I haven't spoken to her about the
incident you're referring to. She is somewhat of a private person,
ensuring she keeps her work and personal life separated at all
times. If you would like to speak to her in regard to said incident,
I would advise you ask Julian to contact her on this email during
her personal time.
Yours Sincerely,
Miss Brielle

I hit send and hold my breath, rolling my fingers on the table as I wait for a reply. Finally, after five minutes, my email notification pings.

From: Julian
To: Bree

My eyes widen when I see the use of our first names, and I

swallow the lump in my throat.

> *Dear Bree,*
> *I understand that you like to keep your professional and personal*
> *life separate, as do Mr. Masters and I. Please assure both of us*
> *that, moving forward, your voyeuristic tendencies will have no*
> *detrimental effect on your future employment. Mr. Masters does*
> *not wish to discuss this subject with you at your place of*
> *employment at any time in the future. I, however, am extremely*
> *intrigued by your thoughts.*
> *Looking forward to your prompt reply.*
> *Yours Sincerely,*
> *Julian*

I smile and I look around the café to see if anyone can see me
sitting here playing this silly game before I eventually reply.

> *From: Bree*
> *To: Julian*
> *Dear Julian,*
> *Please ensure Mr. Masters that I have no intention of telling*
> *Miss Brielle the details of my unexpected visit with you last*
> *night. What happened between us will stay private. What I do*
> *in my personal time is kept completely separate from my profes-*
> *sional life and I would like to keep it that way. I would perhaps*
> *need to investigate this situation further before I can offer my*
> *honest opinion, though.*
> *Yours Sincerely,*
> *Bree*

I close my eyes and hit send. Oh my fucking God. I put my
hands over my face.

I wait for a reply, and I wait some more, but it doesn't come. I
glance at my watch. Half an hour goes by and my stomach is

churning so hard. I order another cup of coffee because I simply can't go home when I'm this nervous.

Why did I say that?

He thinks I'm coming on to him. Have I misread everything?

My email finally pings, and I scramble to read it.

From: Julian
To: Bree
Dear Bree,
Your offer is most tempting.
However, I cannot allow the 'situation' to take place in Mr.
Masters' place of residence ever again. Mr. Masters takes pride in
providing a safe working environment for all his employees.
Any further investigation to determine a solid opinion on the
matter would have to take place off-site.
Yours Sincerely,
Julian

I pack up my bag and leave the coffee shop quickly. I'm going to have to think of a reply on this one, and also think about what I'm actually doing here. I should call Emerson to see what she thinks.

No.

I'm not telling her about this. She'll just try and talk me out of it, and I'm not in the mood.

I glance back to the café. Oh shit, I forgot to wait for my second coffee to arrive. I sit in the car and stare at my phone for a moment.

What do I write? Okay. Let's type.

From: Bree
To: Julian
Julian,
I would be willing to accommodate your off-site request.
Forward me the details of the meeting.
Yours Sincerely,

I start the car and drive home with the goofiest smile plastered on my face.

I can't believe I actually had the guts to write that. I have to talk to Emerson. No, I can't let her know anything just yet. There isn't really much to tell, and besides, I'm not in the mood for a lecture. I want to have frivolous fun, lecture-free.

I pull the car into the garage and my email pings. I scramble through my handbag to retrieve it. I frown as I open it. It's an invitation of some kind.

Julian Masters
Requests the company of: Bree Johnston
Occasion: Situation inspection.
Date: 28th May
Time: 8 p.m.
Place: Scarfes Bar, Rosewood London
Dress code: Slutty

My mouth falls open at the last line. Dress code slutty! What the fuck?

I burst out laughing. What do you wear when the dress code is slutty?

I go over the invitation again and again, until I register the date.

Hang on...that's tonight.

My phone rings, an unknown number appearing on the screen. I answer, "Hello."

"Oh, hello, darling. It's me, Frances." Julian's mother.

"Hello." I smile.

"Julian isn't able to get home from his conference tonight, he just called me. I will come and pick up the children at 6:00 p.m. and they can sleep at my house, if that's okay?"

"No, you don't have to," I reply without thinking.

"No, it's fine. I know you have plans tonight."

I bite my bottom lip to stifle my smile. That's right. I'm inspecting the situation. Visions of Julian wanking flash through my mind, and I smile to myself.

Is this really happening?

"That would be great, thank you," I tell her.

"See you then, darling."

"Thanks." I hang up and get back into the car with renewed purpose.

I've got to get some laser, a pedicure, and some serious slut-wear.

The cab pulls up in the circular parking bay of the ritzy Rosewood Hotel. My heart is hammering so hard in my chest, I have no idea how I'm not in the hospital already. As soon as the children got picked up, I started running around in a mad flap to get ready.

I glance down at myself and shake my head. I'm wearing a large trench coat and looking super serious to the outside world, but underneath is a completely different story.

He wanted slutty...he's getting super slutty.

I'm wearing a white, short, tight dress, with a red lacy bra peeking out. I'm in matching red stilettos, holding a matching clutch too. I wouldn't be surprised if you can see my red G-string through my dress. I'm cringing just thinking about it. I even got a spray tan to complete the whole look.

I look like a hooker—a cheap, dirty hooker.

My hair is down and curled, pinned back on one side, and my lipstick matches my shoes. I reapply my lipstick in my compact, and I smirk. I spent a fortune today looking this cheap.

He'd better appreciate it.

The driver comes around and opens my door, smiling at me as I get out. He's probably hoping I will pay for my cab ride with a blow job.

"Thank you," I offer.

My stomach churns as I walk into the foyer and follow the signs to the Scarfe Bar. I stand at the door and I psych myself up. Should I take the jacket off?

Yes, you've come this far. You came to London to break free of your constraints.

Just do it.

I slide my coat off and give it to the cloak man, and he raises his eyebrows, clearly excited. I look at him deadpan. I don't think so.

I exhale heavily, drop my shoulders, and then I walk into the bar, looking for my date.

Wow, this place is something else. My eyes roam around the exotic space. There is a rosewood bar that runs the length of the large room, with different-colored luxury velvet stools lining it. Behind the mirrored bar there are shelves filled with every expensive-looking drink you could imagine. There's even a huge fireplace in here, as well as beautiful, big sofas in the same exotic colors as the bar stools. A piano is being played and the room is filled with people having cocktails. Their chatter and laughter fill the room.

Oh, sweet Jesus, I'm wearing a white dress and red underwear. Help me! My eyes go over to the fireplace. I scan every chair, then I look over to the bar along the stools in search of him. Is he even here?

I glance at the tables just in front of me, and I see him sitting back in his chair, wearing a dark charcoal suit. His handsome face and big brown eyes are watching me, wearing a sexy grin.

He stands and comes to greet me. "Hello," he purrs.

He kisses my cheek and the skin on my arms bursts to life. "Hi," I whisper.

He stands back and his hungry eyes drop down my body. "Please, come and take a seat."

Julian takes my hand and leads me to the table in the darkened corner he was sitting at. My heart feels like it's seriously trying to escape my chest. I sit nervously, and he takes the seat opposite me. He leans back and rests his elbows on the side of the chair, his pointer finger trailing across his big lips as he smirks. "You look sexy as fuck," he whispers.

Oh man, I may not be able to take this night. It seems so weird seeing him in this context, and I smile awkwardly. I go to pull my dress down and he holds his hand up. "Don't pull your dress down, I want to see."

My eyes widen.

I sit back nervously.

A bartender walks past. "Can I please have a Blue Label on the rocks? And what would you like, Bree?"

"I'll have a margarita, please."

The bartender disappears back to the bar and my eyes fall back to Julian. "This is gorgeous." I smile.

"Like you."

"You make me so nervous," I whisper.

His smirk grows. "You should be nervous. I've never been this physically attracted to a woman before."

I get a much-needed boost of confidence just as the waiter returns with our drinks.

"Thank you." I smile as I reach for mine. I take a sip and lick my lips. "Oh, this is so good."

Julian leans forward and cups my face in his hands, and I feel like I stop breathing. His eyes pierce mine, then he leans in and softly kisses my lips, and then licks his lips. "It does taste good," he whispers.

My breath catches.

I have no words for how hot this man is.

He kisses me softly again and I feel myself lift from my chair. "I have an offer for you."

"An offer?" I ask.

"On these nights out, you can have my body, but you must know that my heart or my private home life isn't up for negotiation. I will not discuss these nights at all with you in my home environment. You are a different person to me when you're at work in my home." He kisses me softly again and my eyes close.

Oh God, it's the perfect kiss. Suction, softness, and a promise of what's to come.

"I know," I whisper.

"You need to think very carefully about what you're agreeing to," he mumbles against my lips. "I'm not wired like most men." He dusts his thumb back and forth over my bottom lip as he watches me.

He's so fucking intense.

He pulls me forward, dropping his lips to my neck, and my head falls back as my eyes close in pleasure.

Oh, sweet Jesus.

I'm in a bar with my red lingerie hanging out, and I'm making out like a prepubescent teenager.

"Do you want to dance with the devil?" He bites my neck hard and I whimper.

His lips continue to roam up and down my neck.

"You need to protect yourself, because I can't protect you from me," he whispers against my skin.

I pull back and my eyes search his. "Are you warning me, Julian?"

"Yes."

"Why?"

"I don't want to hurt you."

I smile softly. "Maybe you'll be the one who gets hurt?"

He kisses me again and smiles as he cups my face in his hands. His eyes have a tender glow to them. "Beautiful Bree and her enchanting optimism."

An uneasy feeling swirls deep within me. He's warning me that he's going to hurt me—to run while I can.

And I know I should.

Alarm bells ring in the distance. Who am I kidding? There is no distance; they scream all around me. I know for certain that this is dangerous territory, but dancing with an honest devil sounds so much more appealing than sleeping with a lying god.

He kisses me softly once more and pulls back to lick his lips. "I would like to go upstairs to our room now."

My nerves return and my eyes search his. "What's the rush?"

"I need to get my tongue between your legs."

What the fuck?

He smiles darkly. "I've needed to know how you taste since you arrived. I'm salivating, and I can't take the suspense a moment longer."

I swallow the lump in my throat. "Let's cut to the chase and get straight to it, then," I croak.

He chuckles, and it's a deep, sexy sound. "I'm not here to romance you, Bree, I'm here to take my pleasure from your body." He leans forward and takes my face in his hands. "And I'm going to fuck you so damn good, no man will ever compare."

The hairs on the back of my neck stand to attention. Run...run the fuck away, right now!

No man can even compare already and he hasn't even touched me yet.

He stands and holds his hand out for me to take. I drain my glass in one gulp and take his hand, and then the two of us walk to the elevator.

Once inside, he rubs his thumb back and forth over the back of my hand.

My nerves are at an all-time high. What if he's into kinky shit?

Anal.

What if he wants anal?

Oh God, I didn't think this through at all.

A trace of a smile crosses his face as he watches me, like he knows what's running through my head, the bastard.

Maybe I'll be the tenth nanny to leave, because I'll be in the hospital with a broken vagina.

What a way to go, though.

Nobody even knows I'm here tonight. I didn't tell Emerson. He could be a serial killer for all I know.

The lift goes all the way to the top. When the doors open, he picks up my hand and kisses the back of it, and the two of us walk down the corridor.

This hotel is out of this world—so luxurious.

He takes the key from his pocket, opens the door, and my eyes widen.

In front of me is a huge sitting room housing a beautiful couch along with two armchairs that sit in front of a fireplace. On the table, there's a silver bucket filled with ice, as well as a bottle of champagne and a bowl of chocolate-covered strawberries to compliment it. There are also two very expensive crystal glasses waiting to be filled.

To the left, there's a king-size bed with velvet coverings draped over the top, and a huge, gilded standing mirror has been placed in front of the window, facing the bed. I can see the white marble bathroom down the hall.

"Wow," I whisper as I look around.

Julian walks to the table and pours two glasses of champagne before he hands one to me. I take a sip, and he cups my face in his palm, licking the remnants of moisture from my lips.

His tongue explores my mouth, and my insides begin to melt.

I pull back and take another sip, my breathing becoming ragged. "Don't be nervous. I won't hurt you."

"I just haven't..." My voice trails off.

"You haven't what?" He holds my glass up to my lips, urging me to drink more.

"I haven't had sex in over a year."

He smiles as his hand roams around to my behind. "Do you have any idea what an aphrodisiac that is?"

His lips drop to my neck, and I take the opportunity to drain my glass.

I need the whole fucking bottle.

His hands roam over my dress, his palm settling on my breast before he squeezes it roughly.

"I need you naked. I need you naked now." In one swift move, he lifts my dress over my head until I'm left standing before him in nothing but my red lingerie.

He smiles as he slowly traces his finger over my breast, and then down my stomach, over my sex. "I've been dreaming about this," he whispers.

"You have?"

"You have no idea how beautiful you are, do you?"

My breathing falters as my nerves take over, and I desperately try to control it, but it's no use.

Julian reaches around and unlatches my bra, removing it slowly. His eyes glow with arousal as he leans back and inspects me, cupping my breast in his hand once again.

"You have bigger breasts than I thought." He bends down, takes one in his mouth, and begins to suck.

My eyes close and my head falls back. Holy shit.

He slides my panties down my legs, removing them from my feet until I'm standing before him, completely naked.

His eyes flicker with arousal, and all his control slips away when he presses forward and kisses me aggressively. His hands are in my hair, rough whiskers against my face, and his tongue delves deeper into my mouth.

Arousal thrums between my legs, and he walks me over to the mirror at the end of the bed, turning me to stand in front of it.

Breaking away, he walks to a large, dark green ottoman that's been placed in front of the fire. He lifts and drags it closer, bringing it to me. "Put your leg up on this."

I frown.

He lifts one of my legs so that it is resting up on the ottoman. He drops to his knees in front of me.

Dear God.

When Julian leans in and presses his face into my sex, I close my eyes and listen to the way he inhales deeply.

Holy fucking hell.

His mouth drops lower and lower. He pulls my sex apart and licks it.

"Watch," he moans against me.

I drag my eyes to the mirror to see him still dressed in his suit, on his knees in front of me, sucking on my sex. His head bobs back and forth, and his eyes are closed, like he's getting as much pleasure from this as I am. I feel like I'm having an out-of-body experience, hovering way above, watching.

He's a god.

All at once he seems to lose control, and he lifts my leg higher to give himself better access. I whimper as I hold the back of his head, pressing him to me.

My mouth hangs open, desperate for oxygen as my breathing gets heavier, when Julian suddenly stands and kicks his shoes off. "Undress me," he commands.

I take off his jacket and then slowly unbutton his shirt. His chest is broad, and he has a scattering of dark hair there.

My body begins to tingle.

I peel his shirt open and push it over his shoulders. My eyes roam over him. He's absolutely perfect. I unfasten his trousers and then slowly slide them down his legs, along with his briefs.

His cock springs free, and my mouth falls open even wider. What the fuck?

He's huge and thick. Oh my God, he's like another species. I stand still, bewildered as I stare down at his dick.

"I won't hurt you," he breathes.

I raise my eyebrow sarcastically.

"We'll take it easy tonight," he promises as his fingers find that spot between my legs. He pauses before he pushes three fingers in.

I cry out without restraint. That's not taking it easy.

"Get on your back," he orders, losing control. He kisses me as he walks me back towards the bed, and then he carefully lays me down.

Julian spreads my legs and positions his body between them, spreading me open for his private viewing, and my back arches off the bed.

Then he is on me, licking, sucking, tormenting. He pumps me

with three fingers, then four, and my back arches off the bed again, making me rise higher.

His thrusts get harder and harder, and the bed begins to rock.

His mouth hangs slack, but all he can do is smile as he watches my face. "You like that, baby girl?" he whispers.

I nod, unable to speak, and he rolls a condom on. Oh fuck...do I ever.

I grip his shoulders as a shudder runs through me. I'm so close to orgasming. "Jules," I pant.

"Let it go. I need you creamy and loose." I begin to moan, and he smiles down at me. "That's it. Give it up for me."

I cry out and convulse, my whole body thrusting forward. Without warning, he forces me back, pressing his body against mine and trapping me beneath him right before pushing himself inside of me.

My eyes widen. Oh... He's big.

He stays still to let me acclimatize to his size. "You okay?" he breathes, kissing me softly.

I nod, and he finally moves to slide out of me, but only for a moment, and then he's sliding back home where he belongs.

He kisses me again as he pulls out and slides back in. He does it over and over until, somehow, we are going hard at it.

His cock is working me, building me up, using my body, and I can do nothing but hold on.

The sound of our skin slapping together echoes all around the room. Perspiration dusts his skin, and I cling to him as his body moves like magic.

"Fuck," he moans. "Fucking hell. This is so..." His voice is unrecognizable, and I smile to myself. I love him like this.

"I knew you would be amazing." He hits me hard. "I knew you would blow my fucking mind."

He starts to lose control and really lets me have it. In another breath, I convulse forward, and he comes in a rush.

He holds me close, his kiss aggressive. My breaths are strained as I try to control my breathing. He moves slowly, still inside of me, and then he pulls out and stands up to take his condom off. He carefully ties the end of it, disposing of it quickly.

He smiles down at me and brushes the hair back from my forehead. I feel so vulnerable lying here naked, weak from orgasm. He rearranges the pillows behind me so that I am propped up.

"What are you doing?" I ask.

"I want you to watch."

"Watch what?"

He lies back down between my legs and his mouth drops to my sex.

Oh God.

His dark eyes hold mine as his tongue begins to explore my sex with long, hard licks.

My heart is racing wildly. No man has ever done this. No man has ever gone down on me after sex.

This is so fucking hot.

His lips are glistening, and I sit with my legs spread wide as I watch him eat me like I'm his last supper.

His hands rest on my inner thighs, and every now and then he smiles into me, as if he can't believe this is happening either.

I frown as I watch him, strangely detached yet completely immersed.

He loves this, he absolutely loves this. This isn't for me. This is for him.

He never stops, continuing his exploration for over fifteen minutes, until I'm writhing on the bed once again.

I need him inside me again. "Jules," I whimper.

He smiles at me and bites my clitoris, causing me to jump. Then he sits me up to kiss me, and I can taste my own arousal on his lips. He's only gentle for a brief moment before he turns me over and positions me on my knees, spreading my legs as far as he can.

I glance up and watch us in the mirror.

He slowly rolls another condom on then runs his hands up and down my back as he studies my body. His hard cock hangs heavily between his legs. He nudges my opening, his mouth hanging open in awe, and his thumb rubbing over my back entrance.

Oh shit. I hold my breath. "No, Jules," I whimper. "Not yet."

He clenches his jaw, moving back to my sex to slowly slide in deep. We both moan in unison. He's so good at this.

He pulls out slowly and slams back in all at once, knocking the air from my lungs, forcing me to cry out. Shit. Then he lets me have it. My hips are in his hands as he aggressively slams me back onto him. I watch him in the mirror and his words from earlier come back to me.

I will take my pleasure from your body.

That's exactly what he's doing. He knows what he wants, he knows exactly what his body needs, and he's just feeding it. There is something so primal about the way he fucks my body, it's turning me inside out.

I shudder as I come in a rush, and I moan.

Our bodies continue to slam together, the sound of skin on skin filling the room. Julian is lost in his own headspace, and he tips his head back, closing his eyes as the ecstasy takes over. He picks up his pace, hitting me harder, and I scrunch the sheets between my fingers as I try and protect myself from the beating my body is taking.

I glance up to the mirror and see myself—hair dishevelled, red lipstick, covered in perspiration, and my breasts bouncing while I'm being fucked hard by God's gift to women. His mouth hangs open as he watches the place where our bodies meet. His thumb sits over my back entrance, and it's clear to see he's in another world, totally oblivious to all that surrounds him.

This is definitely not your average night.

He growls, losing control, and he scrunches his features together, pounding me hard. So fucking hard, I try my hardest to deal with the force of it.

When he comes, he holds himself still deep inside of me before he convulses forward.

His face—oh God, his face. Words cannot describe how beautiful his face is when he comes.

He falls over me and I giggle to myself.

"If that was you going easy on me, what the hell happens when you go hard?" I pant.

He chuckles and falls onto the bed, pulling me over him. "Hmm, slight change of plan," he mutters as he kisses me.

We try to catch our breath, and I lie with my head on his chest, listening to his heavy heartbeat.

I roll off him and lean up onto my elbow so I can watch him.

"What?" he asks.

"Quite the Jekyll and Hyde, aren't you?"

He smirks. "I could say the same about you."

I act offended. "I don't know what you're talking about. I was born to be a sweet nanny."

He smiles, his hand finding that spot between my legs, and he slides one of his thick fingers into me again. "You were born to fuck." He pumps me hard, and I wince. Ouch, I'm sore. "This beautiful body of yours is built for sin."

I smile and pull his hand out of me. "Yeah, well, this beautiful body of mine can't take any more. Down, boy."

A trace of a smile crosses his face. "Until next time."

I lean in and kiss him softly. "Until next time," I breathe.

He kisses me again and again, and I can feel his dick hardening against my stomach. Jesus, how long can he go for?

I thought men's sexual stamina was supposed to decrease with age, but that's definitely not the case here. My sex is throbbing and painful, swollen from the carnage. "I just can't, Jules," I breathe against his lips.

He pulls back from me immediately. "Sorry." He frowns as he stands. "I can be too much to take."

He takes my hand, pulls me from the bed, and leads me into the bathroom to run a shower. He turns toward me and studies my face as he runs his fingers through my long hair. "Do you have a hair tie?"

I nod.

"Where is it? I'll get it for you."

"In my handbag."

He disappears, returning only moments later to carefully tie my hair up into a bun on top of my head. My hands rest on his naked hips as he concentrates on his task. He's gentle and caring— so different from the animal that just fucked me ten minutes ago.

He really is Dr. Jekyll and Mr. Hyde.

He leads me into the shower and washes me tenderly with sweet-smelling soap, caressing my arms, breasts, stomach, my sex, and down my legs. I feel like a child being looked after, and this feels surprisingly intimate. His attention returns to my face, and he cups my cheek in his hand.

"You're quiet," he whispers, his lips lingering over mine. We share a soft kiss.

"I'm in a little bit of shock, to be honest," I say against his lips.

"Why?"

"That was arguably the best sex I've ever had."

He smiles sheepishly. "We've only just started, baby girl."

"Are you sure about that?"

His tongue swipes through my open lips. God, my whole body is open for him. "This is the beginning of a wonderful arrangement."

Arrangement. I don't like the word 'arrangement'. We stay silent in each other's arms for a while longer, and eventually he steps out and wraps me in a towel. He dries me, taking care of every inch of my skin with a tender touch, and then he finds my clothes and dresses me.

It's like this is part of his game, to look after me after he has ripped my body apart. Or perhaps he feels guilty for being so rough.

I'm not sure, but I do feel confused yet cared for, and so fucking satisfied.

I watch him as he dresses back into his suit and then looks around the room. "Do you have everything?" he asks.

Are we going home now? "Yes," I answer.

"Let's get going." He turns towards the door, remembering something and turning back to retrieve his wallet. "I got this for you." He passes me a gold card and I stare at it in my hands.

It's a credit card. What?

"I'm not a hooker, Julian."

He frowns. "I know that, I got it for you for incidentals."

"Such as?" I frown.

"Things that you may need for our meetings."

I stare at him blankly. "Like what?"

"The outfits I want you to wear. Personal care. Lasering. Things like that. Spend it as you wish. The card has no limit."

My eyes drop to the card in my hand. "When did you order this?"

"Last week," he says casually as he looks around the room.

I put my hand on my hip. "So you knew I would be here doing this with you eventually."

He smiles, leans in, and kisses me on the lips. "That was my agenda, yes."

Are you kidding me?

"Come on, let's go."

I glance at my watch. It's 10:30 p.m. We literally just fucked for two hours and now the date is over. He takes my hand and leads me out of the room, back into the elevator and down to the parking lot.

I stay silent because...what is there to say?

He told me he was going to fuck me without any strings attached, and that's just what he did. Except now there is a limitless credit card attached to our arrangement.

Stop overthinking this.

We get to the car and he takes my face in his hands to kiss me. It's deep and erotic, and my feet lift off the ground to get closer to him. "You were amazing," he breathes.

I force a smile but stay quiet.

"Everything alright?" he asks, studying my face.

I nod. "Yes." But I'm just not sure that's the truth. I feel off, and I can't put my finger on which part of the night brought that feeling on.

The drive home is made in complete silence, all the way to him opening the front door to his house.

"Goodnight, Miss Brielle," he says coldly, right before he walks away, making the trek up the stairs to his room. He doesn't look back and he doesn't wait for me to respond.

I stand in the foyer, bewildered, watching his body until it disappears out of sight.

What the fuck just happened?

9

Brielle

I FINISH DRYING my hair and check myself over in the mirror.

It's Saturday morning, and we have Will's soccer game to attend.

I'm wearing black jeans, black ballet flats, and a black singlet with a white linen shirt left open. My hair is down and I'm wearing the smallest amount of natural makeup.

My stomach is alive with nerves. I've hardly slept. My mind was racing at a million miles per minute.

I can't believe I did what I did last night. It was like some erotic movie I had no right to be part of. I can't believe it was that good. The credit card makes me feel uneasy, but I guess I did spend one hundred and fifty pounds on my slut-wear yesterday.

I don't know how I feel about everything, to be honest. I'm going to have to sit on things for a while.

With one last look in the mirror, I leave my room and make my way up to the main house, where I find Willow and Sam eating their breakfast. Frances has already dropped them back.

"Hi." I smile.

"Hello," they both offer, distracted.

"Good morning, Miss Brielle," that velvety voice purrs.

"Oh." I jump. "Hey, I didn't see you there."

Mr. Masters is in the kitchen, with his behind resting on the counter and his sexy smile fixed in place. "I didn't mean to frighten you. My apologies."

He's wearing black jeans and a white polo shirt. His dark hair is hanging loosely, highlighting his messy curls. His eyes are piercing, and that jawline could impregnate anything female with one glance. He looks fucking edible.

My stomach swirls with nervous energy. "How was your trip?" I ask, playing along in front of the children.

His eyes hold mine. "Unexpected."

I smile goofily. Why, I have no idea. He sounds so dreamy when he says the word 'unexpected'.

Oh, cut it out, you pathetic fool. 'Unexpected' is not a hot word.

"How was your time at home"—he pauses, and a trace of a smile tugs at his lips—"without the man of the house here?"

He's playing that game, is he?

I bite my bottom lip to stop myself from smiling. "Fine, thanks." I glance at the children, hoping that they can snap me from my drooling state. Especially with the drool being brought on by their father. "Wasn't it, kids? We had so much fun together."

They both nod and continue eating, not at all interested in conversing.

"What time are we going to football this morning?" I ask.

"You don't need to come, Miss Brielle. I'm well aware that you don't work weekends. It isn't expected," he replies as he sips his coffee.

"I want to watch Will play. I've been looking forward to it all week."

Willow smiles around her mouthful of cereal.

Mr. Masters' eyes hold mine, and if I'm not mistaken, they have a new intensity to them today. Something is different with him this morning. He's playing with me. It's like he's silently daring me to flirt with him, just so he can reprimand me if I do.

I'm screwed if I do and screwed if I don't.

Who am I kidding? Any screwing with him would be good screwing.

Damn him and his all-confusing sexiness.

I raise an eyebrow at him. "I would like to come, please."

"Very well, as you wish. We leave in half an hour," he tells me calmly.

"Okay, call me when we are leaving." I hurry back to my room so I can try to get control of these hormones.

I need to calm my farm.

I sit in a fold-up chair at soccer, with the morning sunlight on my face and my boss sitting beside me.

Julian Masters.

Also known as Hugh Hefner.

Big dick. Check. Arrogant asshole. Check. Off-the-scale fucking hornbag. Double check.

These fucking soccer MILFs are pissing me off. One by one, they all slide up next to him and make small talk. He's always polite, and he flirts with ease as they hang off his every word.

Does he even realize that he does it?

"Oh, I heard you won your tennis semi the other night," he says.

The attractive woman with the dark hair beams with pride. "Yes. It was a great victory." She fakes a laugh. "We still need to get that game in, Julian."

"I know, as soon as time permits. We shall." He smiles. "I'm looking forward to it, although I hope you're prepared to suffer a loss."

She throws her head back and laughs. "Oh, Julian, you kill me."

I fold my arms and roll my eyes. I'm right here, you know. For fuck's sake, he's an idiot.

"Call me." She smiles as she walks off.

We both watch her walk away, and his eyes eventually return to mine.

"I'm looking forward to it," I mimic with a roll of my eyes.

"Why the sarcasm?" he teases. "I look forward to spending time with you, too, Miss Brielle. Don't feel left out."

"Oh, please," I mutter. "I'm not in line with these... these... desperate old hags."

His eyes dance with delight, and I narrow mine. Damn, my jealous streak is showing now.

I fold my arms in front of me. This fatal attraction is beginning to piss me off. I don't need this shit. Who knew that football could be the home to such pickup tricks?

A Blonde from last week walks up next. "Julian, where have you been hiding, darling? I've been searching all over."

Oh God, it gets worse. I keep a straight face as I watch the game in front of me. When it eventually comes to an end, the crowd claps at the result. I have no idea of the score. I was way too distracted by Hugh Hefner here. I shake my head as I get a grip of myself.

Just act calm. This shouldn't bother you, Brielle, I remind myself. It's casual.

Cas. u. al.

It's no bother to me if these women want him. I'm just using him for sex, anyway.

Julian smiles warmly as the blonde kisses both his cheeks. "How are you?"

Ugh, stop being so fucking cute or I will hurt you. "I wanted to talk to you." She smiles.

"About?"

She glances at me and then hands me a twenty-pound note. I look at it, confused.

"Can you go to the cafeteria and grab me a coffee, darling? Just cream. No sugar."

What the hell? Who does she think she is?

I shove the money back into her hand. "No. I'm not your coffee

151

girl, and please don't call me darling." I stand and glare at Julian. "What I am going to do is leave so I don't have to listen to you embarrass yourself anymore," I snap.

Her mouth falls open, and Julian's lips twist as he tries to hide his smile. I storm off towards the dressing sheds. Honestly, these women are ferocious.

Of all the nerve! Get her coffee. Have you ever?

I storm around the corner and see four girls from an opposing team surrounding Willow. It's the same four who were around her last week when she seemed uncomfortable.

I walk up behind them.

"You're pathetic," I hear the blonde sneer at Willow. Willow goes to brush past them, but the girl grabs her arm.

"I would hate to be you. Your poor family must be so ashamed." My heart drops.

Oh no...

"Your mother probably fucking killed herself to get away from you," the blonde hisses, and the other girls all laugh cruelly. "Even death would be better than living with you."

Willows's face drops.

Something feral snaps inside of me—something that isn't supposed to snap with sixteen-year-old girls on the receiving end of it.

I rush forward. "What the fuck did you just say?" I growl. Their faces fall, paling instantly.

Willow shakes her head and grabs my arm. "Leave it, Brell."

"No. I will not leave it," I snap as I pull out of her grip. I point to the blonde. "You listen here and you listen good. If you ever come near Willow again, if you even dare look her way, I will beat down your door, lady. And you better watch out, because it won't be fucking pretty. Do you understand me?" I growl.

The girls all step back, shaken and afraid.

"Not so tough now, huh?" I look them up and down in disgust. "How dare you spew hate like that? You're pathetic."

I grab Willow's hand and pull her away as the girls sprint to the sheds.

She's visibly upset with tears in her eyes, and I pull her around the corner to give us some privacy.

"What's going on, pumpkin?" I ask as I brush the hair back from her forehead.

She shakes her head and wipes her eyes angrily.

"Do they pick on you all the time?" I whisper.

She nods.

My anger hits an all-time high. This is why the poor girl is so angry. She's hurting.

I fix her hair. "Don't worry about them, they're all just spoilt little bitches like their desperate mothers are."

She looks down at the ground.

"Will," I whisper as I take her hands. "Look at me, please."

She drags her eyes up to meet mine.

"Promise me that you will talk to me about this later. I want to know what's going on so I can go around and kick their fake-tanned little asses."

She smiles sadly, and then she looks up at me. "You have a fake tan."

I giggle. "I know. It's ugly, isn't it?"

She offers me a lopsided smile.

I wrap my arms around her and hold her in an embrace, grateful that she lets me.

She stays in my arms and it nearly brings me to tears because I can feel how much she needs me. God, this poor little girl. And she has no one to talk to because her father has his head up his ass. I link my arm through hers. "Come on, let's go and get your bag from the changing room. Then we can get the hell out of this place."

She nods, and we make our way to retrieve her things.

Fifteen minutes later, we find our way back to Julian and Samuel, only to see that blonde is still with him. Only this time, the blonde little bully is standing behind her.

I can tell by Mr. Masters' stance that he is angry. "Go back to the car and wait for me, Will," I say. She stops, as if petrified.

"Will," I say calmly. "Go to the car...now."

Willow heads off to the car, and I approach the four of them.

"Miss Brielle," Julian snaps. "Where is Willow?"

"Why?" I ask.

"Because she is in big trouble." The woman smiles a smug smile.

"Go to the car, Sammy," I say.

He frowns.

"Now," I snap. He runs off into the distance. I glare at the blonde little bitch. "Why, exactly, is Willow in trouble?"

"She's been picking on her teammates," Julian growls. "She's grounded indefinitely."

"No, she hasn't. That's a blatant lie and false accusation." I narrow my eyes. "The bullying is the other way around."

"Miss Brielle, I demand you go and get Willow, bring her to me, and I will make her apologize this minute." His fury is palpable.

Something snaps again, and I step forward

"I will do nothing of the sort." I point to the mother. "But I'll tell you what I will do. If your evil daughter comes near Willow again, I will have her charged by the police for harassment and assault."

The mother gasps, and the other parents all stop to listen to what's going on.

"Why, that's ridiculous," she cries.

I turn to the blonde bully. "Go near Willow again, sweetie, I dare you." I sneer.

Her eyes widen in fear.

"Miss Brielle!" Mr. Masters snaps.

"Who the hell is this?" The blonde asks snootily.

"I'm your worst nightmare. Now get a leash on your girl before I involve the police."

She puts her arm around her daughter. "Come on, dear, let's go home. It's been a traumatic day. This woman is a hooligan." She glares at me and storms off.

I turn to Mr. Masters. "Are you kidding me?"

"Are you kidding me?" he growls.

"How dare you!" I snap, and I storm my way back to the car.

"How dare I?" he calls as he follows me. "How dare you?"

"Oh. I dare, all right," I shout as I arrive at the car.

Willow and Sammy are standing wide-eyed by the car, waiting for it to be unlocked. I don't think they've ever seen someone as angry as I am at this moment.

Mr. Masters drops the chairs on the ground and pops the trunk of his car, and the kids dive into the back seat to escape the fury. I get in the front and slam the door hard.

He opens my door. "Don't slam my car door!" he yells.

I open it and slam it again...harder.

The kids are sitting frozen in the back, afraid to speak or move in case we turn on them.

Their father gets in his precious car and revs the engine before he pulls out in a rush.

Don't say it. Don't say it. I have to say it.

"How dare you?" I cry out.

"How dare I what?" His angry eyes flicker between the road and me.

"How dare you blame Willow for that horrible piece of work." I shake my head. "You need to apologize to her this very minute."

"I've done nothing wrong."

"Unfucking believable. You have the emotional intelligence of a fish. It's blatantly obvious that those girls were and have been picking on your daughter for a while, but you're far too busy chatting up their mothers to fucking notice."

"What?" he cries with incredulity.

"You heard me," I shout back.

"Do not raise your voice at me, and do not curse in front of my children."

"Your children are not robots. Raised voices are perfectly

155

normal everyday occurrences in families. Stop being so damn safe all the time."

"I would rather be safe than a complete lunatic."

I narrow my eyes. "Listen, you big baboon, I'm not afraid of your little high-society sluts and will not tolerate them bullying Willow under any circumstance. I don't care how much money they have."

He glares at me.

"And I am not about to buy their fucking coffee! How dare you not pull her into line about that! Do I look like a servant?"

He clenches his jaw as he drives. "Unlike you, I don't like causing a scene."

"Because you're a wimp!" I yell. "Too scared of what everyone will think to defend your own daughter or your nanny."

He glares at the road and grips the steering wheel with white-knuckle force.

The whole sky feels like it's a shade of red. I can't remember ever being this angry.

Fifteen silent minutes later, we arrive home.

I get out of the car. "Go and get changed, kids. We're going out," I announce.

The kids waste no time and quickly take off in the direction of the house.

Mr. Masters gets out of the car and slams the door. "I hope you're happy with the dramatics you have caused." He brushes past me.

"Do you know what that bully said?" I call. "I heard her. I heard her say it with my own ears."

He turns to face me.

My eyes fill with tears at the sheer memory of it. Poor Willow. "She said that Willow's mum probably killed herself just to get away from her. Do you have any idea what it would be like to hear that being said to you?"

He scowls, clearly torn between disbelief and hurt.

"You're her father, for fuck's sake."

His face falls.

"You were going to ground her without a second thought," I whisper in disgust.

His haunted eyes hold mine as he processes what has happened.

"They are picking on her, and you didn't even bother to ask for her side of the story. You just believed them without question. What kind of a father does that to his daughter?"

He drops his head in shame.

The kids come bounding back to the car, all changed and ready to go.

"Get in the car, kids. We're going to McDonald's." I sigh.

Mr. Masters looks between Willow and me.

"Can I come?" he asks softly.

I shake my head. "You're not invited."

The kids get in the car and we drive away. I watch him disappear in the rearview mirror, standing still, watching us leave without him.

Mr. Masters disappointed me today. I don't think I like him anymore.

I wait on the porch for my Uber driver to pick me up. It's 8:00 p.m. on Saturday night, and I'm going out with Emerson. I'm wearing a pale pink dress and I have my cardigan slung over my folded arms.

I haven't spoken to Mr. Masters since our fight at football this morning, but the kids have spent the afternoon lying on my bed, watching movies.

It seems they're both giving him the silent treatment as well.

Good.

The door opens and Mr. Masters comes out to stand beside me. He puts his hands into his pockets and the two of us stare forward, out into the darkness.

"I didn't know," he says quietly.

I inhale sharply, but I don't answer.

"I'm sorry."

"I'm not the one you should be apologizing to," I tell him dryly. We stay silent for a little while longer.

"When will you be back?" he asks quietly.

"Tomorrow afternoon for Willow's dinner party."

He nods and rolls his lips, unsure whether to speak or walk away.

We stand in silence once again, and I just want him to go back inside the house. I honestly have nothing to say to him.

"I could have driven you."

"No, thank you," I whisper. "I wouldn't want to put you out."

The headlights appear at the end of the driveway, and I watch as the car pulls up to the front of the house.

"Goodbye, Mr. Masters," I say flatly.

He stays silent.

I get into the car and look at him through the car window. He's unmoving, still, with both of his hands in his pockets as he watches the car drive me away.

He looks so lost.

I roll my eyes because he should. He is.

Julian

"Brelly's home!" Samuel yells from his position at the window.

I pretend to continue reading my book on the sofa, but no matter how many times I read a line on the page, I only see the words Brielle repeated to me: *your mother killed herself to get away from you.*

I'm failing miserably at this parenting thing, and I feel as though the weight of the world sits heavily on my shoulders. Willow hasn't uttered a single word to me since Brielle left last night.

Willow comes bounding down the stairs and rushes out the front door with Samuel to meet their nanny.

I clench my jaw and turn the page.

I hate that they prefer her company to mine when she's only been here for all of ten days. I know that says a lot about me.

My fingers flick the page in annoyance. I can hear all three of them coming up the stairs onto the landing.

"Oops, have you got it?" Brielle laughs.

I hear the rustling of plastic bags, and then I hear something bang.

"Ouch, watch it," Willow snaps.

"Oh, that was close to your toe." Brielle giggles.

"I know, just missed it," Samuel answers in his enthusiastic voice.

"Be careful, will you? I don't want to have to take you to A&E," Brielle tells them.

The three of them laugh, and I can't help but roll my eyes as I listen.

They come through the door, ladened with shopping bags. I sit up. "What on Earth?"

"Good afternoon, Mr. Masters." Brielle smiles warmly as she struggles. "How is the man of the house today?"

I raise an eyebrow, surprised that she's talking to me. I rise and take the shopping bags from her hands, taking them through to put on the kitchen counter. "I'm fine. And you?" I ask.

"Happy now that I'm home for Will's dinner party." She smiles. "I'm so excited. Are we ready to cook, pumpkin?"

Willow smiles and nods. "Yep."

I place my hands on my hips as I watch her and Willow unpack the shopping bags. Who is this woman, and what has she done with my grouchy daughter?

"So, what's been going on around here, Mr. Masters?" she asks.

I shrug. "I'm surprised you're talking to me, to be honest," I admit.

Her eyes find mine. "Yesterday was yesterday, and we don't hold grudges in this house, do we?"

"No. Because you did run him over first," Samuel points out.

Brielle points at Samuel. "That's right. I did."

I'm silently grateful that she hasn't come back prepared to launch World War III.

"Do you want me to do anything?" I ask.

"Hmm." She looks around. "I'll get you and Sammy to set the table a little later, but nothing at the moment."

"Okay." I look around, wondering what to do. "Go back to your book and relax." She smiles.

I frown. She is the most confusing woman on the planet. Is she going to spike my food with arsenic?

I pick my book back up and sit back on the lounge.

I sit and listen to her help my daughter over the course of the next three hours. She's teaching her to make fresh pasta as Sammy watches on from his place on the kitchen counter. Brielle is carefree, funny, and the children dote on her.

They are laughing freely, and I have to stop myself from smiling.

I thought I was just pretending to read before, but that was nothing, because now I'm not even focusing on the words on the page.

All I can hear is her voice, praising and directing my children, laughing and joking with them, teaching them little life lessons as she does.

If only she knew she was tempting me to think about things I shouldn't be thinking.

"Mr. Masters?" she calls.

I glance up, hoping she can't read my mind. "Yes, Brielle."

She smiles warmly. "Can you and Sammy go outside and pick some fresh flowers for the table, please?"

"What for?"

"Because this is a dinner party and we want everything to be perfect."

I roll my eyes, thinking this is extreme. "Very well." I get up from the lounge, and with Samuel in tow, go out into the garden.

The doorbell chimes at exactly 6:00 p.m. and I answer it. My mother and father greet me happily.

"Julian, this is so exciting." Mother smiles. "Willow is learning how to cook. We're so thrilled to be invited." She kisses my cheek and my father shakes my hand.

"Yes, yes, I know. Although this is all Miss Brielle's idea," I tell them dryly.

"Grandma and Grandpa!" Samuel squeals as he runs to jump into my father's arms.

"Hello, my boy." He laughs heartily.

Willow comes down the stairs, smiling, and it's the first genuine smile I have seen on her in a long time. She kisses my parents on the cheek and my father's eyes dance with delight. "Where is this new nanny?"

"She's just getting ready," I answer.

I look around the house. It's hard to believe it's actually mine. The place is spotless with the smell of beautiful Italian food filling the space. The table is set and fit for a king, with fresh flowers and the best cutlery out on display.

"Willow," my mother gasps. "It looks so beautiful."

Willow looks around proudly. "It was all Brelly."

"Nonsense." Miss Brielle smiles as she walks into the room.

My face falls at the sight of her. She's wearing a red wrap-around dress with her hair down and full. She may just be the most beautiful woman I have ever seen.

"Miss Brielle." I gesture to my parents. "This is my mother, Frances, and my father, Joseph."

"Hello." She smiles warmly as she kisses them both on the cheek.

My father's eyes meet mine in a 'holy shit, Son, this woman is hot' way, and I smirk.

I know, Dad, you don't have to remind me.

"Come in, come in, please." She gestures to the dining area. "Willow has made us the most amazing feast."

"Have you, Willow?" My mother gasps again. "This is so exciting."

"Would you like a glass of wine?" Brielle smiles. "I bought some non-alcoholic wine for you, too, Will."

Willow's eyes widen with excitement.

I fill everyone's glasses, and my mother holds her glass up for a toast. "To Willow's first dinner party."

Willow beams with happiness, and I unexpectedly get choked up. "To Willow's first dinner party," I repeat.

Over the next four hours, I watch on as Brielle adds my father to her fan club. The food has been amazing, the laughter has flowed freely, and I have to admit, I have had a truly fantastic night.

"So, what do you do back home in Australia?" my father asks. Brielle smiles and glances at me.

"She's an engineer," I tell them proudly.

"What?" my mother squeals. "Really? I had no idea."

Brielle nods and laughs. "You all seem so shocked when you find that out about me."

"What do you do exactly?" my father asks.

"I design machines, but mostly I work on creating prosthetic limbs."

"Prosthetic limbs?" I frown.

"Yeah, and some hearing aids too. I don't actually design them, more fit them to the client's individual needs. I mostly work in the health sector. However, I have designed a few elevators."

I try to process what she's telling me.

"Shall we make our guests a coffee, Will?" Miss Brielle asks, changing the subject.

Willow frowns in question.

"It is customary to offer your guests a coffee or tea to wind down."

"Oh."

"That's what the chocolates in the fridge are for." She smiles as she grabs Willow's hand over the table. "Let's get that sorted, shall we?"

They stand and go to the kitchen. Brielle whispers something to my daughter, and Willow smiles warmly. The sight of it makes my heart constrict. I knew Brielle was perfect on the outside. God knows every man on the planet knows she's fucking perfect on the outside.

But today, she's a new kind of beautiful to me. The kind of beautiful that makes me want to rush closer and kiss her. The kind of beautiful that makes me want to hold her in my arms.

My cock aches at the memory of having her the other night. She was tight, toned, and as loving as she is in everyday life. I want to be alone with her again...right now.

But that's the problem: I will want her to leave soon, too, and then she would.

For the first time since their mother died, my children are happy.

I can't jeopardize this with my carnal desires. Not now, not ever.

I have to put my children before myself, and I have to keep away from Miss Brielle.

My eyes linger on the beautiful woman wearing the red dress who is standing in my kitchen, and my heart constricts at the thought of never having her again.

She glances up, and our eyes linger on each other's face a moment too long.

I drop my eyes and blow out a defeated breath. If only I were normal.

10

Brielle

I WALK along the hallway upstairs, prepared to start the morning routine. "Rise and shine, lovely little people," I call.

I open Willow's door. "Will, time to get up."

"Get out," she sighs groggily.

I continue walking down to Sammy's room.

"Sammy, wake up, little angel," I call as I walk in and sit on the end of his bed. We have a morning routine now. He crawls out of bed, onto my lap, and we cuddle for a few minutes until he wakes properly.

"Good morning." I kiss his perfect little forehead, and he snuggles in closer. "How's my little man today?" I ask.

"Good," he mumbles sleepily.

We sit for a moment longer. "Get yourself washed up and I'll meet you downstairs, okay?"

He nods and toddles off to the bathroom, leaving me alone.

"Miss Brielle?" Mr. Masters calls from his room.

What the hell? I walk into his bedroom to find him with a white towel wrapped around his waist, and he's shaving in his bathroom mirror.

My eyes widen.

"W-what are you doing home?"

He smiles at my obvious shock. "I do believe I live here."

I shake my head. "I meant, why aren't you at work?"

He carefully guides the razor down his cheek through the shaving cream, and I swallow the lump in my throat. The power radiating from his body nearly kills my ovaries; it wrestles them unconscious.

"I don't have court this week. I have a scheduled break, as I have conference meetings. Take a seat, please. I need to talk to you for a moment." He concentrates on his jawline.

My heart begins to beat faster. "Okay," I whisper. My eyes roam over his bare, muscular back, then over his ripped abdomen. He has a trail of dark hair that runs from his navel, disappearing beneath the towel. My mouth goes dry.

He's just so...

I get a vision of his head between my legs the other night and I begin to tingle. This is one hell of a morning show.

I take a seat on his freshly made bed and glance around nervously. The room smells like him—like chocolate body paint that's crying out to be worn.

His eyes meet mine in the mirror. "Unfortunately, I have a very busy week and will need you to do a few extra hours, if that's okay." He hesitates. "Of course, you will be financially compensated."

"Sure," I mutter. God, I wish we had these naked bathroom meetings every morning. This is definitely a sight for the spank bank.

I've never actually seen a man with a body this good. He's chiselled, muscular, and so, so masculine.

"I won't be home tonight, as I have to go out, if that's all right, but I won't be home too late," he says, snapping me out of my little fluffy-white-towel fantasy.

"Sure."

I roll my lips to stop my tongue from hanging out while I watch him.

Honestly, this is next-level perving. I wish I could take a photo for Emerson. She wouldn't believe what I'm seeing right here.

That's if I could frigging tell Emerson. Ugh.

Julian turns toward me and my eyes drop to his broad chest and the scattering of dark hair that dusts it. I can see every muscle in his stomach.

Drop the towel, drop the towel, drop the towel. "...need from me," he finishes.

"Huh?" Shit. I forgot he was talking, and my eyes snap up to meet his. "Sorry. What did you say?"

He smiles a knowing smile. Damn it. I totally just got busted drooling over him. "I said... Is that all you need from me?"

"Erm." My eyes drop down to his crotch, and then back up to his face. "That's all I need from you, sir."

He chuckles as he washes the razor under the hot water, his eyes ablaze with naughtiness.

Something's different about him today. What is it?

"You seem to be especially mischievous today, Mr. Masters?" I smirk.

He smiles as he continues to shave. "Perhaps it's the company I'm keeping."

I smile as I walk out of the room. "You'd better concentrate, or you'll cut your pretty face."

"It's handsome, not pretty," he calls after me, and I smile to myself as I walk down the stairs.

He's certainly right about that one.

I'm fuming. A big, bubbling cauldron of anger is about to blow over within me.

This serves me right. I knew something like this was about to happen, and now I can't even tell Emerson what's really going on.

"Why are we here again?" Emerson asks.

I narrow my eyes as I look at the restaurant across the road from us. "We're spying," I mutter quietly.

Hank looks over as he licks his ice cream. "On who?"

It's 9:30 p.m. and I'm in an ice cream shop with Emerson and Hank—Emerson's flatmate.

He's an odd-looking fellow as well as a raging virgin, but I really like him. We met when he came out with us on Saturday night, and it is Em's—and my—new mission to get him laid.

"Julian has a date tonight," I tell them moodily. Emerson screws up her face. "So?"

"So... I want to see who this Bernadette is, with her stupid toffee voice."

"You like him now?" She rolls her eyes. "You are actually admitting it?"

"No. This is..." I try to think of a suitable answer. "I'm just checking on him for the sake of the kids."

Hank smirks as he licks his ice cream.

"That's a deplorable lie and you know it," Emerson grumbles. "Did he tell you he had a date?"

"No, the girl-woman, whatever she is—rang and left a message with me, asking me to tell him she had changed the arrangements. Apparently, his phone was switched off and she couldn't reach him." I sigh, disgusted.

Emerson frowns as she looks across the street. "What did he say when you gave him the message?"

"He seemed uncomfortable."

She smirks at me.

"What?" I snap.

"I love it when I know something others think I don't know."

I smile and tap my ice cream to hers. "Same here."

I turn my attention to Hank. "Tell me about the concert." He went to a dance concert at the weekend and we set him some tasks.

Hank smiles proudly.

"He did it. Hank kissed a girl." Emerson smiles.

"You did?" I can't hide my excitement. "This is great. Did you get to second base?"

"No." He screws up his face because it sounds so foreign to him.

The doors of the restaurant open, and we all slide down in our seats.

"Here they come," Emerson whispers.

Mr. Masters is wearing a navy suit, and he holds the door open for the woman, and as she walks through, he takes her hand in his.

My mouth falls open. "Are you kidding me?" The girl he is with is blonde, beautiful, and she's wearing a red dress.

"What?" Emerson whispers. "Why are we whispering? He can't hear us. She's pretty. I'm impressed." She raises her eyebrow in surprise.

"She's young!" I snap. "Is he frigging kidding?"

"She's in her late twenties, I'd say," Emerson tells me. "That's not too young. What seems to be the problem?"

Steam feels like it's shooting from my hot ears. "What would a young bombshell want with a middle-aged man like that?"

Emerson rolls her eyes. "Funny you should ask that. I do wonder myself."

Hank snickers. "Touché."

"She's just after his money," I grumble.

Emerson raises her eyebrow. "Remind me again, why we are spying on him?"

"Because he's a fucking idiot," I snap way too loudly.

We sit in silence as we watch them walk around the corner, hand in hand.

Emerson's eyes hold mine. "Tell me."

"Tell you what?"

"What's going on?"

I hesitate for a moment. I'll just tell her a snippet and warm her up to the idea. "I'm really attracted to him. Every time we're in the room together, the sexual chemistry is off the charts."

Emerson's eyes widen, filled with horror. "Will you stop it?"

"What?" I shrug. "We came on this holiday to explore ourselves. I want to explore him." I sigh. "He's fucking gorgeous."

"So what if he's gorgeous? This is a bad idea. Do not engage in any sexual relations with that man or you are going to end up being Monica Lewinsky."

I giggle. "Slight exaggeration."

"Who is Monica Lewinsky?" Hank frowns.

Emerson and I both shake our heads. "Long story." I sigh.

"If he wasn't your boss, I would say go for it, but he is your boss. If you want to explore this, fine, but find another job first."

I point at her. "That's a really good idea."

"I didn't mean you should leave." She frowns. "I meant don't do it."

I lick my ice cream, annoyed with my friend. Emerson doesn't need to know all my business anyway.

I'm sick to fucking death of doing what everyone else expects of me.

If I want him, I'll have him.

"And, of course, there's now the small matter of his girlfriend." Emerson sighs. "He's not even on the market for you to have."

I roll my eyes, annoyed by her fact-finding. I can't believe he's got a girlfriend.

He's now just another fucking asshole notch to add to my bedpost.

Julian

I open the car door for Bernadette and watch as she slides into her seat before I walk around and get in beside her.

Her eyes flicker over to me, and she rubs my thigh. "Let's go back to my place. The kids are with their father."

I take her hand in mine to stop it from exploring, and I pull out into the traffic. "I can't tonight."

Her face falls. "Why not?"

Here we go. I knew this was coming.

"I've got things on tomorrow. I need to get home."

"What's going on with you? I haven't seen you for two weeks

and now you don't even want to come back to my place when we finally get to see each other."

"Nothing is going on with me."

"Are you seeing someone else?"

I roll my eyes. "If I am, it doesn't matter because we, Bernadette, are not exclusive. You've known that all along."

She stays silent, and I find myself glancing between her and the road. "What?" I ask, cutting through the silence.

"You've stopped putting any effort in." She folds her arms across her chest.

"Because you put enough effort in for the both of us. Don't start this shit now, I'm not in the fucking mood," I groan.

"Not in the fucking mood?" she hisses, clearly pissed off. "You know I'm monogamous to you. You know you're the only man I see. Don't treat me like a fool."

I bite my bottom lip, forcing my eyes to stay on the road.

She watches me for a moment. "It's because of what I said the last time we were together, isn't it?"

I clench my jaw and remain silent.

"I told you I love you and this is how you act."

"And that is my precise problem," I yell, losing control. "I told you I don't want a relationship." I glare at her. "You knew. You fucking knew! And then you go and tell me you love me. You lost me with those three words."

"What is so bad about being in a relationship, Julian?"

"It's not who I am. I want a friendship with a woman who I care about."

"But if you don't see other women, why not call it a relationship?"

"Because I don't want to. I don't want the expectation of what's coming next. I don't want to be in love. I don't want anyone to be in love with me."

She watches the road, her face like stone, and we stay silent for a while.

Guilt suddenly fills me, and I reach over to grab her hand. "Let's just leave it."

Her face falls. "You don't want to see me anymore?"

I shake my head. "I can't."

"Yes, you can." She begins to panic. "We'll just go back to being casual."

I exhale heavily and lift her hand to kiss the back of it softly. "I can't continue to see you knowing that you love me when I don't feel the same."

Her eyes fill with tears, and she drops her head.

"I'm sorry," I whisper.

Her tears begin to fall, and she cries quietly for the rest of the trip until I pull into her driveway.

We sit in silence for a moment. I feel like absolute shit knowing I've hurt her.

I've felt this feeling many times before. They all fall in love with me. I always leave them when they do.

"Why?" she whispers as her eyes search mine. "Did I do something wrong?"

I shake my head. "Angel, no." I pull her into an embrace. "It's me. I'm. I..."

"You're what?"

"I'm not wired like most."

"What do you mean?"

I shrug. "I don't know, but at times like this, it's difficult."

"Have you done this before?"

I nod with regret.

She leans over, kissing me softly, and our lips linger over each other's.

"Can't we work this out?" she whispers. "I'll be patient and I won't push you. I promise."

I smile as I look down at her. She really is beautiful. I brush the hair back from her face. "No. I'm going to free you up for a man who can really love you the way you deserve to be loved."

Her eyes crease together and more tears fall. "But I'm in love with you."

I kiss her once more before I open my door and climb out. I go around and open her car door, holding her hand to help her climb out. She clings to me one last time, her pain palpable.

"Julian, please? Please, don't go. Come inside."

"Stop," I whisper as I wipe the tears from her eyes. "I'm going to say goodbye and you are going to walk inside and never think about me again."

The tears stream down her face.

"Okay?" I whisper as I hold her two cheeks in my hands.

She nods.

I kiss her one last time. "You're an amazing woman. Go and find a man who deserves your love."

She smiles despite her tears, and we squeeze each other's hand one last time. When she turns to leave, I put my hands into my trouser pockets and I watch her walk to her front door. She turns back and waves sadly. I smile and wave goodbye.

She opens the door and disappears inside.

I turn and get into my car, and before I know it, I'm opening up my front door. The house is dark, lit only by the kitchen light, and I lie on the living room floor, staring up at the ceiling.

Why am I like this? What's wrong with me?

Brielle

It's 9:00 a.m. on Tuesday morning, and I'm sitting outside the Headmaster's office as I wait for our scheduled meeting about Willow. He couldn't see me before now. I don't know what the hell he does that is so important, but I intend to find out.

I'm already furious because of my stupid twat of a boss. He came home not long after me, so I'm not sure what happened on his date.

Either way, I'm off him.

This Headmaster better not mess with me in here, or he will

meet his maker. My leg bounces up and down as I wait. After speaking with Willow in depth this morning, I now know that it's a group of six girls who are picking on her. They pick on everyone, apparently. Willow's best friend moved schools about a year ago, and that's when they turned their attention to her. She assures me that it's okay and not to worry, but it's not okay. Ever.

I glance at my watch.

Come on. What is he doing? I can't believe I fucked him.

I get a vision of Mr. Masters' face between my legs, and I just want to gouge my eyes out. How can I stop seeing this shit? What an idiot I am.

I exhale as I feel my underarms heat with perspiration.

"Come on," I whisper, my leg bouncing harder as my anticipation builds and builds. "What the hell are you doing in there?"

The office door opens and a man in a grey suit walks out. He's in his early sixties and very distinguished. He smiles kindly and shakes my hand. "Hello, I'm John Edmunds."

"I'm Brielle, thank you for making time to see me."

He gestures into his office. "Please, come in." I walk past him and take a seat at his big, fancy desk.

He sits opposite me and links his hands in front of him. "How can I help you today?"

I swallow nervously. "I have some concerns about Willow Masters getting bullied."

He frowns. "I'm sorry. Are you her parent or guardian?"

I clutch my handbag on my lap with white-knuckle force. "No. Willow's mother died five years ago in a car accident. I'm her nanny."

His face falls. "Oh, I'm so sorry."

"I overheard a girl from this school say something to her that disturbed me greatly."

"What was that?"

"She said that Willow's mother probably killed herself to get away from Willow."

"Dear God," he mutters. "When was this?"

"At the weekend."

He frowns. "On school grounds?"

"No. During football practice, at the playing field."

His face falls. "Unfortunately, we're unable to do anything about weekend activities."

"I know. But I wanted to speak to the school counsellor and see if she has noticed anything going on here at school."

"Yes, of course." He scribbles a phone number on the back of a business card. "Call that number on Monday morning and make an appointment to see him. He's very helpful."

I smile and take the card. "Thank you." I glance at the name.

Steven Asquith

"I'm sorry I can't help more, but I will send out an email today to all of her teachers and ask them to call you, if you like?"

"That would be fantastic." I smile.

"That way we can tackle it at the grassroots level."

"Perfect."

"Shall I schedule a meeting for this time next week so we can update each other on any of our findings?"

I smile gratefully. "That would be great, thank you. I'm sure you can understand that this is a sensitive issue. I don't want Willow to suffer any more unnecessary stress."

"Of course." We both stand and he shakes my hand. "Have a great weekend, and we will meet again next week."

I head out of the office, feeling a little better that we are at least starting to get to the bottom of it, but then I stop dead in my tracks.

The blonde bitch—the one who asked me to buy her coffee, also known as the bully's mother—is behind the reception desk. She's wearing a white dress and black high-heeled pumps, dolled up like mutton with a full face of makeup. She doesn't see me, and she turns and walks down the corridor in the opposite direction.

I stand for a moment, watching her walk away.

I approach the reception window. "Excuse me, can you please tell me what that woman's name is?"

The young girl on reception looks around. "I'm sorry, who?"

"The woman in the white dress who was just here."

"Oh, that's Tiffany Edwards."

"What's she doing here?" I ask, my eyes glued to the back of this Tiffany Edwards.

"What isn't she doing here?" The girl laughs, and I can tell she's not into the politics of the school. "She volunteers here."

"Volunteers?" I ask.

"She practically runs the school."

"Does she?" I fume.

"Yes." The girl looks around to see if her colleagues can hear us gossiping. "You don't want to get on the wrong side of her, that's for sure," she whispers.

"And why is that?"

"She knows everybody."

I glare at Tiffany Edwards's perfect little behind as it disappears, and my blood begins to boil.

"Tell me...where do I sign up to volunteer?" I ask.

"Really?" The girl winces. She leans forward so she can say something the others won't hear. "They can be brutal in there."

I smile sweetly. "Nothing I can't handle."

I drive down the road when my email pings on my phone. I glance over at it.

From: Julian
To: Bree

I narrow my eyes and pull over to park the car. I glance up and see a coffee shop. Before I open the email, I decide to make my way inside. I order a coffee and take a seat, eventually opening the email.

Julian Masters
Requests the company of: Bree Johnston
Occasion: Situation inspection
Date: Today
Time: 1 p.m.
Place: Room 612, Rosewood London
Dress code: Secretary

I narrow my eyes. Of all the nerve. Is his fucking girlfriend busy?

I type back.

From: Bree
To: Julian
Bree wishes to inform you that she is busy washing her hair and will not be attending the secretarial conference.
Yours Sincerely,
Bree

I smirk and hit send. Put that in your pipe and smoke it. A reply bounces back immediately.

From: Julian
To: Bree
What?
A prompt reply is required.
Julian

I narrow my eyes. Conceited prick. I type.

From: Bree
To: Julian
I am not interested in a rematch. Find another candidate.
Yours Sincerely,
Bree

My phone instantly rings, the name Mr. Masters lighting up the screen.

Shit.

"Hello," I answer.

"What do you mean you're not interested?"

"It means what it means. I'm not interested."

"You enjoyed yourself the other night. I know you did."

"Not as much as you, it seems."

He stays silent, and I smirk as I imagine his angry face.

"Don't play games with me," he growls.

"I'm not."

"Is this about Bernadette?"

"Are you deaf, dumb, or just plain stupid?" I snap. "Of course this is about Bernadette."

"I broke up with her last night."

"Why?"

"Because she's not you."

I bite my bottom lip as I listen.

"Meet with me today, give me another chance. I won't be so hard on you, I promise."

I give him the chance to talk me into it. "Why should I?"

"Because you're all I've fucking thought about since Friday night and I'm slipping into a lust-induced stupor here."

I smile. "On a scale of one to ten, how badly do you want to see me?"

"Are you coming or not?" he snaps, unwilling to play my games.

"Yes, Julian, I will come."

"Good." He sighs, relieved. "I'll... I'll see you then."

I hang up and smile. Well, well, well. I do believe I just gained the upper hand.

I sit and stare out the window. I wonder...what the hell does a secretary wear?

11

Brielle

I STAND OUTSIDE the door marked number 612. My heart is hammering wildly in my chest. I'm wearing a black skirt, a white business shirt, and one of his ties wrapped around my neck. My hair is up in a bun, and I'm even wearing tortoiseshell glasses to complete my secretarial look.

Underneath, though, I'm wearing a white suspender belt and lacy underwear, with black sheer stockings hugging my legs. I guess I'm a slutty secretary—the kind you have long lunches with. I did end up charging this outfit to his credit card. I felt guilty at first, but screw it, he did say that's what it was for.

What are you doing here, Brielle? I ask myself.

I didn't like the way I felt the other night when I got home, but the masochist in me wants to see him again, and I know this is the only way it's going to happen. I've been thinking about him constantly. I hate that every time he's in the room with me I can feel his body talking to mine. I'm in a constant state of arousal, and I feel like I was a little boring the other night. I was so overwhelmed with his power, I became a shrinking violet.

I want to blow his mind tonight. I want to leave him begging for more, and then some.

And I'll do what any slutty secretary would do: I'll fuck him out of my system once and for all.

This is it. It's the last time. One for the road.

Just fuck him, blow his fucking mind, and then leave. No strings, no feelings, and no bullshit. I can do this.

I want to really play the part, but I can't imagine myself saying any of the filthy shit I've been thinking of saying. This man makes me feel so naughty.

I knock on the door and exhale heavily as my heart races faster.

The door opens in a rush, and there he stands. All 6ft 3inches of gorgeous man. He smiles sexily when he sees me in my outfit, and I swallow the lump in my throat.

"Hello, Mr. Masters. I believe you wanted to see me, sir."

He smirks. "I did. Please, come in."

I roll my lips to hide my smile and walk past him into the room.

He closes the door behind me.

I turn to him as I continue in my role. "Please don't fire me, sir. I promise I won't do it again."

He lifts his chin, his eyes alight with mischief. "Give me one good reason why I shouldn't. Disobedient secretaries need to be punished."

"Please, no," I beg. "I'll do anything to keep my job."

He licks his lips as his hungry eyes drop to my breasts. "Define anything."

I move closer to him. "There must be something I can do for you, sir," I whisper in his ear.

"I'm not that kind of man," he says calmly.

I lean forward and grab his hard dick in my hand, pushing him back against the wall. "But I'm that kind of woman." I drop to my knees and undo his belt, sliding his pants down swiftly. That beautiful, big cock springs free, and I take it into my mouth.

He inhales sharply, his hands moving to the back of my head.

I look up and smile at him. He frowns down at me, obviously surprised and confused. He was not expecting this, I can tell.

"Fuck my mouth. Punish me, Mr. Masters," I beg around his cock. He closes his eyes, lost somewhere between pleasure and disbelief, and then he grabs my hair in his hands as he begins to slide in and out of my mouth.

I look up with wide eyes, watching him come undone. "Fuck," he moans. I bare my teeth and he hisses, "Fuck."

This is hot—stupid hot—and I know I'm meant to be doing this for him, but it's turning me on big time.

His suit pants drop to his knees, and I get a rush of moisture in my sex. He's lost control.

I stop at once and stand, and all he can do is pant as he watches me, breathless and confused.

"Tell me my job is safe and you can have more."

His eyes darken. "Your job is safe."

I unbutton his shirt and slide it over his shoulders. I take off his pants, and then his jocks before I push him back onto the bed. He's submissive and naked, his cock lying up against his stomach. I stand on the bed over him, making sure he's watching me intently. I slowly begin to take my shirt off, throwing it onto the floor, and then I slide my skirt down my legs and dramatically kick it off.

He's on his back, looking up at me with fire dancing deep in his eyes and his stomach. He reaches out for me, but I move away so he can't touch me.

I take off my bra and my panties, so I'm wearing nothing more than his blue tie, my suspender belt, and my stockings.

"What do you want, Judge Masters?" I whisper as I run my fingers over my nipples.

"Get on me," he growls.

I kneel beside him and take his cock into my mouth again. "Not so fast," I breathe on the upstroke. I turn my behind towards him as I bend over, allowing his two fingers to slide inside me.

He moans and his legs open automatically.

I go up onto my knees and circle my hips to ride his fingers. I play with my nipples, and my eyes hold his. "Oh, you feel so good," I whisper. "I need you," I moan. "You can't ever tell my husband about this."

His fingers pump me aggressively. I can tell he's losing control, and it makes me smile down on him. "You're a very naughty boy, Judge Masters. Do you like fucking other men's wives?" I whisper as I roll my hips.

Oh, man, I feel like I'm in a bad porno here, but who cares? He seems to love it.

"I need a real man to fill me up. A man with a big, hard cock," I moan as I arch my back onto his fingers. Perspiration beads on his forehead. His mouth is hanging open as he watches me, completely in awe.

He's about to lose it.

I glance at the door suddenly. "I didn't lock the door, sir. Somebody could walk in here any moment and see us on your desk."

He closes his eyes and I smile, knowing he's losing his shit.

"Get on me now," he growls.

I hop up from the bed and go to my handbag to grab one of his condoms that I stole from his bathroom cabinet. I open it and slowly roll it onto him.

I bend and take his cock into my mouth and I moan around it. "I want a pay rise," I whisper.

Arousal dances in his eyes. He likes this game. "How much?"

I lick his balls, and he drops his head back in pleasure. "Ten thousand extra, plus a company car."

"I don't have the power to authorize that." He plays along.

I sit up, acting offended, and then I smile darkly as a new idea comes to me. I look him straight in the eyes. "Twenty thousand and you can take the condom off."

His eyes darken with an intensity I've never seen on any man before. A heavy silence hangs between us.

"Do you want to blow inside me, Judge Masters? Do you want to fill another man's wife with your load?"

His body convulses. He's so close to coming. "Fucking hell, Bree," he cries as he loses the last of his control. "Get the fuck on me... now!"

I smile as I lower myself onto him, wiggling from side to side to try and loosen myself up. He's so big.

We struggle for a moment until my body opens up and he slides in deep.

"Oh...fuck," he moans, grabbing my hips.

I ride him, deep and hard. I sit up so that he can fully see me, and I hold the tie between my fingers.

His body rises to meet mine and I know he's completely in the zone.

God, he's beautiful...

"Give it to me," I moan. "Fuck me."

He grabs my behind and starts to fuck me hard. His tie hangs down in his face and my breasts are bouncing up and down.

"Oh God, this is so good," I pant as I bounce. "You're so deep," I whimper. "So, so deep."

His face creases together, and he cries out as he comes, the jerking inside of me setting me off, making me climax too. We move together slowly as we begin to come down, his hands softly running up and down my back.

Our eyes are locked.

He's quiet, shocked into silence, I think. I lie down on his chest and he holds me close. His heart beats hard next to mine as we rest together for a moment.

"I'm glad you're not my secretary for real." He smirks against my forehead.

"I kind of am." I giggle.

"No, don't remind me that you work for me."

I smile. "Don't remind me that you're my boss."

He pulls out, removes his condom, and drags me back down over him. His fingers trail up and down my arm, and I can practically hear his thoughts bouncing around.

I stay silent and can't help but feel he's different to how he was the other day with me. He seems warmer.

"I've got to get going," I whisper.

"What?" His face falls and his arms tighten around me. "No. Why?"

"Willow has golf this afternoon. I promised her I'd take her."

"I've arranged for my mother to pick up the kids. She's happy to take them to their activities," he says.

"No." I sit up as I pull out of his grip. "I promised Will that I would take her."

"But... but we... I haven't spent any time with you yet," he stammers.

I smile and kiss his lips. "You've fucked me. That's all that you wanted me here for, isn't it?"

He frowns, obviously annoyed by me stating the obvious. "I haven't fucked you enough."

"Another time, maybe." I smile.

"When?"

I'm not imagining it. He really does seem needy today. "When my schedule with the kids permits. Next week or something."

He scowls and shakes his head. "Next week? That's not happening." He rolls me onto my back and moves to position himself between my legs. "I need you for an extended time." He kisses me, and my arousal tingles, awakening again.

"Why?" I breathe.

"Because I can't get enough." He nudges my opening.

"You didn't pay the twenty thousand dollars." I smirk. "Get a condom."

He chuckles and growls before he gets up and puts a condom on. Soon enough, he's back on top of me, sliding his dick against my sex.

"I need more of you. Two hours isn't enough," he breathes against my mouth.

"Why isn't it enough?"

"Because I watch you all fucking day, wishing I was inside you."

I smile, and he pushes into me. "You don't act like you do, Mr. Masters," I challenge.

His tempo increases, moving harder. "I shouldn't be thinking about you the way I do. I try my best to control it."

I smirk as he takes my legs and puts them over his shoulders.

Oh God, this makes me nervous. He's too big for me to handle this position. "Be careful with me," I whimper.

He slides in deeper, and he hisses with immediate approval. "Do you feel that? Do you feel how good our bodies fit together?"

My back arches off the bed, and my fragile heart races again. "God, yes."

"The kids are going to sleep at my mother's, Bree. I need a full night with you. Give me a full night." His eyes drop to the place where our bodies meet.

Excitement runs through me. He wants a full night. "When?" I pant.

He spreads his knees wide and holds my feet out in front of him. "Tomorrow." He hits me hard, and I cry out. "Tomorrow night."

"What if...you still need...more?" I breathe.

He takes my face in his hands and kisses me tenderly. "I won't, I promise. Just one more time."

I smile against his lips, but my heart drops.

One more time. He only wants me one more time.

Willow bounces into the car after her golf lessons.

"Hi," she beams.

"Hey, pumpkin. You seem very happy."

"I got talking to that girl who works on the desk. Her name is Lola."

"Really?" I smile and squeeze her thigh. "Great. Tell me all about her."

"She's eighteen. She's at university. She's going to be a doctor."

I smile. "Smart."

"She asked if I wanted to play golf with her this weekend."

"Really?" Oh, this is just what she needs—new smart friends. But all at once my face falls. "Damn, remember you are going to your Aunty Patricia's with Grandma and Grandpa this weekend?"

Her face falls. "Oh no, I forgot."

I don't want her to be disappointed. I know she's lonely at the moment. "Maybe we can reschedule the weekend away so that you can play golf."

Her face lights up. "Really?" she asks excitedly.

"Sure. I can talk to your father and Gran and see if we can reschedule."

Her face beams with happiness—hope. "Would you? That would be so cool."

I smile as I pull out of the parking lot onto the road. "I love that you're having so much fun here. You could be the next Tiger Woods." I roll my eyes. "But with a lot less drama, obviously."

She smiles, clearly happy with herself as she looks out of the windscreen and shrugs. "It's a lot better than I thought, that's for sure."

"See?" I laugh. "I know what's fun. Although, running your father over in a golf buggy is the most fun any of us have ever had."

She chuckles and shakes her head. "You're an idiot." We arrive home and I pull the car in beside his Porsche. He's home.

A rush of adrenaline runs through me. I go through this every day. Whenever I hear or see his car, excitement fills me, even if I never show it.

When we walk into the house, I hear his deep voice echoing through the halls as he talks to Janine in the kitchen.

He is back in his customary suit, looking neat and respectable for all the world to see. Nobody would ever know that he was on his back two hours ago with his nanny riding him hard.

I smile at him, and his sexy eyes hold mine. It's as if he's silently asking me if I can still feel him deep inside of me. My answer is yes.

Hmm, he's so hot.

"Hi, Dad," Sam calls, walking in behind us.

"Hello, Samuel." He smiles as he messes up his hair.

"Hi, Janine," I say as I approach her.

She turns and smiles warmly before she kisses me on the cheek. "Hello, my beautiful girl."

Janine and I have become quite close. I hang out in the kitchen every day while she cooks, and the two of us chat away. She's a lovely woman.

Julian seems surprised when he sees our interaction.

"You picked a winner when you hired this one, Mr. Masters. The sunlight in this house, she is," Janine says.

I laugh. "Oh, please, you exaggerator. Tell Janine your news, Will."

Willow shrugs, clearly embarrassed.

"She has plans this weekend with her new golf friends," I say for her.

Janine turns to Willow. "Really? This is great news."

Janine and I have been brainstorming as to how we can help Willow navigate this whole bullying saga, and we both believe making other friends is the key to her finding confidence.

"How were golf lessons, Will?" Julian asks her.

"Good." She shrugs. "I really like it."

"And she's so good at it," I add as I grab her hand in mine. "I got there early today so I could watch her, and I was so amazed at her skills." I smile at Willow. "She's very professional."

Willow grins and Julian's smile softens, his eyes lingering on my face.

"Do you want to work on your essay now, or should we do it later?" I ask her.

She frowns. "Can we do it later? I might take a shower."

"Sure." I turn my attention to Sammy. "Come on, kiddo, let's go shoot some hoops."

"I'll get my ball." He runs upstairs to get his basketball. Janine disappears into the bathroom.

Julian's eyes hold mine. "Is this what you do every afternoon when the man of the house isn't around?"

I bite my bottom lip. "Yes." I pause. "Sometimes I have secretarial meetings, too, though."

"How are those?" His eyes drop to my lips.

"They're the highlight of my week, sir."

The air between us zaps, and damn it, I want to go back to the hotel right now.

"Mine too," he whispers.

We stare at each other. The sexual tension between us is thick. God, I can hardly believe we had sex just a few hours ago. He was deep inside of me and now I'm dying for him all over again.

Janine comes back into the room, effectively destroying our moment, just as Sammy walks in with his basketball under his arm. I bat it out of his grip, steal it, and run.

"You snooze, you lose, sucker," I call.

"Brell!" Sammy calls as he runs after me. "That's not part of the rules."

"Rules are for breaking, Sammy," I call as I bounce the ball down the front steps. "Come at me."

Julian

I stare at my two friends as they sit across the table from me. We're at our favorite breakfast restaurant. They're talking about something printed in the newspaper today, but my mind is on other things.

"You're quiet today, Masters," Spence says.

I chew my food and raise my eyebrows as I cut into my omelet. "I did it."

They both frown.

"I fucked my nanny."

Their eyes widen with perfect synchronized timing. "What? I thought you said she was off-limits," Seb says in shock.

"She is."

"Wait." Spencer looks between Seb and me. "This is the hot nanny who ran you over at golf last week, right?"

I nod.

He leans against the table. "Where did you do it?"

"She caught me jerking off in my bathroom the other night."

"What?"

I close my eyes, the memories of it washing over me. "What did you do when you saw her?" Seb gasps.

"I kept going, finished off, and then I rubbed my jizz onto my stomach for added effect." I put a forkful of food into my mouth and shrug.

Their mouths fall open right before they both begin to laugh.

"What the fuck?" Seb whispers. "Then what?"

"Then I asked her to meet me at a hotel."

They exchange looks.

"The hot one...?" Spencer repeats again. "With the long dark hair? The bad driver?"

"Yes!" Seb snaps, annoyed. "How many fucking nannies do you think he has?"

I continue eating my breakfast as they both wait for me to speak.

"And?" Spencer frowns. "What happened then?"

I shake my head and wipe my mouth with my napkin. "We screwed, and it was the hottest fucking sex of my life."

Their eyes widen even further, if that were at all possible.

"We met again yesterday, and she fried my brain with dirty talk, and then fucked me stupid. Afterwards, she left, and I've been hard ever since."

"That's insanely hot," Spencer whispers. "What are you going to do?"

I sip my orange juice. "Meet her again at the hotel tonight."

"That good?" Spencer whispers. "Two nights in a row?"

I nod and exhale heavily. "I have to get a handle on it, though. My kids love her. I'm not going to fuck it up for them."

Brielle

Julian Masters
Requests the company of: Bree Johnston
Occasion: Situation inspection
Date: Tonight
Time: 7 p.m.
Place: Room 612, Rosewood London
Dress code: Formal

I read the information again on my phone. Formal? What the hell constitutes formal?

Damn him and his confusing sexy invitations. I flip through the rack in the department store, annoyed.

That's too short, that's too tight, that's too daggy.

It's not like I'm going to be wearing these clothes for long, anyway, is it? He's going to rip them off my body the moment he sees me.

I smile to myself. What a problem to have. A bottomless credit card to buy something pretty to wear for a date with a big-dicked, sexy god.

What is my life? I've turned into Pretty Woman.

Julian has meetings on and off all day today, but something has changed between us since our meeting yesterday. He's openly watching me now. He didn't do that last week. In fact, he avoided eye contact at all costs.

My phone rings and an unknown number pops up. "Hello," I answer.

"Hello, Brell, this is Frances."

Julian's mother. "Oh, hello." I smile nervously. Shit, what does she want? Oh my God, does she know?

"I wanted to take you out for lunch today, darling."

I inflate my cheeks, knowing that I don't really have time for that today. I want to prepare for my formal porno meeting.

"You don't need to do that," I tell her kindly.

"I want to. I'll pick you up at 12:30 p.m."

Damn, she's pushy. "Umm, I'm already in town, can I meet you somewhere?"

"Okay, dear. Let's go to Polpetto. It's on Berwick Street."

"Yes, okay, I'll see you then."

"Great. I'm looking forward to getting to know you better." She hangs up.

Fuck. She knows.

Does she know? I bite my thumbnail, knowing she could only really know if he's told her, but there's no way he would have told her...would he?

I dial his number. It rings and my stomach flips. I've never called him before.

"Hello, my beautiful Bree," he purrs.

"Hi." I smile goofily. He makes me giddy.

"How can I help you?"

I get tingles from the sound of his voice.

"Bree? Hello?"

I frown. "Oh, sorry. Did you tell your mother?"

"Tell her what?"

"About us."

"No. Of course not. Why?"

"She just called me saying she wants to take me out to lunch."

"What?"

"I know, but she was being pushy and I couldn't say no."

"Don't worry, I'll call her."

"N-no," I stammer. "If you call her now and cancel for me, she's going to know something is going on between us for sure."

"Hmm."

"You're absolutely positive she knows nothing?" I frown.

"No, and don't you tell her anything either."

I scowl to myself. "I can't lie, Julian. If she asks me if we're sleeping together, then I have to tell her the truth."

"Don't you dare. Don't go if you can't keep your mouth shut."

I bite my lip. This is a disaster because I really can't lie for shit. "You're certain she doesn't know?" I ask one final time.

"Bree, my mother is taking you to lunch to milk you for information. She's as sharp as a whip. Don't be fooled by her friendly demeanor."

My eyes widen. "What information?"

"Information on us."

"Right. So I can't tell her that we meet in hotels and fuck each other stupid, then?"

He chuckles, and the sound permeates through my bones. "Why don't you tell her that you are pussy whipping her son, and he's on the verge of needing sectioning because of his sexual addiction to you?"

I smile. "Great idea."

"I'm looking forward to tonight." I can tell he's smiling.

"Me too." I flick through the clothes on the rack.

"Wait, I bet I know what she wants to meet you for," he says, as if he's suddenly remembering something.

"What?"

"I asked her if the children can stay at her house every Thursday night."

"Why?" I frown.

"Because I want a whole night with you every week."

Hope blooms in my chest. "You do?"

"That's if you'll have me every week."

"I'd have you every day if I could, Jules," I whisper.

"Keep talking like that and you may not be walking for a few days."

I giggle. "Walking is overrated, anyway."

"What have you got for me tonight?" he breathes.

"Whatever you want." I look at the shoppers all around me, who are oblivious to my awesome dirty-talking skills.

"Just the sound of your voice makes me hard, even when I'm sitting at my desk."

I'm going to play with him. "Tell me about that beautiful cock of yours, Mr. Masters. Do you have any idea how often I think about it?" I whisper.

"You're a very naughty nanny, Miss Brielle. My cock is going to have to punish you for the things you make me think while at work."

"I'm your naughty nanny," I breathe.

He inhales sharply. "Yes...you are."

"Goodbye, Mr. Masters."

"Goodbye, Bree." He hangs up.

I grin to myself and continue looking through the racks, when my phone rings again. The name Mr. Masters lights up the screen.

"Hello."

"Stop distracting me with your sexiness," he says, and I smile. "I told my mother that I have a legal meeting every Thursday night for a while and that you can't mind the children because you're taking a class at the college."

I frown. "What course?"

"I can't actually remember what I told her, but I think it may have been sculpture."

"What?" I frown. "Sculpture? Why the hell would you say sculpture? What even is a sculpture class?"

"I don't know."

"Oh, great." I throw my hand up in the air. "Not only do you have me lying to your mother about us not being fuck buddies, but now you want me to tell her a stupid lie about me being interested in sculpting—a subject I know nothing about. What am I supposed to say when she asks me about it?"

He chuckles. "I'm sure you'll think of something."

I roll my eyes. "I'm going to tell her that I can't mind the children on Thursday nights because I will be too busy sucking her son's pea- sized brain out through the end of his dick."

He laughs out loud. "That's a great idea." He laughs some more. "Not you telling my mother part, but definitely the sucking part. We should practice that technique tonight."

"Goodbye, Julian," I respond sharply.

"Goodbye, Bree," he says with nothing but warmth in his voice.

I flick through the clothes rack. Screw the shopping. I should turn up in a garbage bag tonight.

Let's see how sexy he thinks that is.

I walk into the swanky restaurant at exactly 12:30 p.m. Frances stands and waves to get my attention, and I make my way over to her.

"Hello." I kiss her on both cheeks.

"Brell, thank you so much for coming." She gestures to the table. "Please, take a seat."

I fall into the chair.

"Would you like some wine?" she asks.

"I can't, I'm driving, but thanks."

She pours herself one and calls a waiter to the table. "What would you like, Brell?"

"Just a Diet Coke, please." I look around at the Italian restaurant we're in. It's beautiful, filled with leather chairs and the air of ultimate opulence. "This place is amazing."

"It is. The food is divine too," she says with enthusiasm. "So, tell me...how are you settling in?"

I shrug. "Okay, I guess. I'll be a lot better when I get to the bottom of Willow's problems at school."

My drink arrives. "Thank you." I smile as I take it from the waiter.

Her face falls. "What's going on?"

"These stupid little bullies are picking on her."

"Who are they?"

I roll my eyes. "Pathetic little rich spoilt brats. I completely lost my cool with them at the weekend."

"Why?" She sips her wine, listening intently.

"Because I walked around the corner to find Willow, when I heard one of the bullies suggest that Will's mother probably killed herself to get away from her."

Frances's face drops, and her eyes fill with tears.

"I know. Isn't it the most horrible thing you've ever heard?"

She shakes her head, unable to believe it. "What did you do?"

I roll my eyes. "I lost my cool and caused a huge scene. I dared them to come near her again so they can deal with me. I was swearing and completely losing control."

"And where was this?"

"At her football practice."

"Where was Julian?"

"He's useless. Those stupid mothers are all too busy trying to marry him, and he's so busy fighting them off that he sees none of it. When I approached the mother of the bully and admittedly"—I hold up my hand to admit my faults—"I was losing my temper and threatening to call the police to have her charged, but Julian defended the bully, not his own daughter, without even knowing what had happened."

"What?" She narrows her eyes. "Why does he always do this? He makes me so mad."

I widen my eyes. "I know! Me too. We had this huge fight, so I took the children to McDonald's, making it quite clear that Julian wasn't invited." I sip my drink. "But...in his defense, he didn't hear what they said to Willow, I guess."

She smiles and rests her elbows on the table. "You're good for him."

I fake a laugh. "I'm sure he thinks I'm a giant pain in his ass." If only she knew that he really wants into my ass.

"Thank you so much for our dinner last weekend. It was lovely seeing the children so happy." She takes my hand over the table. "I can't stop thinking about the change in them since you arrived. Especially Will."

I grin as I squeeze her hand in mine. "Thank you for coming. They are such beautiful kids. I'm so lucky to be able to get to spend time with them." I widen my eyes. "Oh, I forgot. Willow has been invited to play golf with her new friend this weekend."

"Willow's playing golf now?"

"Yes. I enrolled her in lessons. I thought it could be something that she and her father could do together."

She narrows her eyes. "Are you in a relationship, dear?"

"No."

"Hmm." She smiles against her wine glass.

"What are you thinking?" I smirk.

"Nothing." She smiles sarcastically. "I was just going to give you some tips, you know, in case you ever had an inkling or urge to"— she shrugs and waves her wine glass around in the air—"date my Julian."

I fake a laugh to cover my lying ass. "Oh, you're so funny." I should've got wine. Hell, I should've got tequila.

She falls serious. "Am I? Or do you want to hear my advice?"

I frown.

"I know why every single woman who tries to snag him fails."

I sip my coke; I need to know the tips without her knowing I need to know the tips.

"You are a character," I tease as I down my drink.

"Julian hasn't had a girlfriend since Alina died."

"His wife?"

She nods. "It did something to him."

My face falls.

"He closed off when he met her, and he never recovered after she died."

"That's so sad," I whisper.

"It is, but now he's very lonely."

"I know he sees people...women," I tell her to try and make her feel better.

"Yes, but only on his terms."

"His terms?"

"He only wants to see a woman to use her for sex. As soon as they fall in love with him, he breaks it off every single time."

"He told you this?" I can't imagine him ever telling anyone this, let alone his mother.

"He doesn't have to. I know that's what happens. He calls them needy."

"Why is it so bad if anyone falls in love with him? I don't understand."

"He doesn't want the responsibility of making anyone else happy. He's guarded. A lot of women want him for his money, and he's more than well aware of that."

It's not the money I want. It's his huge jackhammer dick, I think to myself.

"Why would any woman chase a man just for his money? It's an absurd way to live." I tut.

She sips her wine as she studies my face. "Do you know anything about Julian's money, or about the Masters Group, dear?"

"No, and I don't want to. Just talking about money makes me uncomfortable."

She smiles, as if impressed, making me feel like I'm at a job interview.

Our meals arrive. "About those tips you have," I say as I take my first mouthful of food. I know I shouldn't be hinting, but this is need-to-know information. I could sell it on the black market.

She smirks at me. "Well, if I were to date Julian, I would keep my cards very close to my chest, because he will run if he senses a relationship blooming."

I frown.

"And we wouldn't want to scare him off too soon, would we?" She takes a mouthful of her food. "We would wait until he's unaware of his emotions."

I can't believe it. She's actually come here today to tell me how to snag him. Julian was right, she is as sharp as a tack. I put my knife and fork down on my plate and pick up my drink. "You do know that Julian and I are not suited, right?"

"Julian is not suited to anyone. He's troubled, dear, but he's different with you."

I sip my drink as I stare at her. "What do you mean?"

"He knows his money doesn't interest you. He knows his children adore you. He can't take his eyes off you whenever you're in the room. You don't even know it, but he is already putty in your hands. What you do with that putty and how you knead it will determine the outcome."

I wipe my mouth with my napkin. "I can assure you that Julian and I are just platonic co-workers," I lie through my teeth.

She smiles and sips her wine. "Of course." She reaches over and taps my hand on the table. "I believe you."

Fuck. She definitely knows.

Her knowing eyes hold mine, and I'm so close to cracking and telling her the truth, it's not even funny.

Don't say it. Don't say it.

I stuff my mouth full of food so I can't speak. I need to be muzzled.

I slide into my car at around 2:00 p.m. We've had a long lunch, and I really do like Frances. We talked about books, movies, and, surprisingly, we do have a lot in common.

One thing she said to me has my mind ticking over.

Do you know anything about Julian's money or the Masters Group?

What did she mean by that?

I Google Masters Group and wait for it to load.

Masters Group – United Kingdom
CEO – Joseph Masters
General Manager – Julian Masters
Estimated worth - Sixteen billion dollars.
Oil, Stock Market, Gas, IT, Banking, Property

I frown as I stare at the screen in front of me, and I blink. What?

Sixteen Billion Dollars

Who the fuck am I sleeping with?

12

Brielle

I STAND in the corridor of the swanky hotel, my shoulders dropping as my nerves take over.

I'm wearing a black strapless evening gown tonight.

I feel nervous—more nervous than ever before—and I'm not sure why. Maybe it's because I actually love this dress, I feel like a princess, and this kind of feels like a real date.

I know it's not. Of course I know it's not. But I can let myself forget the reality of the situation for just one night, can't I?

My timid hand knocks on the door, and Julian opens it in a rush, smiling as he sees me. My breath catches immediately.

He's wearing a black dinner suit. His hair is styled to perfection, and the way he's looking at me might set me on fire.

"My beautiful Bree."

My heart races. "Hello." I smile and walk in. He closes the door behind us, taking my overnight bag from me to carefully place it on the luggage stand. When he turns back to me, he takes my face in his hand and kisses me softly.

"I've been looking forward to this all day long."

I smile against his lips, my hands resting on his hips. "You only had me yesterday, Jules."

"It wasn't enough. How could I possibly get enough of you in two hours?"

Oh, man. I'm totally screwed when he's being sweet.

We smile against each other's lips and I put my arms around his broad neck.

"What are your plans for me tonight?" I ask.

He smiles down at me. "I thought we would go out for dinner, and then maybe enjoy some dancing."

My eyebrows rise. "Really?"

He smiles at my excited reaction and then pulls me into an embrace, holding me tight. "Really."

God, he's beautiful. I close my eyes as I rest my head against his shoulder.

Stop it. This is nothing more than a façade—a part of his game.

Don't fall for it, whatever you do, Brielle.

He steps back and takes my hand in his, slowly lifting it to his mouth to kiss the back of it. "Where does my girl want to go tonight?" His eyes hold mine.

His girl.

Fuck, he was safer when he was a typical asshole who just wanted to fuck me.

I shrug shyly, overwhelmed by his tender seduction. "I have no idea where to go in London."

He holds his arm out for me and I link mine through it. "It looks like I'm in charge, then." He smirks.

I giggle and rise up onto my toes to kiss him. "Are you ever not in charge, Mr. Masters?"

"Not if I can help it."

We walk out of the room to where the elevator is waiting for us.

Not if I can help it.

What does he mean by that? Is that why he doesn't want to fall in love, because he won't be in charge anymore?

The lift arrives at the ground floor, and we step out hand in hand.

Hmm, that's a very interesting thing to say. I'm going to come back to it.

Three hours later, and I'm practically melting across the table from him.

We are at Closs Maggiore, an exclusive restaurant in Mayfair, and we're sitting in the courtyard. The tables are lit by single candles, and fairy lights hang above us. Relaxing music is being piped throughout the entire outdoor space.

The champagne is going down well, and we've had an amazing meal. The conversation has been flowing easily. Julian is actually the most relaxed he's ever been around me, laughing freely and being his charming, witty, intelligent self. We've talked about college, his work, my work at home, friends, and family. It really does feel like we're on a real date.

The reflection of the open fire dances across his face, and he's watching me intently as he takes a sip of his champagne.

"So, what did my mother have to say to you today?"

I giggle. This alcohol has gone to my head already. "She wants me to pursue you."

He smiles and winces. "She actually said that to you?"

"Yes."

"My apologies. She's shameless."

I smile and sip my champagne, remaining silent for once.

His eyes hold mine. "What did you say to her, Bree? What did you say to her when she said you should pursue me?"

This answer is important to him, I can tell. "I told her that I don't pursue men."

He raises an eyebrow. "Is that true?"

"Yes." I lick my bottom lip. "A relationship with a man is the last thing I want."

He sits forward, his eyes darkening. "What do you want?"

"What I've already got."

Our eyes are locked. "What's that?"

I smile softly. "A hot boss with a huge jackhammer dick."

He chokes, laughing out loud. "Honestly, Bree, you are out of this world."

I laugh and then our eyes linger on each other's as we fall serious. "Your mother is trying to marry you off," I whisper.

"Yes."

"Promise me that when the time comes for us to part..."

A frown crosses his face. "Promise you what?"

"Promise me that you won't make me the other woman." His eyes hold mine, and I know I've hit a nerve.

"Promise me that you'll make a clean break and pursue any future wife without me on the side."

He sits back slowly. "I can assure you that I'm not in the market for a wife."

I pick up his hand and kiss the back of it. "And I'm not in the market for a husband. We don't have long together, Jules. I'll go home to Australia eventually." I kiss his hand again, and he frowns as he watches me. "Let's just make the most of the short window of time that we do have."

He turns his hand and cups my face, his thumb dusting over my bottom lip. "You may be the most beautiful woman I have ever met," he admits softly.

I can feel myself getting stupidly emotional because I know for a fact that he is the most beautiful man I've ever been with. His mother's confirmation that he's really lonely and troubled has opened up a can of worms in my heart. The grief he has been through alone, while bringing up his two beautiful children... I can't imagine the pain. No man should have to go through that. It's no wonder he's so closed off to the world. He's afraid to let anyone get close.

I just want to make everything right for him and help him find his way. To be honest, I'm grateful for Frances's little lunch meeting today. Now I see Julian in a new light entirely.

A beautiful, tortured light.

I smile, trying to snap myself out of these sappy emotions. "You said you were taking me dancing."

His hand rests under his chin. "Where would my girl like to dance?" he whispers.

My eyes hold his. "Anywhere, as long as I'm with you."

We hit the wall with a thud, his lips crashing against mine and his hips pinning me to the wall. "Open the door," I pant. "Open it."

He struggles to get the key from his pocket, but eventually the door creaks open. He grabs me again and kisses me as he walks me backwards into our suite.

We've danced for hours, kissed for hours, and now we're back at the hotel, I can't wait one minute longer to have him.

He turns me and unzips my dress, letting his lips linger on my neck. He unhooks my lingerie and it falls to the floor, leaving me in nothing but my black sky-high stilettos. His hungry eyes drop down my body when he turns me back to face him, and then they rise up to my face.

"I want you," I whisper. "Please. I can't wait any longer."

He loses control and tears his suit jacket over his shoulders, throwing it on the floor.

I slip out of my shoes and pull back the covers on the bed, lying down and placing my head on the pillows.

His eyes hold mine as he slowly unbuttons his shirt and removes his pants.

My eyes drop down his body, to the broad, muscular chest, his ripped abdomen, down to the thick, hard cock hanging heavily between his legs. I can see every vein on it, and pre-ejaculate drips from its end.

Heaven.

"How do you want me?" He leans over to kiss me.

I cup his face. "On top of me, holding me close." We kiss. "I need it slow tonight, baby."

He closes his eyes and his lips take mine.

He's right here with me. He feels it too. Whatever this is.

Julian moves over the top of me. My open legs cradle his large body, and I smile at him as my hands roam up and down his broad back. He slides in slowly and we both close our eyes, moaning blissfully.

Our kisses are tender, his cock is deep, and in this moment, I feel so unbelievably close to him. He slowly pulls out and slides back in. "Fucking hell," he groans. "You're going to be the fucking death of me."

Steam fills the bathroom.

I have no idea what time it is, but we've just made love for hours, and now we're sitting in a deep, hot bath together. It's like we don't want to go to sleep because our night will be over. He lies back and I'm lying on top of him, my weary head on his chest. He rubs his face back and forth across my forehead as he holds me close.

I feel closer to him than I should.

"How did you lose your virginity?" I smile to myself.

"Oh God, don't remind me of that balls up." He tips the hot water over my shoulders. "Literally."

I giggle.

"Janika Merris."

I smile against his skin, already knowing I'm going to like this story.

"She was older than me. She wanted me badly." He hesitates. "She offered me a head job at our school dance."

"What?" I giggle as I look up at him in surprise. "How old were you?"

"Sixteen."

I shake my head before I put it back down on his warm, strong chest.

"She sucked my dick at the back of the school hall." I chuckle as I imagine the scene he's setting.

"And then she had sex with me as my two friends watched on."

I sit up in shock. "What?" My mouth falls open. "Your friends watched you lose your virginity?"

He smiles and pulls me back to his chest. "Yep, and then she had sex with them too. We all lost our virginity on the same night to the same girl."

I burst out laughing. "Oh my God. That's the worst virginity story ever."

"Appalling." He winces. "Funnily enough..." His voice trails off.

"Funnily enough, what?"

"I've never told anyone that story before."

"Good. You shouldn't." I laugh.

I can feel him smile above me, and he kisses my forehead, tightening his arms around me.

"Do you still see those friends?" I ask.

"They're still my two best friends. Sebastian and Spencer. We see each other all the time."

"Well, I suppose you do have a special bond now."

He chuckles. "Yeah, it's a funny story that we often discuss when drunk."

We let the silence linger for a moment longer. "Jules, can I ask you something?"

He softly kisses me on the temple. "What?"

"Why the skits?" He stays silent. "When you invite me here on these nights, why do you want me to dress up and not be here as myself?"

He pauses for a moment before he eventually answers.

"Because the beautiful woman who lives in my house and cares for my children is too good for me."

I listen in silence.

"I couldn't fuck her the way that I fuck you."

I frown against his skin, weighted down by his fingertips as they trail across my back.

"Why couldn't you fuck her like you fuck me?" I whisper.

"Because she's the kind of girl you fall in love with, and I'm not wired to love. I'd only let her down."

My eyes tear up. Good God, he is broken.

The two of us become lost in our own thoughts, and I know I need to lighten the mood.

"That girl who lives in your house is frigid and would never fuck your friends anyway." I look up at him.

He smiles and kisses me softly.

"You should stay away from her." I smile against his lips.

"I intend to, don't worry. She's the devil in disguise."

I giggle, and we kiss again.

And just for tonight, all is right in my world.

It's now Friday, and Julian is due home at any moment. He's taken the afternoon off to come with me to the meeting at the school. I'm looking forward to what this counsellor is going to say to us both. Hopefully it's not as bad as I'm imagining.

I put some things away in Sammy's room, and I walk down the hall and glance into Julian's bedroom, frowning when I see something out of place.

There's a book, upside down, left open on his bedside table. I walk in and pick it up.

When Children Grieve:
For adults, to help children deal with death.

My eyes instantly fill with tears, and I sit on his bed with the book in my hand.

Sadness engulfs me. I wish a book like this never had to be written. I wish nobody ever needed it. How do you ever teach your children to live without their mother?

I sit for a moment with tears in my eyes.

They've been through so much. I imagine them at the funeral, and then at the wake. Willow would have been ten, Sammy only three. He probably doesn't even remember her. I get a vision of them all dressed up, of Samuel in a little suit in his father's arms. Julian would have had to organize the funeral.

Was she buried or cremated? Where is her grave? Has the house been silent and sad ever since?

I hear his car come up the drive. I carefully place the book back on his bedside table and run down the stairs to meet him.

I want to tell him everything is going to be okay.

But she wasn't my wife, I'm not grieving, and it's not okay because she's never coming back.

For the first time, I can understand why he's the way he is, so closed off to the world and afraid to get too close to anyone ever again.

The door opens, and he appears in front of me, smiling warmly. He's wearing a grey suit with a white tie, looking like everything but a man swallowed in grief.

"Hello, Miss Brielle."

My heart skips a beat. I just want to throw my arms around his neck and hug him. "Hi," I breathe.

"You ready to go?"

I nod, but I hesitate. This really isn't any of my business.

"What?" he asks, sensing my need to say something.

"You're doing a really good job."

He frowns, waiting for me to expand.

"With the kids. You're doing a really good job with the kids. You're a great father."

He smiles softly, offering his thank you in silence. "Let's go."

We're sitting outside the Headmaster's office, waiting to be called in. Julian is next to me, his hands linked in front of him, staring straight ahead. We went out for breakfast this morning and made love again. Scratch that. He fucked me like there was no tomorrow, and his vow to make it impossible for me to walk for a week may actually come true. After, he kissed me goodbye and went to work, slipping back into his cold, indifferent persona.

It's like he's two different people. The man I fuck in the hotel is warm, sexy, and tender.

The man I live with is reserved, cold, and doesn't show his emotions at all.

I'm not sure how to reach out to him at home, or if I even want to.

He came back to pick me up for the meeting we're here for regarding Willow, and now it's like last night didn't even happen.

Did it?

Did I imagine the whole beautiful thing?

The office door opens. "Please, come in." The Headmaster smiles. "Julian Masters," he asserts as he shakes the two men's hands. "I'm the Headmaster, and this is our school counsellor."

I smile and take a seat next to Julian.

"So, Miss Johnston, last time we spoke, you were concerned about Willow and how she is getting on at school."

"Yes." I clutch my purse in my lap.

"Well." The counsellor raises his eyebrows, seeming uncomfortable. "I've had a meeting with each of her teachers throughout the week and, unfortunately, I've heard some things that have left me feeling very uncomfortable."

"Such as?" Julian asks sharply.

"Willow." He grimaces. "Doesn't actually appear to have any close friends at the moment."

My face falls. "What?"

"Since her only friend left nine months ago, she sits alone at lunch and doesn't really mix with anyone."

Julian frowns. "What do you mean?"

"She goes to the library alone." He shrugs. "I was unaware of this until the teachers started asking other students questions."

I squeeze my hands together on my lap. Oh no.

"Is there a problem?" Julian asks.

The counsellor frowns. "Apparently, and this is just what I've heard and hopefully it may not be true, there is a problem. There's name-calling going on, for a start. Everyone calls her Weird Willow."

Julian frowns.

"Is there a certain incident that triggered this?" I ask.

"I'm not sure, but we're getting to the bottom of it."

"How is this the first I've ever heard of it?" Julian snaps. "This isn't good enough. I pay thirty thousand pounds a year and the school doesn't even keep me informed when my daughter is suffering under their watch."

"Excuse me, Mr. Masters, I'm sorry, but you've never been to a parent-teacher evening before. Nobody in this school knows you on a personal level. Willow's previous nannies attended any functions or galas we had. We didn't even know that Willow's mother had passed away."

Julian drops his head and stares at the carpet. I see him internally start blaming himself.

"This isn't his fault," I snap. "Don't try and blame him. The school counsellor, which is you, should have been aware of a problem long before I got involved. She is in your care and one of you should have noticed and called Mr. Masters to discuss what's been going on here. If a child has no friends, it's a huge issue."

The counsellor lifts his chin defiantly. "I can assure you that I'm aware of it now and we will be handling it."

"How, exactly?" I snap. "And I want to know what you are going to do about the bullying. Willow is being attacked daily about her mother's passing, and we will not tolerate it."

The Headmaster and counsellor exchange looks.

"Are you aware of the destructive effects of bullying on young teenagers, and how deeply it's linked with depression?" I ask.

"Yes...but—"

"There are no buts! I want the girls reprimanded for saying what they did to her."

"It wasn't on school grounds."

"I don't care," I hiss, losing my temper. "This simply isn't good enough. I warned you before that if I have to bring the police into the school to press charges, I will."

"Miss Johnston, please calm down."

I glance over at Julian, who is still staring at the carpet, lost in a world of regret.

For God's sake, he's useless.

I scramble through my handbag and retrieve the piece of paper I brought from home. "Here, these are the six girls involved. I would like a meeting with their parents as soon as possible."

Emily Edwards
Michella Topan
Kiara McCleary
Teigan Hoslop
Bethany Maken
Karen Visio

The Headmaster's face falls as he sees the names. "I'm sorry, this isn't going to be possible. This matter is confidential, and until something happens on school grounds, the parents and children won't be involved."

"What?" I snap in horror. "This is simply not good enough. I don't want another incident. She can't take another incident. More to the point, she shouldn't have to." I hit Julian on the leg to drag him out of his daze.

"There won't be another incident, because if there is, I'll personally have you charged with neglect of a minor who has been placed in your care," he growls.

The Headmaster sits back in his seat, unsure what to say next.

Julian stands. "I'll be back next Thursday evening at 6:00 to meet all of her teachers in this office." He pauses as he glares at the two men, and they wither under his glare. "Are we clear?"

"Yes, sir."

"If one thing—one more thing—is said to my daughter about

her deceased mother, I'll bring hell and all its fire down on those involved."

The two men glance at each other.

Julian glares at them intensely, and then he turns and storms out of the door.

I smile proudly. That's my man.

I power walk to catch up with him. He marches to the car, not forgetting to open my door for me.

Ah, ever the gentleman, even when furious.

He gets in the car and pulls out into the traffic like a maniac. "You handled that well." I smile over at him.

He shakes his head. "I didn't even know. What kind of a fucked-up father am I?"

"Don't say that." I reach over and take his hand to comfort him.

He rests it on his thigh while we drive in silence.

His hand is warm, strong, and I feel myself begin to weaken.

We stop at the lights and he glances over at me, his eyes dropping to my lips.

"I'm furious with myself," he whispers.

"I know."

Oh God, take it out on me.

He slowly lifts my hand to his lips and kisses the back of it. This is the first time he's ever touched me outside of our arranged night together.

"You should really get some of that anger out," I breathe.

He closes his eyes, as if he's imagining the same thing.

The air in the car begins to buzz. Hot, hard sex is all I can think about.

What would he be like when he's angry and naked?

"We should get home," I whisper.

His eyes darken, and he pushes down on the accelerator, sending the two of us flying back in our seats. "We should do a lot of things, Miss Brielle."

The adrenaline hits me hard. Let's do this. Let's fuck at home.

We tear up the driveway, and my stomach drops when I see his mother's car waiting there.

Damn her for interrupting my angry sex. Julian exhales heavily, obviously annoyed too.

"Your mother is here."

"I see that," he mutters flatly. "I am not in the fucking mood for her shit today."

I wince. "Be nice, please." He glares at me.

"Let's take the kids out for dinner tonight?" I try to diffuse his annoyance.

"Fine." He gets out of the car and slams the door, marching into the house without me. I find myself smiling goofily after him.

I think he's even hotter when he's angry. How is that possible?

13

Brielle

WE WALK DOWN the busy street together. I'm holding hands with Sammy, and Will is walking behind with her father.

"Where is this restaurant, Miss Brielle?" Julian calls from behind.

"Just up here." I crane my neck to look up the street. "I hope," I mutter under my breath.

It's Friday night. After our meeting at the school earlier, I talked Julian into taking us to a new Texan restaurant that just opened up in town. It's the opening week, so they have extra attractions there. It seemed like it could really be fun from what I read in the brochure. Hopefully, it will cheer Willow up.

"What exactly is Texan food?" Julian calls.

I smirk and wink at Sammy. "Horse."

"What?" Will snaps, outraged. "I'm not eating horse."

I giggle.

"They do not eat horse," she calls. "You twit, Brell."

Sammy and I giggle. Moments later, we arrive at the restaurant.

TEXAS RANGERS

The restaurant has huge double wooden doors, and the décor has been set up to make it look like a big barn. It seems so out of place compared with the snooty parts of London Julian insists on frequenting.

"Oh, wow, sick," Sammy whispers, looking around in awe.

"Yes, there's no doubt what we'll all be after eating here," Julian mutters dryly.

I elbow him. "Stop being such a snob."

The attendant walks up to us. "Table for four?"

"Yes, please." I smile as I go up on my toes, completely excited to be here.

The attendant hands me a small silver bucket of beer nuts. "Nuts are on the house." She begins to walk off. "This way, please," she calls over her shoulders.

The children follow her, but I hang back, hunching my shoulders and smiling broadly at Julian. "I love it when nuts are on the house."

He looks at me, deadpan. "Or in your mouth."

I laugh. "That too."

We weave through the busy restaurant and take a seat at a bench seat. Country music is blaring through the space, and the back area of the restaurant opens out onto a huge courtyard. They have attractions out there, obviously because it's the opening week. There are donkeys, horses, and a baby-animal petting zoo, with a bucking bull set up in the corner.

"I love this place." I smile as we sit down.

"Me too." Sammy beams. I hold my fist up and he punches it with his.

Julian turns his attention to his daughter. "What do you think of the place, Will?"

Will looks around and sees the peanut shells on the floor. "It's a bit feral, if you ask me."

"Thank you. At last, someone who knows what they're talking about." Julian sighs, relieved.

Sammy and I pull a face at one another, and we open the menus.

"Wow, I'm definitely getting the ribs." I keep reading. "It's called The Huge Rack."

A look of disgust washes over Julian's face. "I have to sit opposite you and watch you chew meat from a bone that's called The Huge Rack?"

I giggle. "Aha, and I'm drinking beer straight out of the bottle too."

Willow giggles. "You are so uncouth, Brell."

"That's why you all like me so much." I bat my eyelashes playfully. "What are you getting, Sammy?" I ask.

He studies the menu. "Chicken wings, maybe."

"Hmm." I nod. "Sounds great, but we'll have to make sure we ask for them plain, not spicy."

"Yeah." He shakes his little head. "Definitely not spicy."

"Will, you getting the ribs with me?" I keep looking at the menu. "Oh, we have to get the Yam Taters."

She concentrates as she reads the menu. "Yam Taters? This food is weird."

"I know. It's great, isn't it?" I smile. "What are you getting, Mr. Masters?"

He frowns as he peruses the menu. "Food poisoning, no doubt."

I roll my eyes. "Will you stop being such a killjoy? Just pick something."

"Chilli Tex-Mex." He closes the menu.

I giggle. "Are you serious?"

"Yes, why?"

"You have no idea how hot that could be."

He smirks. "My dear Miss Brielle. May I remind you that I like my life extra hot."

I smile down at the table. He's being a bit flirty tonight. "If you have an upset stomach all night long, don't be blaming or calling me," I tease.

The children both laugh, and Julian rolls his eyes.

"Oh, look, the horse." Sammy smiles excitedly as he looks out to the backyard.

"Do you want to go see?" Will asks.

"Can we?" Sam asks me.

"Of course." I smile.

They both get up and disappear out the back, leaving Julian and me to watch them in silence for a while.

"Thanks for coming tonight," Julian says. "I'm not sure how to handle this whole thing."

"It's okay. I'm not going to go out this weekend."

"Why not?"

"I want to stay with Will."

"Oh, so you'll stay home for her, not me?" he teases.

"That's right." I smile as I watch his eyes hold mine. He's so lost in all this Will business, he has no idea what to do for the best. "I thought maybe we could do something fun, both on Saturday and Sunday. You know, to try and take her mind off it all."

He nods as his eyes drop to the table.

"Did you think any more about getting them a kitten?" I ask hopefully.

His eyes snap up to mine. "I don't want pets, Bree. We go away a lot. The children stay at my Mother's every Thursday now." He frowns.

"The cat can go with them."

He shakes his head. "No."

I roll my eyes. "Fine."

The waitress comes over and we order the meals and drinks, and then she disappears through the crowd once more.

"What do you want to do all weekend, then?" he asks.

"Whatever you want."

His eyes darken as they hold mine. "Whatever I want isn't on the menu at home."

"Why not?"

He shakes his head. "Because it needs to be kept separate."

"Why?"

"It just does."

The kids bounce back to the table, interrupting our conversation, and we fall quiet again.

I watch the bucking bull trying to throw somebody off. "Who wants to come watch me ride that bucking bull?" I ask.

Julian's face falls.

"Yes," both kids squeal.

I stand. "Come on, then."

"You're not going on that death trap, Bree. I forbid it," he suddenly snaps. "Sit back down this minute."

"It's completely safe." I huff.

He glances over at it as it picks up speed, and he shakes his head in a panic. "No. No. You're not allowed. I don't want you getting hurt."

"I'm not going to get hurt, pussy boy." I smirk as I walk off, watching the kids rush ahead.

He stands abruptly. "Bree!" he barks. I turn to him. "What?"

"Please. I really don't want you to go on it."

"Look at you, getting all protective."

"This isn't funny."

I grin. "Yeah, it kind of is. Loosen up, Jules."

He exhales heavily and follows me down the steps. "I'm not taking you to the hospital if you die."

"Good. I would expect to be taken to the mortuary anyway." I smile.

"Christ All-fucking-mighty."

Ten minutes later, I'm sitting on the bucking bull as it begins to slowly circle. Willow and Sammy are bouncing up and down, but Julian looks like he is about to throw up. I give them a wave and laugh out loud.

"Go, Brell!" Willow shouts.

I put my hand up in the air, pretending to swing a rope, and then throw a lasso over them. Julian pinches the bridge of his nose, exasperated.

It only makes me laugh more. I'm so embarrassing to him.

The bull picks up speed and I hang on with my thighs. The kids scream and Julian puts his hands on the top of his head, fear-stricken. The bull begins to buck, but I still hold on.

The kids are chanting and I'm laughing out loud.

Julian's eyes are like saucers as I go around and around, up and down. I can hear Sammy squealing with laughter. Suddenly, the bull becomes really violent, and I begin to get thrown around.

"Oh my God," I hear Julian cry. "Stop it this minute," he yells at the controller.

"No, don't!" I cry with laughter.

All at once it lurches forward and I'm thrown from the bull, down onto the cushions. I land hard on my back, staring up at the sky.

Ouch...that hurt.

Julian rushes over me. "Are-are you injured?" he stammers as he looks down, filled with worry.

I laugh up at him. "That was so much fun." He grabs my hand and pulls me up, helping me dust the straw from my body. "I'm going to do it again," I tease.

"Over my dead body," he growls, grabbing my hand and dragging me back to the table. The kids fall in behind us, hysterical with laughter.

"Children, control your lunatic nanny." He guzzles his Corona straight from the bottle. "She's completely out of control."

I laugh and pick up my beer, holding his gaze as I sip it slowly.

"Behave yourself," he mouths.

I throw him a cheeky wink. "Now it's your turn to dice with death, Mr. Masters," I tease.

"How so?"

With perfect timing, the waitress places his meal down in front of him. There's a huge pile of meat stew filled with green and red chillies on his plate, and a dollop of sour cream on the top. It's so hot, steam is rising from it.

The four of us all stare down at it in silence.

He frowns and looks back up at me. "Maybe the bucking bull was the safer option."

"Don't worry." I grin. "I'll take you to the mortuary."

Julian

"Spotto!" Brielle calls.

"Huh?" I frown over at her in the passenger seat. It's Saturday afternoon, and we're driving through the countryside. I have a surprise for the children. We went to football practice this morning, then to the park to play ball. I can confirm that Brielle Johnston is a complete and utter maniac.

She laughs and jokes constantly, never taking herself seriously for a single moment. She always knows exactly how to make fun in every situation.

No wonder my children adore her. Just being around her is addictive because she oozes happiness.

I've never known anyone quite like her. "What is Spotto?" I ask.

Her eyes widen as she watches me. "You've never played Spotto before?"

I shake my head and she turns in her seat to the children. "Oh my God, have neither of you played it?"

They both shake their heads.

She throws her arms up in the air. "This is unbelievable. Do you all live under a rock?"

We remain silent, waiting for her no doubt long-winded explanation.

"So, when you are driving and you see a yellow car, you have to be the first person to yell 'Spotto'."

I scowl harder. "What for?"

"Because that's the game. You have to be the first to spot the yellow cars."

I raise my eyebrows. "Good grief, you must be hard up for entertainment in Australia."

The three of them giggle.

"Oh." She holds up her finger. "And..." She turns back to talk to the children. "If you see a yellow Volkswagen, you need to yell 'punch buggy'."

My eyes flicker between her and the road. "Punch buggy?"

"Yep. Because you then get to punch the person sitting next to you in the arm as hard as you can."

"Yes." Willow laughs from the back. "I'm spotting one of these babies."

I chuckle and shake my head. What next?

"Punch buggy," Brielle yells, and my eyes flash to her. She laughs out loud and points at me. "Ha! Made you look."

I smirk as I pull into the drive. "I'm going to punch you in the buggy in a minute."

The car falls silent as we pass the animal shelter sign. "What are we doing here?" Willow asks.

I stop the car and turn toward them. "I thought we might get a puppy."

"What?" they all screech.

"Oh my God."

The children jump out of the car and run up into the building.

I turn my attention to Bree, and she smiles over at me with an affectionate glow in her eyes.

"That may just be the hottest thing you've ever done."

I smile, nodding as I look out through the windscreen. "I don't know whether to be offended that my previous attempts to be hot have been so...underwhelming. Is that supposed to be a compliment or an insult, Miss Brielle?"

She giggles as she hops out of the car. "Compliment, you baboon. Now get out of the car."

We walk down the aisle of the shelter, inspecting the puppies.

"This one!" Samuel calls out, filled with excitement.

I peer in to see a shaggy-looking mutt. I screw up my face. "We need a dog that doesn't grow too big."

"Right," Bree hums as she studies the dogs. "What kind do we want?"

"Something friendly that doesn't bark a lot," I reply. "Or make a mess."

Bree raises a sarcastic brow and I shrug. It sounds good in theory.

"Look at this one," Sammy calls as he drops to his knees beside a cage.

A little brown and white puppy with droopy ears and big brown eyes looks up at us.

Willow falls to her knees beside them. "Oh my God, it has to be this one," she cries.

I read the ticket:

Female Beagle 10 weeks old
In need of loving home
Gentle temperament
Great with children

The puppy stares up at me with her big brown eyes. Bree drops to the floor. "Look at her sweet little face."

"Let's just keep looking, shall we?" I mutter, swiftly moving along.

I get to the end of the aisle and glance back to see that the three of them haven't moved from their position beside the female beagle.

"Have you looked at every dog?" I ask them.

"We want this one," Willow tells me with confidence.

"Bree, can you Google beagles and see what they are like, please?"

"Sure." She takes out her phone and begins to read the information. "Great with children, lovely housemates, gentle, loyal. Not messy. Very quiet."

I study her face. "Are you just saying what you think I want to hear?"

She giggles. "Totally."

I roll my eyes. I can't believe I'm doing this. "Are you sure this is the one you want?"

The three of them all smile enthusiastically.

"Fine. That was easier than I imagined." I walk over to the assistant. "Excuse me, can we take the ten-week-old beagle, please?"

The young girl smiles and then goes through a series of questions and then finally replies. "Great choice. She's a beautiful little girl. I'll get her ready." She takes the puppy from her cage, and Willow and Samuel start to bounce on the spot, unable to control themselves. "I'll meet you out the front in ten minutes." She smiles before she disappears through the office door.

We walk into another section of the shelter and my face falls.

It's filled with kittens.

"Oh my God," Willow gasps.

"Look at this one!" Bree shrieks.

We walk over to see a little white fluffy ball of fur staring back at us.

"This one," Samuel calls to us. "He looks like the one that attacks bears."

The three of them all burst out laughing.

I go to the front counter and wait for the girl to return with our puppy.

"Oh no, he got me." Willow laughs, and we turn to see a little ginger and white kitten standing on his back two legs. He's put his paw through the cage and somehow got it snagged in Willow's knitted jumper.

She giggles as she tries to unhook herself, and Samuel and Bree begin to help her. The kitten is a livewire, playing with them through the cage.

Willow's eyes find mine. "Dad, can we have this kitten too?"

"No."

"Please," she begs. "Oh, please, Dad. I'll look after him. I'll even pay for his food from my pocket money."

"Willow, we just got a dog."

She smiles sadly at the kitten and continues to play with it through the cage.

"Why can't she have it?" Bree whispers.

"I don't want a fucking cat," I mutter under my breath.

"This isn't about you. This is about taking her mind off the situation at school. This cat could be the perfect friend for her."

"That's what the dog is for." I frown.

"Do you think Sammy's going to take his hands off that dog? I'll look after it." She puts her hands together, pleading with me as she bounces on the spot. "Please. I'll beg," she whispers.

I look at her flatly. "Bree, if this isn't already you begging, I dread to think what is." I exhale heavily and glance over at Willow, who is currently smiling down at the ugliest cat in the world.

Fuck's sake.

The lady appears with the puppy, handing it to Samuel, but my focus is on Willow.

Fine...

I've totally lost control of this situation. "We'll take the ginger kitten, too, please."

Willow and Bree start to shriek and clap their hands. "Dad, you're the best!" Willow cries.

Bree smiles up at me, and her eyes linger tenderly on my face. "Don't say a word," I warn her.

She giggles and links arms with Willow as they continue to play with the cat.

Great. Not only do I now have to deal with having blue balls, but I have to watch out for a cat attacking my dick in my sleep.

Brielle

"The movie is starting, guys," Sammy calls.

The microwave pings right on cue. Willow takes out the second bag of popcorn and tips it into the bowl.

I've just made a beautiful dinner, and the house is alive with playful baby animals. It's been a wonderful day.

I walk into the living room to find it dark, with the kids lounging on their beanbags and Julian on the couch. He's covered himself with a huge blanket, and he pats the sofa next to him. I smile, liking that he wants to sit next to me.

Tillie, our puppy, and Maverick, our kitten, are now curled up on their little beds next to the children.

I lie down and Julian covers me with the blanket, pulling my feet onto his lap. God, I just want to kiss him.

Seeing him trying so hard with the children is literally exploding my ovaries.

"What are we watching?" I ask.

"*The Terminator*," Willow tells me, her eyes glued to the screen.

"I'll be back," I say in my best Arnold Schwarzenegger voice.

Julian rolls his eyes.

"I feel like I should get up and go to the bathroom just so I can say I'll be back," I chuckle.

"God help us," Julian mutters dryly.

I giggle. "I crack myself up."

"We know."

I laugh again, and for an hour I sit, completely lost in the movie. "How much do you reckon he would eat to be that size?" I ask.

"Please don't talk." Julian sighs.

So serious. I wiggle my foot on his lap to annoy him and he grabs it and grinds it against his cock, staring straight ahead at the TV, stony-faced.

Oh, this is fun.

He rubs my foot over his dick again, flexing it so I can feel it move beneath my skin.

My insides begin to melt.

I wonder what it would be like to have him in this house? To have him sneak into my bed at night, and to hold him as I slept. I have this nagging little voice in my mind telling me that I'm developing feelings for him. Especially after today.

I'm not. I know exactly what this is.

It is just fucking, right? But somehow it feels like more, and we bounce off each other so well. His flirty little comments, his constant worry over me, his eyes lingering on my face when he thinks I'm not looking, and his comfortable complaints about my terrible sense of humor...they all leave me thinking things I shouldn't be thinking.

Stop it.

He rubs my foot over himself again, and I smile to no one in particular.

I want to have sex in this house. I want to break him so that he can't help himself. If we have sex here, he'll have to accept the fact that the woman he thinks is too good for him is also the woman he can fuck.

They're both me. I'm the same person. I don't know why he wants to keep us separate, but I think fear has a lot to do with it.

When I'm in the hotel, it's on his terms. His mother said that he is happy when things are on his terms. Then and only then. I need to move this whole thing to be on my terms...but how?

He grinds my foot again and I watch him, knowing he's turned on. He needs it. He's so sexual. I imagine he's the kind of man that would want you every day if you were his wife.

His wife.

What would that be like?

What would it be like to have him love me and take care of me forever?

I close my eyes. Stop it.

I feel his cock jerk beneath me, and my eyes flicker up to him.

His eyes are rolled back in his head. My mouth falls open and he smirks to himself.

Is he for real?

He just came in approximately four minutes.

The movie ends and he jumps up. "I'm going to shower." He disappears up the stairs without another word, leaving me to shake my head.

I help the kids with their new pet routine before bed, when my email suddenly pings.

Julian Masters
Requests the company of:Bree Johnston
Occasion: Situation inspection
Date: Thursday
Time: 7 p.m.
Place: Room 612, Rosewood London
Dress code: Bondage

My eyes widen. Bondage?

What the fuck?

14

Brielle

I WAKE to a bang on the door, and I jump, startled.

"Brell, come quick," Sammy's panicked voice calls through the door before I hear him tear down the hallway.

Huh? I frown as I look around the room. What's going on? Then I hear Julian's voice bellowing throughout the house.

What's going on out there? I grab my robe and throw it on before I open my bedroom door.

"You can't be serious?" I hear Julian yell. "This is fucking unbelievable."

Shit, he's cursing in front of the children. What on Earth is the matter? I run up into the house and my eyes widen as soon as I step foot inside.

Julian, Willow, and Samuel are all standing frozen still as they survey the damage.

The puppy has ripped open the two beanbags, and there are tiny beanbag balls spread all over the house.

My mouth falls open as I assess the damage. The entire living room is in disarray. The cushions are on the floor, not on the sofa where they should be. The potted plant has been chewed to within an inch of its life. It now has no leaves left and is turned on its side. The tiny beanbag balls are spread over the floor like thick snow, even covering the floor throughout the kitchen and dining room. There are even skid marks where she has been running and sliding in them. My eyes rise to find Sammy and Willow, who are standing with wide eyes in silence, horrified and clearly unsure what to say about the catastrophe in front of us. The cat appears through the white snow, covered in the white balls, hundreds of them now stuck to his fur.

I can't help it. I put my hand over my mouth and burst out laughing.

"This is not funny, Miss Brielle," Julian barks.

I belly laugh even harder, picking up a handful of the white balls before I throw them at Willow and Samuel. "Look! It's snowing."

The puppy comes running into the room like a rock star, diving into the white balls at full speed.

"That dog is a damn menace," Julian growls. "Look at this place! It's completely destroyed."

"She's just a little baby." I laugh and dive into the balls beside her. "You're a naughty puppy." She jumps on me and starts to paw my hair. "Get down here, you two, and play with your baby."

Sammy and Willow exchange looks, and then Sammy dives onto the floor without a care in the world. It isn't long before Willow bursts out laughing and falls down beside us. The puppy goes ballistic, barking and growling as it gets excited with us playing with her. I throw some white balls over Willow's head. Then I lie on my back and move my hands and feet. "Look, make a snow angel." I laugh.

Sammy and Willow follow suit. I glance up and see Julian staring at the three of us, frozen and disgusted.

"What the hell are you three doing?" he snaps. "The house is completely ruined, and all you three can do is laugh and play in the mess?"

I throw a handful of balls at him. "Take some photos of us, you cranky pants."

He folds his arms over his chest and raises an eyebrow. "Miss Brielle, must you find everything funny?"

The puppy growls, leaning back on her back legs right before she pounces towards him in full attack mode. I giggle and get up with two big handfuls of balls. "Get him, kids," I cry as I pelt the balls toward Julian's head. We all jump up and chase him.

"Stop it," he shouts as he tries to get away.

"Get him!" I order.

"What the hell?" he cries, and he starts to run into the kitchen. The children squeal in delight and we grab his arms, the three of us dragging him to the floor and completely covering him in balls. I flop down beside him. Willow and Sammy do the same, and our little rock star puppy prances out and sits on Julian's chest, proud as punch of her handywork. Julian shakes his head and looks to the ceiling for some kind of divine intervention.

"This is unbelievable," he mutters.

I throw some balls into the air. "Tell someone who cares."

Willow giggles. "Yeah, Dad, tell somebody who cares."

I read the email again. It's now Tuesday morning, and I'm preparing for my date night.

Julian Masters
Requests the company of: Bree Johnston
Occasion: Situation inspection
Date: Thursday
Time: 7 p.m.
Place: Room 612, Rosewood London
Dress code: Bondage

What the actual fuck does he mean by bondage? Does he expect me to turn up to the date tied up in a mummy suit with a ball gag in my mouth? Bondage is what you do, not what you wear. At least, that's what I thought. Not that I would really know, I suppose. I've never been with a kinky bastard before I met Mr. Masters.

I soon find myself walking through the heavy metal door of the sex shop, anyway. It's completely soundproofed, and the windows are painted over. A porno is playing on the televisions displayed on the walls. It's 9:30 a.m. Jeez, these guys are hard-core. I glance up and see a girl on a bed. She's on her hands and knees with three naked men standing over her. God, this place is seedy.

"Can I help you?" the young man asks. He looks about nine-teen, like he's straight out of school. What the hell is he doing here?

Does your mother know where you work, young man? "No, thank you. Just browsing."

I really do need his help, but I'm not dealing with him explaining to me the ropes of bondage while literally showing me the ropes of bondage. The back wall is filled with whips, chains, and all kinds of tools that look like they belong in an archaeological dig. I see a photo of a woman tied up, suspended from the ceiling. The ropes are wound around her breasts so tight, they've turned her flesh blue. Surely that can't be fucking healthy for breast tissue? I fold my arms over my chest, somewhat uncomfortable with what I'm seeing. What the hell does he think he's actually going to do to me, anyway?

I take out my phone. I'm calling him. I'm not into this. He is not doing that to my boobs. Over my dead body is he doing that shit. I dial his number, and he answers on the first ring.

"Good morning, my beautiful Bree," his deep voice purrs.

I smile goofily and put my head down so the young guy can't hear me. "I'm in the sex shop," I whisper.

"Are you?" he replies sexily.

"I don't know what bondage is, but I assure you that you are not bruising my boobs."

He chuckles. "And I can assure you that there will be no marks left behind."

"Jules, no," I whisper.

He chuckles again. "Only buy what you're comfortable with."

I glance over and see a huge black strap-on dildo. "Fine. I'm going to get a huge strap-on dildo and fuck you up the ass."

He bursts out laughing. "I can also assure you that is not happening. I don't take it up the ass. Yours, however, is up for discussion."

"It is not!"

"I've got to go to court now, babe. See you tonight." He hangs up.

I frown. Great lot of help he was. Judge Pervert, that's what he is.

A young woman comes out from the back room, walking in my direction with a smile on her face. "Do you need some help?"

"Umm." I frown. "I suppose. I'm looking for something bondage-y that doesn't look like that." I point to the photo of the poor woman who has been turned into a rolled roast.

"You're more of a dabbler, I take it."

I nod. "Yes. I'm definitely dabbling, but not..." I wave my arms around. "Bruising."

She narrows her eyes as she looks around. "Okay. Over here we have some really cute black leather lace-up lingerie sets. You could maybe get some handcuffs or something to go with them."

"Yes, that. That I can do."

I wait in the park for Emerson. It's Tuesday lunchtime and she is on her lunch break. We haven't been seeing each other as much as we would like to. Not since she met Alastar and I began sneaking around with Julian. In a bid to solve that problem, I've started making lunch for us both in the morning and meeting her here each day.

"Hello, my beautiful friend." I smile as she drops down onto the picnic blanket beside me. I open a can of drink for her and put the straw in for her, passing it over with a smile.

"I'm missing you."

She frowns. "I know, me too."

I hand her a sandwich. "How's work going?" I ask.

"Yeah, it's okay. I don't really know what I'm doing, though." We chew our food. "How's your spunky boss?"

I smile. I'm going to try and ease her into the idea of Julian and me. "Spunky?"

She watches me, waiting for more information.

"We watched *The Terminator* together the other night."

"Yeah?"

"Yeah. The room was dark and the kids were on the floor in front of us."

She frowns as she chews. "And?"

"He used my foot to wank himself off."

Her eyes nearly bulge from their sockets. "What?"

"He grabbed my foot under the blanket, and then he rubbed it over his hard cock."

"Fuck off! He did not?"

I smile. You don't know the half of it. "Oh, he did."

She chews her sandwich, her eyes the size of saucers. "What happened then?"

"I let him."

Her mouth falls open. "I don't believe this."

I grin. "He's so fucking hot."

"How was it?" Her eyes hold mine. "How's his dick?"

"Huge."

She puts her fingers over her mouth in surprise.

"He came."

"He came?" She gasps.

"I felt the jerk, and then the movie ended, so he jumped up and went to bed."

She chews her sandwich slowly, never blinking. "I can't fucking believe that story. What happened after that?"

"Nothing. He's just being normal again now."

"Wow."

I fall back on the blanket and grin to myself as I enjoy the sunrays on my face. "Yep, I'm officially a foot wanker."

She shakes her head. "Now I've heard everything."

It's 4:00 p.m. I'm pissed.

I just got my period and it's my date night. I get to see him one fucking night of the week and I go and get my stupid period. The worst part is that I'm now going to have to call him and tell him I can't come. I can't put it off any longer. He'll be leaving his office soon to go to the hotel.

I dial his number.

"Hello," he answers in that sexy voice of his. I can tell he's in his car.

Damn it, he's already left. "Hi," is all I can say.

"You on your way?"

"No." I frown. "Are you alone in the car?"

"Yes."

"I..." I pause because I really don't want to have to say this. "I don't think I can come tonight."

"What? Just a minute..." I hear a rustling, and then he picks up his phone and I can tell he's just pulled over. "What's wrong?" he asks.

"It's not a good time of the month for me."

"Since when?"

"Since just now."

He listens for a moment. "So you're not coming...just because of that?" He sounds annoyed.

"Well, we can't have sex."

"It's just all about the sex for you, is it?" he snaps angrily.

I bite my bottom lip to stifle my smile. "You were the one who said it was always going to be just about the sex."

"Well, it's not. Get in the car and get to the hotel. It's been a long week without you."

I stay silent on the phone. Did he just admit that this is something more for him, too?

"Okay, I'll leave soon." I grin, unable to stop myself.

"Good." He exhales heavily. "See you soon."

What was that?

I walk into the hotel an hour and a half later. I had to drop our mischievous fur babies and the children at their Grandma's on the way here. I'm nervous, just not like before. I'm a different kind of nervous today. Julian said it wasn't just about sex. It never was for me, but I thought that's exactly what it was for him.

I knock on the door and he opens it in a rush. "I thought you weren't coming," he says, his tone clipped.

I smile softly. "I'm here, Jules."

His features relax, and he takes me into his arms, holding me tight. We stay locked in our embrace for some time. I can't help but feel like he seems off.

The dominant man who fucks me into submission isn't here today. This is someone new. Someone I haven't met before.

"Are you okay?" I whisper as he holds me.

"Yes," he breathes into my hair. But he's not, I can feel it. Something is definitely wrong. He kisses me and then studies my face as he stares down at me.

"Look at you being all gorgeous," I whisper as I kiss him. "I like this Julian."

"It's been a long week without you."

I dust the backs of my fingers down his face. "This is a hard arrangement some days."

He kisses me again and walks me into the room, kicking the door shut before we lie down on the bed.

"We're not having sex tonight." I smile against his lips

233

"I know that. I'm simply kissing you. Don't get ahead of yourself."

"How was your day?"

"Long," he mutters, distracted as his hands roam all over my body and his lips drop to my neck.

"What are we having for dinner?"

"Who cares?"

I giggle. God, he makes me feel so desired.

I roll over and grab the remote to turn the television on. "Let's watch a movie."

It's only 6:00 p.m. I need to distract him or he will be humping the chair any moment. I flick through the movies. "What do you want to watch?"

He shrugs and rolls his eyes. "Whatever you want."

I put *Ocean's Eleven* on and snuggle against his chest, enjoying the way he holds me tight, and I smile dreamily to myself. I think this is my favorite date night so far.

Four hours later and Julian is somehow naked and on top of me. I'm in only my panties. My legs are wide open and he's grinding his body against my pubic bone. I'm so hot for him, it's just ridiculous.

He didn't watch the movie. I watched the movie while his hands ran all over my body. For hours now he has been touching me like I'm the most beautiful woman in the world. I don't know how much more I can take.

"God, I need you," he moans as his tongue dives deeper into my mouth.

Fuck, I need him too.

He rocks his hard cock against me. It feels so good—so big. "Please," he begs as his open mouth brushes my jawline.

"No, Julian." I pant. "It's too...too intimate." He pulls back to look at my face.

"I need intimacy from you tonight."

"Why?"

His lips hover over mine. "I don't know, I just do."

We kiss again and I begin to lose control of the situation. He pulls my leg back to entice me further. His large body drives forward, and I clench. God, he feels good.

"I've never done it before," I admit quietly.

"Neither have I."

I frown and pull his attention back to my face. "What?"

"I've never done it before either. Not at this time of the month."

Huh? How can that be? Not even with his wife?

"Why not?" I ask.

"I've never wanted to."

"Then why do you want to do it with me?"

"You tell me and then we'll both know." Our kiss turns frantic, his large body lurching forward.

This amount of arousal is crazy. He turns me into some kind of animal.

"Let's get in the shower," he suggests, unable to hide the quiver in his voice. He's desperate for it.

"Jules..."

"Please. I'm fucking begging here," he whispers.

Hearing him admit he's begging is my undoing, and I find myself nodding.

"Okay, we can take a shower." He pants against my lips.

"Just...give me a minute," I whisper.

I stand and glance down at his body as he lies back on the bed. His hard cock is up against his stomach, and a smear of pre-ejaculate glistens across his ripped abs. I'm so turned on, I really am. My sex is throbbing, aching to be filled.

I go into the bathroom, remove my tampon, and get into the shower. I stand under the hot water with my heart beating hard in my chest. He said he needs intimacy tonight, and this is as intimate as it gets for me.

He walks in, his eyes holding mine intensely. I hold out my

hand and he takes it in his, stepping under the hot water slowly. He holds me close, kissing me.

"Are you sure?" He stares down at me.

The water is running over his face, and he looks so damn beautiful and tortured...

He looks like he's mine.

"I'm sure." Our lips collide and his tongue slides deep into my mouth. He lifts me off the floor, pinning me to the wall, and with one hard pump he's deep inside of me.

We both moan softly because, oh God, this is beautiful. Julian moves slowly, gently, and I can feel every damn vein on his cock.

The physical feelings I'm having... The emotional.

I feel so much closer to him than I should.

He hooks my thighs up over his forearms, gripping my behind and bringing me onto him to slide in deep.

I whimper, "Jules."

"I know, baby." He drops his head and begins to give it to me slow and deep. The slapping of the water on our skin echoes all around, and I cry out, unable to hold my orgasm in any longer.

Julian inhales sharply, pushing himself deeper than he's ever been, and he comes in a rush inside of me.

Our bodies jerk and shiver as we ride our waves of pleasure. We kiss a slow, gentle, loving kiss. His touch is electric.

"What are you doing to me?" he eventually whispers as the water runs down over his head.

"I'm taking care of my man," I answer quietly.

His eyes search mine, and I feel there's something more he wants to say.

Instead, he kisses me softly and I smile against him, my heart melting even more. I can't believe we just did that.

Every day we take another few steps up the intimacy ladder, and no matter what we tell each other, we both know this is more.

. . .

The clock strikes midnight, and I'm still trying to put my finger on what's going on with him this evening. We're in bed together and his head is resting on my chest. He's soft, relaxed, and so fucking beautiful, it hurts my heart.

Something's changed. Everything's changed.

"You said something the other day, and I can't stop thinking about it," he says.

"What's that?" I kiss his temple.

"You said that your ex-boyfriend had psychological problems and that you stayed with him to try and fix him."

I frown to myself. How does he remember that? "Yes."

"What was wrong with him?"

I brush my cheek against his. "He's a beautiful man...but he was abused as a child by an uncle, and that fucked with his head."

"As it would."

"Most definitely." I sigh. "But it rewired something inside of him."

Julian looks up at me. "He turned gay?"

I shake my head. "No, just the opposite. He had to prove to himself that he wasn't gay."

He frowns and waits for me to continue.

"If a woman came on to him, he had to go through with it. He couldn't knock her back because, in some sick way, he thought that was confirmation that he was, in fact, gay."

Julian runs his hands up my thigh, waiting patiently for me to tell him the full story.

"He would come home and confess everything to me. Then he would be disgusted with himself and beg for my forgiveness." I narrow my eyes as I remember the horror of living that life. I never knew what the day would bring. Stability wasn't an option. "We would both go back to his therapist for an intensive couple of weeks. He would be fine for a while...until it happened all over again."

"How many women did he sleep with while he was with you?"

"Too many," I admit in a whisper. "Towards the end, I just

237

couldn't deal with it anymore. I knew he was broken. I knew that he loved me. But what about my heart? I deserved better, you know?"

He nods, his eyes turning sad. "How did it end?"

"He worked in the city. Things had always happened there, so he kept it completely separate from me. Nobody ever knew. Hell, I wouldn't have known if he didn't come home crying guilty tears every time and confessing his sins."

Julian exhales heavily.

"Then one day he slept with a girl I knew. She knew we were together." I frown and my eyes fill with tears. The pain is still as raw as the day I found out. "He crossed the line with her. Everyone knew her and me. They thought it was the first time he'd strayed, but little did they know I'd been suffering alone for three years while I tried to save him."

"God, Bree," he whispers.

"It would have been easier to leave, but he was so broken. I thought if I couldn't help him when he loved me that much, nobody would be able to."

He stays silent.

"I couldn't save him," I whisper with regret. "I had to cut all ties in the end because I couldn't deal with him constantly begging me to come back. I couldn't deal with the guilt I felt."

Julian listens, his eyes penetrating mine.

"After I left, he went totally off the wall and just started fucking everything that moved. He's had two overdoses since."

"Fuck," he whispers as he picks up my hand and kisses it.

I think for a moment. "A lot of people said I was weak for staying with him."

"You weren't."

I exhale heavily. "That's when I decided to just be happy and grateful for every single day."

He rolls over to face me. "So I guess you're done with damaged men?" His eyes search mine.

I smile down at him and softly kiss his big, beautiful lips. "I've got room for one more."

He kisses me, and as if he is overloaded with emotion, his face creases against mine. I don't know what the hell his story is, but I need to find out.

My phone rings at exactly 11:00 a.m. and the name Mr. Masters lights up the screen.

"A daytime phone call? This must be important," I tease as I answer it.

"Very funny," he mutters, unimpressed.

I smile. "How can I help you, Judge Masters?"

"Do you have any plans tonight?"

"No." I bite my bottom lip as my heart dances to the sound of his voice.

"Would you like to go to a fundraiser thing with me?"

"I would. Like...on a real date?"

"Like...on a real experiment."

I giggle. "A science experiment?"

"Good grief. Yes or no?" he snaps, and I can tell he's edgy.

"Yes, of course, yes." I frown. "What's the dress code?"

"Not bondage." He chuckles.

"Damn it." I widen my eyes. "That's annoying."

"Pick you up at seven?"

"Okay." I do a little jig on the spot. "Seven it is."

It's just after seven when I hear a knock on my bedroom door.

I close my eyes and put my hand on my stomach to try and calm my nerves.

I've never been so nervous, and I know it's not about what I'm about to do. This is about what I'm ignoring.

My gut is telling me to run. This is a bad idea.

I shouldn't be going out with Julian tonight. I know we should be keeping things separate. What if this turns pear-shaped?

We live together, for Christ's sake.

I open the door and there he stands—my tall, beautiful man in his black dinner suit.

He smiles sexily as his eyes drop down to my tight, coffee-colored evening gown. I inhale when I'm teased with his heavenly aftershave.

"You look beautiful," he whispers.

I smile softly as my heart tries to escape my chest. "Thank you." His dark eyes hold mine. "You ready to do this?"

I swallow the lump in my throat. "As ready as I'll ever be."

He leads me through the house by the hand, and then out to the car. As usual, he opens the door for me, but then backs me against the car before he leans to kiss me.

I smile as I put my arms around his neck. "We can kiss in the garage now?"

"We can kiss in the garage." His large hands roam down to my ass and he drags me onto his hard body. We stay in each other's arms as he looks down at me, taking in every detail of my face. His brow creases suddenly, and then he falls serious.

What is that look?

He straightens and pulls away. "We need to go."

"Okay." I climb in, and without a word, he closes the door behind me and gets into the driver's side.

Once we're driving on the main road, I find myself watching him. He's deep in thought when he glances up and catches me watching him. Julian takes my hand in his and places it on his thigh.

"Everything all right?" I ask.

He focuses back on the road, picking my hand up to kiss the back of it. "Why wouldn't it be?"

"You're just quiet."

He smirks. "I'm trying to tame this roger in my pants, if you must know. It seems to have a mind of its own when you're around."

I smile over at him, relieved that my playful man has returned. "Maybe you should give me a good rogering, then."

He chuckles. "Don't worry, my beautiful Miss Brielle." He kisses the back of my hand again as his eyes remain on the road. "You will be well and truly rogered by the time I'm finished with you."

He called me Miss Brielle. I fake a smile and my eyes turn back to watch the road in front of us.

His force field is back on. Finished with me.

Why are those the only three words I heard in that whole sentence?

We both remain lost in our own thoughts for the rest of the trip.

I'm wondering how this is going to go. I don't know what he's thinking about, but I know it's more than the roger in his pants.

He's always thrilled to be touching me in the hotel, but when we just stood cheek to cheek and had that brief moment of perfect intimacy at home, I felt him pull away.

I don't even know why it's bothering me. It shouldn't. I know what's going on here. He warned me, and I know how this game works.

There are no false pretenses—no promises or need to pretend to have feelings that don't exist.

Don't mistake this for anything other than what it is, Brell.

What we have is a friendship with a few orgasms on the side.

Nothing more, nothing less.

In his words...we have an arrangement.

Twenty silent minutes later, he pulls up outside a fancy sandstone building, into the car valet parking service. He climbs out, handing the keys over to the attendant before he makes his way to my side to help me out of the car. He's such a gentleman, always opening doors and walking behind me. It must be his fancy schooling. At least all those school fees get you something for your money, I suppose. I wonder if Sammy is being taught this kind of stuff.

Julian takes my hand in his and we walk up the front steps. The building is pure luxury. "What is this place?" I whisper.

"Spencer House," he replies, clearly distracted as he looks around.

The ceilings are domed and covered in amazing paintings. The carpet is red, and the furnishings are out of this world. This is antique architecture in its finest form.

"My God, it's gorgeous."

He smiles down at me.

"I thought you'd like it. It's from the seventeenth century and perfectly preserved."

I bite my bottom lip to try and hide my excitement. He's constantly telling me little facts of history, knowing I love it.

"It once belonged to the Earl of Spencer," he adds.

My eyes widen. "Really? Lady Diana was the daughter of the eighth Earl of Spencer."

He smiles softly.

"That's right. Her brother is the ninth."

"Wow," I whisper. People are everywhere inside. The men are in their dinner suits, while the women are dressed up to the nines. Waiters are carefully walking around with trays of champagne.

"What is this function for again?" I ask.

"It's a fundraiser for a mental health program for reformed criminals."

"Oh." A waiter walks past with a tray and Julian takes two glasses, passing one to me.

"Thank you." I smile.

He clinks our glasses.

"Do you come to all these things?" I ask.

"We take turns. Only one of us ever comes to these events. They are mostly filled with sponsors."

"We?" I frown.

"The other judges and me."

I sip my champagne as I watch him. "You know, it amazes me that you're a judge. An actual judge."

He smirks. "Why?"

I shrug. "I don't know. I've just never known a judge before." I frown. "I've never even known anyone who knew a judge."

He lifts his glass in the air and tilts it towards me. His eyes smolder. "Here's to getting to know this judge quite well."

I smile softly and feel the nerves in my stomach simmer. I've never been with a man like Julian Masters. He's a higher level of hot that I haven't experienced before. I don't imagine many women have. He's deep, guarded, mercurial, and sexy as all hell. With his black dinner suit, his dark hair, square jaw, and those piercing eyes, everything about him screams domination.

Is it because he's older and forbidden that makes him take up most of my thoughts? I do have to wonder if I'd be this attracted to him if he were my age and nothing but a normal guy.

Hmm, that's an interesting thought, actually. Why am I attracted to him?

What if he were my age and he met me first? Would we have ever dated? I mean, if he met me before he fell in love with his wife.

Sadness fills me. She's missing out on so much of her beautiful children's lives. They are so precious, and they need her. I drop my head and stare at the carpet for a moment. She should be here with him. He was her husband. It's my worst fear to not be able to see my children grow up. So tragic.

I wonder what she looked like.

I frown as a strange thought crosses my mind. Why are there no photos of her in the house? Not even the kids' rooms. Wouldn't he want the kids to remember her? I concentrate and go through the house in my mind, room by room. No. I've never seen a photo of her anywhere.

That's so weird. I'm going to ask Sammy to show me one tomorrow.

"So, you never know anyone at these types of events?" I ask, changing the subject.

"No." He sips his drink. "We get invited for the sake of it, and like I said, they are filled with sponsors. It makes for a lonely night if you come by yourself." He glances down at my dress and licks his lips. "Have I told you how beautiful you look tonight?"

I glance down at myself and dust my hands over my hips. "You did, but you can tell me again."

He chuckles. "You"—he pauses for effect—"are undoubtedly the most beautiful woman here tonight."

My face falls, and I act offended. "Just here? You mean that there are more beautiful women than me out there in the world?"

His eyes dance with mischief. "None that I know of."

"Good save." I smile.

He raises an eyebrow and sips his drink as he looks over the crowd, but my eyes linger on his face. I feel like a little girl going to my first rock concert.

He glances back and catches me staring at him. "What are you thinking?"

"Now?" I ask.

"Right now."

"That I would like you to kiss me," I whisper.

Electricity buzzes between us, and he gives me a slow, sexy smile. "Here?"

I nod.

"You want me to kiss you right here?"

I giggle. "No, but can we find somewhere where you can?"

He puts his hand on the small of my back and leans down to whisper in my ear. His breath tickles my neck, giving me goose bumps. "Why do I get the feeling that you're going to make my secret hard to keep?"

I lean even closer. "Because I am."

His eyes darken, and he looks at me for a moment. "From the time your meal arrives, you have approximately eight minutes until I drag you to my car."

"What are you going to do to me?"

He leans in and gently kisses my lips. "Whatever I want."

Our lips touch again. Suddenly, I don't care where we are or who can see us, because he is the only person in the room.

He has this intensity about him. It's like he's trying to make me lose my mind with these soft, gentle kisses hidden among hard words.

And it's working.

He's only kissed me a few times since we left home.

He could talk me into doing anything with that kiss. It's pure perfection.

His attention is a damn addiction...

I'm like a drug addict on the precipice of a high, and I need the hit.

His hand slides down, and he subtly grabs a handful of my behind. "My beautiful Bree." I can almost hear the electricity buzzing in the air between us, and I know he can too.

"That does something to me," I whisper. He raises his brow in question.

"Hearing you call me that." He only calls me it when we are alone.

That's probably why I love it so much.

His tongue darts out, sweeping across his bottom lip as he watches me.

"Bree," he mouths, and I giggle just as a large bell rings out to signal their opening of the ballroom.

We wait for the crowd to clear a little. He takes my hand, leading me into the ballroom and through the crowd. He checks where we are sitting on the map, and we make our way over to the table.

Julian suddenly stops mid-step. "Fuck," he whispers.

"What?"

"One of my work colleagues is here."

"So?" I frown.

"I don't want them to fucking know about you." He drops my

hand like a hot potato and strides to our table, pulling my chair out angrily.

What the hell? It's not my fault his work friend is here, but I take a seat anyway.

"Drink?" he snaps.

Is he kidding me? I've done nothing wrong. "Please," I reply calmly.

He disappears to the bar, and I sit alone as people slowly begin to make their way in, one by one, filling the tables up.

"Hello, I'm Veronica." One lady smiles as she sits down beside me.

"I'm Ted," her husband says, and they begin a conversation with me about the entertainment that's scheduled for tonight. I'm too distracted.

What's taking Julian so long?

I glance over to the bar to see him talking to a lady and a man, deep in conversation. I take out my phone.

There's a message waiting for me from Willow.

Hi, Brell,
We can't forget the uniforms tomorrow.

I close my eyes. Shit, the uniforms.

I completely forgot about them. It was our turn to wash the jerseys after training on Thursday night. We threw the big bag of them in the trunk. They're still in there, all dirty. Damn it.

Yes, of course.
What time are we leaving again?

She texts back.

Eight o'clock.

I blow out a breath. Great. Looks like I'm washing when I get home. I text back.

Are you guys okay at Grandma's?

A reply bounces in.

Yes
Goodnight.

I smile.

Goodnight.

I sit at the table alone for a full twenty minutes while people try to make polite conversation with me. With every moment that passes, I get a little more agitated. I glance over and see him laughing out loud, having a great time as he talks, while he leaves me sitting here alone.

I don't get it.

I sip my champagne, wishing I could drain the whole bottle.

The entrees come out, but he still doesn't return to the table. He and the woman are the only two standing by the bar now, and it's apparent that he's avoiding sitting down beside me.

Okay, now I'm getting pissed.

I roll my lips and push my chair out. I'm going to the bathroom.

I make my way out to the bathroom and sit in the cubicle for a while. Why would he bring me to a dinner and not even make an effort to sit with me? I know he doesn't want anyone to know who I am, but would he really treat a friend like this if he took her out? I don't think so.

My heart is hammering in angry beats.

Stop it. He's probably talking about some very important case and I'm just being melodramatic. After fifteen minutes, I make my way back to the table. He's now sitting on the chair next to mine, and the woman he was talking to at the bar is on the other side of him. The main meals have finally arrived too.

I pull my chair out, and he smiles over at me as I sit down. I give him a lopsided smile in return.

"Miss Brielle." He gestures to me. "This is Anna, a work colleague of mine."

I smile over at the pretty redhead. She's around the age of forty and has an incredible body. Her shoulder-length hair is down and full, and she has olive skin that is complimented by her green eyes. She really is stunning. "Hello."

"Hello, Miss Brielle." She turns to Julian. "Is she one of Willow's friends?" she asks sarcastically.

Julian's eyebrows rise in surprise before he chuckles nervously. "No, no. She's just our nanny. She has a love of history and this building, so I wanted to bring her to see it. She's new to London. All the way from Australia."

Anna laughs and says something I can't hear, and the two of them fall into a muffled whispered conversation.

I drop my head as my blood begins to boil. Just the nanny.

I pick up my glass and drain it in one mouthful. Who the fucking hell does he think he is?

I push my plate to the side.

"Not hungry?" he asks.

I glare at him. "I just lost my appetite."

For the next forty minutes, I sit in silence as the rest of the table eats and chatters amongst themselves. He hasn't said one nice word to me in over an hour and a half, but he and Anna haven't stopped talking since she arrived. Other members of the table, who obviously feel uncomfortable, are trying to make idle conversation with me because they feel sorry for me.

Why did he bring me? I feel so stupid.

He says something, and Anna bursts out laughing. The lady opposite me gives me a sad smile.

Fuck this, I'm leaving.

I put my serviette down and grab my bag from underneath the table.

"Where are you going?" he asks quietly.

I can hear my heartbeat ringing in my ears, I'm so angry. "Home." I stand and walk out of the ballroom and into the foyer, and then through the front doors to the valet parking man.

"Excuse me, can you get me a cab, please?" I ask.

"Of course."

I stand with my arms folded in front of me as he goes out onto the street, and I just wish that Emerson wasn't on her date tonight, or I would go back to her house and not come back till Monday. If ever.

"What are you doing?" Julian asks, approaching me from behind.

I roll my eyes. "What does it look like?"

"I'll drive you home."

"Don't bother."

A car pulls in and the valet driver—the one who was trying to get me a cab—has to come and take the car to the parking lot.

"Back in a minute, Miss," he calls.

I blow out a breath. "Great."

"Excuse me, can you get my car, please?" Julian asks the other attendant.

"Of course, sir."

He stands next to me, silent.

"Go back inside, Mr. Masters." I sigh.

"Why are you pissed?"

I raise my eyebrows in disgust. "If you don't know, I'm not telling you."

He stays silent, unsure what to say or understand just how angry I am. His car arrives and he opens my door. I glance around. It's either stay here in the cold or get a lift with him. Fuck it, I just want to get home. I climb in and he shuts the door behind me.

He pulls out into the traffic. I stare through the windscreen, watching as heavy raindrops begin to fall and the automatic wipers come on.

"I didn't want anyone to know that we were together." He sighs.

"Well, you won't need to worry about hiding me anymore."

He glances over. "Why?"

"Because I have too much self-respect," I snap.

"Why are you carrying on?"

"What the fuck?" I yell. "You take me to a dinner and spend two hours chatting up another woman, and then you proceed to tell her that I'm just the nanny."

He glares at me.

"That suits me just fine, Judge Masters." I sneer.

"What's that supposed to mean?"

"It means that tonight, while you were playing judges with Anna, I was judging you. And I didn't like what I fucking saw."

"Is that so?"

I turn to him, outraged at his behavior. "I don't know how you usually treat women, Julian, but let me tell you this...you will never again get the fucking chance to make me feel like you did tonight."

"How did I make you feel?" he growls.

"Like a cheap slut you are taking home to fuck when the night is over."

His jaw clenches and he grips the steering wheel tightly, not saying a single word. We ride the rest of the way in silence. He pulls into the driveway and parks the car under the carport. I get out, slam the door, and march up to the front door, fumbling with my keys.

He moves in front of me, unlocks the front door with his key, and pushes it open. I barge past him and storm through the house.

"Stop!" he calls after me.

I turn toward him sharply. "I have never been so furious. You arrogant prick, to think that I will put up with that kind of treatment." I shake my head. "Who do you think you are?"

He narrows his eyes. "You don't get to tell me what to do. This isn't a relationship."

I smirk, speechless, offering nothing but a huff in response. I don't bother replying.

"Bree," he says softly, grabbing my arm.

I hit his arm away. "I don't want a relationship with you!" I cry. "The mere thought of sleeping with such an arrogant pig turns my stomach now. Don't you dare call me that again. My name is Miss Brielle to you, and I am just the nanny. Stay the hell away!"

He glares at me. "You're taking that out of context and carrying on for no reason."

"Go fuck yourself."

I turn and walk to my room, slamming the door behind me. I'm so mad that tears begin to well in my eyes.

I can't believe he's even justifying treating me like that. He didn't say one word to me for two hours while he chatted up another woman, for Christ's sake.

I hear the front door slam and then his car start. I rush to the window and see him driving off like a madman on the loose.

He's gone back out.

I flop onto the bed and swipe the angry tears away from my eyes. His words ring through my head.

This isn't a relationship.

No shit, Sherlock. This isn't a relationship—this is a train wreck.

15

Brielle

AN HOUR HAS PASSED, and I'm still on my bed, staring at the ceiling. Just how did I get myself into this situation? What did I honestly think was going to come of going out with Julian Masters?

When we were at the hotel and it was just the two of us, things were safe. It was controlled.

It didn't hurt.

I take out my phone and flick through Instagram and Facebook to try and take my mind off how shitty I'm feeling. Nothing works.

I throw my phone down in disgust. Ugh. I hate Facebook. It should be called Fakebook, the way every idiot in the world posts pictures and shows off how good their lives are. All their gorgeous, caring boyfriends and husbands, babies, kids—they all seem to have everything I don't. You never see anyone posting pictures saying 'Oh, I went out with my older boss tonight, who, by the way, treated me like I was a stupid slut and embarrassed the hell out of me', do you? I roll my eyes.

Fake fuckers.

My phone beeps, and I scramble to read the message from my mum.

Hi, Brell, How's everything?
We're missing you.

I read it and tears fill my eyes. Before I even think about it, I'm dialing her number. She answers on the first ring.

"Hello, my beautiful Brell."

"Hi, Mum." The sound of her loving voice gets to me, and I instantly choke up.

"You okay, darling?"

I close my eyes. How does she always know when something is wrong?

I nod, even though I know she can't see me. "Yeah," I lie, despite my obvious tears.

"What's wrong, Brell?" she asks.

I went on a date with a guy who is closer to your age than mine, who turned out to be a real asshole, and now I'm alone in this big, scary house with nowhere else to go. "Nothing, Mum." I smile. "I'm just a bit homesick." I twist the blanket between my fingers. "Everything will be fine in the morning."

"Are you going out and sightseeing?"

"I am." I puff air into my cheeks. "Emerson met someone."

"Oh, is he nice?"

"He's dreamy. His name is Alastar. He's Irish." I smile. "He's different."

She laughs. "And what about you? Any men in your sights?"

"No." I frown. "All the men I meet are idiots." I hesitate for a moment. "I'm like a magnet to them."

"He's waiting for you, Brell. Somebody very special is sitting and waiting for you to come along. Any day now, he's going to show up."

I get a lump in my throat. I used to always think that someone, somewhere, was waiting for me, but I just don't know if I believe that anymore.

"How are you and Dad?" I change the subject.

"We're good. Actually, we're thinking of coming over for a trip."

My eyes widen. "Really?"

"Yes. It wouldn't be for another six to eight weeks, but we thought we might come and stay in London for a week and then go on to Prague."

"Oh, could you? That would be so great." My eyes fill with tears again. "I would really love to see you."

"Are you okay, darling? You sound off. It's Friday night. I thought you would be out."

"I'm going out tomorrow night with Em. She has a date tonight."

"Have you met anyone else that you can go out with?"

"Emerson's flatmates are really nice. I guess I might start going out with them if Em really likes this guy. I'm not sitting around this big old house alone, that's for sure," I mutter, almost to myself.

"And how's your job going? Are you getting everything done that you're supposed to be getting?"

My eyes widen as I remember the uniforms that are still in the trunk. The uniforms. Shit.

"I am," I lie. "Mum, I have to go, one of the kids is calling me."

"Okay, dear. I love you," she says lovingly. "I'll get back to you about my trip."

"I love you too. Bye, Mum."

I hang up and go down to the darkened garage. I kick my toe on something that's sticking out.

"Fuck it!" I snap as I hop around. Pain shoots through me. I flick the light on angrily and go around to the trunk to take out the huge bag of jerseys.

Are you kidding me? There are at least two loads in here. I drag the big bag back into the house. The light is on in the garage, but I don't care, he can pay the damn bill. Now, to top off a great night, I have to stay here alone and do his washing, while he has no doubt gone back to the work function to continue to crack on to the stunning redhead.

I shove the first load of washing into the machine and turn the dial with force. My blood has risen to boiling temperature.

Stupid fucking asshole.

Where's his fancy scotch? I'm drinking the lot of it.

Buzz, buzz, buzz, buzz.

I frown. What the hell is that? I punch my pillow, roll over, and close my eyes.

Buzz, buzz, buzz, buzz.

"Shut the hell up," I mumble into my pillow. Why the hell is the alarm going off on a Saturday?

I hit snooze and close my eyes again. Why would it be going off? I didn't set it?

Wait...

My eyes spring wide open. The uniforms.

I throw my robe on and race to the laundry, pulling the jerseys from the washing machine and throwing them into the dryer. I go into the kitchen and flick the coffee machine on. I glance at the time on the oven. It's 6:00 a.m. and it's very quiet around here.

Oh, that's right. The kids slept at Grandma's, and Judge Stupid is still asleep upstairs. I wonder what time the jerk got home.

I go to the window and peer down at the garage to see if I can see his Porsche in the driveway. Nope. He must have parked in the garage. Weird. I didn't hear the garage door like I normally do. It annoys me that it sometimes wakes me up.

Damn it, I'm supposed to be on a post-date high right now, feeling relaxed and refreshed. Instead, I'm tired, menstrual, and I'm pissed—not a good combination to be in any situation. I hope that Tiffany bitch gets in my way today at soccer. I need an excuse to end somebody.

I make myself a cup of coffee and sit at the dining table. I want those jerseys dried and put away before anyone wakes up. Nobody will ever know I'm shit at this nanny gig.

My mind goes over last night's events, and I think I'm angrier now than I was last night, if that's even possible. I get a vision of him being all witty and charming, and my blood boils.

I wonder...did he pick up that redhead in the end? I roll my eyes in disgust. Imagine if he brought her back here. What would I actually do if she walked down the stairs?

I pinch the bridge of my nose as I imagine them together or her in this house. I'd go batshit crazy if I saw her here now, no doubt about it. I'd probably lose control and karate kick Julian in the dick too.

I smile as I imagine him doubled over in pain, begging for me not to kick him in the balls again.

Fucking twat.

God, I hate feeling like this. I thought my days of feeling like this were over.

I walk back to the laundry and open the dryer in a rush. The clothes are still wet. Damn it.

I walk back out into the house and look up the stairs. He wouldn't have brought her home. No way in hell. I frown. Would he?

I blow out a deep breath because who knows? I mean, I never thought he would have treated me like he did last night.

Anything is possible now. I bite my lip, looking left and right to check that nobody can see me.

There's nobody down here, stupid, I remind myself. He sleeps with his door a little ajar. If he brought her home, his door will definitely be closed. If it is... Heaven help him.

I tiptoe up the stairs. I just need to take a peek. I peer down the hall and see his door is open.

I put my hand on my chest in relief. Thank God. But then I frown.

His door, it's too open.

I walk down the hall and look into his room to see his empty bed, unruffled, still made.

What?

He didn't come home.

Are you kidding me? I storm back down the stairs like The

Hulk. I go to the laundry and open the dryer, cursing when I see the clothes are still wet.

"Dry, motherfuckers!" I yell at the jerseys. "Do not mess with me today. Do you understand me?"

I get the second load out of the washing machine and begin to hang them around the heater on the small fold-up clothesline. Why didn't I think of doing this last night?

"Your stupidity astounds me," I mutter under my breath.

I sit back down and make another cup of coffee, drinking every bit of it in silence.

He must be picking the kids up on the way home from Fucksville. I get a vision of him walking in the door and me punching him fair and square in the nose, knocking him out. I'm sure if I looked in a mirror right now, the whites of my eyes would be red. I'm like the exorcist before a kill.

I put my head into my hands. Calm, calm...just keep calm.

He's an idiot and you're too good for him. He had sex with strawberry fucking shortcake last night.

I hear the car drive up the driveway, and I run to the window.

Oh no.

They're here.

I run to the laundry and start pulling the jerseys out of the dryer at double speed when something falls on the floor. Huh? I glance down and see a white thing. What's that? I pick it up and see that it's a very hot number seven.

My eyes widen.

I pull a jersey out of the dryer to see the number on the back of it is melting and hanging off.

Oh no.

What the hell?

I scramble through the jerseys. Sure enough, all of the numbers on the back are either completely fallen off or are half hanging off.

"Brelly!" Sammy calls from the kitchen.

I put my hands over my mouth. What the ever-loving fuck??

This can't be happening. No... Dear God, no.

"Go and wake her up," I hear Julian say to Willow.

"I'm awake," I growl. "And in the middle of a nightmare."

Willow comes into the laundry and her eyes widen when she sees the jersey I'm holding up.

"Oh my God," she cries. "What have you done?"

I wince and put my hands on the top of my head. "I don't know!" I yell.

Julian walks into the laundry and his face falls as he sees the melted number two.

"What the hell's going on here? You can't put those in the dryer. Don't tell me you put those in the dryer!" he snaps.

"Of course I did!" I yell.

Willow starts crying and takes off upstairs, having a complete meltdown.

I know how she feels, because I want to have one myself. This is un-fucking-believable.

Mr. Masters picks up the jerseys and starts to go through them. "They're all ruined," he growls.

"What kind of crap jerseys can't go in the damn dryer?" I cry.

"Every jersey in the damn world."

Sammy snaps and punches his father on the leg as hard as he can. "Don't yell at her," he cries. "Stop it." Then he bursts into tears.

My face falls. "Sammy, no, baby. It's okay." I pick him up and he howls into my shoulder. "Dad didn't mean it." I rock him as he has a meltdown too. "You can't ever hit Dad."

Julian glares at me and storms up the stairs to comfort Willow. I put my head on top of Sammy's head as I rock him.

Yep...

Saturday's off to a flying start. Bring on the alcohol.

I sit in the fold-up chair with Sammy on my lap as we wait for the game to begin. Julian took over the jersey situation this morning, because clearly, I couldn't handle it. It turned out that there were two sets of jerseys in that bag, and combined with the ones that weren't in the dryer, we nearly had a full team. Only four numbers were missing, and he ironed them back on temporarily while I freaked out. They are definitely going to fall off on the field, but at this point, who cares? I'm not talking to Julian, and Willow isn't talking to me. Sammy isn't talking to anyone but me, and this is one hell of a traumatic weekend.

Julian stands behind us with his arms folded, too wound up to sit down.

"Samuel, why did you hit me this morning?" he asks, unable to hold it in any longer.

I roll my lips, but I somehow keep my eyes on the field. "Because I wanted you to stop it," Samuel answers honestly.

"Stop what?"

"Yelling at Brelly. You're going to make her leave."

Oh no. "No, Sammy," I say. "I'm not leaving. We were just having a discussion. You can have a discussion without anyone leaving." I wrap my arms around him. Poor little kid.

"Do you promise?" he asks as he looks up at me with his worried little face.

"I promise. I'm not leaving," I reply. "You don't ever have to worry about that."

My eyes rise up to Julian, and he glares at me, furious that his own child chose to defend me over him.

I may kill your father, but I'm not leaving you, Sam.

He snuggles into my lap and the game begins. Soon enough, Sammy sees his little friend on the other field and runs off to play with him.

Julian and I watch the game in silence...until he chooses to speak. "I'm sorry about last night," he says quietly.

I stare at the field, unable to answer him.

"Aren't you talking to me?"

I ignore him again. If I talk to him, I'm going to lose my shit, and I have way too much dignity to do that here.

"What did you expect me to do?" he pushes.

"Stop talking," I hiss. "I'm trying to watch the game."

"Brell?" I hear a woman's voice behind me, and we both turn to see Mr. Masters' mother and father, Frances and Joseph, walking closer.

Oh, great. Just what I need. "Hello." I smile as I stand to greet them.

They both kiss me on the cheek and stand beside me and their son.

"How's she doing?" Frances asks as she watches Will on the field.

"Great."

Julian's eyes flicker over to me, silently accusing me of being a liar.

"Julian?"

We hear another woman call out, and we all turn to see that stupid Rebecca.

"Hello." He fakes a smile.

"Have you been hiding from me?" She laughs, putting her hand on his chest.

He chuckles uncomfortably.

I roll my eyes in complete disgust.

She flirts and laughs with him for ten minutes, making everyone cringe until I can't take it anymore.

"I'm going to check on Sammy," I say.

I check on Sammy, and then I strategically go and stand on the other side of the field.

I can't listen to that woman flirt with him for one moment longer.

Frances comes and stands beside me. "Good Lord, Brell, don't leave me with that stupid woman."

I roll my eyes. "I know, you need a bucket to listen to them fawn over him."

She pulls a face and fakes a shiver. "Julian has this knack of attracting the worst women."

"He likes it," I reply, deadpan.

"Would you and Julian like to come over tonight...for dinner?" she asks hopefully. "I would love to repay the favour."

Damn it, she's being nice. "I can't, I'm so sorry. I have plans."

Her face falls. She thinks for a moment. "Do you have a date?"

"No." I shake my head. "I'm going out with my friend, Emerson."

"Oh." She fakes a smile and links her arm through mine. "How lovely."

"Don't get any ideas." I sigh.

She taps my arm. "I wouldn't dare."

Julian and his father walk around the field to stand with us. "Mother, would it be alright if you took the children back to your house this afternoon? I would like to have a meeting with Miss Brielle in private."

Her eyes widen in excitement. "Yes, great idea. Take Brell out for lunch for a meeting." She taps my arm. "And if you can talk her out of cancelling her date tonight, I can have the children so you can take her dancing."

Why, that old snake...

Julian's face falls. "You have a date tonight?" he asks, horrified.

"Yes." I hesitate because I'm the worst liar in the world. "I do."

"Who with?" he snaps.

"A doctor," Frances replies as she squeezes my arm.

I frown at her. What are you doing, you senile old woman?

"What doctor?"

His father smirks as he pretends to watch the game.

"None of your business," I tell him. "Why don't you go and ask one of the desperate, dateless soccer mums to go dancing." I pretend to watch the game. "Or Strawberry Shortcake. She's always up for a good time."

He narrows his eyes, knowing exactly who I mean.

"Who's Strawberry Shortcake?" his mother whispers under her breath.

"Julian's rude work friend."

"She's not rude. It was a business meeting," he defends.

"She's more than just the nanny," I offer sarcastically.

Julian fakes a smile.

"I'm lost," his mother whispers, thinking only I can hear. "Who's stupid?"

"He is," I reply.

His father smiles at the field, entertained by our conversation.

"Oh, because putting the jerseys in the dryer is so intelligent." Julian sneers.

I glare at him and squeeze his mother's arm. "I'm sorry, but in Australia, we can put our jerseys in the dryer. I'm not used to these United Kingdom inferior products...or men."

His father chuckles again as he looks at his phone. "Oh, I see. Strawberry Shortcake is a doll from the eighties with red hair." He holds the phone out to show us.

Julian rolls his eyes, and I bite my lip to hide my smile. Has his father really been googling Strawberry Shortcake all this time?

"Julian?" A woman calls from the other side of the field. We look over and see a woman smiling and waving in an exaggerated manner.

He fakes a smile and waves back.

"Good grief." His mother sighs. "These women are unbearable."

"They're a perfect match for him," I mutter as I watch the game.

"Julian, go over and stand with her so she doesn't come over here talking, please."

Julian's mother giggles and taps my arm that's still in hers. "Oh, I really like you, Brell." She glances at Julian. "Are you sure you two can't go dancing tonight?"

"Positive," we both say at the same time.

I need to get out of this conversation. "I'm going to get a coffee. Anyone want one?" I ask.

"Yes, please," Julian and his father both say.

"I'll come with you, dear." His mother smiles, keeping her hand tightly linked through mine as we walk across the fields.

"Who's Strawberry Shortcake?" she whispers.

I roll my eyes. "You're very nosey."

"This is true. Go on."

"You can't tell him I told you."

She crosses her fingers over her chest. "God's honor."

"I went out with Julian last night as a friend."

Her eyes widen in excitement. "You did?"

"Don't get excited. It was a disaster."

"Why?"

"He ignored me for two hours and spoke to a hot redhead from his work."

Her eyes narrow. "Strawberry Shortcake?"

I nod.

"I always hated that doll," she mutters.

"Anyway, I left, we had a fight, and then he went back out and didn't come home all night."

"Well, he was at my house."

"What?" I frown.

"He came back to my house to get the kids and ended up falling asleep on the sofa, so he decided to stay the night."

"Oh."

She frowns. "You didn't think..."

I shrug.

"No, Brelly." She taps my arm and pulls me closer. "He was with us."

I shake my head in disgust. "It doesn't matter. We're just friends, so..." I shrug. "That's it."

"That's it?" She frowns. "That can't be it."

I look at her, deadpan. "That's totally it."

"Talk to him this afternoon. Maybe you can go out and work it out tonight."

I pull from her grip. "I'm not working it out with him. He's weird, he's a weird person..." I hesitate because that sounded so rude. "No offence, he's a lovely man, but—"

"None taken. He is weird." She laughs. "And this is exactly why I like you. You are so refreshingly honest. Julian needs someone like you in his life."

I pat her arm and link it back through mine. "I don't like Julian. He's not the man for me." I sigh. "But do you want to have coffee and cake on Tuesday?"

She smiles broadly. "I'd love to."

The drive back to Julian's house is made in complete silence. The children have gone back to his mother's, so we can talk about last night.

Too bad for him, I've got nothing to talk about. I'm going inside, I'm packing my things, and I'm going to Emerson's for the weekend. I don't even care if she's not home and I have to sit out on the curb, waiting for her. Anything is better than being with Julian right now.

I'm still so mad that it's not even funny. He parks the car and I get out, marching up to the house.

"Can we talk, please?" he asks.

"I have nothing to talk about, Julian," I call over my shoulder.

"I do."

"Call somebody, then, because I'm not talking."

I walk through the house, into my room, and I take out my overnight bag.

What shall I wear out tonight? Hmm, something insanely hot. I begin to go through my wardrobe and lay things out on the bed. I take out some cute black, lacy underwear and lay it on top of a black dress.

He walks into my room.

"What are you doing?" he asks.

"Packing my stuff."

His eyes roam over the underwear on the bed. "You have a date tonight?"

"Yes." I continue looking through my drawers.

"Where did you meet him?"

"None of your business. Get out."

He exhales heavily. "Can we talk about last night, please?"

"No." I bend and begin to look through my shoes in the bottom of my walk-in wardrobe.

"I didn't want anyone to know that we were together."

I throw my high heels onto the bed with force. "We're not together."

"She's just a girl that I work with," he adds.

"I don't care who she is. This isn't about her."

He puts his hands on his hips. "What is it about, then?"

My eyes rise up to him. "You can't be that fucking stupid."

"Try me."

"This is about you and your inability to communicate."

"I communicate," he hits back, outraged. "I communicate very well."

"You have no idea how to communicate with anybody, not even your children."

"That is not true."

"Okay then, smartass. You found out what that girl said to Willow last week about her mother at the soccer game. Did you bring it up and talk to her?"

He frowns. "I don't want to upset her."

"Ignoring her is upsetting her!" I yell. "Tell me. Tell me the last time you talked about anything with either of your children that was about them."

"What? I talk to them every day. What are you on about?"

"You talk to them about what's on television, world events, what they are eating, homework, school-related things. You have trivial conversations, nothing more, nothing less."

He frowns harder.

"When was the last time that you asked them about something personal? Willow played golf last week and she was really, really good, but you didn't even discuss it with her. Why? Why are you like this?"

"Because I don't have the pleasure of being the fun parent. I have to be the disciplinarian."

My face creases. "They are good kids. They don't need a disciplinarian. They need a father to show them how to love."

He drops his head and then his eyes flash up to me angrily. "This is none of your business. I will not discuss my children with you."

"You wanted to talk. This is me talking." I fold my arms over my chest. "While we are at it, why are there no photos of their mother anywhere in this house?" I add.

His eyes flare with anger. "Don't go there."

"No. I want to know. Why is there no evidence that she ever existed? Her kids deserve to remember her. They are a part of her, but they're being brought up as if she never existed."

"Fucking get out!" he roars.

"You're in my room. You get out!" I scream.

His eyes hold mine, and I can see that the comment about his wife hurt him. Regret fills me. "Julian, childhood is supposed to be filled with mess and love and laughter." We stand in silence for a moment. "I just don't want you to look back one day and wonder why you're not close with your children."

"I love my children. More than anything, I love my children," he replies sadly.

"I know you do."

"Well, what are you saying, then?"

"I'm saying that you need to learn to give yourself to them."

"I do. I give them my all!" he cries.

"You give them stability. They need compassion and understanding. They need you to be their friend too."

His eyes narrow and fall to my underwear on the bed. "And what about last night? I was just trying to protect you from gossip."

"I don't need protecting. Like your children, I want compassion and understanding."

He shakes his head, pausing for a moment. "Before we went out... when we were here..." His voice trails off.

"When we were here, what?"

His eyes rise to meet mine. "You threw me."

I frown. "Threw you?"

He runs both of his hands through his hair in frustration. "I don't know. You just did." His eyes rise to meet mine. "I was genuinely excited to be going out with you..."

"What's wrong with that?"

He shrugs. "I don't do normal relationships, Bree. I have no fucking idea what's going on between us." He throws his hands in the air. "I'm fucking confused, okay?"

"Julian," I sigh.

He grabs my hand. "Don't go out tonight. Stay here with me."

I exhale heavily and he puts his arms around me to pull me close.

"I just..." He hesitates. "I just—" He stops himself talking again.

I pull out of his arms. "Julian, I get that you don't want a relationship. I get that we have no future. But I will never understand the way you made me feel last night. I would never treat a friend like that."

His face falls.

"You need to get your shit together. I can't be in a friends-with-benefits setup if there isn't even a friendship."

"Bree." He goes to grab me again, but I pull away from him.

"Don't Bree me."

His eyes search mine. "Are you really going out with someone else tonight?"

"Yes."

His jaw clenches in anger. "Consider us done if you do."

I smirk and shake my head in disbelief. "You ended us last night, Jules. Don't put this back on me."

He drops his head and stares at the floor.

"Can you get out, please?" I ask. "I want to get ready."

He turns and walks out, and I watch the door close behind him. Regret curls deep in my stomach

That feels unexpectedly final.

Julian

I SIT at the table and rub my fingers over my forehead, back and forth.

Stop her from going out. Go in there and apologize.

I'm hot, I feel sick.

Make her stay.

I close my eyes and blow out a heavy breath, swallowing the lump in my throat. An unfamiliar feeling of regret swirls in my chest.

If she wants to go out with someone else, that's her business. I don't do monogamy. So what's with this sick fucking feeling I get from even thinking about her going out with another man?

Stop it.

I get up to pour myself a scotch, and then I sit back at the table and take a sip. Maybe she won't go.

Her words run through my mind on repeat.

I don't need protecting. Like your children, I want compassion and understanding.

I give my children compassion. I give up my whole fucking life for my children. Who is she to throw the blame on me when she knows nothing about our situation?

I take a large gulp of my scotch and she walks out with her overnight bag in her arms.

Tell her not to go.

I press my lips together so that I don't beg her out loud. I sip my scotch again with my leg bouncing underneath the table.

"Are you okay?" she asks.

"Why wouldn't I be?"

"Well, you're drinking scotch at 10:30 a.m." She stands and watches me for a moment. "I didn't mean it to sound like I think you're a bad father." She hesitates. "That's not how I meant it."

"That's how it sounded."

She takes a seat at the table opposite me.

"Julian."

I stare at my glass on the table.

"Will you look at me?"

I drag my eyes up to hers.

"I know you don't want a relationship."

I clench my jaw.

"I don't know how you think this is going to go between us, but you upset me last night. You really hurt my feelings, and it surprised me because I wasn't expecting it. I was completely blown over, both by how you treated me and how it felt."

My stomach twists.

"And it's not a good sign for me to feel hurt by you when we aren't even in a relationship."

Her eyes hold mine. "You told me to protect myself from you."

I sip my scotch, an intelligent reply escaping me.

"This is me doing that."

"By going out with someone else?" I reply.

Her eyes hold mine. "I just want a friend I can rely on."

"You can rely on me."

"No, I can't. You showed me that last night."

"Last night was an exception."

"Last night was our first date, for Christ's sake."

I clench my lips together so I don't say anything to embarrass myself further. I'm not begging. I get a vision of her kissing someone else and I feel my temperature rise. I rub my hand through my stubble in frustration. Stop it! You don't do monogamy.

What is this stupid fucking feeling? Is this jealousy?

I bounce my leg under the table as I try to get a hold of my emotions.

Her eyes hold mine. "These barriers you put up."

I frown, not understanding.

"Why do you do it?"

I screw up my face. "You don't even know what the fuck you're talking about."

"What are you protecting yourself from, Julian?"

I stand abruptly. "I'm not sitting here and listening to this psychobabble bullshit." I shake my head in frustration. "I don't need protecting. I'm happy having friends with benefits. Don't twist this to be what you think I should want."

"Are you?" She watches me intently. "Because you looked pretty pissed off when you thought I was going out with someone else tonight."

"Because you are fucking dismissing me!" I yell. "I do not get dismissed. Nobody dismisses me!" I turn my back to her as my breath quivers. It's been a long time since somebody got to me enough for me to lose my temper. I exhale heavily as I try to control my anger.

Walk away. Walk out of the room right now.

"Let me in and we can try again."

I turn toward her. "I have no idea what you're talking about."

"You shut down on me. The other night, when we were in each other's arms, we had this small window of intimacy and you immediately shut it down."

"I did not."

"Yes, you did, and the more I think about it, the more I think this is a behavior pattern for you. You don't bring up certain topics with the children because you don't want to give them the opportunity to ask hard questions."

I turn toward her, our eyes locked.

"You protect yourself from them, too, Julian, whether you're aware of it or not."

My stomach drops at her insinuation. "That's ridiculous."

"Is it? Can you at least think about it after I leave?"

I stare at her, and I have to say it because it's eating me alive. "I don't want you to be with anybody else."

"What are you saying?"

I frown, knowing I need to say more, but I can't make the words leave my mouth.

Her eyes search mine. "Do you really think I'm going to go out with another man when you hurting me is all I can think about?"

My face falls. "I didn't mean to hurt you, Bree."

"Yet you did it anyway."

I look to the floor, filled with shame.

"Maybe I need to learn how to work my own barriers," she whispers.

I swallow the lump in my throat as my eyes rise to meet hers. "Do you have to go out?"

"Yes."

Anger fills me, and I glare at her. Dismissed again.

A car horn sounds outside.

"My Uber is here."

I exhale heavily.

She walks towards the door and turns back. "Just talk to me, Julian. Tell me what you want."

I clench my jaw, and the strong urge to lash out and hurt her for leaving me takes over.

"I want a woman who isn't needy." I sneer.

Her sad eyes hold mine, and I want to kick myself the moment the words leave my lips.

Why did I say that? I drop my head, and then I hear the door shutting quietly behind her.

Brielle

I apply my lipstick and roll my lips in the mirror.

"Do you think I should wear the black dress or the grey?" Emerson asks, holding up the two dresses in front of her body.

I frown as I look between them. "The grey."

I'm at Emerson's place, getting ready for our night out. I'm trying to push Julian out of my mind.

I want a woman who isn't needy.

"I'm sorry I can't go sightseeing tomorrow." Em sighs. "I had no idea I had to work."

"It's okay, I'll go and do something on my own. We can go next week."

"So, Thomas, hey?" Emerson smiles. "He's so funny. Honestly, I'm always laughing the whole time he's around."

"Yeah, he's nice," I agree.

"Well, at least he's a lot nicer than that foot-wanking boss of yours." She tuts as she sits down beside me and begins to apply her mascara. "Please tell me that you're over this fascination with him."

I watch her for a moment. I've hardly told Em anything that has happened between Julian and me. Why, I'm not really sure.

"What don't you like about him, Em?" I ask. "You don't even know him."

She glances over at me. "You're right, I don't, but I know you."

"And?" I frown.

"He said he wanted casual sex."

I pick up my mascara. "So?"

"So then he takes you to a dinner and totally ignores you for two hours."

I look at my reflection in the mirror and press my lips together again.

"And then there's all this sexual tension, and he tells you that his kids come first."

"That's an admirable quality in my books," I reply, unimpressed.

"It is." She stops what she's doing and looks at me. "If they're your kids."

I watch her for a moment.

"I just know you, Brell. I know you won't do casual because you're not wired to be a casual kind of girl. So why would you waste the next twelve months on a guy who doesn't want commitment and who'll probably be sleeping around while you are at home, looking after his children? It's not like you won't run into him—you live with him. You care for his kids. Bottom line is, you'll be loyal and he won't."

I exhale, pick up my blusher, and begin to brush my cheeks. "You never know what could happen."

Emerson stops and shakes her head. "Brell, he is not the guy for you."

I put my blusher down on the dressing table. "Why are you so sure?"

She thinks for a moment. "Okay, let's look at it like this: you could meet a twenty-five-year-old guy who is your soul mate. You fall in love and have wild fun, maybe date for a few years. You're a team. You decide together where your home will be and you save for one. You get married, have children, and be on equal grounds for the rest of your lives."

My eyes fall to hers in the mirror, and I watch her.

"Or...you could hook up with Mr. Masters, who has already fallen in love with his soul mate and lost her. He's a widower and you will always come second to her no matter what. His house, his job, his children...and you're left to fit in somewhere around them."

I swallow the lump in my throat.

"Even if he did want a relationship—and he doesn't—you will never come first to him, Brell. You will always be fourth or fifth down the line. He can't move home to Australia. He can't go out and be spontaneous. He can't put you before his children. He can't give you something that a younger man can."

My face falls.

"I just want what's best for you, Brell, and Mr. Masters is not it. He's the complete opposite." She puts her arm around me, and we stare at our reflection in the mirror. "You stayed with your last boyfriend for three years too long because you felt sorry for him, because you're a good person and you wanted to fix him."

"I know." I sigh.

She bumps her shoulder with mine. "You can't fix Julian, no matter what you do. You can't turn back time for him. He's already been there and done that with somebody else."

I smile sadly.

"Just whatever you do, don't sleep with him. Everything will just get complicated and messy if you do."

I blow out a deep breath and pick up my lipstick and begin to reapply. This is the first secret I've ever held from Emerson.

And I know why: because in my gut, I know it's wrong too.

"This way, ladies." Thomas smiles as he leads us through the crowd. "Make way, gorgeous women coming through," he calls to the crowd, and sure enough, they part for us.

Emerson and I giggle. "You're an idiot," I whisper.

"At your service." He smiles, flashing me a sexy wink.

We're at the art gallery at one of Emerson's work's art auctions. Alastar—Em's new man—is an artist and has some of his artwork auctioning tonight. Thomas is his brother. Apparently, he's very talented, or so Em has heard.

I met both Thomas and Alastar on the second weekend we were here, and while Alastar—or Star for short—is quiet and broody, Thomas is the exact opposite. He's funny and outgoing, and I laugh the whole time he is around. He's flirty, but I think he's like that with everyone. Either way, I feel very comfortable around him.

"I have to go and see some people. Back soon," Star says.

"Okay." We smile.

"I'll get us some drinks," Thomas suggests. "What will it be?"

I frown. Hmm, what will it be? "I'll have some Sauv Blanc, please."

"Me too." Em smiles.

The room is full and buzzing. The two of us look around in awe.

Men are wearing their expensive suits, and the women are dressed in their designer clothes. Everyone is milling around while the expensive art auction takes place in the background.

"Wow," I mouth to Em.

"I know. Can you believe that this is actually happening?"

"No." I laugh. "What the hell? Look at us at a fancy art auction."

Thomas returns with our drinks, and we take a look around as we sip them.

We went to a restaurant and had dinner with the boys first, as well as way too many cocktails. Star's art auction starts at 10:30 p.m., so we arrived in time. In fact, we have half an hour to spare.

I'm wearing my tight black dress that hangs just below my knees. The spaghetti straps expose my shoulders, and a long string of gold beads adds a little flare, matching my gold heels and clutch bag. My hair is down and I'm wearing red lipstick. I put in a little extra effort tonight because I needed a boost. My mind is weighed down with thoughts of Julian at home, as well as what Emerson said about him when we were getting ready earlier.

She's right about everything. I've made a mistake. It's annoying that I can't stop thinking about him and how he dismissed me with such coldness.

I feel like shit, to be honest.

Thomas says something, but I can't hear him over the crowd.

"I beg your pardon? I can't hear you," I tell him.

He leans in and puts his arm around me at my waist, pulling me closer so I can hear him.

"I said...do you want to go and grab a coffee sometime next week?"

Oh.

"Like, on a date?" I ask, surprised.

He chuckles and pulls me closer to kiss my cheek.

"Of course on a date. What do you think?"

I look up across the room, my eyes landing straight on the cold, hard glare of Julian Masters.

I immediately stiffen.

What the fuck?

He's standing with a group of six men, all around his age, good looking, and each one wearing an expensive suit.

I smile awkwardly and drop my head. It's then that I notice that Thomas still has his arm around me.

Holy fucking shit.

I look back up and Julian is still glaring, openly furious. This night just took a gigantic nosedive.

What the hell is he doing here?

_____

17

Julian

MY RAGE RINGS in my ears.

She's here with someone... On a date?

His hand is on the small of her back, and when he says something, she smiles up at him. Bree's wearing a little black dress that hugs her every curve.

She looks edible.

I snap my eyes away angrily. No wonder she was so fucking keen to get out of the house.

My blood begins to boil.

"What's wrong with you, Masters?" Seb frowns. "You look like you just saw a ghost."

Adrenaline starts to pump through me, and an unfamiliar burn of jealousy starts to take over.

"Nothing." I glare at Brielle across the room, and then I turn my back to her.

"I'm going to bid on the Panton," Seb says as he flicks through the program. "I've got another two of his in the beach house."

"How much are you going to pay?" Spencer asks as he reads through the listings.

"I'll check what I paid for the last ones first." He pulls out his phone and begins to trawl through his emails.

I clench my jaw to stop myself from turning back to look at her.

"Brielle's here," I tell them quietly.

"Who?" Seb frowns.

"My nanny."

"Jesus." He smiles. "Where?"

"Across the room. The one in the black dress. Long, dark hair."

Seb searches the room and then releases a low whistle. "Fuck me, she's gorgeous."

"Who's gorgeous?" Spencer asks, finally joining in the conversation.

"Masters' nanny is here."

"Where?"

"Black dress, long hair. The brunette, remember her from golf?"

He looks across the room too. "Holy fuck, yeah, she's hot."

"What's she doing?" I ask through gritted teeth.

"She's talking to a guy, but she keeps looking over," Seb whispers.

I close my eyes and inhale a deep breath as I try to calm my beating heart. It doesn't matter that she's here with another guy. I don't give a damn, as long as she gives me what I want.

I drain my glass of scotch, and my heart pounds furiously.

Spencer grins smugly. "Look at you, Masters. Are you fucking jealous?"

"Don't be stupid," I snap.

"You are. You're sweating." He laughs and elbows Seb. "Masters has done his nuts."

"I have not," I bark.

"Julian, can I speak to you for a moment, please?" Bree asks, grabbing my elbow from behind.

I turn to her and lose control. "You're on a fucking date?" I growl.

Bree's eyes widen, and they flicker to my two friends, filling with embarrassment.

Spencer smirks and sticks his hand out to shake hers. "I'm Spencer."

"I'm Sebastian," Seb tells her. They stand smiling as they watch me, clearly enjoying the show.

"I-I'm Brielle." She smiles meekly.

"We know exactly who you are," Seb says arrogantly.

Bree frowns at him and turns her attention back to me. "Can I speak to you outside? Now...please?"

"You're on a date. I can't fucking believe you," I grind out.

She purses her lips. "You're not getting needy, are you, Julian?" She puts her hand on her hip. "There is nothing more unattractive than a needy man."

I narrow my eyes. The bitch, throwing my own words back in my face.

The boys chuckle, and Spencer holds his hand in the air. Seb instantly high-fives it. "Boom." Spencer smiles. "Take that, Masters."

"Fuck off," I snap, and storm towards the door.

"What the hell are you doing?" she whispers angrily as we burst through the doors, out onto the courtyard.

"What the fuck are you doing?"

"I'm out having fun. What does it look like?"

"You're on a date? I can't believe you."

"You told me I was being too needy."

I put my hands on my hips angrily, my ears burning with rage. "I thought we had something."

"So did I."

"Then what are you doing?" I whisper angrily.

"Trying to get over you."

"What? Why?"

"Because you don't want what I want," she snaps.

"What is that?"

"A friendship."

"We're fucking. Of course we have a friendship. Have you gone mad?" I swear, I'm about to lose my shit.

"I want you to talk to me."

"I am talking to you." I growl as I run my hand through my hair, completely exasperated.

"Why are you acting like this, Julian?" she whispers.

"Because I can't stand the thought of someone else touching you."

"Why?"

"Because you belong to fucking me," I admit, losing control.

She raises a brow and smiles softly, all while I glare at her and struggle to catch my breath.

I can't believe I just said that.

We stand staring at each other—me with my hands on my hips, panting heavy breaths, her looking relaxed and serene.

"Everything okay out here?" my stupid friend interrupts.

"Fuck off, Spence," I shout without looking his way.

"Okaaaay then." He turns and walks back inside.

"What's happening between us, Julian?" Bree asks.

I stare at her, helpless.

"Don't tell me that you don't have feelings for me, because I know you do."

I scowl, confusion and pain written all over my face. "You don't know shit."

"Then what is this?" She gestures to me. "Why are you acting like this if you don't give a fuck?"

I clench my jaw.

"I know you care for me, Julian. Save us some time and just admit it."

I drop my eyes to the floor.

"You can either man up and take me dancing now, or you can go and be with your friends for the rest of the night, and I'll go back to dance with Thomas." She slides her hand underneath my suit coat and around to my behind.

"Don't threaten me, Bree. You won't fucking like me when I'm angry."

"I like you however you come." She smiles sexily.

"Witch."

She rises up on her toes. "Do you want to know a secret?"

"What?" I say as I kiss her quickly. I'm still mad.

"I like you too."

I bite back my smirk. "Let's go home."

"Nope." Her tongue sweeps over my lips, and my cock twitches in appreciation. "Let's go out. I want to dance with my man."

An unexpected thrill runs through me at her calling me her man, and I lick my bottom lip, my eyes holding hers. "Then let's go out."

We walk out of the art gallery and text our friends to let them know we are leaving.

I open the door of my car and she glides in, leaving me to run around to the driver's side and get in beside her.

She puts her hand on my cock as I start the engine, and I inhale sharply, trying to reverse out of the car park.

The adrenaline is still pumping through my body.

"Julian."

I glance over at her.

"Drive it like you stole it."

I drop the clutch, hitting high speed in first gear, and I glance over to her. "Then I'm going to fuck you like I hate you."

She laughs a husky laugh, and for the first time in a long time... I feel alive.

After a hot and heavy make-out session in my car, we stumble into a bar half an hour later. It's small, out of the way, and there's a lady singing a Lady Gaga tribute song, putting on a whole show. Bree walks to the bar and leans over it, resting on her elbows.

"What will it be?" the barman asks.

She smiles mischievously and looks up at the drinks board. "We'll have four tequilas and four margaritas, please."

I frown over at her, but all I see are her eyes dancing with delight.

"Let's get fucked up."

"Oh no," croaks a scratchy voice. "Jules."

Huh? My eyelashes flutter as I try to open my heavy eyelids.

The room begins to spin, and nausea rolls my stomach. "What the fuck?" I whisper. My voice is hoarse and barely there.

I look around to find we are on the living room floor. Bree looks over at me and giggles.

I frown and put my head back down on the carpet with a thud. "Oh...my God. What the hell happened?"

She gets up slowly, resting on her elbows.

Just the sight of her makes me smile. "Look at you," I say.

She looks down at herself, and then back over to me.

"Oh no."

She's completely naked and has my tie tied around her head like a sweatband. Her hair is wild and loose. I drag myself up to a seated position, too, and she bursts out laughing. Something hangs in front of my eyes, and I bat it away. "What's that?"

Bree laughs loudly as she looks over at me. I glance down at myself. I'm wearing one sock and I have her gold beads tied around my head like a sweatband.

I lick my sandpaper lips. "My mouth's so dry," I groan.

I drag myself up to get two glasses of water, returning to the living room as quickly as I can. I pass her her drink, and it's then that I notice the room is destroyed. The sofa is pushed against the walls and there are crisps scattered all over the carpet. A bottle of scotch is spilt all over the coffee table. I pinch the bridge of my nose. "This is like that fucking Hangover movie."

Brielle downs her glass of water in one go before she stands and moves to stand beside me. She kisses me as she smiles against my lips.

"I had a good night." She pauses and then narrows her eyes. "I think."

I frown as I get a vision of us dirty dancing to the song "*Poker Face*." Where was that?

She picks up her phone from the coffee table and snaps a selfie of the two of us just as I hit the beads tied around my head out of the way.

She laughs again.

"I've got to shower before I die." I grab Bree's hand and drag her up the stairs, into my bathroom. We stand next to each other and stare at our dishevelled reflections in the mirror.

"Oh, man." Bree frowns. "What the hell happened, and where are the kids?"

"At my mother's."

I turn the shower on and untie the gold beads from my head. "I've got to go get them." My eyes widen as horror dawns. "Where's my car?"

She puts her hands over her mouth and laughs out loud.

"Oh, that was a great idea, Einstein. Let's get fucked up." I roll my eyes.

I stand under the water and Brielle gags over the sink.

"I think I'm going to die," she grumbles.

"Serves you right, you fucking maniac."

She climbs under the water with me, and we wrap our arms around each other. I kiss the top of her head as the hot water runs over us. "Did we have sex?"

"I'm on the pill, so it's okay if we did." She kisses my chest.

We hold each other for a long time and I smile to myself as the memories filter back to me. I don't remember the last time I had fun like that.

Bree kisses my chest and looks up at me.

"So...you're going to be my boyfriend now?"

I frown down at her. "What?"

"Don't." She kisses my lips. "Don't take it back."

"I'm not any good at boyfriend stuff." I sigh sadly.

She kisses my chest again. "I know this must be hard for you after losing your wife. I know why you don't let anyone close. You're such a good husband to grieve so deeply for her."

What?

I step back from her as my blood runs cold. My eyes hold hers as the hot water runs over my head and down my face.

Time seems to stand still. "I'm a good husband?" I ask. "You think I'm a good husband?"

She nods.

"You have no fucking idea what you're talking about." I sneer.

She pales but doesn't speak.

"My wife died on the day I asked her for a divorce."

Bree's face falls, and her eyes search mine. "How? How did she die?"

"She killed herself."

18

Brielle

"W-WHAT?" I whisper.

His eyes hold mine. "You heard me."

He grabs the shampoo and begins to soap up his hair while I stare at him.

She killed herself.

He rinses the shampoo out of his hair and then looks down at me.

"Shocked into silence?" he asks sarcastically. "Or just too horrified to speak?"

I raise my eyebrows and casually take the shampoo to wash my own hair.

I am shocked into silence *and* too horrified to speak.

Why didn't Janine, our cook, tell me this? "Who knows about this?" I ask.

"My parents."

"Who else?"

"Sebastian and Spencer. Nobody else. I've never told another woman before."

I stare up at him, and I don't know whether to be flattered or mortified that I'm the first one he told. What do I even say to this?

I narrow my eyes. "You've carried this secret around for five years?"

He nods, and the water runs over his face. His haunted eyes hold mine, like he's expecting me to run. He really is broken. It's as clear as day now.

I knew it. I knew something was hurting him. I picked it up weeks ago.

I cup his face in my hand. "Jules," I whisper.

He drops his head and I reach up and kiss his lips tenderly. At this moment, he needs me. He needs my acceptance, and for whatever reason that is, I'm going to give it to him.

"It's okay, baby," I reassure him.

He drops his head to my shoulder and I hold him tight.

His arms are around me and I can just feel the sadness seeping out of him.

This is the first time he has let me see him completely vulnerable this way.

And he is more beautiful than I could have ever imagined. "It's okay, baby. It's over now."

His eyes are glazed, and he crashes his arms around me, burying his face deep in the curve of my neck.

How does it feel to finally tell someone a secret like that after you've kept it inside for so long?

We stand for a long time with our arms around each other, and I know for certain that I should be doing some psychobabble talk about suicide or something right now, but I have no idea where to even start.

I choose to remain silent instead.

He will tell me when he is ready, and I'll wait for as long as it takes.

"You do know that I'm probably going to throw up all day," I whisper.

I feel him smile against my neck. "Serves you right."

286

I giggle against his shoulder. "I just wanted to have some spontaneous fun with you." Everything is so planned with us, and Emerson's words about his inability to be spontaneous must have spurred me on.

He leans back, regaining his composure. He begins to wash my hair under the water, deep in thought.

"Mission accomplished." He smirks. "I don't even know where my car is. Is that spontaneous enough for you?"

I giggle up at him, and then we fall serious again. I push my fingers through his hair. "Thank you."

He frowns.

"It means a lot that you told me."

He purses his lips together, as if trying to stop himself from saying anything else, and I kiss him tenderly. "Just know, Jules, that I am always on your side."

He pulls me closer and closer, and then I pull back.

"You should also know that if we have sex right now, I will throw up on you."

He chuckles, leaning farther away from me. "That's definitely not on my bucket list."

He finishes washing my hair out and then he gets out of the shower and dries himself. He holds a towel out for me to step into, and he wraps me in it before he begins to dry me as carefully as he can. We kiss, again and again, and I smile against his lips. "You're going to have to wait until tonight. We have a trashed house and kids to pick up." I sigh.

"Golf." He sighs. "I promised the kids I would take them to play golf."

I giggle and say something that I know I'm going to regret. "That's okay. I'll come too."

I sit on the sofa with my eyes fixed on Julian. Unlike other days, I know his silence is heavy. He's sitting and pretending to watch television, his mind a million miles away. He's been quiet today, lost in his own thoughts, and I know that after he confided in me this morning, he's now going over it again in his head. The children are sprawled on the floor with their beloved baby animals.

Eventually, I stand. I'm exhausted and falling asleep here.

"Take Tillie out to the bathroom before she goes to bed, Sammy," I tell him.

"Okay." He runs outside with his puppy, and I smile as he disappears.

"Bedtime, Will," Julian says.

"Yeah." She bends and picks up her kitten, Maverick. "Goodnight," she calls as she disappears up the stairs.

My eyes find Julian's across the room, and the overwhelming need to kiss him goodnight fills me. "Goodnight," I say.

He looks over at me. "Goodnight, Bree. I'll be asleep before I hit the pillow tonight."

"Okay." I walk over to stand in front of him. "If I could kiss you goodnight, I would."

He smiles up at me. "Same."

Our eyes linger on each other, and this warm affection between us rolls in. I hate this. I hate that I can't get a minute with him alone unless it's at a hotel. Why can't we just make love at home? Is it really going to make a difference?

"Thanks for wrecking me last night." He smirks. I grin and throw him a cheeky wink.

"Anytime."

"See you tomorrow night?" he asks.

"Sure will."

I walk to my room, shower, brush my teeth, and then I finally climb into bed. When I turn off the light and stare into the darkness, my mind begins to tick.

How must it feel to be him—to be left alone with his guilt? His children's mother...gone.

Never to return.

I toss and turn, rolling over and over, and I even end up punching my pillow. I keep seeing Julian's haunted face when he told me his secret. I'm so overtired, I just want to sleep. I have no idea what time we went to sleep last night. I get a vision of Julian, naked, with my gold beads tied around his head this morning and I smile to myself. He looked so carefree and happy. I reach over to grab my phone and scroll through social media for a while, but still, my mind won't switch off. Without thinking, I send a text to Julian.

Goodnight, my man.
My bed is cold without you.

I wait for a reply and it doesn't come. He's probably asleep already. I roll onto my back and stare at the ceiling. I have this horrible, sad feeling deep inside of me, and I just don't know how to shake it. I'm lost in so many thoughts when I feel my bed dip, and I turn suddenly to see Julian beside me.

"Hey," he whispers.

I smile up at him, and he takes me in his arms, falling down beside me. Our lips touch and we kiss softly.

He's here. He's here in my bed.

Something changed between us in the shower this morning. His secret has somehow gotten under my defenses. Now I just want to make everything all right for him. "You okay?" I whisper as I hold him in my arms.

"Yeah, baby, I'm okay." He kisses me.

We hold each other tight and my eyes fill with tears. He's been through so much. We kiss again and again, and I just can't get close enough to him. He sits up at once and peels my nightdress from my body, somehow removing his own clothes too. Last night, us acting fun and crazy was all for him. Tonight, I feel his tenderness is for me.

He can tell I need it from him. Maybe he needs it from me too.

He rises above me and he carefully rocks himself between my legs, kissing me as he does. My fingertips run up and down the muscles in his back then up through his hair, our eyes never straying from each other.

"You're perfect," he whispers.

I smile up at him and wrap him in my arms. We continue to get lost in our kisses, until he rises above me and slides deep inside my body.

We moan together and his breath quivers.

I love how his breath quivers when he's on the verge of losing control.

He slowly pulls out and then goes deeper. Our lips are locked and our bodies take on their own rhythm.

Julian goes deeper and deeper, and my legs are open as wide as they go.

He's so big. So fucking perfect.

In, out, around and around, he moves with perfect timing, and I cling to his shoulders.

"Jules," I whimper, knowing I'm close.

He rises above me and starts to pump me deep, never taking his eyes off mine. His hair falls over his forehead, and I smile up at him. He has the best sex face—completely focused on his task.

He lifts my leg up, puts it over his shoulder, and he really lets me have it.

Our skin slaps together as he takes over my body.

My mouth hangs open as I become lost in the pleasure. He's so deep.

Oh God. He's so good.

"Fuck. Fuuuck," he moans as he holds himself still, and I feel the jerk of his orgasm, and I know he's come deep inside me.

It sets off my orgasm, and I convulse as I cling to him with white-knuckle force. He takes my face in his hands and kisses me. It's soft and tender, and he holds me close. I know this is supposed to be a booty call, but fuck, it's not.

It's so much more than that. I can feel it.

He slowly moves to empty himself completely, but our lips never part.

"How did you get me to do that?" he whispers. "I'm dead tired." He kisses me again. "You're a bad influence on me, Miss Brielle."

I giggle. "Excuse me, I was just lying here, minding my own business, when you accosted me in my bed."

"You shouldn't be so damn irresistible." He chuckles as he pulls out of my body and rolls off me. He brings me closer and I kiss his chest, enjoying the feel of his smile against my forehead. I can feel and hear his heart beating hard in his chest.

We stay that way for a few moments as we come down from our high.

"It's Monday tomorrow." I sigh sleepily. "Don't remind me."

I glance up at him. "What's it like being a judge?"

He scowls softly. "Serious."

I smile. "Would I make a good judge?"

He chuckles and kisses my forehead. "You would be a terrible judge."

"Hey! I can be serious, you know."

He rolls his eyes. "No, you can't. Just admit it." He thinks for a moment and then smiles. "Don't change a thing, though. You're perfect as you are."

I half sit up and my mouth falls open. "Are you admitting that you like my ditziness, Judge Masters?"

His eyebrow rises. "Perhaps." He pulls me down to kiss him again. "Don't tell anyone."

I fall back down beside him. "Well, nobody knows about us anyway, so it will remain a secret."

We remain silent for a while. "Big weekend, huh?" I smile.

"Hmm."

"How long has it been since you just let loose like you did last night?"

He shrugs, frowns, and pulls me over his body again. I wait for him to answer with my head on his chest. "I was twenty-two when I met Alina."

What?

"She was at the same university as me and I'd seen her around. She was pretty."

I smile, imagining him younger.

"We hooked up one night after going to a nightclub."

God, he would have been a good-looking twenty-two-year-old.

He's insanely hot now at thirty-nine.

"We slept together again a few weeks later after another night out. I didn't see her again until she turned up at my dorm room three months later. She was pregnant."

My heart drops.

He licks his bottom lip as he stares into space.

"What happened?" I ask.

"I did the right thing."

My stomach twists. "You married her?"

He nods softly with his bottom lip caught in his front teeth, and I wait for him to keep going, but he doesn't.

"Did it go okay?" I whisper softly.

He shrugs. "I tried. I tried every damn day to fall in love with her." My eyes fill with tears.

"Twenty-three with a wife and a baby," he mutters softly.

I kiss his chest and rub my cheek on his skin. I hate this story because I already know how it ends.

"It wasn't so bad at first. We both put a front on for the sake of the other. Until she fell in love with me, but I didn't fall in love with her..." His voice trails off.

A tear falls free, and I quickly swipe it away. Stop it.

He clenches his jaw and I know he's right back there, all those years ago.

"I couldn't even force myself to make love to her."

Oh, this is a horrible story.

"Jules," I whisper, and he wraps his arm around me and pulls me closer.

"Samuel was conceived when I came home drunk one night. That's the only time it would happen." I close my eyes.

"Then...she started drinking."

God.

"It got so bad that I had to have a full-time nanny to care for the children even while she was home." He stares into space. "Some days, she never got out of bed."

Oh, this poor woman.

"I tried, I tried to get her help. I just didn't do enough."

My chest hurts for both of them.

"I couldn't take it anymore. I told her before I left for work one morning that I was filing divorce papers that day."

I scrunch my eyes shut as I wait for the next part of the story.

"She said goodbye to the children."

A lone tear rolls down my face onto his chest.

"And she drove drunk down a dead-end street at around 130 miles an hour, straight into a tree."

The lump in my throat hurts as I try to hold my tears back. He stares straight ahead, almost frozen.

"Do the children know?" I whisper.

"No. How could you ever tell your child that their mother killed herself because their father didn't love her?"

I sniff as the tears roll down my face. "I'm so sorry."

He kisses my temple. "Me too."

_____

19

Brielle

"ARE you going to watch the movie with us?" he asks me.

"Yes."

We've had the kids with us all day and haven't had a moment alone.

He slowly brings his hand up to cup my face, and my eyes close. His touch is magic.

"I need you to know how much I regret how I treated you at that dinner," he whispers. "It's playing on my mind."

I nod. "I know."

He shakes his head. "I don't know what came over me. I just handled the whole thing so badly."

I watch him as he struggles with this conversation.

"I know."

His eyes search mine. "My children have to come first."

"For me too," I whisper. "Their needs will come before mine or yours."

Our eyes are locked, and I feel like I'm agreeing to a deal here. He wants me to secure his children's happiness for him. How do I assure him of that?

Kiss me.

"This is harder than it should be," he admits quietly. "I can think of nothing else but you." He dusts his thumb over my bottom lip. "Promise me. Promise me that when we fall apart, you won't leave them."

Why is he so sure that we are going to fall apart?

I frown and nod before I can stop myself. "I promise that your children will always come first."

His eyes drop to my lips, and my heart begins to race. Right on cue, we hear someone bounding down the stairs, and we jump back from each other. He goes to the fridge and gets out a bottle of wine as a cover.

Sammy comes into the kitchen.

"Come on. Let's watch the movie." He disappears into the living room and I hear Willow and him talking. They get comfortable on their new beanbags, snuggled with their baby animals.

Julian comes up behind me and snakes his arms around my waist, pulling me back onto him aggressively.

"Go and change into a skirt," he whispers into my ear. He nips my lobe and goose bumps ripple my skin.

What? Holy fuck.

I walk into my room and start going through my wardrobe quickly. What the hell? I don't even have a skirt that isn't tight.

Shit. I think for a moment.

I know. I have a nightdress and gown. I take off my underwear and throw on my black silky nightdress, along with my white fluffy gown to cover it, and then I walk back out. My heart is beating fast as my adrenaline takes over.

He's going to touch me.

"Hurry up, Brell," Willow calls.

I walk into the living room to find the kids on the floor facing the television, and Julian at one end of the sofa. He pats the space next to him as his tongue darts out to wet his bottom lip. "Turn the light off."

Fuck's sake, there isn't a hotter man on Earth than him.

I turn the light off and sit down next to him. He throws the large blanket over both of us.

Terminator 2 starts playing, but I have absolutely zero interest in the movie.

"Lie down," he mouths.

I do as I'm told and put my legs on his lap. The blanket is completely covering us.

He grabs my foot and rubs it over his hard cock through his pants, and I close my eyes when I feel how hard he is.

With his eyes fixed on the television, he undoes my robe and then puts my back leg up on his shoulder along the sofa. He pushes my other leg forward, effectively opening me right up.

What the hell?

He smiles darkly as his eyes stay fixed on the television, and I watch as the shadows of the television flicker on his face. His hand runs up my calf, and then up my thigh, under my nightdress, to my stomach and my bare breast. He clenches his jaw as he grabs a handful of my breast and squeezes it hard.

I try to concentrate and control my breathing. What the fuck are we doing?

There are two kids in the room, completely oblivious, but nonetheless...

He goes to the other breast and kneads it in the palm of his hand. I can feel the desire in his touch, and I nearly combust. He trails his hand down my stomach as he explores my body. His fingers follow my hipbones and my ribs. He grabs my bottom foot and rubs it over his cock again.

Fuck, he's rock-hard.

I close my eyes and enjoy the way my body tingles. This is insane.

For fifteen minutes, his left hand explores every inch of my torso as he touches me tenderly, while his right hand is on my foot that's over his cock.

Every time he grabs my breast, he flexes his cock beneath me, and we both close our eyes and become lost in the moment.

Touch me...

Touch me...

Touch me there.

My pelvis begins to lift off the sofa towards his hand.

I'm losing control. He grabs my foot and grinds himself harder, and I can see his chest rising and falling in the shadows.

God, he's as hot for this as I am.

He lowers his hand and we both hold our breath. My chin tilts towards the ceiling in anticipation.

His fingers dust through my pubic hair. I don't have much—an inch square and cut super short—and I see a trace of a smile cross his face. He feels how wet I am and his eyes close and his mouth falls open in awe.

He tips his head back and mouths the word, "Fuck."

Oh God, I'm so hot for it right now.

His thumb glides back and forth through my open flesh, and he turns, his eyes holding mine as he pushes his thumb inside me.

I clench, and he shudders.

He's going to come. He's going to come, just from touching me.

Manic killing breaks out on the blaring television, and everyone is screaming with gunshots ringing out all around us, but all I can feel is tranquil ecstasy.

He grinds my foot hard onto his cock, and we both clench to hold the orgasm off.

He pulls my body down towards him with force, so that my hips are nearly on his lap, edging towards losing control.

He wants right-handed access.

Our eyes lock as he slides two fingers deep inside of me. His mouth hangs open as he starts to ride me deep.

Thank God it's dark. Who knows what this looks like?

With his left hand clutching my breast, his right-hand fingers are deep within my sex, and he slides them all the way in, and then all the way out. In and out. Every time he slides them in, I feel the burn of the stretch, and I know that's his aim.

This is so damn good.

In, out, around and around, all while trying to keep his arm as still as possible. We do this for nearly an hour. Every time I get close, he takes away the pressure and moves back to my breasts. I'm going out of my mind and I don't give a single fuck if the Terminator gets killed.

Kill the motherfucker and just end this damn movie already so I can fuck Julian stupid.

We get into a rhythm—one that I am not going to be able to stop. The pumps are hard and deep with three of his thick fingers penetrating me. It feels so good. Too good.

My pelvis lifts off the lounge again as I silently beg. Give it to me.

Give it to me.

He rides me hard with his fingers, and I start to see stars. Oh. That's it.

My body rocks with the pressure of his strong hands jerking me, and I throw my head back as an orgasm rips through me. I close my eyes and I shudder, contracting around him.

Our eyes meet and triumph flares on his face. This guy is too much.

He continues to slowly pump me as I watch on, and I feel like I'm having an out-of-body experience. That was the strongest, most perfect orgasm I've ever had. An hour of fingering attention is every woman's dream.

Julian took his time. He got it right. He made sure I was well and truly pleasured. He slowly slides his fingers out of me, and I frown at his withdrawal.

Don't leave. Stay in there.

He lifts his fingers to his mouth and my heart stops. What's he doing? In the diluted light of the room, he puts his fingers in his mouth and begins to suck my arousal from them.

My mouth falls open. Oh dear fucking God. His eyes close when he tastes me.

I pant as I watch on. Who is this man? How the hell did he get so hot?

He grabs my foot and grinds it onto his cock as he goes down on his fingers covered in my come.

I hold my breath. Holy...

He throws his head back and his cock jerks beneath my foot, and my sex contracts again as he comes to the taste of me.

He came to the taste of me.

I didn't even have to touch him. That's it. The game is over.

It doesn't get any hotter than this. I'm forever ruined.

For the next twenty minutes, his hands roam all over my body and continue to slide into my sex, but surprisingly, it doesn't feel sexual.

It's like he's worshipping me, needing to touch every inch. He's making sure that he still can. His hand slides up my thigh, and then into my sex and back up to my breasts in complete reverence.

I lie with my legs wide open, giving him full access as I watch him. He's fucking beautiful. I thought he was hot when I was chasing the orgasm, but watching him touch me like this is another level entirely.

Another level I've never had.

The movie is coming to an end when he pulls my nightdress down and readjusts my gown so it's closed. I wriggle up the sofa, moving away from him a bit. His hand stays firmly on my foot, though, as if he won't let that go.

He flicks the blanket back a bit so that they can see us. The credits begin to roll.

"That was awesome," Sammy says. "Did you like it, Dad?"

Julian widens his eyes. "Best movie I've ever seen in my life."

I giggle, and he squeezes my foot playfully.

"You two, off to bed. I'll be up in a second," he tells them.

"Goodnight, Brell," Willow calls as she disappears up the stairs with her little ginger kitten in her arms.

Sammy jumps up and comes to hug me. "See you tomorrow, Brell." He leads his puppy out the back to go to the bathroom before bed.

"Okay, Sammy." I smile at him.

Julian turns towards me, and I sit up on the lounge, suddenly alone with him.

He leans in and kisses me softly as he holds my face. "I'll be down to your room in half an hour," he promises against my lips.

We kiss again.

"Are you ready for me?"

"God, yes," I whisper. "Hurry."

He gets up and then bends to kiss me again. "See you soon."

Half an hour later and I'm in bed, freshly showered and back in my nightdress. The room is lit only by my lamp.

I'm counting the minutes until he gets here, until he makes me feel like that all over again.

There's a quiet knock at the door and my heart rate picks up. "Come in," I call.

He walks in, smiling. "Hi."

I sit up and lean back on the headboard.

"Hi."

He has a shopping bag with him for some reason.

"What have you got in there?" I ask.

"Oh. I brought champagne and glasses." He turns and flicks the lock on the door. "Thought it might take the edge off."

I giggle. "My edge has well and truly been taken off already, Julian."

His eyes dance with mischief. "And what a beautiful edge that was to witness."

He takes the glasses out of the bag and opens the bottle to pour us a glass each before he comes to sit on the side of my bed.

I hold my glass up. "To *The Terminator*."

He chuckles and clinks his glass with mine. "To *The Terminator*."

Julian places his glass down and kisses me, and he's all tongue and power as he lies me back down on the bed. His mouth drops to my nipple and he bites it through the silk.

300

"Bree," he whispers, moving against my neck. He swiftly lifts my nightdress over my shoulders, and I lie before him completely naked. He looks down at me, his eyes flickering with arousal.

"You're so beautiful."

Suddenly, I'm desperate. "Get naked." I grab the bottom of his T-shirt and tug it over his head. "I need you." I kiss him. "I need you now."

He stands and tears his shirt off, followed by his jeans and his black briefs.

My eyes drop down his body, and when he moves to kiss me, I hold my hand up in the air. "No. Don't move. Let me look at you."

He stands still, naked at the side of my bed as he waits for the all clear to touch me.

His chest is broad, his stomach ripped, and he has the perfect 'V' of muscles that drop down to his groin. I lick my lips. I've never seen such a perfect specimen. My eyes drop lower to his large penis that hangs heavily between his legs. Thick veins run down the length and girth of it. My heart begins to race and my eyes rise back up to find his. I swallow the lump in my throat and lie back down, about ready to have a heart attack. This is the most nervous I've ever been in my life.

His eyes roam over my body as if wondering where to start, and I shake my head.

"I just want you. I don't want more foreplay. I don't want one more minute without you inside of me."

His eyes rise to meet mine. He falls down beside me to kiss me, and we both smile into the kiss as if we've been waiting for a long time for this.

We cling to each other and he opens my legs to rise above me. His eyes are dark and he begins to rock against me. His touch is tender and loving. His kiss...perfection.

Our tongues dance together for a long time and he rocks harder against me. My legs are wrapped around his waist as I wait for him.

We pant as we become desperate. "Jules," I murmur.

"I know, baby," he whispers into my mouth. "I know."

He nudges my opening, and I open my legs wider for him to slide in deep in one quick movement.

We moan together. "Oh God, this is so good," I moan.

He slides out and then back in, and we both hiss again. Oh, fuck. He feels like he hits the very end of me. He's the perfect size, and it makes my eyes roll back.

"How's this?" he whispers.

I grab his face and kiss him in pure desperation. "Make it go away. Make this ache stop," I beg.

He rises above me and slides out, then back in deeper. Again and again, each time deeper than the last, each time harder.

We get into a rhythm and he begins to really let me have it. Deep, hard hits force the bed to bang against the wall. His hand rises to my thigh and he brings it up higher, giving himself greater access.

"Fucking hell, Bree." He moans as he begins to lose control. "How will I ever get enough of this?"

If I could answer that, I would, but my eyes are rolling and my mouth is hanging open.

He loses control and lifts my legs, hitting me harder and harder until the sound of the bed hitting the wall is all we can hear. I cry out as my world flashes in bright technicolour. His body is covered with a sheen of perspiration, and he lifts my hips to where he wants them, pumping deeper, and then holding himself still when buried inside of me. His body jerks hard as his own orgasm tears through him.

We gasp for air and he leans down to kiss me. We smile at each other's lips as his body slowly moves in and out of mine.

"You're fucking perfect," he says, like it's the most important thing he's ever said.

I smile shyly, overwhelmed with emotion.

He kisses me again and again, until finally, ten minutes later, he pulls out and falls on his side next to me. We lie facing each other, and he runs his fingers through my hair, obviously deep in thought.

"What?" I ask with a smile.

"Just you."

We lie in comfortable silence. I feel so relaxed, and my eyes begin to close.

"Don't go to sleep on me, baby. I want to spend more time with you."

I smile against his chest. "You can have me every night, Jules. I'm yours," I whisper sleepily, letting my eyes close properly.

"Until you leave," he mumbles quietly as if distracted.

I smile against his skin. "Yes." My eyelids are so heavy that I can't keep them open. "Until I leave."

20

Brielle

It's still dark in my room when I wake. Julian has already left for work, and the light is just peeking through the side of my drapes. I rub my eyes and stare up at the ceiling, unable to believe what a weekend we had. So much happened. I'm having trouble processing it all.

Alina. Poor Alina.

My mind is weighing heavy with thoughts of her and how sad her life must have been. She fell pregnant so young, and then Julian couldn't love her, but that didn't stop her from falling in love with him. That hurt changed her to the point of her becoming an alcoholic and dying of loneliness.

I get a lump in my throat when I imagine how alone she must have felt.

What a terribly tragic story. Sadness fills me as I imagine her lying upstairs in despair, desperate for a way out of what her life had become.

No wonder this house is so heavy and serious.

It's never been any other way.

And my beautiful Julian, trapped into marrying a woman he

didn't love. He tried to do the right thing and take care of his responsibilities. He never had a chance to pursue his own happiness. I can't imagine the guilt he must feel every day, knowing that his inability to love a woman had inadvertently caused her death.

His mother told me that he had issues. Hell, she wasn't joking, was she? I now know exactly why he doesn't bring up hard subjects with the children. How could you ever explain that story without them being resentful to him?

Sorry, kids, I just couldn't love your mother after I knocked her up, so it's my fault she became an alcoholic and killed herself.

Not happening.

I drag myself up to go to the bathroom and take a shower. I have this new, overwhelming urge to protect Julian. He's a good man, an honorable man who tried his best to make a bad situation right, but in the end, he just couldn't.

I'm not going to let him blame himself for one more day. I know why he's scared of relationships and of having someone love him. Of course he'd never want to be responsible for anyone else's happiness ever again. I wouldn't either, if I were him.

The hot water runs down over my face, letting me get lost in my thoughts.

I'll only let you down. His words come back to me. He's terrified of letting anyone down again—of letting anyone get close.

That's too bad, Julian, because I'm already close to both you and the children, and I'm not going to let you push me away out of fear.

As I stand in the shower, I feel my reservations about Julian Masters disappear down the drain along with the hot water.

I want him as a boss, as a lover...as my boyfriend. I want the full package, kids and all.

Willow and I are sitting at the kitchen counter, eating breakfast.

"I'm looking forward to our girlie day, Will." I smile against my coffee cup. I've coerced Julian into letting Willow have the day off school for some appointments. He doesn't need to know it's for our nails. We need some time together, and I want to try and get her to talk to me.

"What exactly do you do on a girlie day?" she asks.

"Well, we'll get our nails done, and then we might get our hair cut. Afterwards, we could go somewhere nice for lunch." She gives me a lopsided smile.

"We might even go and buy you some new clothes." I widen my eyes, trying to make her as excited as I am.

"Really? Like what?"

I shrug. "Whatever you want."

She finally begins to smile.

"And Emerson has the day off too. I thought we might go and have a coffee with her this afternoon."

"You want me to meet your friend?" she asks, surprised.

"Uh-huh." I smile. "You're my friend and she's my friend, so it's a lot easier if my two friends become good friends too."

"Oh no, Tillie." We hear Sammy cry from upstairs.

Willow's eyes meet mine.

"What is that naughty puppy up to now?" I ask.

"Oh, man, she's exhausting." Will sighs, and we make our way upstairs to see what the commotion is about.

Woof, woof.

Tillie leans back on her back legs, then jumps up and attacks Sammy.

"Tillie," he calls.

Our eyes widen as we assess the damage.

Tillie has been in Willow's makeup case and chewed everything inside of it. There is blush and lipstick all over the upstairs carpet, as well as down the stairs. She now has a powder sponge in her mouth and is running away from Sammy, enjoying the chase, thinking that this is the most fun ever.

"Oh no, naughty," I whisper.

She barks and then runs. We take chase, running after her as she sprints down the stairs.

"Oh my God, somebody get her," Willow cries.

I'm terrified she is going to swallow the sponge.

"Tillie," I call as I run down the stairs. "Come back here."

Maverick the cat thinks that this looks like a good game, and he starts pulling himself upside down along the leather sofa by the claws so that Tillie doesn't get all the attention.

"Stop that, Maverick," I cry as we run past. "These baby animals are very naughty today."

"Sammy's going to be late for school at this rate," Willow cries.

We corner Tillie in the kitchen and she goes feral, bending her back legs as she straightens her front legs. She's having so much fun.

Woof, woof.

I look around at the three of us in our pyjamas, chasing a tiny little dog as she completely destroys the house, and I get the giggles. "Come here, you naughty girl." I hold my hands out wide to try and entice her.

She begins to chew the sponge in her mouth, and we all scream "Nooooo!"

Willow dives on her, and I pry her tiny mouth apart and take the mangled makeup sponge from her grip.

She latches onto Sammy's finger and bites down hard.

"Ahhh!" he yells.

"No," I snap. "No biting, naughty!"

Willow puts Tillie back down on the floor, and the pup sprints back upstairs on a mission to wreck something else.

"Oh my God," Willow cries as she runs after her.

Sammy rolls his eyes and takes chase. I laugh and turn around to see Maverick climbing the curtains by his claws. He's looking at me upside down. "Get down, Maverick, you naughty cat." I rub my hands through my hair.

These pets are completely out of control.

"What about this shirt?" I ask Will.

We've had our nails done and now we're perusing the shops with Daddy Warbucks's gold credit card. This is essential spending—way more important than bondage lingerie, that's for sure.

Will looks at the shirt and frowns. "It's okay, I guess."

"What style do you like?" I think for a moment. "You're at that age where you are transforming from a duckling into a beautiful swan."

She rolls her eyes at my dramatics and then twists her lips together. "Well, I've always liked grunge clothing."

I nod as I listen.

"But I was thinking of maybe trying to get something a bit..." Her voice trails off.

"A bit what?" I ask as I keep looking around the shelves.

"I don't know. Something a bit more"—she raises her eyebrows —"attractive?"

I smile, knowing she does like that boy from the golf club after all. "That's an excellent idea." I link my arm through hers. "Let's get you a whole new look."

Two hours later, we have six bags in our hands, filled with some of the most beautiful clothes you could imagine, as well as four pairs of shoes. I have totally blown out his credit card. But honestly, who cares? It's not like he can't afford it.

We are walking down the street, on the way to meet Emerson, eating chocolate waffle ice cream cones. "Tell me about school," I say as I lick my chocolate heaven.

She shakes her head. "Nothing to tell."

"Why do you think those girls pick on you?" I lick my ice cream as I pretend to be blasé about the answer.

She frowns. "I'm just different."

"How so?" I watch her. I've spent the whole day preparing her to have this conversation with me, and if it takes all of Julian's money to get more from her, then so be it.

"I don't have a mother." She shrugs as she looks to the ground. "I don't like what they like."

I watch her. "Like what?"

"The music, the stupid boys. Everything. I have nothing in common with any of them."

"But that's okay, right?" I frown. "Does it bother you that you have nothing in common with them?"

"It used to."

"But not anymore?"

"I'm used to it now, I guess."

I link my arm through hers as we walk. "You know it's okay to be different, Will. I'm different, and not everyone likes me."

"Everyone likes you, Brell." She tuts.

"No, they don't. Do you know how many times I get called a bimbo because I choose to be outgoing and happy? People assume I'm dumb because I laugh a lot." I shrug. "Think about it...both you and your dad thought I was a bimbo at the very beginning."

She frowns as she watches me, my words falling into place.

"I choose to be how I want to be." I bump my shoulder with hers. "I don't care what people think. You need to choose how you want to be and forget what everyone else says or thinks about it."

She listens intently.

"Because the people who matter will love you however you are."

"What about Dad?" she asks. "Will he?"

"Your father loves you so much. He just wants you to be happy, Will. He doesn't always say what he feels, I know, but it's the truth, and deep down you know it."

She smiles softly, her eyes holding mine.

"He's going to wet his pants when he sees you in these beautiful dresses." I smirk.

She giggles.

"How about we call into Grandma's and show her your new clothes on the way home?" I say.

"Okay." She smiles.

We arrive at the café where we are meeting Emerson, and we walk in to find her sitting at the back. "Hello." I smile as I kiss her cheek.

"Hi, Will." She smiles

"Hi," Willow replies nervously.

"Jesus, have you two bought the whole shop?" She gasps as she looks over at all our bags.

"Yep." I sigh as I fall into my seat. "We needed a pick-me-up. Some spoilt rich little bitches are giving Will a hard time at school."

Emerson narrows her eyes and punches her fist into her palm. "Who do I have to take out?"

I'm lounging on the sofa. "Put the grey dress on," I call out.

Frances sits in the wingback chair as the two of us watch Will's fashion show. The butler brings out a tray of tea and scones, placing it on the table. "Will that be all, ma'am?"

"Yes, thank you, darling." Frances smiles. I can't believe she has house staff. It's like being part of the royal family or some shit.

Willow breezes out of the study in the flowing grey dress, proudly placing her hands on her hips.

"Oh my goodness," Frances exclaims as she begins to clap her hands. "Simply gorgeous. You look at least twenty-one in that outfit, Will."

Willow rises up on her toes and looks down at herself.

"Put the black skirt and top with the high heels on." I smile. Will disappears back to the study to change into her next outfit.

We are at Frances's house, or should I say palace, having a fashion parade of Will's new clothes, and I have never seen her so excited. This is so much fun.

"Put your hair up for this outfit," I call from my position on the sofa.

I've been here a few times over the last week to visit Frances. It gets lonely in that big old house of ours when everyone is at school and work. Julian's mother is actually a really cool lady, and I enjoy her wit and sarcasm. We don't discuss Julian at all when I'm here, but I have a sneaking suspicion that she's reading between the lines and knows exactly what's going on. She really is as sharp as a tack.

Willow appears before us again with her arms spread out. "Ta-dah."

"Oh, my." Frances slaps her hands to her cheeks. "Lord have mercy, you are divine."

I laugh. "She is, isn't she? Turn around and show us the back." Willow does a twirl, and we both gasp.

Willow laughs and disappears back into the changing room. Frances's eyes fall to me. "Thank you," she whispers.

"What for?"

"For taking the time to get to know Willow."

My eyes fill with tears. How many people actually take the time to see beneath her scars to admire the beautiful girl she really is?

"It's been an honor to spend time with her."

She smiles knowingly. "Have you thought any more about marrying my son yet?"

I giggle. "No."

She sits beside me on the sofa and takes my hand in hers, staring at me with hopeful eyes.

"We're just friends, Frances. Don't get excited."

She taps my hand in hers and smiles broadly. "Of course, dear. I believe you."

Willow appears again in a blue fitted dress this time. "And I can wear this one if I ever go out." She puts her hands on her hips proudly. "Like...on a date."

I clap my hands together. "Oh my God, Will, yes. This is a definite first date outfit."

Frances stands and embraces Will in a hug. "I'm so proud of you, darling."

My face nearly splits in two, I'm so happy. It's been a good day. The best, actually.

. . .

"You scrape it in, just like this." I watch as Willow scrapes the last of the mixture into the bowl. "That's it." I smile. "Now pop it in the oven."

Willow has developed a taste for being in the kitchen, and I'm trying to do it with her as much as I can. Sammy is sitting on the bench, watching us, and Lady Gaga's "*Poker Face*" is blaring through the house. It's starting to turn dark outside, and dinner is in the oven.

I feel him before I see him.

I turn to find Julian standing in the doorway, watching us. He's wearing a navy suit and holding his briefcase down by his side. I've never seen a man looking so damn divine. His big brown eyes hold mine, and he gives me the best *come fuck me* look I have ever seen.

"Hey." I smile.

"Hello," he replies, his eyes smoldering, making my sex clench in appreciation.

He gives Sammy a hug, and then he gives Will a kiss on the cheek.

"We're baking, Dad," Will tells him.

"I can see." He smiles. "What am I eating for dessert tonight?"

"Apple Danish." She smiles proudly with her hands on her hips.

He peers at the oven and then turns to her. "You're going to make me overweight and unattractive, Will," he teases as his eyes fall back up to me.

I smirk at him, *as if*.

"Go wash up for dinner, guys," I say. "Will, why don't you bring your new clothes down to show your father?"

She looks to Julian for approval before she sees his returning smile, hunches her shoulders, and runs upstairs with Sammy on her tail.

I go to the fridge to put the ingredients away. Julian's arm snakes around me from behind. He pulls me back against his body, and his cock is already hard.

My body weakens instantly.

Julian pushes my hair around to one side, and his lips find my neck where he softly bites me, making goose bumps scatter up my arms.

"I've been hard all day thinking about you," he whispers in my ear.

Arousal pumps through my body.

"Why?" I whisper as his face rubs against mine over my shoulder.

He jerks me closer so his erection digs into my behind. "Because I wanted to be home, here, inside of you." He kisses my ear.

Woof, woof.

Tillie grabs the bottom of his suit pants and tries to pull him away using all her strength, tugging and dancing around.

Damn you, Tillie, for ruining my moment. This dog will be the death of me.

"Don't!" he snaps as he shakes his leg to try and detach the naughty puppy. "If you rip my suit, there'll be hell to pay, pooch." He bends and pushes her away but she just goes crazier and bounds back to grab his sleeve between her sharp little teeth.

I giggle as I watch her. "Tillie, stop." She growls as he pushes her away.

Maverick jumps up on the bench and Julian's face falls. "Get down this minute."

I lift the little ginger ball of fluff up and put him back on the floor. "He's just a little baby. He doesn't know the rules yet," I tell Julian.

"He's a damn health hazard."

Willow comes down wearing her blue dress and holding her arms out proudly. As soon as he sees her, Julian's mouth drops open, and his eyes flicker to me then back to her.

"Will..." he says breathlessly. "You look so beautiful."

Will beams with pride, and I have to blink through my tears. I'm getting soft in my old age.

"Are you crying?" Will asks.

I wave the tea towel around in the air. "It's all those onions I chopped."

She giggles. "You're an idiot."

I sniff. "I've been called worse."

Julian's eyes linger on my face before he turns his attention back to Will. "What else did you girls get up to today?"

"We got our nails done, went shopping, and then we visited Grandma."

He frowns. "You went to Grandma's?"

"Of course. We had to show Grandma Will's new clothes," I interject.

"Oh, and we met Emerson. She's really nice. And did you know that it's Brell's birthday on Wednesday?" Will adds.

His eyes come back to me. "You didn't tell me that." He looks between Will and me. "What do you want to do for your birthday?"

I look over at Will. I was thinking about this earlier today, actually. "I was hoping that Will could cook dinner for us."

Her mouth falls open in surprise. "You want me to cook for your birthday?" She gasps as she looks between Julian and me. "Of all the things you could do, you want *me* to cook for you?"

I nod and smile. "Only if you have time."

"I would love to." She waves her arms around in front of her. "Can we invite Grandma and Grandpa? Oh...and Emerson?"

Julian smiles at her enthusiasm. "If you like."

"Yay! We can have a whole dinner party. Oh... I'll have to make a cake." She flits around and then runs back upstairs like a giddy child at Christmas. Tillie begins to bark and run behind her. We hear the commotion as they disappear up the stairs.

Julian's eyes come back to me and he takes my face in his hands. "You're going to get yourself fucked tonight, Miss Brielle."

I stand on my tippy toes and kiss him on the lips, sliding my arms underneath his suit coat. "Good. Make it hard, Mr. Masters."

"Happy Birthday to you," the tableful of people sings loudly.

The birthday candles light up my smiling face. It's my birthday, and one of the happiest days I have ever had.

Julian woke me up this morning—wearing his sexy suit—with a cup of coffee in his hand for me—a luxury I haven't had before. The children made me birthday cards, bought me a jumper, and even picked me flowers from the garden.

Tillie chewed up the rug and Maverick fell asleep inside the washing machine. That stupid cat clearly has a death wish.

And now I'm sitting here with Julian, Will, Sammy, Emerson, Frances, and Joseph, watching as they sing Happy Birthday to me. Will has made a beautiful dinner, and the conversation has been fun and light. The table is set perfectly. It feels like everything I have been trying to teach Will has finally paid off.

I blow out the candles and they all cheer. My eyes meet Julian's across the table and he smiles softly.

I can't wait to hold him in my arms after everyone has gone for the night.

It's different now between us. Since he told me about his past and we had sex in the house, he comes to my room every night, staying until he has to get up for work. I look forward to going to bed now because I get him to myself. Even the sound of him asleep beside me is soothing.

I'm in love with him.

It happened somewhere between the crazy hotel hook-ups and now, despite the serious persona he puts on to the world. I know what a tortured man he is, and yet the tenderness he gives me when we're alone melts my heart. Every damaged inch of him is perfect to me.

"Make a wish." He smiles.

My eyes search his and I blow out the final candle.

Don't let this end.

The guests are gone, the house is quiet, and I'm waiting for my man in my bedroom. This is the worst part of my day, when he's upstairs waiting for the children to fall asleep before he can come to me.

Eventually, he knocks quietly and walks in. I turn and smile at the sight of him wearing a navy robe over his boxer shorts.

"How's my girl?" he whispers into my hair.

I close my eyes and wrap my arms around him. "Better now that you're here."

He steps back and takes out a gold envelope with a red ribbon around it.

"What's this?"

"I could lie and tell you it's a present for you, but it's really a present for me."

I frown as I stare down at the envelope. "Open it."

I untie the silk ribbon and pull out a cream card.

I giggle when I see that it's actually an invitation, but this one looks like a proper wedding invitation.

Julian Masters
Requests the company of: Bree Johnston
Occasion: Birthday
Date: This weekend Time: 6 p.m.
Place: Rome
Dress code: As you are.

"Rome?" My eyes rise to meet his. "W-what?"

"I thought you might like to go to Rome for the weekend..." He pauses, as if he's suddenly nervous. "For your birthday."

My mouth falls open. "Really?"

He raises his brow and throws me a sexy smirk. "Really."

I jump into his arms.

"Oh." I pull back and stare at the invitation. "You want me to come as I am?"

His eyes search mine. "It's you that I want."

I bite my bottom lip to stifle my stupid smile. "I'm twenty-six today, Julian."

"Then I owe you twenty-six orgasms. Get on your back and open those pretty legs."

He pushes me back and I fall onto the bed with a giggle. He crawls over me, and I can feel his erection against my stomach as his lips trail down my body. He pushes my legs apart aggressively, and his tongue sweeps through my wet flesh, making my back arch off the bed.

"Happy Birthday, baby," he whispers to me. "Let me in."

21

Brielle

I STAND at the airport check-in desk like I'm a groupie waiting to be let into a rock concert.

Julian Masters *is* my rock god.

He's checking us in for our flight, and it's clear to see that the stewardesses are all swooning over his every word. He's wearing a charcoal suit, a light blue shirt with a navy tie, expensive shoes, and his customary designer watch. My man is tall, dark, and handsome. He oozes power, money, and enough sexual energy to light up a universe.

Sorry, girls. He's all mine and he's taking me to Rome for my birthday to give me twenty orgasms. Suck it and weep, bitches.

I smile goofily to myself. What is this frigging life? I have a hot man taking me to Rome and shit.

This is how the other half lives. Now I'm doing it in style. I take a quick picture and send it to Emerson with the caption:

Ready for Rome xx

Julian turns back to me, frowning when he sees me and my exaggerated smile.

"What's that look?" he asks.

"This is my 'I'm so happy I could burst' look."

He smiles softly.

"I'm sure you see it on my face all the time," I add.

He shakes his head. "I've never seen it before in my life."

I take his hand in mine. "I've been wearing it for a week now, Mr. Masters."

"Oh, *that*. I did wonder if you were ill." He smirks. "You're very easily pleased, Miss Brielle."

I smirk back at him. "Just the opposite, my love." His smile fades as his eyes hold mine.

Shit, I just called him my love. Why did I do that?

I reach up and kiss him softly on the lips to try to distract him. He takes my hand in his. "Let's get going."

I stare at my reflection in the bathroom mirror. My hair is down, full of soft curls. My makeup is smoky, and I'm wearing a soft pink evening gown, which I bought yesterday, along with some matching pink stilettos. I know why he gave me his credit card now. He knew I had nothing to wear that was up to the standard of the places that he would be taking me.

"Are you ready?" he asks from the door.

I feel like a queen. Our room at the Rome Cavalieri is nothing short of spectacular. It has a huge, gilded bedhead over the king-size mattress. Oversized paintings of angels line the gold walls, and tapestry rugs cover the floors. I've never seen such luxury.

He holds my hand out to open up my body to him, and his hungry eyes drop down every inch. "You look so fucking beautiful, I can't stand it."

"You don't look too bad yourself, Masters." That's the understatement of the year. He's wearing a black dinner suit, and that beautiful face of his shines for me. He's one hell of a date. His two-day stubble shows a hint of salt and pepper in his whiskers, and it's enough to drive any female insane.

We recovered from our little *my love* slipup this afternoon. I don't know why I said it, but the fear on his face when I did took me back a little. I thought that maybe he was softening to the idea.

Maybe not...

He leans down to kiss me, and his hands roam to my behind so he can pull me close. I can feel his erection through his pants.

"Is that thing always hard?" I ask.

He smirks. "When I am around you. Yes."

"How do you manage to think when all the blood in your body has travelled down to a dick that size?"

He chuckles as he takes my hand and leads me out to the living area. "Flattery will get you everywhere." He glances at me. "I got you something."

"What?"

He guides me to the drawer of the desk and takes out a black velvet box.

"What's this?" I whisper when he passes it to me.

"Your birthday present."

"*This* is my birthday present." I gesture to the room. "*You* are my birthday present."

"Having you all to myself in this room for the weekend is a present for me, not you. Open it." He smirks, watching me intently.

I open the box and my breath catches, my eyes rising to meet his. "Jules, no. This is too much."

"Nonsense."

He's bought me diamond stud earrings. They're rose gold surrounding two huge diamonds. "I can't accept these."

He kisses me as he pushes the hair back from my face. "Yes, you can. You're the first woman I've ever wanted to spoil. Let me do it."

I nervously take out my earrings and put the new ones in. Then I look at myself in the mirror and my eyes fill with tears.

His face falls. "What's wrong?"

"Nobody has ever bought me a gift like this before."

"If it's any consolation, I've never bought a gift like this before, either."

My eyes search his.

Ask him now. Just do it...ask him.

This question has been burning a hole in my brain for over a week.

"Have you ever been in love, Julian?"

His eyes hold mine and he shakes his head softly. "No."

My stomach flutters with excitement and my traitorous smile breaks free.

"You like that answer?" He smirks down at me as he brushes the hair back from my forehead.

"Yes. I like that answer a lot," I breathe. I feel my confidence return. Is it evil that I'm excited that he's never been in love before? There's a chance that I could be the first woman he loves. It may be small, but still, a chance is a chance.

"I'm ready to be romanced in Rome now, Mr. Masters."

He raises his eyebrow. "You are aware that you are with somebody who has no idea how to romance, right?"

"Any time spent with you, Julian, is blissful and romantic to me." I smile up at him.

He chuckles and pulls me towards the door. "This is why you are perceived as ditzy, Miss Brielle. You really don't have any idea what you're talking about."

I giggle as he pulls me down the corridor by the hand. This is the best night of my life already.

Julian

I'm listening to her breathing as she sleeps. Bree's on her side, facing me, her small hand resting in mine. Her long, dark hair has been braided into a loose plait for bed. Her beautiful big lips are slightly parted, and her dark eyelashes fan out above the cheekbones of her porcelain skin. They begin to flutter every now and then, as if she's dreaming. I can't take my eyes off her, just in case I'm the one dreaming and she won't be here with me when I wake up.

The white blanket pools around her. I lift it carefully and tuck her back under it to keep her warm. She becomes restless for a moment and then kisses my hand before she drifts back to sleep.

This is it—the stuff you read about. Peace.

I smile and tuck a piece of hair behind her ear, then I lean in and kiss her lips softly with complete reverence.

She's fucking perfect in every way. I've never met a woman like her. We connect on every level: mind, body, and soul.

She's got me.

I don't want to be anywhere else on Earth but here with her, doing this.

It's weird.

We went out for dinner last night, and we talked and laughed for hours. Then we danced and she sang to me. I get an image of her singing up at me on the dance floor and my heart constricts, making me frown. After that, we came home and made love, and she sang to me some more while I laughed at her terrible voice.

What is this feeling?

She rustles about.

"Jules?" she mumbles sleepily.

"I'm here, baby," I whisper, wrapping my arm around her to pull her close.

She smiles, her eyes still closed, and snuggles into my chest. Moments later, I can tell she's asleep again by the rhythm of her breathing.

I need to go to the bathroom, but I'm not getting up because then I'll have to let her go. I kiss her forehead and close my eyes.

Having her in my arms is as close to heaven as I've ever been.

Brielle

The candle between us flickers, casting a subtle shadow on Julian. We're in a romantic Italian restaurant, drinking champagne limoncello cocktails after devouring the most beautiful meal in the history of good food.

"Can I ask you something?"

He smiles. "I assume you're going to anyway."

I giggle and hold my glass up to him. "Your mother told me about Masters Group and what your role is there."

"Okay."

I frown. "Why are you a judge when your family's business is so successful?"

"I studied law at university so that I could work in the family business. But then..." His voice trails off for a moment. "I had all the stuff happen with Alina and I needed a distraction, so I threw myself into studying harder. Somewhere along the line, the family business wasn't enough for me."

I watch him as I try to imagine him back then.

"What happened when she told you she was pregnant?"

"I demanded a paternity test."

I frown.

"I slept with her on the first night we met." He shrugs. "I knew she slept around. She knew who I was, about my family's wealth."

"Is that what you thought? That she was after your money?" I ask.

He sips his drink and his eyes glaze over. "I did."

"Until?"

"Until she died."

"Did you fight often? Sorry for asking questions, I'm just trying to get my head around being married to someone and not be in love with them."

"It's okay. I've never talked about this stuff with anyone other than Spencer and Sebastian."

"Spencer and Sebastian?" I frown.

"My two friends." He sips his drink and smiles. "You know, the ones from the back of the school hall?"

My eyes widen, and I giggle. "Oh, them. Spencer and Sebastian. Even their names sound naughty."

"They're trouble, that's for sure."

"What do they do?"

"Sebastian is an architect. He's divorced, no kids." He smiles fondly. "And Spence owns a steel company and has fucked his way around the world...twice. He designs skyscrapers, and he chooses to live between here and New York."

I smile. "You're close to them, I can tell."

"They've kept me sane over the years. They know me better than anyone. We've been through a lot together." He puts his hand up to the waiter, silently asking for two more cocktails.

I eye the golden fluid in my fancy glass. "These things are super potent."

"Oh, like you can't handle a good drink, Little Miss Let's Get Fucked Up."

I giggle, and then another question comes to me and my face falls serious.

"What?" he asks.

"I have another question, and I don't want you to get annoyed with me, but these are the things I think about when I'm alone. I just want to lay it out on the table, you know?"

He rolls his eyes. "Go on."

"You're the most sexual man I've ever been with. When we're together, we have a *lot* of sex and you can't keep your hands off me. Every night we sleep together we have sex in some shape or form. I can't imagine you ever going without it."

He sits back in his chair and rubs his thumb back and forth over his bottom lip. "Where are you going with this?" he asks.

"You said you didn't have much sex with Alina. That it only happened a handful of times."

His eyes hold mine.

"Did you have affairs?" I whisper.

He sips his drink and his gaze slowly drops to the table.

The answer is important to me, though. I need to know who I'm in love with.

His eyes rise to meet mine. "I never had an affair. I wouldn't do that to someone."

I hold my breath as I watch him.

"I had sex with multiple high-end prostitutes instead." My brows crease together.

He sits forward and takes my hand across the table, trying to read my shocked expression. "And it was lonely, cold, and nothing like what we have."

"How long have you used prostitutes?"

"From the age of twenty-four up until the day you walked into my house."

What?

"And the other women you dated?" I frown.

"I continued seeing prostitutes while I was seeing them."

"Why?"

He shrugs. "I had no real attachment to them. I only saw them once a week. I need sex more than that."

I narrow my eyes. "No attachment at all?"

He shakes his head and frowns. "Up until I met you, I didn't think I had the ability to love anyone."

Did he just say... No. Stop it.

"And now?" I whisper as I pick up his hand and hold it in mine.

His eyes glow with tenderness. "I think you're a witch who has turned me into this pathetic, lovesick schoolboy."

I lift his hand and smile against it. "Why?"

"Because I think about you all day, and the thought of being with someone else, having someone else touch me..." He frowns and shakes his head. "It turns my stomach."

The air swirls between us. What is it about Rome that is making him all open and swoony?

"You know, I'm beginning to think that I've never been in love before, either," I whisper.

He leans over and kisses me softly. "So what were the other men in your life, then?"

"Just...practice."

"For what?"

"For you."

He smiles against my lips and we completely forget that we are in a crowded restaurant, our kiss turning passionate.

"I have a new favorite truth serum." I smile.

"What's that?"

"Champagne limoncello cocktails."

Julian is spinning me around the dance floor, even though it's now 1:00 a.m. We've laughed, drunk, and eaten our way around Rome. "*Your Song*" by Elton John plays as I smile up at my man. We are the only two on the dance floor and the club is nearly empty. My arms are wrapped around Julian's broad neck, while his hands rest on my hips as we sway. He's happy, carefree, and everything I knew he could be. I smile as I listen to the words. I've never liked this song before, but being here with him, I think it may be the most perfect song in the world.

"I have a confession to make, Mr. Masters."

"What's that?" He grins.

"From the moment I met you at the airport, I knew you were special."

His eyes search mine and he frowns as if battling something internally. "I also have a confession to make, Miss Brielle."

"I'm listening." I smile goofily up at him.

His eyes widen, and his lips soften. "When I told you I have never been in love before... I lied." He swallows the lump in his throat.

I stare into his big brown eyes.

"Because I'm in love with you," he whispers.

I frown as my world stops. "But... I thought you didn't know how to love?"

"I don't." He kisses me softly. "But apparently my heart does, with or without my permission."

I smile as tears well in my eyes. "Oh, Julian, I'm so in love with you," I confess.

Our lips touch in a perfect moment of intimacy, and he crushes me to him, holding me close.

We keep dancing on the dance floor to Elton. Just the two of us...alone.

Staring at each other.

On what may just be the most wonderful night in the history of my life.

Julian

We walk into the room, our lips locked as I guide her inside. My cock is hard and weeping, and I kick the door shut behind me. I've never felt like this—this overwhelming need to fuck a woman so damn bad, yet thinking about caring for her the morning after too.

Loving her.

I bend and lift her dress over her shoulders in one fell swoop. She stands before me in white lacy underwear. My eyes roam down her body and my cock hardens to a painful level. Her breasts are large and firm, her stomach slightly rounded, her hips curvy, and her face...

Her beautiful, pure face.

"Take it off." I kiss her aggressively. "I need you to take it off." I tear my jacket and shirt off over my shoulders while she fumbles with my belt, panting in desperation as she slides them down my legs and I finally stand naked before her.

Her eyes roam over my torso. "You're so insanely hot." She smiles to herself.

I swipe my fingers through her flesh. My girl is swollen and wet, so ready for me.

I put my hand on top of her head and push her down. "On

327

your knees." I take my cock in my hand and smear the pre-ejaculate across her lips.

She looks up at me and licks her lips. Our eyes lock and nothing else matters when she looks at me this way.

"I'm going to blow in your mouth, and then I'm going to fuck you so damn hard, you won't even remember that we're in Rome."

I slowly pump my cock in my fist and Bree opens her mouth. Just the sight of her on her knees with her mouth open sends me into a stupor. My fist jerks harder and harder in response.

"Touch yourself," I whisper.

Her hand drops to between her legs, and her eyes close as the ecstasy takes over in her body. A fire rages in my balls.

Fucking hell...

I grab a handful of her hair and guide myself inside her mouth. My eyes close. Holy fucking hell, her mouth is perfection.

I slide out and then back, making it deep. Her dark eyes watch my every reaction.

"You like that, baby?" I whisper roughly.

She nods around me. My hands grab the back of her head as I push my cock into her mouth.

Be gentle. Be. Gentle, I remind myself, but I can never be gentle with her. She makes me lose all control. She's the hottest fuck I've ever had, and it blows me away that she's also the one I love.

This is rare. I know this is rare. Is this really happening?

I build a rhythm, making her moan around me. My hands are gripping her hair with white-knuckle force, and I feel myself begin to jerk.

Fuck it, not yet.

I pull her aggressively and really start to fuck her mouth, hissing with nothing but appreciation as she takes all of me.

"Good girl," I pant. "That's it." I keep pumping.

"Bare your teeth." I growl.

She smiles as she bares them, and I cry out as my orgasm rips through me. My cock jerks and thick white semen gathers in her mouth. Bree struggles to swallow it all, and I tenderly wipe the hair back from her forehead as I look down at her. My heart is hammering in my chest, and she licks me up and down, making sure I watch on. No matter how many times I've watched her do this, it'll never be enough. I drag her to her feet and kiss her deeply. I can taste my own arousal, and it sets me off again.

She's so fucking hot.

I push her down onto the bed, my lips taking hers as I slide three fingers inside her. She's hot, and her muscles ripple around my fingers, making my cock clench again. "This beautiful cunt needs to be fed," I whisper.

She moans and arches her back off the bed.

"Doesn't it?" I whisper, jerking my fingers harder.

"Yes," she moans. I add another finger, making it four in total.

"Oh, careful."

My eyes darken. "Don't you careful me, Bree. You know the rules in my bed."

She nods and closes her eyes. I know I'm a lot to take in the bedroom, but if she wants to love me, she needs to get used to who I am. I've tried to control myself with her so far, but knowing she now belongs to me has released the animal I've been keeping caged.

I only fuck one way.

I pump her with force as I feel her dripping flesh contract around me. We're moving hard and fast and the bed is rocking, hitting the wall.

She loves this—loves it when I fuck her with my hands. "You ready?" I ask.

Her eyes hold mine, and I swipe my thumb over her clitoris. Her body instantly contracts around my fingers, and my cock jerks as she lurches forward, her orgasm all-consuming.

"Ah, Julian," she cries out.

I close her legs, push them to one side, and bend them at the knees. Then I slide in deep again. My eyes close. "Fuck, yeah," I whisper.

Her legs are together, making her super tight around my cock. I slap her on the ass and she cries out,

"Ouch."

I slap her again for whining, and she closes her eyes, taking it this time. "That's it."

I grab her hip bone and ride her deep—so deep she's thrashing and moaning, sending me out of my fucking mind.

My body is covered with a sheen of perspiration when I look down at the place where our bodies meet. My hard cock disappears into her soft, wet, pink flesh. The sound of our skin slapping together echoes around the room.

"Fucking hell, Bree," I growl.

"Julian," she whimpers. "Oh God, it's so good."

I look down at her flushed face and her dark hair splayed across my pillow. "Clench," I demand, slapping her again. She does as she's told and clenches around my cock. I throw my head back and I come in a rush, pumping her hard. She cries out at once, and I don't know if it's in pleasure or pain. Either way, it sounds so fucking good.

I slowly ride her through her orgasm before I lie down on top of her and kiss her gently.

"I love you," she whispers as she clings to me.

I smile against her lips, still panting for breath. "I love you too."

22

Brielle

I HEAR the car pull up and I grin to myself. Julian has just been to pick up the kids. I've really missed them. We flew in from Rome a few hours ago after the best weekend ever. He dropped me at home first, and then he went to get them. I hate that I couldn't go, but his parents think he went away with Sebastian for the weekend. I don't know how long we're going to keep this secret of ours. I need to talk to him about it. I hate lying to the children. I hate sleeping downstairs when the rest of the family is upstairs.

I want to be up there with them.

Dinner is in the oven, and it's then I realize how good it feels to be home.

The front door bangs open.

"Brelly!" Sammy squeals as he sprints into the kitchen and throws himself at me.

"Hello, baby." I kiss his forehead. "Oh, I missed you." I smile as I squeeze him in my arms.

Tillie comes sprinting into the kitchen and jumps up on my legs.

Then Will appears, and I wrap my free arm around her.

"Hello, my pumpkin." I kiss her forehead.

Julian soon follows behind them and he finds me with a child under each arm and a dog jumping up my legs.

"I didn't get this reception," he mutters dryly, throwing his keys onto the bench.

I giggle as I stare into his eyes.

"I've got so much to tell you, Brell," Willow says, her voice filled with excitement.

"You do?" I smile.

She holds her hands out. "You won't believe it."

"What?"

"Lola invited me to her birthday party."

"She did?"

"Yes, and *everyone* is going."

My eyes widen. "You mean the boys from golf?"

She smiles and nods. "And all her friends from university."

"This is great news." I point at her. "You should wear the blue dress, and I'll do your hair. We should practice some styles tomorrow."

"Yes, can we?"

Julian rolls his eyes as he takes a seat at the counter. "May I remind you that the blue dress is for wearing at home only?"

I smirk as my eyes rise to him. He hates that his little girl is growing up.

"So, when did you speak to her?" I ask, focusing back on Willow.

"She's been texting me all weekend."

"She has?" I smile broadly. "Look at you, being all friendly and social."

She smiles, filled with pride.

"Dinner is about half an hour away. Why don't you kids go shower and get ready for school tomorrow?" I ask.

"Okay." Sammy scoots back into the living room. "Oh no! Maverick, no," we hear him cry.

Willow walks into the living room. "Oh...shit." She gasps.

"What's going on out there?" Julian calls.

"Nothing," Willow tells him calmly.

Something is *definitely* going on out there. I put my hand on Julian's shoulder as I walk past him.

"Pour us a wine, babe. I'll get the kids sorted." That's code for 'please stay here while I sort out the wild animals we call pets'.

I walk into the living room to find Willow standing on the couch, trying to reattach the drapes which Maverick has ripped from the window. I walk over to inspect them to see that they have actually torn at the top.

Julian comes in and frowns when he sees the destruction. "This bloody cat has been home for five minutes," he cries. "How can he ruin the drapes in five minutes flat?"

"He's just a baby," I say.

"Oh...and he doesn't know the rules yet," Julian mimics with an eye roll before storming away and calling over his shoulder. "That cat is going back to the shelter if it doesn't learn the damn rules soon."

I giggle as I watch him disappear. My Mr. Cranky Pants is back.

Julian Masters
Requests the company of: Bree Johnston
Occasion: Situation inspection
Date: Thursday night
Time: 6 p.m.
Place: Room 612, Rosewood London
Dress code: Bondage

I smile as I read the invitation that's sitting in my email. He really is set on this damn bondage thing, isn't he? Maybe I should just go all out and buy some whips. He already slaps my behind when he's getting into it anyway. Not that I really feel it.

He was mortified in Rome when he saw his red handprint on my behind while we were showering, post-sex. He must have apologized at least ten times.

My phone rings, and I smile. Speak of the devil. The name Mr. Masters lights up my screen. "Hello, Mr. Masters."

"How is my naughty nanny today?" he purrs.

"She's feeling especially naughty."

"And why is that?"

"I'm wishing my man was here with me."

"I'm missing you too," he whispers.

Who is this man, and what has he done with the emotionally disabled Mr. Masters I met six weeks ago?

"I'm just about to leave work. Are you on your way yet?" he asks.

"Not yet. I'm about an hour away."

"Okay. Drive safely."

I hang up and stare at my phone for a moment. He's started saying that to me since we got back from Rome: *drive safely*.

Does it ever cross his mind, the phone call he got when Alina died? Is he scared he's going to get that call again?

We have so many bridges to cross, so many inner demons to fight —both of us do. I keep thinking this horrible thought—and I hate that I do—but what about his addiction to prostitutes? Would he ever go back to that?

I mean, if I were pregnant and unable to have sex for an extended period of time, would he still be satisfied?

Stop it. Stop thinking this shit. It isn't healthy.

His past is his past. It can only hurt me if I let it.

Knock, knock.

I stand outside room 612 at the Rosewood, smiling to myself. I'm wearing one of his black trench coats. Beneath it, I'm wearing leather bondage lingerie, as well as thigh-high, black lace-up boots.

I can be as dirty as he wants me to be.

He's bringing out a side of my personality I didn't know existed.

I'm craving this submissive sexuality.

When we are at home and he sneaks into my bed, we make gentle, silent love. We whisper the words *I love you* to each other all night long. But when we stay in hotels, we fuck like animals, and I am completely addicted. I'm addicted to the hit. I love the contrast of hard and soft.

Of loving and fucking.

Of Mr. Masters and Julian.

Julian loves me.

Mr. Masters loves to fuck me...hard.

He opens the door to me, already undressed, wearing nothing but a robe. He has a glass of scotch in his hand and I know he will already have an erection beneath his robe. A thrill runs through me, a sick thrill, because I know what we are re-enacting here: his time in the brothels. And the only sick thing about it is that I fucking love it.

I love being his whore.

"Hello, Mr. Masters," I whisper.

His eyes flame with arousal. "Hello, Miss Brielle." His voice becomes deeper when he's aroused. I can tell the difference between his personalities now.

Mr. Masters has a deep, commanding tone. Julian has either a playful or sad tone, depending on his mood.

He takes my hand and lifts it to his mouth, kissing it softly. "I've been waiting for you."

He leads me into the room and I glance over and see a bottle of baby oil on the bedside table. I swallow the lump in my throat and try to ignore the nerves dancing in my stomach.

He pours me a scotch. "Drink this." He leans in and kisses me on the cheek. "You'll need it."

My heart races and I sip the rocket fuel. It brings memories of our nightcaps together. They seem like a lifetime ago now.

I down the glass in three gulps, and he smiles darkly.

"Atta girl," he whispers.

I hold the glass out. "I'd like another."

He smirks and refills my glass slowly. Once it's full, I sip it, ignoring the way my hand shakes.

I'm so nervous, I have no idea what he has in store for me, but the baby oil tells me it's something we've never done before.

"Undress," he orders coldly, slipping smoothly into his role-play.

I down the rest of my second scotch and take my jacket off, throwing it on the chair.

He smiles darkly and his hungry eyes drop down my body. I'm wearing a lace-up black leather corset that pushes my breasts to the moon, along with tiny leather panties. He walks around me like the hunter circling his prey. He slides his robe over his shoulders, and my breath catches.

He's naked and hard. Muscles ripple in his abdomen, and he has a 'V' of perfect definition that drops to his groin. His large cock hangs heavily between his legs. I can see every vein on its engorged head. Pre-ejaculate drips from the end and he hasn't even touched me yet.

My body begins to tingle, from my arousal *and* from the scotch, but mainly because of him.

He walks over to his suitcase and takes out a black leather whip.

My eyes immediately widen.

Fuck.

"I'm going to hit you three times." His dark eyes hold mine. "And then I'm going to fuck your ass."

I swallow the lump in my throat. "Yes, sir." I look around the room. "Can I have another scotch, please?"

He smirks at the sound of my consent, and he nods before pouring me another drink. When he comes back to me, he kisses me softly, as if he's already apologizing in advance for what I'm about to endure. His lips linger over mine and our foreheads touch.

"You know that I love you," he whispers.

"Yes."

"I won't hurt you."

"I know," I mumble, my heart racing wildly. I really don't know if I can do this.

But I want to...for him.

I want to be everything for him.

I tip my head back and drain the glass of scotch, and all at once he grabs me by the hair to kiss me. He's all suction and domination as his tongue sweeps through my mouth and he holds my head the way he wants it.

"On your back, baby."

His finger slides underneath my leather panties and through my sex, where he grabs me aggressively. "I want to suck on your beautiful, creamy cunt." My sex tightens, wanting him...needing him.

Jesus Christ, he's so fucking hot.

I lie down on the bed and he slowly rolls my leather panties down my legs. He slides his fingers through my sex and pulls me open for him to study.

I hold my breath.

He bends and tenderly kisses the inside of my thigh, enticing a quiver from my body. His eyes hold mine as he blows on me. What for, I'm not sure, but there could be a fire down there. I wouldn't be surprised.

He strokes himself a few times, and I watch the pre-ejaculate drip. God, this is one hell of a show. Imagine getting paid to do this. There's a lot to be said for prostitution when you're dealing with clients like him.

Julian bends and presses his tongue through my open flesh, and I have to clench to stop myself bucking. He grabs my thighs, pulls them open, and begins sucking on my sex. His dark eyes never leave mine.

Oh God, heaven have mercy.

My hands go to the back of his head, holding him close as his eyes close. The sounds of his moans vibrate against me. He builds me up to an almost-orgasm, and then he stops right at the edge of it. I have to close my eyes to block him out. The mere sight of him is arousing enough to send any red-blooded woman insane.

"J-Julian," I pant.

"You can't come," he growls.

"Why not?"

"You'll come on my cock and not a moment before."

Again and again, he sucks me, teases me, bringing me to the edge of ecstasy before he takes it away, leaving me writhing on the bed and begging. "Please," I moan. "Julian, now."

He lifts his head momentarily to kiss my inner thigh. "On your knees."

I roll over, doing as I'm told, and I get on my hands and knees. "Drop to your elbows," he commands.

I do as he says, and that's when he grabs the baby oil and pours it all over my ass and thighs.

Christ...

He begins to rub it in, letting his fingers slide into my open sex. "You feel so fucking good, baby." He pumps me for a while, and I close my eyes, allowing the pleasure I'm feeling to take over.

He kisses the small of my back as he slides a finger into my back opening.

"Oh..." I scrunch my eyes shut.

"Let me in."

I try to control my breathing and relax as he slides another finger in deep. His lips stay on my back. I can see his cock through my legs, and I swear, he looks like he's about to come. It makes my mouth fall open.

This is off-the-fucking-charts hot.

He slowly works me, pulling me by the hip bone until I'm backed onto his fingers. I close my eyes as the pleasure shoots through me.

"You like that, my dirty girl?"

"Y-yes," I whimper.

He spreads his two fingers, and then he adds another. I have to close my eyes tighter to deal with it. This is unlike anything I have ever experienced. It's so wrong, but so, so fucking good.

I feel a sharp sting as the whip connects on my ass, but he immediately follows it with a deep thrust of his fingers.

I moan from deep inside.

Julian repeats that action twice more, each one more pleasurable than the last, and then he removes his fingers. That's when I feel his cock at my back entrance.

He pours more oil over my behind, rubbing it in with his thumb before he lines himself up and pushes forward. My face plants into the mattress as a searing pain burns through me.

"*Oh!*" I cry out.

He bends and places a kiss on my back. "You're doing great, baby. I'm nearly in."

His hand comes around to my clitoris and he circles his fingers at just the right pressure to make me feel pleasure instead of pain. My eyes roll back in my head and he lurches forward again.

"*Ah!*" I cry into the mattress.

"That's it." He pulls out and pushes back in as slowly as he can. I scrunch my eyes shut. He pulls out and slides deeper, never stopping his fingers moving over my clitoris.

"Come on, baby," he whispers. "Fuck me."

The sound of his voice pulls me from my trance, and I push back a little.

"Yeah, that's it," he rasps. "You're doing great."

I push back again and he hisses.

God, he loves this.

He slides in and out a few more times, and then I think I've actually got the hang of this. I begin to bounce back onto him, relieved that the pain has stopped and the pleasure is building. He grabs my hip bones and begins to ride me as I hold my breath. Holy fuck...*this is an insane amount of pleasure.*

The sound of the oil slipping between us is all I can hear, and I look up to the mirror to stare at our reflections. His eyes are fixed on the place our bodies meet. He's wet with perspiration and he's taking my body just how he wants it: for his pleasure only. I've never seen anything so hot in my entire life.

Every muscle in his stomach clenches as he pumps, and then, as if he needs more leverage, he lifts one of his legs and puts his foot on the bed beside me to really let me have it.

I scream into the mattress as a tornado of an orgasm tears me apart. Julian tips his head back, groaning his appreciation as he comes deep inside my body.

For a while, he moves slowly in and out on repeat. Eventually, I feel his gentle kisses trail across my back as he comes to lie over me, his cock still inside me.

He turns my head and gifts me with a kiss.

"I love you," he whispers against my mouth.

I can't answer him. I'm still dealing with myself. I think the term 'hot mess' was made for this moment. He's all around me, all I can see. He's deep inside my body, his tongue taking over my mouth.

He's etched on my heart. "I love you," I confess.

He smiles and holds my head to his. "How the hell did I ever get you?"

"Smithson Employment Agency," I pant.

He chuckles and slowly pulls out of me. I feel the sharp sting of his withdrawal, and I'm surprised by how much I want him to stay there.

He kisses me and pulls me up by the hand.

"I need to wash you."

I smile sleepily. "I know. I'm a very dirty girl."

It's Saturday night, and Willow is finally going out with Lola. This isn't to the party—that's next weekend—but she's really nervous, anyway. Even I'm nervous for her. This is the first time since I've been here that she's gone out with anyone her own age.

"Where exactly are you going?" Julian frowns as he sits in his wingback chair with his book in his hands and his feet up on the ottoman.

"Just dinner and the movies."

"What time will you be home?"

"The movie ends at eleven."

"You're only sixteen, you know, Will. I don't want you out all night."

She rolls her eyes at me. "I know, Dad."

"Am I driving you?" he asks.

"No, Lola drives."

He looks up from his book. "I don't want you driving around in a learner's car."

He looks to me. "Bree, did you know that this girl is old enough to drive?"

"Julian, she's fine." I sigh. "She has her license, and I've met Lola at golf and she seems lovely."

Well, not really, but we did say hello. Willow seems to like her, anyway.

"I'm going to get dressed." Will smiles before she bounds up the stairs.

I hunch my shoulders. "I'm so excited for her."

Julian goes back to concentrating on his book. "I'll be excited when my dick is in your mouth tonight," he mutters to himself.

I bend over and lean down to whisper into his ear, "You are a very filthy man."

He smirks and slaps my ass. "With an even filthier, totally fuckable nanny."

Twenty minutes later, there's a knock on the door. "You get it," I whisper.

"You get it," he counters.

"This is your house. You get it."

He begrudgingly stands and opens the door.

"Hello, Mr. Masters. I'm Lola." She smiles and shakes his hand.

"Hello, Lola," he replies. "Lovely to meet you." He turns to me. "This is Brielle."

I smile and she shakes my hand. "Hello, Brielle."

Oh, she's gorgeous, naturally pretty, and she's wearing navy pants with a white shirt.

"Hi, Lola. It's lovely to meet you again."

She runs her hand over her thighs, obviously nervous, and Will comes down the stairs. Lola looks up at Will and smiles softly when their eyes meet.

Willow is wearing her blue date dress, as well as her heels. She looks absolutely beautiful. Her hair is down and curled, and she has soft makeup on which highlights all her best features.

She walks down the stairs, and Lola watches on. I glance between the two of them and start to feel like I'm having an out-of-body experience.

My heart beats wildly in my chest as I watch the two of them silently interact with one another.

Oh my God.

Why didn't I see this before? You stupid fool, Brielle.

This isn't a friendly movie night. This is a date.

I think Willow might be gay.

I sit in the car outside Will's school on Monday afternoon. She finishes at 2:00 p.m. today. I've been wracking my brain all weekend about how to talk to her about her sexuality. I didn't say anything to Julian. How could I when I don't even know if my suspicions are true? I spoke to Emerson at lunch yesterday about it in great length, and we both came to the conclusion that Willow has to tell me herself. I can't approach her about it. It may just be a stage, and I don't want to make it a bigger thing than it needs to be. All I can do is support her and be here for her when she needs me.

The school bell rings, and I sit and wait as the children all start streaming out of the school. Eventually, the cars all start leaving. Most of the children are gone, so where is she?

I glance at my watch. It's now 2:17 p.m.

I wait and I wait.

The parking lot is completely empty now. I call her cell, but there's no answer.

Where is she?

2:35 p.m.

What the fuck?

I begin to bounce my leg. I have to leave now or I'm going to be late picking Sammy up. I try to call her again.

No answer.

I call Frances.

"Hello, darling," she answers.

"Are you at home? Can you do me a favor?" I ask.

"Of course, what's wrong?"

"I can't find Will, and I'm going to be late picking Samuel up if I wait."

"That's fine, I can get him."

"Oh, could you? Thank you."

"Of course, but where's Willow?"

"I don't know. She hasn't come out of the school yet. I'm going to go in and look for her now."

"Okay, dear. We'll see you back at your place."

I call Julian.

"Hey, babe," he answers.

"Have you heard from Will?"

"No, why?"

"She hasn't come out of school. I've been here for nearly an hour now."

"She's probably in detention or the library or something. I'll call her now. I'm just about to leave for home anyway," he says. "Court has finished for the day."

I frown. "Okay, see you at home."

I get out of the car, make my way into the main block of the school, and I head down the corridor. The school is completely deserted.

What the hell? Where are all the teachers? Does the school just completely clear out in half an hour?

I walk down to the Math block and back over to the library, but there's nobody in sight.

Is she even at school today? I begin to panic.

Has something happened? This isn't like her at all.

I begin to jog down the corridor, dialing her number again as I run with my heart racing in my chest.

I hear her phone ring, and I quickly look around. I find her school bag outside a science lab. I bend down and open up the bag, taking out her phone as it rings. The name Brelly lights up the screen.

It's definitely her bag.

Where the fuck is she?

"Will?" I call. "Willow, are you here?" I open the classroom door. "Willow?"

I hear a bang on a storeroom door, and I run to find it locked on the outside. I turn the lock and pull the heavy door open to find Willow wet with tears and perspiration. She falls into my arms. "Baby, what happened?" I whisper, horrified.

She sobs against my chest, shaking with fear.

"Did they lock you in there?"

She nods as she cries in complete distress.

"Oh, pumpkin."

I hold her tight. She's so distraught that she slides down my body and I can't hold her upright. We end up sitting on the floor together in an embrace.

I take out my phone and call Julian. He answers on the first ring.

"Where was she?"

"I found her. She was locked in the storeroom. Call the police and get to the school right now. I think she needs to go to the hospital."

"Jesus Christ, is she okay?"

"No, Julian," I cry. "She's not."

Her body begins to convulse as I hang up the phone. She's going into shock and I hold her tight, calling an ambulance myself.

"It's okay, baby," I whisper as I rock her. "You don't have to come back here. Not ever." I continue to rock her. "I promise you, you won't come back here ever again."

Guilty tears run down my face. I should have done more to protect her.

I should have done *more*.

Willow stares out of the window, devoid of emotion.

The hospital room is dimly lit now. She's been given medication to calm her down. It's 10:00 p.m. and they won't discharge her tonight.

Julian sits on a chair on one side of the bed with Sammy on his lap, while I sit on the other side in a big chair. Willow hasn't let go of my hand for over two hours.

Julian's furious—like, thermonuclear furious. The police have been to take a statement, but Will burst into tears as soon as they arrived. I asked them to leave and come back another time. She just can't deal with it right now.

Julian hasn't spoken to me since we got here. I can tell he's annoyed that I stepped in and overruled him. He stares at the floor in front of him. I know he's blaming himself as much as I am.

This is just one big fucking mess.

"I'm tired," Sammy whispers, rubbing his eyes.

"I know, buddy," Julian murmurs as he kisses his head. "We'll get going soon."

"You're going?" Willow whispers in a panic, her eyes flickering between us.

"No, baby, I'm staying," I reassure her.

Julian's angry eyes rise to meet mine and I look away. Jesus, don't start your angry shit now. I am not in the fucking mood.

"Do you want to stay with her, Julian, and I can take Sammy home?" I offer.

"No, Brell, I want you," Willow whispers.

Julian clenches his jaw and stands, openly annoyed that she wants me to stay with her over him.

"I'll go, then," he says. Firmly.

"Julian," I sigh.

"It's fine," he snaps before he kisses Willow on the forehead. "I'll be back in the morning."

With one last look at the both of us, he takes Samuel's hand and leads him out into the corridor.

Willow squeezes my hand, and I push the hair back from her forehead, smiling softly. "You should try and get some sleep, pumpkin," I whisper.

"You're not leaving me, are you?" She frowns with worry.

"No, I'll be right here all night."

She relaxes and closes her eyes, snuggling into my hand. I take out my phone and text Julian.

Goodnight, Jules I love you

I wait for his reply but it never arrives.

I exhale heavily and slink back into my chair. It's going to be a long, long night.

23

Brielle

I WAKE in the chair with a start. It's early morning and Julian is sitting beside Will with his hands clasped in front of him. "Hey," I whisper.

He smiles. "Hey."

"You okay?" I ask.

He nods. "Sorry about last night." He shrugs his shoulders. "Tough day yesterday."

My eyes roam to Will. She's sleeping peacefully.

I gesture to the bathroom and make my way inside. Moments later, Julian follows, shutting the door behind him. He takes me into his arms and we stand in an embrace.

"I missed you last night," I whisper.

"Me too." He kisses me softly. "Did she sleep okay?"

"Yeah, she was zonked out the whole night."

"Have you slept?" He looks down at me and tucks a piece of hair behind my ear.

"No, I just napped. I'm fine, though." I kiss him again. "I'm sorry she wanted me to stay last night. I've felt bad about it all night. You should have stayed with her. She's your daughter, not mine."

"No, it's okay. I'm just not used to having someone else to rely on." He blows out a deep breath. "I acted like a spoilt brat last night when she didn't want me."

I smile up at him. "I love my spoilt brat."

He smiles as his hands squeeze my behind. "Let's get the hell out of this place."

"Brell?" I hear Will call.

Shit. I take off out the door. "Here I am."

She frowns. "I thought you'd left."

"No, I'm here, baby. I was just talking to your dad in the bath-room. We didn't want to wake you up."

Julian walks out of the bathroom. "Hey." He kisses her on the forehead and takes her hand in his.

Watching him be so caring and gentle with his children really hurts my ovaries.

"Hi, Dad," she whispers. "Sorry about all this fuss."

He smiles sadly. "This isn't your fault, Will. Please don't think this is your fault."

She falls silent.

"I spoke to the doctor. You can come home now," he tells her.

"I can?"

"Yes." His eyes rise to mine. "You have to have a few appoint-ments over the next few weeks, but all is fine."

She smiles sleepily. "Good. I'm really missing Maverick."

"Hmm." He rolls his eyes. "You'll be pleased to know that I couldn't find that damn cat when I got home last night. I had to spend three hours outside searching for it, only to come in and find it had been asleep under my pillow the whole time."

I find myself grinning.

"I was tempted to smother it with said pillow when I found it there."

Willow giggles. "Thanks for looking for him."

He widens his eyes and flashes a little smug smirk. I really have to stop myself from grabbing his hand.

Who is he kidding with this tough-guy act? He's a big pussycat underneath it all.

He pulls Willow up by her hand. "Let's go home."

The house is quiet, the weight of yesterday playing heavily on our minds. It's 3:00 p.m. and Frances and Joseph are picking Samuel up from school and then dropping him home. Julian has been down to the police station, determined to press charges against whoever locked his daughter in that cupboard. The police are interviewing kids at the school right now, hoping to get some answers and find out who is responsible.

We're sitting at the kitchen table, drinking coffee, both lost in our own thoughts.

"What happens if they don't find out who did it?" I ask.

"They will." He blows into his coffee cup. "The police will get to the bottom of this."

"We need to look for a new school for her."

Julian frowns. "What for?"

"Well, she can't go back there."

"Why not?" He shakes his head dismissively. "The person responsible will be charged and expelled. After that, she can return."

"Julian, twenty-five children were in that class. Not one of them stepped in and told someone she was locked in there."

His brows furrow.

"This problem runs much deeper than a few mean girls."

"Don't be so dramatic."

My face falls. "Can you hear yourself? Teenage depression is the number one cause of suicide in the world right now. Your daughter is being bullied. She's trying to find herself."

"She's not suicidal," he snaps.

"Like you can tell when people are suicidal!" I cry in outrage.

His face falls and he rubs his fingertips over his lips, clenching his jaw.

"Sorry." I shake my head, instantly regretting the words I just spat at him. "I didn't mean that."

"Yes, you did."

I grab his hand over the table. "Julian, please, let's change her school. She doesn't need to put up with this. She's just a baby."

"This is the best school in England. I want her to go there."

"Why?" I scowl. "So you have bragging rights? It's the best school with the meanest girls." I throw my hands up in the air. "The best school means nothing if she is fucking miserable and depressed."

"She needs to learn to toughen up."

"You have *got* to be joking?"

"The world isn't all hearts and flowers, Brielle."

"You think she doesn't know that?" I lose my temper. "Growing up without a mother isn't exactly hearts and flowers, Julian."

His eyes fall to the table.

"She can't go back to that school. Over my dead body is she going back to that school."

"This isn't your decision," he says, his voice rising in anger.

"I don't believe you. Is your head stuck that far up your own ass that you can't see the wood for the trees? Money means jack shit if you're miserable, Julian."

He stands abruptly. "Don't you think I know that?" he growls. "I, more than anyone, know that." He shakes his head. "This is none of your business."

"None of my business." I throw up my hands in despair. "What the hell am I doing here then if Willow is none of my business?"

"Making my life fucking difficult."

My eyes fill with tears. "You're really going to make her go back there?"

"Yes." He lifts his chin defiantly. "She can have the rest of the week off until the police find whoever was responsible and press charges. Then she is going back to that school."

350

I shake my head in disgust. "You poor, delusional man. You think that the police are going to change anything? You think that the school is going to change anything? They don't give a fuck, Julian. The whole system is about protecting the criminals. You know that more than anyone. You're a fucking judge, for Christ's sake. A criminal gets bashed in prison and the whole world is up in arms."

He glares at me.

"What about the ten children he raped before he was sent to prison? Nobody hears about the silent victims, do they? You only hear about the criminals. The whole judicial system is geared towards saving them. Schools, the law, you fucking name it." I shake my head as angry tears fill my eyes. "It's all about protecting them, protecting their privacy and reputation, making sure they get counselling." I swipe a stray tear away. "Well, I'm not letting her become another statistic just because you're that much of a fucking snob."

"You have no say in this. You are not her fucking mother!" he growls in my face.

"I'm the closest thing she's got to one, and I'm choosing to defend her like you should be."

He steps back from me, contempt seeping from his every pore. "She is *my* child, and I will not have you telling me how to bring her up. How dare you fight with me over this?"

"I promised you I would always put the children first," I counter.

"Over me?" he cries. "You're putting her over our relationship?"

"Yes, and you can hate me all you want for it. My loyalties lie with Willow and what is going to make her the happiest she can be." The tears roll down my face. "Whatever path she chooses to take, I will be behind her one hundred percent."

"Then you'll be on your fucking own," he growls. "Parenting isn't a popularity contest, Brielle. It's about making the hardest decisions." He slams his hand onto the bench. "The right decisions. I've looked after her for the last sixteen years, and it will be me who looks after her for the next sixteen. This has *nothing* to do with you!" he yells, losing complete control.

"Dear God, Julian. What's going on?" Frances whispers as she walks into the room. "Why are you speaking to Brielle like that?"

I swipe the angry tears from my eyes and drop my head.

"What's going on, Son?" Joseph asks.

Sammy floats into the room, his face immediately falling when he sees me in tears. "What's wrong, Brelly?"

"Nothing, baby, I'm fine." I force a smile. "Can you take Tillie outside for a walk, please?"

He nods, his eyes holding mine. "It's okay. Out you go."

He begrudgingly does as he's told. The rest of us stay silent.

"What's going on?" Frances eventually asks.

Julian's breath quivers as he tries to control his anger, placing his hands on his hips.

"I don't want Willow to go back to that school," I tell them quietly. "She has no friends and she's miserable. I'm scared for her mental health."

Julian glares at me, his fury palpable.

"I agree with you," Joseph says firmly. "She doesn't even need to go to school. She's finished year ten. She already has a position in the family business. She can do the rest of her schooling through correspondence at work."

"The whole world isn't about the fucking family business, Dad!" Julian yells.

"You wouldn't know because you refuse to work in it," Joseph hits back. "This is about you not wanting to work there, not Willow."

I put my hands on my head, knowing this is getting out of control. "Stop it," I whisper angrily. "I only care about Willow. I want what's best for Willow."

"What's best for Willow is you butting out," Julian growls.

My anger rises and I glare up at him with fire in my eyes. "Fine," I hiss, and then I turn and storm to my room.

I've never felt so hopeless in all of my life.

. . .

The house has been silent all afternoon. Julian and I aren't speaking to each other. Willow is holed up in her bedroom, while I have been hovering around her, trying to make sure she's okay.

I'm sitting at the kitchen table, trying to work out what to say to Julian to make this right. I just don't believe that she can go back to that school safely.

It's 8:00 p.m. when the doorbell rings and Julian goes to open the door.

"Lola, hello." He smiles. "This is a nice surprise."

My face falls. What's she doing here?

"I just came to check on Will. Is it okay if I visit with her for a while?"

"Of course." He says. "Come in, come in."

Lola walks in and smiles when she sees me. "Hello, Brell."

"Hello, Lola. How thoughtful of you to visit." I stand nervously. "Willow is upstairs, I'll just get her—"

"No, I'll show her up," Julian interrupts. "This way." He leads her upstairs and I put the kettle on. He returns only moments later.

"Would you like a cup of tea?" I ask.

He nods and slides into place on a stool at the kitchen counter.

I dunk the teabag into the water. "I'm sorry about this afternoon. I just..." I pause, wanting to get this right. "I'm scared for her."

He nods to himself. "I am too." He scratches his head. "I'm also sorry. I shouldn't have said what I said to you."

We sit in silence, neither of us knowing what to say to the other. "Our first fight," I whisper. "Over the kids."

He frowns and smiles at the same time. "I hate that you said you'd choose her over me."

"Julian, I wouldn't choose anyone over you. But I have to do what I feel is right." I take his hand over the counter. "I'm genuinely concerned for her. If something were to happen, I would never forgive myself."

His eyes search mine. "Do you really think she's in danger of becoming depressed?"

"Yes. I think she already is, a little bit."

He drops his chin to his chest.

"We can help her, but..." I pause as I watch him. "The path that you choose for her may not be the path she wants to take." I squeeze his hand. "You need to trust her choices. If she says she can't go back there, then you need to listen."

He reaches for his tea and takes a sip. "This Lola seems nice, though."

I smile to myself. If only he knew how nice Will thinks she is.

Right on cue, Will walks into the kitchen, and Julian quickly drops my hand. Shit.

"Hey." He smiles at his daughter. "You're looking better."

"Can Lola sleep over?"

"Sure."

I frown. "Where will she sleep?"

"In my room, on my trundle bed."

What?

"That's fine, sweetheart." Julian puts his arm around her. "Have fun, hey?"

What the fuck? She's sixteen and vulnerable. She's not in any state to be having her first sexual experience with an older woman right under her father's nose.

Jesus Christ. Can this day get any harder?

Willow smiles. "Thanks." She bounces back upstairs.

My pulse seems to blare in my ears. I need to tell him my suspicions. But they *are* just suspicions. Julian stands and puts his arms around me. "Let's go to bed early and have makeup sex."

"Uh, yeah," I say, distracted.

Maybe they are just friends...

I know they're not. She's only sixteen.

What if something happens and Willow goes completely off

354

the rails? She's too fragile to be doing this right now. I have to stop it, so I stand.

"I'm going to go and make sure they have enough blankets."

"Okay, babe. I'll lock up."

I walk up to Willow's room and stand outside the closed door.

Sammy is already asleep after staying up so late last night looking for Maverick.

My heart is hammering in my chest. How the hell do I approach this?

I knock on the door as quietly as I can.

"Just a minute," Willow calls, already sounding guilty. Shit, does she have a lock on this door?

She opens it in a rush, and I glance in. Lola is lying on her bed and Willow already looks disheveled. Jesus, were they making out?

"Can I speak to you for a minute, Will?"

Willow frowns. "Sure."

I take her down the hall until there's nowhere else to go. I quickly pull her into Julian's room. "Take a seat."

"What's wrong?" she asks.

I take both her hands in mine as we sit on the bed. "You know I love you, right?" I whisper.

Will frowns.

"I don't think that it's appropriate that Lola stays over just yet."

"Why not?"

I swallow the lump in my throat. "Well, you only just met."

She watches me, and I can tell she's trying to figure out if I know.

"So? We want to get to know each other better."

My eyes search hers. "Will..." I whisper.

She frowns. "How do you know?"

I smile softly. "I could tell as soon as I saw the way you looked at each other."

Tears fill her eyes. "Are you going to tell Dad?" she whispers in a panic.

I shake my head. "No, baby. You have to do that when you're

355

ready." I brush my hand over her hair. "But you're only sixteen. I can't, with a clear conscience, let Lola stay over."

She drops her head and tears fill her eyes. "Do you hate me now?"

"What? No." I take her in my arms. "Why would I hate you? There is nothing wrong with this. You are perfect exactly as you are." I kiss the top of her head.

"Please don't tell Dad. I'm just trying to figure this out," she begs.

"I know." I hug her tight. "And you will, I know you will."

"I love you, Brell," she whispers against my shoulder. "You're the first person who has ever been on my side."

"I love you, too, baby." I kiss the top of her head and she holds me tight.

"What are you two doing up here blubbering?" Julian asks as he casually walks into his room.

We pull back from each other and wipe our eyes. "We've just had a shitty week, haven't we, pumpkin?" I smile.

"Yes." Willow stands, still wiping away her tears. "Dad, Lola can't stay now. She has to work in the morning."

"Okay." He shrugs. "Whatever."

Will walks out and disappears down the hall.

"What was that about?" Julian frowns.

My heart drops. I have to lie to him, even though I know it's wrong.

It's not my secret to tell.

"Nothing, just emotion overload," I say sadly.

Julian's hand cups my jaw and he brings my face up to his. "You okay?" he whispers as he studies my face.

I smile and nod. The lump in my throat hurts as I try to hold back more tears. Willow has such a hard road ahead of her. It's overwhelming, and my chest hurts.

I'm not okay.

. . .

An hour of crying and a shower later, I finally crawl into bed. I'm exhausted from not sleeping last night, and I'm hoping everything will seem better in the morning. Julian had to wait for Lola to leave before he could come down. He's probably fallen asleep by now. He's tired, too, after searching for our mischievous kitten all night. I get a vision of him walking around outside in the dark with a flashlight and it makes me smile.

He makes out he's so tough, but I know the truth.

The door creaks open slowly, and then I hear the lock click.

Knowing he's here makes me smile into my pillow.

He comes around to my side of the bed.

"Hey," he whispers.

"Hi." I smile up at him. Last night was the first night we slept apart since we became a thing. I missed him.

He slowly undresses and crawls under the blankets beside me, taking me into his arms. The second I cling to him, my emotions rise again and I tear up.

"What's wrong, baby?" he whispers.

The lump in my throat aches so bad. "I'm just tired, and I'm scared for Will."

"It's okay. She'll be okay, I promise you." He leans up to rest on his elbow, offering me a kiss of reassurance.

"Promise me that whatever happens, you will always be on her side," I beg him softly.

He frowns down at me. "You know I will. I love her. Of course I'll always be on her side."

I imagine how he is going to react when he finds out she might be gay and it makes more tears run down my face. He won't cope with it. I know he won't. I can't imagine how scared she must be.

He leans closer. "Hey," he whispers, pushing the hair back from my face. "What's causing all these tears?"

I shrug and force a smile.

"Roll over," he tells me.

I roll over so that my back is to him, and he wraps his arms around me and kisses my cheek. "Go to sleep, baby. You're delirious."

I feel so safe in his arms, and I close my eyes as he trails kisses over my shoulder.

"I love you," he murmurs into my hair.

Guilt hits me in the chest. "I love you too."

It's been two weeks since Will has been to school. The two girls who did it were expelled, but it doesn't really matter to us anymore. Joseph and Frances thankfully talked Julian into letting Willow leave that school, and now she is working at Masters Group as a trainee, and a tutor is coming in and doing lessons with her every afternoon. She's happy and smiling for the first time in a long time. Today is her first soccer game. She's not playing against any of the nasty girls, and we all agreed that her sporting activities are something she should never give up.

I sit in my fold-up chair next to Julian so we can watch the game.

"Julian?" Rebecca calls as she power walks over to us. "Have you been hiding from me, darling?" She rests her hand on his shoulder. "What are you doing tonight?"

My eyes flicker over to him and I give him the look. I'm sick of this bitch cracking on to my man in front of me.

Julian seems to get the hint. "Can you take your hand off me, please?" He sighs.

"What?" Her face falls in surprise.

"I don't like the way you touch me every time you talk to me," he mutters dryly.

I keep my eyes on the field and bite the inside of my mouth to stop myself from smiling. *Awkward.*

"Oh." She frowns, as if flustered. She straightens her shirt to try and regain her composure. "Well, what are you doing tonight?"

"I'm going out with my girlfriend."

I keep my eyes on the field, pretending not to listen.

"You have a girlfriend?" she asks, even more horrified than before.

"Yes."

"Who?"

"That's none of your business."

Her mouth falls open. She's never heard him be so blunt, and I just want to punch the air to celebrate.

"Oh." She frowns harder. "Well, it's not serious, is it?"

"Very. I'm completely off the market."

I can't help it. My smile does break through this time, and I stand in a rush. "I'm going to get coffee," I blurt out.

"I'll come too." Julian stands.

"Oh." Rebecca's face pales completely. "Catch you later, then, I suppose."

I walk towards the coffee van with my arms folded and my smile aimed at the ground.

"What are you smiling at, Miss Brielle?"

"I like that you're off the market, Mr. Masters."

He chuckles and raises his brow. "Surprisingly, so do I."

24

Brielle

Ten weeks later.

I WAKE to my body trembling, my orgasm close. The light of dawn is peeking through the side of my drapes. My legs are open, I'm naked, and Julian is eating his breakfast.

He does this often—wakes me up with an orgasm. My alarm clock is his tongue, and I am the luckiest bitch on the planet. My hands drop to the back of his head. "Good morning, Mr. Masters." I smile as I run my fingers through his hair.

"Good morning, my beautiful Bree," he whispers before he kisses my inner thigh. He spreads me open with his fingers and continues to suck.

God, he loves this. I've never been with a man who gives oral just because he craves it so much.

This is Julian's favorite thing, which means I've died and gone to heaven.

Knowing that I'm the only woman he's ever loved and the only woman whom he has had a real relationship with has taken our relationship to a higher level. It's as if nobody else came before me. He looks at me like I'm the only woman in the world.

He pushes my legs back to the mattress and slides two fingers in, making my back arch off the bed. I smile sleepily, knowing he's warming my body up to take his.

It turns out I'm in love with a sex maniac.

He fucks me every morning before he goes to work, and then he makes gentle love to me every single night. I get the best of both worlds. He's never had this, a body to call his own to do what he wants with, whenever he wants.

Maybe one day he'll tire of sex, but at this moment, my body is his absolute favorite thing, and he worships every inch of it.

He rides me hard with his hand, and I linger somewhere between awake and asleep. The morning light drifts through the crack in the drapes, and I smile to myself. How many mornings have I watched the sunrise with the feeling of intense pleasure between my legs?

He rises, leaning over me, and I can see the glimmer of my arousal on his lips as he looks down at me.

"How do you want me this morning, Mr. Masters?" I whisper.

He lifts both my legs over his shoulders, and then he slides in deep as his eyes hold mine. "I can feel every muscle inside of you," he whispers.

I take his face in my hands, rolling my lips as I watch him.

He spreads his knees to get better leverage and I close my eyes to try to deal with him. It's so deep like this. He's so focused on what he needs from my body. He starts to pump me with slow, deep, hard hits, and I can feel the muscles in his behind contracting as he flexes. My head falls back onto the pillows.

"Oh God," I whimper. "So good."

"You like that?" He turns his head and kisses my ankle.

I nod as I watch him, seeing his beautiful face in between my feet.

It's one hell of a wake-up call.

"What's my girl doing today?" he grinds out as he continues to ride me slowly.

"Hmm," I sigh. Fuck, who cares? This day is already perfect.

"Fuck, yeah. That feels so good." His eyes close as he starts to work his own orgasm into a frenzy, and he picks up the pace. His eyes darken and he hits me hard. "I just love fucking you."

I smile, knowing what's coming. Here he goes. He can only be gentle for so long before he starts to lose control.

His arms straighten and I can see every muscle flexing in his chest as he holds himself up.

My body begins to contract, and I grab his arms. "Oh God," I whimper. "Fuck me." I turn my head and kiss his wrist next to my head. "Give it to me, baby."

He hisses and starts to pound me. My sex clenches around him, and I scrunch my face up to stop myself from crying out.

"Fuck. Fuck. Fuck." He lurches forward and holds himself deep inside me. I feel his cock jerk as he ejaculates.

Then his lips take mine and he slowly lowers my legs. Our kiss is tender and beautiful, and I swear it's the reason I was born.

I'm so in love with this man, I can't even see straight. I cling to him.

"I love you," I whisper.

He smiles against my face. "I love you more."

Ding dong.

The doorbell rings.

Tillie tries to grab the laces out of my shoes as I walk to the door. "Tillie, cut it out," I scold her.

I open the door to find a delivery driver standing in front of me with the hugest bunch of red roses I've ever seen.

"Delivery for Miss Brielle Johnston?"

I grin. "That's me." I dance on the spot and take them from him. "Thank you."

I close the door and walk into the kitchen to lay them down on the table. The buds are huge and a deep red. Their perfume is strong and beautiful.

I open the small card.

Twelve weeks today since I told you
I love you.
The happiest twelve weeks of my life.
I still love you
Julian xx

I smile goofily as my eyes fill with tears. This man makes me weak at the knees. I take out my phone and text him, even though I know he's in court and can't speak.

Look at you getting sentimental.
I loved you long before that.
Thank you for my flowers.
Hurry home xoxox

"Would you like to dance?" my sexy date asks me from across the table.

I smile. "You know I would."

It's Saturday night, and Julian and I have the luxury of being out. Sammy is sleeping at his friend's house and Willow is at dinner and the movies with Lola. We're in a cocktail bar and lately, we've found a penchant for dancing. Julian stands, taking my hand in his to lead me to the dance floor. I put my arms around his neck. "Thank you." I smile up at him.

"For what?" His hands drop to my behind.

"Can you put your hands back on my waist, please?" I smirk. "There are other people here, you know."

He widens his eyes and places his hands back up to a respectable level. "That better?"

"Not really."

"Thank you for what, Bree?" he repeats.

"For showing me what it feels like."

He frowns down at me, clearly puzzled.

"To be loved wholeheartedly."

He chuckles and spins me around. "I think you mean wholedickedly."

I giggle. "That too." Our lips touch. He glances up and his face falls, making him step back from me immediately.

"What?" I frown as I look around.

"My parents are here."

"So?"

"So...we can't be on a fucking date," he whispers, dragging me to the back of the restaurant.

"They're going to have to find out about us eventually." I frown.

"No, they're not," he whispers angrily, pulling me toward the exit.

What?

He drags me from the restaurant and out to the car, not forgetting to open my door for me.

"I didn't want to go." I pout, annoyed.

"Well, we had to." He pushes me into the car, closes the door, runs to his side in a rush, and gets in.

"Why?"

"I don't want anyone to know about us." He starts the car.

"Why?" I frown over at him. "Are you ashamed of me?"

He scowls as if the very thought is ridiculous. "No, I'm not ashamed of you."

"Then what's the problem?" I snap.

"I don't want us to be a thing."

I glare at him as he drives. "Newsflash: we *are* a thing."

He glances at me, annoyed.

"You don't have a problem with us being a thing every morning with your dick out, do you?"

He rolls his eyes. "Stop being so crude."

I raise my eyebrows. "Crude?"

"Yes, crude."

"What's the problem with people knowing about us?"

"I just want to keep you to myself."

"For how long?"

He shrugs.

I watch him as he drives.

"Julian, we've been together for months now. We're in love. I want to tell the children."

His face pales, his eyes widening. "We are not telling the children. No way in hell!"

"Why not?"

"Because they will only get excited and think we're getting married."

My brain tries to catch up with what he just said. "Where exactly do you see this relationship going, Julian?"

His eyes find mine. "Don't start."

"Don't start?" I shake my head. "What do you fucking mean, don't start?"

"It means I'm not having this conversation."

"So that's it? As far as you're concerned, we're just going to keep going on like this?"

"Like what?" he snaps.

"Sneaking around."

"And what's wrong with that?"

Oh my God. I shake my head and stare out the front windscreen.

"What do you have in that head of yours, Bree?" he huffs.

My face falls and my anger begins to simmer. "Oh, I don't know. Maybe a future with a man who is actually proud to be seen with me."

"Don't start that fucking shit." He sneers. "You know how I feel about you."

"Fucking shit?" I repeat. "I don't know what part of '*I love you*' you don't understand, but I want to be with a man who one day has plans to maybe marry me."

He looks at me like I've gone completely mad. "I'm not marrying again. No way in hell am I ever getting married again, Brielle. Get that shit out of your head right fucking now." He grips the steering wheel and shakes his head. "So if that's what you want from a man, we should probably end it."

"What?" I gasp. I watch him for a moment as he grips the steering wheel with white-knuckle force.

"I am not going to be fucking controlled again with a wedding ring!" he yells.

My mouth falls open in shock. He's actually serious.

"What about children?" I ask, feeling my blood run cold. "Do you want more children?"

"I'm thirty-nine, Brielle."

"So?"

"I'm not having any more children. I'm too old."

My eyes instantly fill with tears. "Then what are we doing here?" I cry. "I thought we were in love?"

He falls silent and stares at the road. "And I thought you were happy with simply having me," he says flatly.

"I am happy with you, but what about my needs? I'm twenty-six. I've never been married, and I want my own children." I put my hands up to my chest. "I want your children *and* my children."

He inhales deeply, not saying another word. Julian keeps his eyes on the road and we drive home in silence.

When he parks the car, I get out and slam the door shut before I march inside. Willow and Lola are sitting on the sofa, watching television.

"Hello." I smile as I walk past them. "I'm beat. Going to bed."

I hear Julian put the keys down on the bench in the foyer as he walks in behind me.

"Hi, Dad," Willow calls. "What's wrong with Brell?"

"I don't know. I just picked her up on my way through. She was out with Emerson."

I close my eyes in disgust and walk into my bedroom. What a gutless wonder.

. . .

It's 2:00 a.m. when I feel my bed dip and Julian climb in behind me. I pretend I'm asleep. I don't want to talk to him. He wraps his arms around me from behind and kisses my hair.

"I can't sleep without you, baby," he whispers.

I close my eyes. If I open my mouth now, we're only going to fall into a huge screaming match. Maybe he just needs time to get his head around everything.

I suppose we've never had this conversation before. I just assumed that he knew I would want these things. I lie in the dark for a while, thinking. Maybe if I just let it lie for a while, he could come around to the idea. I roll over and face him.

We stare at each other in the darkness. "I'm not Alina, Julian."

"I know." He pulls me to him. "I never loved her."

My eyes fill with tears. "Yet she got to be your wife and have your children," I whisper.

He holds me tight and kisses my forehead. "I don't want to talk about this anymore, babe."

I close my eyes against his shoulder, and I know this conversation is far from over. "Me neither."

Julian

I'm sitting at the bar in a pub with Sebastian and Spencer. We're twenty-two years old, and it's the morning of my wedding. Dressed in our suits, we're ready for the church, but the mood is somber. They're trying to comfort me the best they can.

I'm devastated about what I'm about to do—for the way I fucked up everything.

If I were going to prison for life, I would be happier than I am right now.

I stare at a small droplet of beer that has spilt next to a coaster, and I release a shaky breath.

"Did you organize a honeymoon?" Spencer asks softly.

"Yeah." I shrug. "Scotland."

"How long are you going for?"

"A week." I sip my beer.

We all stay silent and stare straight ahead.

"Any luck, she'll fuck a Scotsman and ask you for a divorce," Seb offers.

I nod without emotion, and I close my eyes in regret. Another wave of nausea rolls through me. I've been throwing up all morning.

"Don't do this, Masters," Spencer begs. "This is the worst fucking decision you'll ever make."

Seb and he exchange looks. "She trapped you, man. She's after money. Just give it to her. Give her fucking all of it."

My eyes rise to meet his. We've had this conversation a million times. Even my parents have begged me not to go through with it.

"I'm not letting another man bring up my child," I tell them sadly.

"So you're sacrificing your whole fucking life for a baby that you don't even know?" Spence snaps in disgust.

"Yes."

"I don't think I can stand next to you and watch you do this," Seb says, his voice monotone.

I get a lump in my throat. "That's okay. You guys don't have to come if you don't want."

The driver arrives at the front door of the pub.

"We need to get going for the church or we'll be late," he says.

I nod, watching as he disappears out the door. My heart begins to hammer in my chest.

"Let's just fuck off," Spencer splutters, his panic rising. "We can go to the States. Yeah. We'll live there and you can send her money." He shakes his head. "Just don't fucking do this, Masters."

I drag myself off the stool.

Beep, beep.

I'm snapped back to the present by the car honking its horn behind me. I look up to see the traffic lights have now turned red, meaning I've completely missed them.

I'm on my way to work. The horror of my younger life has been playing heavily on my mind this week. It's as if I'm back there, dealing with it all over again.

The lights change, and I click into first gear to floor it. I can't go back there again.

Not now. Not ever.

Brielle

I'm sitting on the sofa as the movie plays on the television. It's Thursday night—date night—but we're home. I didn't get my email invitation this week, and that hurt. Sammy is snuggled up beside me while Will is lying on the floor. Julian is sitting in his wingback chair with his book, uninterested in what we are doing.

It's been a week since we had our fight about marriage and babies, and we haven't discussed it since. I'm too scared to bring the subject up.

Julian has pulled away from me; the force field is back up. His heart is locked safely back into the freezer, never to be defrosted. I know he's scared, terrified that he's going to be trapped in a loveless marriage again.

But that marriage would be to me, and it hurts that he doesn't trust me enough to let himself fall.

Maybe he will. Maybe he will come to me any day now, and the two of us can sit and openly talk about it. He can explain why he feels the way he does. But until he does, there's a huge elephant in the room, in our bed, everywhere between us.

"I'm going out with the boys tomorrow night straight from work," he says quietly as he continues to read his book.

I turn and watch him until he looks up at me, and I raise a brow in question.

"Mother will have the children, so you can go out if you wish."

"I don't want to go out."

His eyes hold mine. I just want to scream and call him a coward, but I'll only push him further away.

"I won't be late," he says after a moment.

I nod and turn back to the television. The lump in my throat hurts again as I try to hold in my tears. I can't stand this. Screaming, yelling, or anything would be better than this.

My mind goes to Alina. Is this what she dealt with? The silent treatment?

While he fucked prostitutes on the side.

Stop it.

I close my eyes in disgust. Stop thinking about her. This is different. He loves me. He wouldn't do that to me, I know he wouldn't.

Would he?

I kiss Sammy on the head. "I'm going to bed, baby." I stand. "Goodnight, Will," I say.

Julian doesn't say anything.

"Night, Brell," Will and Sammy call.

I walk into my room, get into the shower, and I cry.

I can't stop thinking about Alina and worrying that we're falling into that same pattern. He's hardly touched me in a week, and we haven't made love once.

He's pulled away from me without any regret.

I scrunch my eyes together and let the tears roll down my face.

My heart feels like it's being torn out of my body in slow motion.

Maybe my fairy tale is already over.

"Come on," I laugh as I run about outside with Tillie at the end of the driveway. It's 4:00 p.m. and Willow is still at work while Sammy is at his little friend's until later tonight, after dinner.

Julian came to my bed last night, and we made love. Well, not really. We basically fucked with no emotion attached to it. But I felt like he was sad too. We lay in silence after we were finished, clinging to each other, as if hoping the other one would take back what they said last week.

I can't take mine back because it's true, I do want children. I may not be gifted them by God's hand, but I want to at least try. I can live without marriage, but motherhood...not so much.

The mailman pulls up, and I smile and wave as he hands me the letters.

"How are you today?" he asks me.

"Fine, thanks." I smile. "It's a beautiful day."

"It is, it is. See you later."

"Come on, Tillie." I begin to walk back to the house as I flick through the envelopes. Boring, boring, boring. I come to a letter in cream paper.

Julian Masters

I turn the letter over to see who the sender is.

Dr Ellards Rosedale Clinic

Hmm, I wonder what that is? I continue to look at the letter as I walk back up to the house. I stop to take out my phone and I google Dr. Ellards, Rosedale Clinic.

Dr Edwards is the leading vasectomy specialist in London.

My heart roars, racing wildly in my chest. No. He wouldn't?

I run back to the house with the letter in my hand. I put it on the kitchen bench and stare at it.

My blood is pumping hard through my body as I begin to pace. Why is he getting a letter from this doctor? For fifteen minutes, I stare at it until curiosity gets the best of me and I tear open the envelope.

Mr. Masters,
Thank you for your enquiry this week regarding our vasectomy services.
Please find below a quote as requested.

Your initial appointment is on the 17th and then the procedure is booked for the 25th as requested.

The words go blurry as tears fill my eyes, and I put my hand over my mouth.

He's going to have a vasectomy without telling me. I stagger back in shock.

Oh...this hurts.

I grab the car keys and I get in the car with the letter in my hand. There's no thought as I tear down the driveway.

He wants a fight. He just fucking got one.

Brielle

I SPEED to the courthouse with my heart beating wildly the whole journey there. He wouldn't do this to me. I know he wouldn't.

He loves me.

Why am I even going to see him when I know that there must be a reasonable explanation for this? Maybe he's getting a reversal? Yes!

My eyes widen. Yes, of course.

My face falls. No, that's not it. We used condoms in the beginning because he was scared he was going to get me pregnant. If he'd already had a vasectomy, he wouldn't have been worried about that at all.

My stomach rolls and the tears well again. He's going out tonight with his friends. I can't deal with not knowing what's going on.

I need to talk to him.

I glance down at the letter on the seat. I screw up my face in tears and I sniff loudly.

He wouldn't.

I stop at the traffic lights and glance at my watch. Shit, hurry up. If I don't catch him as he's walking to his car, I won't know where he is, and I am not having this conversation over the phone. I need to see his face when I confront him.

I glance at the car next to me. The lady is looking at my crying face with a worried expression.

No, I'm not okay, bitch.

I shake my head and wipe my eyes with my forearm.

I know this has to be a misunderstanding. He wouldn't do this to me. Of course he wouldn't, because that would be the end of us and he knows that.

Please don't let this be the end of us.

I'm not ready to let him go.

Please, please, please, baby. Don't let this be true.

I turn into the underground parking lot and drive around until I see his car in his reserved parking space.

He's still here.

I park my car and get out with the letter gripped firmly in my hand. I glance down at my watch. It's 4:30 p.m. and he's finished for the day. He should be coming out at any moment. I walk over to his car and lean on it and wait.

Twenty minutes later, he appears, talking and walking beside another man in an expensive suit. I immediately stand up straight, my racing heart driving me wild. He glances up and frowns when he sees me.

"See you later," he says to his friend as he walks over to me. His eyes hold mine, and I know he can tell I've been crying. "What's up?" he asks.

I should say something intelligent, or ask a calm question—anything that will help me not look like a complete lunatic—but I just don't have it in me.

I hold up the letter. "You tell me."

He frowns, takes the letter out of my hand, and reads it. His eyes come back up to my face and he rubs his tongue over his teeth.

"You opened my mail?"

"Tell me it's not true," I whisper.

He closes his eyes and opens his car to throw his briefcase in his trunk, slamming it shut with an almighty thud. "This is not the time or place to discuss this," he says calmly.

"Is it *true*?" I scream, completely losing control.

He puts his hands into his suit pockets and swallows the lump in his throat. "Yes."

I stagger back from him, shocked.

"What?" I whisper. Pain shoots through my chest.

He raises his eyebrows and looks at me. "I told you... I don't want more children."

I stare at him in shock, his silhouette blurred because of my tears. "So you were going to just do this without telling me?" I whisper.

He drops his chin to his chest. "No, I was going to tell you."

"To make me leave?" I frown.

His haunted eyes rise to mine.

I screw up my face. "You said that you loved me," I whisper.

"I do."

I sob loudly, all my control gone.

He steps forward. "Bree, baby." He pauses. "We...we're at different stages of our lives. We want different things."

I frown, the tears still rolling down my face.

Is this happening?

"I can't give you what you want," he confesses sadly. "I wish I could. I just can't."

"Yes, you can," I whisper. "You just don't want to."

His jaw clenches. "You're right. I don't."

If he hit me with an axe, it would be less painful. I gasp as my chest constricts.

I step back from him. How can he knowingly hurt me like this? *Oh my God, I need to get away from him.*

He steps forward, taking me into his arms, and I screw up my face and let myself cry. My shoulders are shaking violently.

"Baby, listen to me," he whispers into my hair. "I love you. More than anything, I love you. But I can't go back there."

"I don't want you to go back there," I sob. "I'm not Alina, Julian. Stop punishing me for her mistakes."

"I don't want to hurt you."

Anger hits me all at once, and I pull out of his arms. "Well, you have!" I cry.

"It's my body," he snaps.

"It's mine too," I whisper. "How could you take away my chance of happiness without even talking to me about it?"

He presses his hand to his forehead, unable to give me an answer. I stare at him.

"I don't even know you," I whisper.

His face falls. "Don't say that."

"Where's the beautiful man I fell in love with?"

He gestures to himself. "He's right here."

"No." I shake my head in disgust. "Alina's husband is here, and I don't love him. He's a fucking coward."

His eyes well with tears. "Bree..."

I turn and walk to my car on autopilot. I've never been so hurt before in my life. Even my ex, the adultering prick, didn't hurt me this badly.

I start the car and drive out of the parking lot. Julian stands behind his car with his hands in his suit pockets, watching me, devoid of emotion.

I begin to howl, trying desperately to see the road through my tears.

That's it... We're done.

Julian

I walk into the bar to find my two best friends at the back booth, and I fall in beside them. My beer is already waiting for me.

"Hey." Seb smiles. "You look like fucking shit, man."

I roll my eyes. "Don't ask." I pick up my glass and drain it, quickly putting my hand up for another.

"What the fuck's wrong with you?"

"She wants marriage and babies."

They both frown and glance at each other.

"And?" Seb asks.

"I don't."

They both raise their eyebrows and sip their beer, afraid to comment.

I stare at the television on the wall with a huge lump in my throat as I picture her heartbroken face. I close my eyes and exhale heavily.

Seb is frowning when I look up again.

"I'm lost." He points his beer at me. "Why do you look so shit if you *don't* want marriage and babies?"

"Because I love *her*," I whisper.

They exchange looks and Seb holds out his hand. "Well... I mean, she is twenty-two."

"Twenty-six," I correct him.

"Of course she's going to want marriage and babies. Where the hell did you think this relationship was going to go?"

I rest my elbow on the table and drop my head into my hand. "I don't fucking know. Not here."

"I take it she didn't take the news too well?" Spencer asks.

"We argued about it last weekend." I sip my beer.

They both frown as they listen.

"Today she opened a confirmation letter for a vasectomy I had booked this week." I rub my hand through my hair.

"Ouch." Seb winces at Spencer. "That's got to hurt."

I close my eyes. "You should have seen her face," I whisper sadly.

"Fuck. If I were her, I would have given you the vasectomy on the spot with my knee," Spencer murmurs.

"He hasn't gone home yet. That's probably going to happen tonight."

They both chuckle at their stupid joke.

"What are you going to do?" Spencer asks.

Another round of drinks arrives.

The walls start to close in around me and I feel my chest tighten as I consider both my options. The thought of repeating what I've been through with Alina terrifies me so badly, it nearly brings on a panic attack.

But how am I supposed to live without Bree?

She's everything to me.

I drain my beer and stare at the television screen on the wall above us. Not that I can see it. All I see is Bree's heartbroken face. All I hear is the disappointment and sadness in her whispered voice. Her words come back to me.

Alina's husband is here, and I don't love him. He's a fucking coward.

I can't be here. I put my glass on the table and stand. "I've got to go home."

"I thought we were going out tonight?" Seb frowns.

"Yeah, I got bigger fucking worries than a night out with you two losers. Catch you later."

I don't remember getting home. I don't remember walking up the front steps or unlocking the door. I stand in the dark foyer and look around the silent house.

Is she here?

She's left already...

"Bree?" I call. No answer. "Bree?" I walk down to her room and open the door, peering in. "Bree?"

The boys could have been onto something about that castration. The shower is on, and I walk in to find her curled up in a ball, crying as the hot water runs over her.

My heart breaks. "Baby," I whisper.

I take off my clothes and climb in, immediately pulling her

onto my lap. "Shh," I whisper. "I'm sorry. I'm so sorry." I kiss her forehead as I hold her tightly and she cries on my chest. I can't stand seeing her this hurt. "It's okay. I won't get it. I won't get it, I promise," I whisper into her hair.

She clings to me and I hold her. I don't know how to make this better.

I don't want more children. I don't want marriage.

But I love her so much.

This is an impossible situation. One of us has to live a lie for the other to be happy.

Brielle

We sit in the bottom of the shower for over an hour, me on Julian's lap. He lets me cry as he whispers apologies for hurting me. I don't know how to deal with this, only that tonight he is back with me and isn't blocking me out like he has been for the last week.

"Come on," he mutters. "Let's get you out of here, you're going cold."

He pulls me to my feet and wraps his arms around me. I cling to him. I feel like we're close to the end of our time together, and I know he does too.

"Bree," he whispers.

I keep my head on his chest. "Look at me, baby."

I drag my eyes up to his and he takes my face in his hands. "I love you so much. Please know how much I love you."

I stare up at him, numb.

"I won't get a vasectomy." He kisses me softly. "I promise. Okay? I don't know what I was thinking. I freaked out and..." His voice trails off.

I nod, mollified for the moment.

"Just give me some time." He kisses me softly. "I just need some more time."

My eyes search his.

"Please?" he whispers. "I don't want to lose you. I can't stand seeing you like this."

I drop my head to his chest and he holds me tight. Maybe we *can* work through this.

"You hurt me," I whisper.

"I know." He presses another kiss to my lips. "I'm sorry."

Our kiss turns passionate and my face creases against his. It's been a long week of tension, and I've missed my man. Maybe we just needed to have it out and now things will be okay?

He wraps me in a towel and dries me before we move to lie down together on the bed.

He runs his fingers through my hair, never taking his eyes off me. He seems miles away. What's he thinking about? We're staring at each other as he dusts the backs of his fingers down my cheek, a small smile creeping onto his face

"What are you smiling at?" I ask.

"You." He leans in and kisses me. "Your lips go blue when you cry."

"That's the frostbite from your heart."

He smiles. "I deserved that."

"How is this going to work, Jules?"

He frowns. "I don't know." His eyes hold mine. "Do we have to decide now? Can't all these big decisions wait?"

"For what?"

He shrugs. "I don't know, but I feel like I've only just found you and we've been together for two minutes. Suddenly we have to make a decision on the rest of our lives." He shrugs. "What's the rush?"

"I don't want to fuck you in the dark, Julian. I want to love you in the light," I whisper. "I can't lie to Willow any longer." I shake my head. "Every time I lie to her, I die a little inside. She deserves the truth."

He exhales heavily and rolls onto his back, staring up at the ceiling.

Ding dong.

"Sammy," I whisper, sitting up. "He's getting dropped home. I completely forgot."

Julian jumps up, grabs his clothes, and throws them on. "You stay here, I'll sort it."

He disappears out of the room, closing the door behind him. I turn off the light and crawl under the blankets. My eyelids are so heavy. I'm exhausted from all my crying.

I close my eyes and try to forget today ever happened. If only.

I wake with a start to find Julian lying on his side, watching me.

"Hi," I whisper. I vaguely remember him crawling into bed late last night and wrapping himself around me as I slept.

"Hi." His gaze falls to my shoulder as if he's too ashamed to make eye contact. We say nothing for a while, until he eventually spits the words out like they're poison.

"I'm sorry."

"About what?"

"For last night." He pulls me close and holds me in his arms. "I shouldn't have gone out and left you."

I frown. *That's not what I'm upset about.* But I stay silent, unsure what to say.

"Bree. I just—" He pauses, searching my eyes. "I just—"

"You just *what*, Julian?"

"I don't know what you want me to say."

"How about you start with the truth?"

He swallows the lump in his throat as he watches me. "You know I love you. I don't want to lose you."

I watch him intently.

He frowns as he struggles with his words. He brushes the hair back from my forehead. "What's the rush?"

"There is no rush."

His eyes search mine as if he's hoping to read my mind. "On a scale of one to ten, how important are marriage and babies for you?" he asks softly.

I swallow the lump in my throat. "A hundred."

His face falls and he rolls to his back to look at the ceiling, exhaling heavily.

I watch him, and I feel guilty for pushing him when he's obviously not ready.

"Let's just leave it for the time being. We can come back to this subject in six months. You're right, we haven't been together long enough for this," I admit.

He listens, not saying a word.

I lean up on my elbow and kiss his lips. "Okay? We won't think about this for a while. I don't want to stress you out about this."

He purses his lips, and I get the feeling that the subject is already closed in his mind. I don't know what else to say, so I get up.

"Where are you going?"

"To shower." My eyes hold his, and after a moment, when he doesn't respond, I turn and walk into the bathroom, closing the door behind me.

I have no words for him. I don't know what to say.

Willow is sitting at the table, her face solemn. It's 6:00p.m. on Saturday night and Lola has just cancelled plans with her. She's clearly disappointed. Julian is cooking dinner and Sammy is in the bath.

"What's happening, pumpkin?" I ask as I blow into my coffee cup. "Nothing." She shrugs.

Julian glances at her, and then he frowns at me in question. I force a smile and shrug.

I've kept myself from Julian today and given myself time to lick my wounds. I'm still hurt. I keep wondering what would have happened if I hadn't found that letter. Would he have gone through with it?

It's going to take *me* some time to get over yesterday. I still can't believe he actually booked a vasectomy.

A little voice inside me keeps telling me that we really are incompatible. He has to be unhappy for me to be happy, and vice versa.

I have no idea what to do with this new information or how to feel about it.

I just know I can't deal with the thought of losing him, so I'm pushing it to the back of my mind to deal with later.

"Do you want to go see a movie and have some dinner tonight?" I ask Will. "Just the two of us?"

Her face lights up. "Really?"

I look at Julian. "Is that alright?"

He shrugs. "Yeah, if you want. Sam and I will watch a movie."

This could be just what I need, a night away to clear my mind. Willow smiles broadly and hunches her shoulders.

"Have a look what's on." I smile at Willow.

She excitedly takes out her phone and googles the movie timetable. "There's one on at nine. That would give us time to get dinner beforehand."

I smile at her excitement. "Okay."

She jumps off the chair excitedly.

"You're the best."

She runs off upstairs.

"I'm going to get ready."

I smile to myself. Julian comes over and places his hands on my shoulders. He bends and whispers into my ear, "She's right. You are the best."

I put my hand over his and smile sadly. "And you're still on my shit list."

"I wouldn't have gone through with it."

"But you thought about it." I sigh.

He bends and kisses my cheek. "I'll make it up to you when you get home."

"You are banned from my body," I whisper sadly. "Forever."

He turns my head and kisses my lips. "We'll see."

. . .

Willow and I walk out of the movie at 11:45 p.m. The movie was funny, and we laughed out loud the whole time. I needed this night with her to regroup. Our arms are linked as we walk back to the car.

"So what happened with Lola tonight?" I ask.

"To be honest, I think she's out with someone else."

I frown. "Why do you think that?"

"I was reading on her phone the other night after she fell asleep on the sofa at our house, and a message came through from a girl asking her to go to a club called Kitty Cats tonight."

I listen as I watch her. "Did you ask her about it?"

She shakes her head. "No."

"Why not?"

"I didn't want to be the jealous girlfriend."

"Maybe they're just friends?"

"No. I searched on Facebook and Instagram. They only became friends a week ago."

My face falls. "Oh."

"And then, when she messaged me tonight to cancel..." She shrugs again. "I don't know."

"Well, maybe she didn't go to this club Kitty Cats." I smile, offering her some hope.

She rolls her eyes. "God, I'm off dating already."

I widen my eyes. "That makes two of us." I sigh sadly.

We get into the car, and I glance across the road and see a hot pink neon sign.

KITTY CATS

My mouth falls open. "Oh, look, is that it?" I point.

Willow's eyes widen and she cranes her neck as we both peer through the front windscreen.

"Google it. See if it's the same place," I whisper.

She takes out her phone and reads the address out. "That's it. Gay and Lesbian bar. Kitty Cats."

384

We both stay silent as we watch a few groups of girls and boys walk in.

"I wish I knew if she was in there," Willow whispers.

"Yeah, I know, right. To be a fly on the wall."

We continue to watch on as people pile in.

"Can you go in and see if she's there?" she asks me.

"What?" I glance over at her.

"Can you just go in for five minutes and see if she's there? Please."

"What are you going to do while I'm in there?" I frown.

"Stay in the car. I'll lock the doors."

"And what are you going to do if she's in there with someone else?"

"Break up with her." She widens her eyes at me like I'm an idiot.

I scowl and cringe. "I don't think that's a good idea, Will. I don't want to leave you in the car."

"You'll be five minutes and the bouncers are right there. Nothing is going to happen to me. At least then I'll know for sure."

I think on it for a moment. How else will she find out if Lola is a snake? It's not like they know any of the same people. She could cheat on her for another two years until Will is old enough to go out, if she's that way inclined. I bite my thumbnail as I stare across the road.

"If I go in, I'm just going to do one lap of the club and that's it. If I don't see her, I'm coming out and we are leaving straight away."

"Yeah, okay," she says as she stares through the windscreen.

I glance over at her. "What do I do if I do see her with someone?"

Willow frowns. "Don't let her see you. Just leave."

I bite my bottom lip as I think on it. "Fine. I'll scope it out a bit." We both stare out the front window at the club in front of us. "Are you going to lose your shit if she's in there with her?"

She shrugs. "I'd rather know so I can break it off before she does." I exhale heavily.

"Yeah, okay." I grab my bag, take my phone out, and grip it in my hand. "Call me if you need me. I'll be five minutes... max."

She smiles and hugs me. "Thank you. You're the best."

"Wait. What do I do if a girl cracks on to *me*?" I whisper.

She smirks. "Tell them you're in love with my dad."

My mouth falls open.

She laughs softly. "I'm not stupid, Brell."

I raise my eyebrows. "At least one of us isn't." I sigh.

I have no idea what else to say, so I get out of the car, cross the road, and walk up to the doorway.

"Fifteen pounds, thanks," the doorman says flatly.

"Jeez," I mutter. "Expensive." I pull out my purse, pay the fee, and walk into the club. It's dark with a large dance floor in the middle. It's completely packed, mostly with girls.

Jesus, this scene is alive and kicking.

I look around and try to get my bearings. The song "*Let me Think About It*" by Freddy Le Grande is playing. I love this song, so I begin to groove a bit as I walk through the crowd. This song reminds me of my situation with Julian at the moment. *Let me think about it.*

Okay, focus. I'll just do one lap.

I'm not going to find her even if she is in here, anyway. It's completely packed. I begin to walk through the club to the beat of the music, looking around as I do. The dance floor is going off, and I smile as I watch the girls getting down and dirty as they dance.

This place is cool.

I get to the back corner, and all at once the music stops and the lights come on. What the hell? I frown as I look around.

A voice comes over the loudspeaker. "Identification check." Huh?

What the hell? I turn to walk out and see about twenty police checking identification at the door.

Jesus, it's a sting operation.

I push my way through the crowd, and I'm just about at the door when my eyes widen.

386

A policeman has a hold of Willow by the arm and he's dragging her towards the door.

What the fuck? I run after them. What in the hell is she doing in here? I told her to wait in the car. They bust through the front door as Willow struggles to break free.

"What are you doing?" I call. "She's with me."

"Show me your identification?" the policeman says to her. Oh no.

"I...I haven't got my wallet on me," she stammers.

"She's with me, we're leaving now anyway," I say as I grab Willow's arm. My heart is beating wildly.

The policeman jerks her backwards. "Not so fast. Give me your wallet," he snaps.

Willow slowly retrieves her wallet and passes it over.

The policeman goes through it and reads out her student card.

Willow Masters, Aged 16

"We got one," the policeman calls to his friend.

I shake my head frantically. "No, no. This is a mistake. She was just picking me up."

"Yeah, yeah. Sure, lady." He continues to drag Willow to the police car.

Willow's eyes are like saucers. She's petrified. "W-what are you doing with her?" I stammer.

"Taking her to the police station."

My eyes widen. "What for?"

"She's under arrest. Her parents will have to come get her." I shake my head.

"I'm her parent. I'll take her home now."

He pushes her into the back of the police car and takes out his cell phone to call the number on Willow's identification.

Oh my fucking God.

"Hello, this is Detective Rogers. Do you know a Willow Masters?" he asks.

He listens for a moment.

"No, she's fine," he snaps. "You'll have to come down to the police station and collect her."

"What for?" I hear Julian asking, as clear as day through the phone.

"She's just been caught underage in a gay nightclub." The blood drains from my face.

Holy.

Fucking.

Shit.

26

Brielle

I SIT in the police station waiting room, feeling nauseous. A sense of dread hangs over me like a storm cloud.

I fucked up. I fucked up *bad*. I'm supposed to be the adult here.

What a stupid mistake to make.

Why did I go inside that club? And why did Willow follow me? I would never have gone in there if I'd thought for one moment that she was going to come after me.

This is one big fucking nightmare. The door opens and Julian comes into sight. His eyes find mine across the room and he glares at me.

My stomach sinks. God.

"Hello, I'm here to collect my daughter, Willow Masters," he announces.

"Ah, yes," the policeman answers over the reception desk. His eyes rise up to Julian.

"Judge Masters. This is unexpected."

Julian glares at the policeman and I slump farther into my seat.

Fuck, the policeman knows who he is.

"Has she been charged with anything?" Julian asks.

"No, but she was found underage in a gay nightclub. It's mandatory that she be brought back here until a parent can collect her. You can sign her out now and take her home."

Julian's jaw clenches. "I see." His angry eyes flick to mine, and I sink into my seat again.

Fuck.

I twist my hands together in front of me.

He signs the paperwork in silence and the policeman disappears.

I peer up to see Julian is staring at me with his two hands tucked into his suit pockets, his face stony.

I stand and walk out the front door. I'm just going to wait outside for them both. It's dark, cold, quiet, and I stare at the pavement beneath my feet.

The door opens and Julian strides to the car.

"This way," he barks.

He opens the passenger door and I hang back.

"Willow can sit in the front."

"It's you I want to speak to," he says as his cold eyes hold mine.

"Thought you might." I swallow the lump in my throat, and Willow and I exchange glances.

I slide into the seat and gently close the door. Willow climbs into the backseat of the SUV.

He pulls out into the traffic and his furious eyes flick over to me.

"What the fuck, Brielle?" he shouts at the top of his voice as he hits the steering wheel with his open hand.

I jump in fright at the bang as his hand connects, and my eyes instantly fill with tears. "I'm sorry." I shake my head.

"This isn't her fault," Willow cries. "I followed her in. She didn't know I was coming behind her."

His eyes find his daughter's in the rearview mirror. "I thought you were going to the movies? What happened to the fucking movies, Willow?" he yells.

"Don't you swear at her!" I cry.

His furious eyes come back to me. "I will speak to *my* daughter however the fuck I want." He sneers.

Oh God, I've never seen him this angry. We drive in silence for a little while.

"What in the hell were you two doing in a gay bar?" I close my eyes. Dear God.

"We were looking for Lola," Willow tells him softly.

Julian frowns and his eyes rise to the mirror, back to his daughter. "Why would Lola be there?"

I drop my head.

"Because she's gay," Willow answers.

I roll my lips.

Julian's confused eyes turn to me, but I stay looking down at my hands in my lap. "Did you know this?"

I stay silent.

"Brielle!" he bellows. "Did you know this?"

"Yes," I admit.

"Why are you hanging out with a gay eighteen-year-old, Willow?" His concentration flickers between the road and the rearview mirror.

"Because I think I'm gay too."

I squeeze my eyes closed.

He hits the steering wheel with force. "You are not gay! You are fucking sixteen," he shouts.

Tears fill my eyes as I hear the hurt in his voice. He looks at me again. "Did you know about this?" I stare at him through tears.

"Did you...know?" he growls.

I nod.

He punches the steering wheel again. "You are not gay, Will. You are a child. You're just confused!" He turns his attention back to me. "How dare you not tell me this!"

I close my eyes, wishing this was over.

"Don't you blame her. She's the *only* one who supports me," Willow cries.

"I am your father!"

391

Tears roll down my face and I wipe them away as discreetly as I can.

"So let me get this straight. My daughter confides in you with some ridiculous pubescent revelation, and you decide the best way to handle it is to lie to me and take her to a gay nightclub."

I shake my head quickly. "It wasn't like that."

"That's exactly how it is," he screams like a madman.

"We weren't even going there, Dad. It was just near the car and I wanted to see if Lola was in there. Brielle went in to find her for me. I was supposed to wait in the car, but the doorman left, so I snuck in," Willow blurts out. The stress begins to get to her, and she starts to cry.

Julian grips the steering wheel, staring straight ahead, and his eyes fill with tears.

Oh, he's hurt.

"Julian," I whisper.

He shakes his head. "Don't."

Willow begins to sob in the backseat.

"It wasn't my secret to tell you," I whisper.

"She's *not*. Your. Daughter." He hits the wheel again. "Get it through your thick head. She will *never* be your daughter."

I watch him as we drive in complete silence. Sadness hits me like a freight train.

"You're right," I whisper. "She's not."

I stare through the front windscreen with my heart in my throat.

Willow's soft sobs can be heard through the car.

What am I doing here?

This isn't my family, and no matter how much I love them, I will always be an outsider.

He was right. We are on different paths.

Love just isn't enough. I can't change what I want and he can't change what he doesn't want. This is never going to work.

The tears roll down my face as we pull into the driveway.

Willow gets out of the car and slams the door. She disappears into the house and starts up the stairs before either of us can chase her.

"Willow," Julian calls.

She stops and turns on the step to look down at him.

"You are not gay. You *are* confused."

"Let her work this out for herself. Don't judge her," I say quietly.

"What?" He turns on me sharply. "What did you just say?"

"I said don't *judge* her!" I cry, the last of my patience fading away. "This is not a decision you can make for her. She is not a criminal in your courthouse, open for judgement." I shake my head, disgusted with him. "She's a young girl going through a very confusing time, and she needs your goddamn support."

He glares at me, contempt oozing from his every pore. "When she's eighteen we'll talk about it, and not a moment before."

My face falls. "She needs to talk to you about it now."

"What she needs is guidance from an adult who knows what they're fucking doing. She is too young to think about this right now. She doesn't need to label herself."

Our eyes are locked and his chest is rising as he struggles to remain in control.

"She should still be at fucking school, but I let you talk me into letting her leave when I knew it was wrong." He shakes his head, throwing his keys onto the sideboard. "You have no fucking idea what you're doing when it comes to parenting."

Something breaks inside of me.

I know what I have to do.

"Don't you talk to her like that. She's a much better parent to me than you are. I hate you!" Willow cries angrily.

Julian's face falls.

I look up to Will. "Don't speak to your father like that, Will. Go to bed. I'll see you Monday."

"Where are you going?" Will whispers in a panic.

Julian's eyes come back to mine.

"I'll still be your nanny, but I have to move out."

Julian lifts his chin defiantly.

"I'll work business hours to mind the children, but I won't be living here anymore."

Julian clenches his jaw in anger and points at me. "You leave me now and that's fucking it. We're done."

The lump in my throat hurts as I try to hold it in. "We were done long before we started, Julian," I whisper through tears.

His eyes hold mine.

I turn and walk to my bedroom.

"Brielle," he yells, and Willow cries as she runs up the stairs. "Brielle, get back here right now!"

Once inside, I lock my bedroom door and slide down the back of it to sit on the floor. I hear a glass smash as he completely loses his temper in the kitchen. All I can do is drop my face into my hands and cry.

I just need to be gone.

I zip my suitcase up slowly and look around my empty room. Five months of memories are coming to an end. I remember arriving and how excited I was to start my new adventure. It seems like a lifetime ago now. I get a vision of Julian sneaking into my room every night and the beautiful moments we shared...the love that he made me feel.

It hurts that this is how this story ends.

Not all love stories have happy endings.

I've cried all night, but I know this is right. I've known it since I opened that letter from the doctor.

I hear the beep of a horn outside, telling me my Uber has arrived. I've booked a hotel. In a cruel twist of fate, Emerson has had to go home this week, rather unexpectedly.

I'm all alone. If it wasn't for the children, I would be on the first plane back to Australia as well, but I can't leave Willow yet. I feel like she needs me now more than ever. At least for a short while. I just need to get through this weekend.

I pull my heavy case down the hall and find Julian sitting at the dining table.

His haunted eyes hold mine.

Don't look at me like that.

He stands abruptly. "Don't leave me," he says quietly.

I cup his face in my hands. "I have to."

He shakes his head. "We can work this out."

"No, baby, we can't." I kiss him softly on the lips. "I want you to be happy."

He puts his arms around me. "*You* make me happy."

"I don't. I make you feel obligated. Confused. Guilty. That's not happy."

He swallows the lump in his throat, and I know he knows I'm right.

"What am I going to do without you?" he whispers as he dusts the backs of his fingers down my face.

My eyes hold his. "Keep living with Alina's ghost and go back to your prostitutes. You're safe there."

He closes his eyes, and I take the opportunity to place a soft kiss on his lips. "I love you," I whisper.

His face creases against mine. Eventually, I pull out of his arms and drag my suitcase through the front door to the car. The driver gets out and puts it in the trunk.

I get into the car and stare out the window.

Julian doesn't come out to say goodbye. I look up and see Willow at her window, watching me leave. I give her a small wave, and I try my hardest to hold it together.

The driver gets into the car.

"Where will it be, Miss?"

Straight to hell?

Oh, wait. I'm already there.

Roses are red,
Violets are blue.
I'm in love with a broken man,

And there's nothing I can do.

They say everything has a reason, a lesson to learn.

Haven't I had enough fucking lessons? Haven't I had enough emotionally damaged men in my life already? When am I going to be someone's lesson? When will someone love me more than people from their past?

And what can I possibly learn from feeling this much pain? It's complete bullshit.

I stare at the hotel room's wall from my position on the uncomfortable bed. I haven't gotten out of it since I arrived yesterday.

It's been the longest twenty-four hours of my life.

I'm broken—so broken. I can't eat. I can't sleep. I wish I couldn't feel.

A week ago, I had a home, children to take care of, and naughty pets that chewed stuff up. I had a man who worshipped the ground that I walked on, but it was all some kind of optical illusion. They were never really mine.

They were borrowed... From Alina.

She still controls him from her grave. He still lives in the dark shadow she cast.

He always will.

I don't know if I've done the right thing by sticking around, and I'm dreading going back to the house tomorrow morning. I just know that I couldn't leave Will and Sam at this stage—not with a clear conscience. I need to prepare them for my final absence. I need to prepare myself to live without them.

I'm not ready to say goodbye yet. My chest physically hurts at the thought of not seeing them again.

Ever.

More tears roll down my face. I don't even try to wipe them away anymore. My pillow is soaking wet. If I let this poison seep out for long enough, then maybe the infection will start to heal and the pain will stop.

I won't feel so empty and cold. Alone.

. . .

The Uber pulls up out the front of the house at 6:45 a.m. sharp. I pay the driver and climb out. The front porch light is on, even though the sun is just coming up over the hills.

The air is getting colder, and a small cloud appears in front of me as I exhale.

I wring my hands in front of me, walk up the steps, and knock on the door.

Julian opens it swiftly.

"Hello," he says on autopilot.

I smile awkwardly. "Hi."

He steps back to let me in, walking into the kitchen without another word, and I close my eyes.

His force field is back on.

Probably a good thing, to be honest. This is hard enough as it is.

Heaven help me if he showed any real emotion now.

"Just take the car through the week," he says matter-of-factly. "I won't be needing it. On Fridays, I can drop you back home for the weekend. I'll have a car pick you up Monday mornings."

I nod and clench my hands by my sides. "Thank you."

He's wearing a navy suit with a crisp white shirt beneath it. Then there's the usual accessories: a grey tie, his immaculate black shoes, and his expensive watch. His dark hair is shaped to perfection, and that's when I know his controlled persona is fixed firmly back in place. He's freshly showered and his aftershave smells like things dreams are made of. It's the very same aftershave that got me in this trouble in the first place.

Damn it, I should have smashed that damn bottle the minute he caught me snooping in his bathroom cabinet. Perhaps it would have saved me a lot of heartbreak.

I watch him as my heart gets on her knees and begins to beg to be back in his arms.

Cut it out.

He watches his finger as he runs it along the edge of the kitchen counter as if he's contemplating saying something else.

His eyes finally rise up to mine. "I'll see you later, then."

I nod, unable to speak through the lump in my throat. He picks up his briefcase and walks out the front door, never looking back or giving me any indication of how he's feeling.

Sadness rolls over me.

I hope he feels as bad as I do.

Julian

I stare at the television on the wall, my mind a fog.

"Hey, Masters?"

I frown as I'm pulled from my thoughts. "What?"

"Jesus fucking Christ, I'm taking you to the vet. You need to be put down, you're so fucking miserable." Spencer tuts.

We're all in a bar, having lunch. My mind is anywhere but here with these two.

I force a smile on my face. "I'm fine."

"So, do you want to do that, then?"

"Do what?"

Spencer slaps his forehead and rolls his eyes. "Stay in Sussex for Andrew's wedding next weekend."

I frown. "Oh, I'm not going to that."

"You *just* said you were coming with us."

"Did I?" I exhale heavily and sip my beer. "I don't remember that."

"Why don't you want to come? Do you think you're going to combust into fire when you walk into the church or something?" Seb asks.

"We probably all will," Spence mutters sarcastically. "Do you reckon there're hookers in hell? Like, are we all just going to be naked, getting our rocks off down there or what?"

"Yeah, drag queens that are going to fuck you up the ass," Seb retorts as he sips his beer.

Spencer winces as he considers the prospect. "That would be hellish." He nods to himself. "Guess it makes sense."

I roll my eyes. Seriously. The conversations we have. "You two insult my intelligence."

They exchange looks.

"Of course we are going to be naked and fucking down there," I add, holding my hand up.

Spencer slaps the table. "Jolly good, then I'm down for hell."

"Are you coming to the wedding then, or not?" Seb asks.

"Not," I reply. "I hate weddings, you know that. I would rather go to a funeral than a wedding."

They roll their eyes at me.

"You need to go to a quack," Seb says. "You've got some serious fucking issues."

"Oh, like you don't," I hit back.

"No." He points at me. "I'm no longer married because my wife is a fucking slut who fucked our gardener."

"Here, here," Spencer cheers, holding his beer up. "Fucking slut."

I chuckle. Spencer hates Seb's ex-wife with a fiery passion.

"But you"—he shakes his head as he talks—"are walking around brokenhearted like a lovesick puppy, pining for a woman you love, who your children love, and most importantly, who loves you...all because you're too fucking gutless to marry her."

"I'm not gutless," I snap. "I just don't want to get married."

"Whatever," he grumbles. "Are you coming to the wedding or not?"

"Not." I sip my beer. "Stop pissing me off."

"When can I have my phone back?" Willow asks me.

I stare at her, expressionless. "When you're thirty."

She exhales heavily and sips her hot chocolate. We're sitting at the kitchen counter. It's late at night, and Samuel has already gone to bed. Willow has been hovering around me since Brielle left last week. It's like she knows I'm a man on the edge.

"Have you spoken to Brell yet?" she asks.

"No." I sip my hot chocolate.

"It wasn't her fault, Dad."

I nod once. I don't want to get into this with her.

"Why didn't you tell me you were in love with her?"

I shrug as I stare at the counter.

"You need to fix this. Call her and ask her to come back."

"Will, it's not that simple. I wish it was."

"Is this because she didn't tell you about me being gay?"

I frown. "You're not gay. Stop saying that." I shake my head, exasperated. "Will, if you were caught in a normal nightclub last week with an eighteen-year-old boy and you told me that you thought you were interested in him, I would have had the same reaction."

She watches me.

"If you came out and said to me, 'Dad, I'm a Republican now', I would tell you that you're too young to make that decision. If you came home and said, 'Dad, I'm an atheist now', I would tell you that you are too young to label yourself."

She frowns in confusion.

"Will." I sigh. "I'm not going to like the first person you date."

Her shoulders slump.

"I'm probably not going to like the second person you go out with, either, or the third. Maybe not even the fourth."

"Dad..."

"You know why?" I ask.

"Why?"

"Because until you find someone who loves you as much as I do, they will never be good enough."

She smiles softly.

"You're one in a million, and so, so special—too special for just anybody. And one day you will meet that person and they will love you. That's when I will finally be able to relax and you will have my blessing."

She takes my hand in hers and I kiss it.

"I don't care if that person is a man or woman, Will."

Tears fill her eyes.

"But I care that you're sixteen, and these are adult labels that you don't need to put on yourself yet. Why don't you just see how it turns out? Stop trying to analyze everything."

She smiles, and her eyes twinkle under the lights because of her tears.

"Okay?" I whisper.

She nods, and I put my arm around her and hug her. "You should go to bed. It's late."

She kisses me on the cheek and begins to walk off, suddenly turning back.

"Dad?"

I glance up. "Yes?"

"Brell loves you as much as I do, you know."

I drop my head and exhale heavily.

"She's special, Dad. Don't let her walk away."

I point to the stairs and she smiles, quickly turning and disappearing out of sight.

Don't let her walk away.

Too late. I already did.

Brielle

"Dad's home!" Sammy calls from his place at the window.

I fake a smile and get up to collect my bag. I have to leave as soon as he walks in so that I don't start blubbering like a baby and drop to my knees.

It's been two weeks since I left.

Two weeks without him.

I've moved in to Emerson's old apartment with Hank and his

flatmate. I even went out at the weekend. I had a shitty time and came home early, but hey, at least I tried.

Julian comes through the front door. His eyes find me across the room and I frown and snap mine away. I can't even make eye contact with him without getting tears in my eyes.

We haven't said one word to each other since I left. Not one that isn't about the children, anyway. Looking back, I have to wonder if he *ever really* loved me.

He doesn't seem affected at all. I'm over here dying of a broken heart, gasping for air, and he's looking like he just stepped out of a *Vogue* modelling shoot.

He's unaffected and totally in control.

My mind has started playing fucked-up games on me. Has he gone back to the brothel? The high-class hookers? His therapist—the one who sucks his dick without questions?

I'm going crazy. Today I even counted the condoms in his bathroom cabinet, just so I know if and how often he's had sex.

Why am I doing this to myself?

I need to leave, but I just can't. As soon as I'm stronger, I will. I promise I will.

I hug Willow and kiss her forehead. Then I kiss Sammy before I turn to Julian.

"See you tomorrow."

He nods and rolls his lips. It's like we don't even know each other anymore.

Maybe we never did.

Julian

ALINA MASTERS
1984 – 2013
Wife and beloved mother
In God's hands, we trust.

The rain pours down around my umbrella as I stare at her headstone.

Trapped.

I'm trapped in a sadness so deep, I don't know how to escape it. Every morning she comes to my house.

Every night I die a little when she leaves.

I read the words carved in front of me again.

ALINA MASTERS
1984 – 2013
Wife and beloved mother.
In God's hands, we trust.

I lean down and brush the dust from her name. I rearrange the pink lilies I've placed in the vase. I touch her face in the small oval photo, watching as she stares back at me, unblinking.

I step back and put my hands into the pockets of my black overcoat. I come here twice a week to pay my respects to a woman who gave me my children.

My wife.

A woman who was good. A woman who deserved a better man than the one she married.

I always blamed Alina for my sadness, but Brielle has taught me that my problem isn't Alina. My problem is me.

I don't know how to love a woman and not cause her pain. I see it every day. The look on Bree's face nearly breaks me.

As I stand here, I can feel the blood pumping through my veins. My body is working, keeping me alive, but my heart has completely stopped. I exhale heavily. I've got to stop this.

I can't go on feeling like the world is about to end. I frown as a realization dawns on me.

I need to do what makes me feel better. The only thing I know that works.

. . .

Half an hour later, I arrive at Madison's, my therapist.

I always leave here relaxed. I don't have to talk. I don't have to think. I don't have to feel. I walk through the front doors on autopilot.

"Good afternoon, Mr. Smith." Hayley, the receptionist, smiles. "Good to see you back, sir. It's been a while."

"It has."

"Would you like your normal room, sir?"

A frown creases my brow. "Yes."

"Just go up to the penthouse and someone will be with you in a moment."

I catch the elevator to the penthouse and pour myself a scotch.

I stare out of the smoked-glass windows that overlook London.

I hear the door click behind me, and I close my eyes, already regretting what I'm about to do.

"Hello," the feminine voice behind me says.

I turn to see Veronica, and my stomach drops. "Hello."

She's blonde and wearing a sexy black dress. She has a killer body—a body that has pleasured me many times before.

I sip my scotch with a shaky hand, my eyes holding hers. She kneels in front of me and begins to unfasten my belt. I swallow the lump in my throat.

She kisses my thigh.

"You like that?" she whispers.

I stay silent.

Her hand reaches for my cock and she strokes it three times. I clench my jaw.

Her lips brush the end of me. My cock jerks in appreciation and I close my eyes in disgust.

I see a vision of Bree. My beautiful Bree.

No.

I step back from her. "Stop."

She frowns. "I haven't even started yet." She crawls closer and I immediately step back again.

"Leave."

"What?" She frowns.

"I said *leave*," I whisper.

I turn my back to her and zip my pants back up.

I need to get out of here. I grab my wallet and my keys, and then I rush from the room. I hit the button on the elevator three times to try and make it arrive quicker. My heart is racing, and I'm losing control.

I fall into my car and put my head into my hands. Tears fill my eyes, and I sob out loud.

I'm in a dark place.

Help me.

Brielle

I'm sitting in the café with Frances. We have lunch twice a week.

I still adore her, despite it now being two months since Julian and I broke up.

I miss him every single day.

To the outside world, he seems fine, but I can see in his eyes that he's not.

I can't help him. He needs to work through this, whatever *this* is.

His mother told me he's been seeing a therapist twice a week, and not the kind who gets on her knees. A real one. One who I hope is getting through to him. I want him happy; he deserves to be happy.

My email pings.

Julian Masters
Requests the company of: Bree Johnston
Occasion: Conversation
Date: 31st September
Time: 7 p.m.

Place: Room 612, Rosewood London
Dress code: Ears

Dear God, he wants to talk.

27

Brielle

I RAISE my hand to knock on the door, hesitating and closing my eyes. I'm so nervous, I feel sick. I have no idea what today is about. Because it's here at our hotel, I'm hoping it may be about us on a personal level, but I'm well aware that he may just want to fire me without the children overhearing.

But it *is* our Thursday, and it is 7:00 p.m. I have hope.

I drop my shoulders, exhale, and knock.

Knock, knock, knock.

The door opens and there he stands, dressed in a navy suit. He towers over me as his big brown eyes hold mine.

"Hello," he says softly. "Thanks for coming."

He gestures to the room and I walk past him to step inside. My heart beats like crazy.

Being this close to him and the smell of his aftershave brings back so many memories. I can already feel the lump in my throat beginning to close over.

Don't cry.

Don't beg.

I wring my hands in front of me as his eyes hold mine.

"How are you?" he asks.

I nod, unable to speak properly. "I'm okay," I whisper in a barely there voice.

He runs his hand through his hair, his pause creating tension.

"Thank you for staying for the children." His eyes drop to the carpet. "It would have been easier for you to leave."

"I couldn't leave them."

His eyes rise to meet mine.

"But you left me."

"I had to."

"It's been...difficult," he admits.

"For me too." I tear up, unable to hold it in any longer. "I miss you," I whisper.

He presses his lips together and nods, clearly struggling to speak, but I feel that he has so much to say to me. The room is heavy and silent. I know I'm going to have to lead this conversation. He's clearly unable to. I take his hand in mine and lift it closer to my mouth.

He watches me. His eyes become glazed, his pain palpable.

My face falls at his upset. "Baby," I whisper as I take him in my arms. "Don't look at me like that." I hold him tight, and he clings to me as if his life depends on it.

"I can't fucking stand being without you," he whispers into my hair.

I smile sadly and kiss his lips. His face screws up against mine. "Oh, Julian," I whisper as I stare up at him, cupping his face in my hand. He's so hurt.

"I've been working through things, and..." His voice trails off. "I'm trying."

"I know you are."

Why am I doing this to us?

"I don't care." I shake my head. "I don't care if you don't want to marry me. I don't care if I don't have children. I just want you," I whisper through tears. "I can't live one more day without you," I breathe. "I just want you. I don't care about the other things anymore." I frown. "I'm sorry for doing this to us."

He stares at me as his eyes cloud over. "You would give up what you want for me?"

I nod. "I would."

"But you being happy is what makes me happy."

I smile softly. "I'll be happy as long as I'm with you and the kids. I don't need anything else."

His eyes hold mine, and then, without a word, he drops to his knee, and his shaking hands pull out a black velvet box.

My lips part as my world stops.

His breathing quivers and he looks up at me, filled with hope. "Brielle Johnston, will you marry me?" He opens the box to reveal a huge oval diamond ring.

My hands cover my mouth instantly.

"Please?" he whispers.

My eyes search his for a beat too long, and I drop to my knees in front of him. "W-what did you just say?"

He pulls my face to his. "Marry me, Bree." His face is filled with so much hope, and my heart melts at the sight of him.

"But you said..."

"Forget what I said." His hand cups my jaw and he presses his lips to mine. My cheeks are wet with tears. "I had no fucking idea what I was talking about back then."

He takes the ring out, and with his hand still shaking, he slides it onto my finger.

"Answer me, baby," he whispers.

I frown, confused, still ringing with shock, until reality finally catches up with me and I smile broadly. "Yes."

He stands, pulling me to my feet, and we kiss the best kiss we've ever had. I hold my hand up in the air to look at my ring.

It's huge—like, stupid huge—and I smile goofily.

Is this really happening?

"Do you like it?" he asks, uncharacteristically uncertain.

I shake my head in awe. "This doesn't look like the kind of ring a nanny would wear."

He smirks as he takes his jacket off and tosses it to the floor. "That's because you're not my nanny anymore."

My eyes hold his. "Then what am I?"

"You will be my wife, Mrs. Masters. You'll be the mother of our children." He kisses me softly. "The only woman I have ever loved."

Goose bumps scatter down my arms, and my throat feels dry.

Emotion overload.

I sob against his lips the second he kisses me.

"For God's sake, stop crying, woman, and just fuck me," he breathes against my mouth.

I giggle as he walks me back towards the bed, lifting my dress over my shoulders and unclipping my bra.

I stop suddenly. "Julian, did you have sex while we were apart?"

"No." He frowns. "But I can confirm that I now have carpel tunnel in my right wrist." His eyes have such a tender glow. "How the hell could I have sex with another woman when I belong to you?"

Another tear rolls down my face and he wipes it away with his thumb. "I promise you, baby, you will never shed another tear because of me again."

I nod, overwhelmed. He pulls the blankets back and lays me down, sliding my panties down my legs. His fingers gently circle through my sex before he slowly begins to undress himself.

Our eyes are locked.

His chest is broad, his stomach chiseled, and oh, how I've missed him.

He lies beside me and I pull the covers over us both. Julian takes me into his arms. The feeling of his warm body against mine is familiar. He's warm, hard, and so fucking perfect, I can hardly stand it.

"I missed you," he whispers.

We kiss and kiss and kiss, and I can feel how strong the love between us really is.

He pushes the hair back from my forehead to study my face. "The last eight weeks have been hell." He kisses me softly. "Every day when you left, you took a little piece of me with you."

I run my hands over his broad shoulders and up the back of his hair, never taking my eyes off him.

"It feels so good to be in your arms again," I tell him.

Our kiss turns desperate, and I can feel his erection against my legs as his body moves itself forward, trying to find its release.

"Now," I whisper, almost desperate. "I need you now."

He kisses me, and then his fingers find that spot between my legs.

He slides two in and I wince. "Careful," I breathe.

He watches me as he slowly pumps my body to prepare it for taking him again.

A rush of cream rises to meet him, and he smiles darkly down at me.

"There's my girl."

I smile, and he pushes my legs back, riding me a little longer with his hand. Then he rises above me and positions himself. He pushes in a little.

"Ouch." I wince.

"Relax." His lips take mine and he surges forward again.

Oh God, the burn. It's so good. I'm stretched to the max. I forgot how big he is.

"Open, baby. I need you open." He pushes my legs back to the mattress and moves forward with force, slicing through my body.

I throw my head back onto the pillow, and his dark eyes hold mine.

"Oh, fuck, yeah." He moans as his eyes roll back in his head.

He slides out and back in again, and I cling to him as our kiss turns desperate.

"I love you," I whimper.

Our breathing becomes ragged and he pumps me hard.

"Don't fucking leave me ever again," he whispers with a hard pump.

I shake my head. It's too good. I begin to thrash beneath him. Nobody can fuck like Julian Masters can.

He's a god.

"I won't, I promise," I pant.

His dark eyes hold mine and, as if he loses control and wants to punish me for hurting him so deeply, he lifts my legs up around his rib cage.

"Careful," I whimper.

He spreads his legs wide and begins to pump me deep and slow.

His arms straighten and his dark eyes penetrate mine.

His hair hangs over his forehead, forcing me to smile up at him. "I've missed you inside of me. I felt like I was dying without you."

The last of his resistance crumbles, and he begins to ride me hard, taking what he needs from my body.

"Come." He hits me hard as he watches his cock disappear into my body. "Come now," he growls.

And like the slave my body is to him, I convulse on cue. Julian holds himself deep, crying out as his own orgasm rips through him.

We pant and gasp for air, our hearts racing out of control.

Our lips meet. The kiss is soft, tender, and gentle. My beautiful man is finally back where he belongs.

"I love you," he whispers as he falls against me.

I hold him close and can't help but smile. "I love you, too, Mr. Masters."

"Dad's home!" Sammy calls from his place at the window.

Excitement instantly fills me. Julian had to go to work today, but we want to tell the children about our engagement together. I had to take my ring off and everything.

I stand in the kitchen with my nerves dancing in my stomach. As soon as he walks into the house, his eyes find me across the room and I melt.

I haven't seen that look from him in such a long time, and it feels so good.

It feels like home.

Willow is doing an assignment on the kitchen counter when Sammy rushes to meet him.

Julian walks in and puts his briefcase down. He seems nervous too.

"Hi, Will."

"Hi," she mumbles, distracted.

"I thought we might go out for dinner tonight," he says. "To celebrate," he adds.

Willow looks up from her assignment. "To celebrate what?"

He holds his hand out for me to take. I walk to him and he puts his arm around me. "We have some news."

Willow smiles instantly, but Sammy simply frowns as he looks between the three of us.

"Brielle and I are getting married."

Julian pulls me close to his body and kisses my forehead. The children stare at us in shock.

I wait for their reaction... And I wait.

And I wait.

Oh no. Aren't they happy?

"What?" Will frowns.

My eyes rise to Julian. I frown, unsure what to say.

"Brielle is going to be my wife. That means she'll be your step-mother. She'll be moving in to live with us," he explains.

They both look at each other, then us, and then each other again.

Finally, Willow screeches, "Yes!" She jumps from her chair and nearly knocks her father and I over as she wraps her arms around both of us. "Oh my God. I'm so happy. This is awesome."

I laugh at her excitement, and then my attention turns to the beautiful little boy in the room.

Sammy's face falls.

"What's wrong, baby?" I whisper.

"I don't want you to marry Dad."

I crouch down in front of him. "Why not?"

He twists his little hands in front of him. "Because if he gets cranky then you will leave."

I smile and Julian rolls his eyes. "No, I won't, baby. I like your dad... even when he's cranky."

Julian smirks.

"That's just who Dad is." I smile. "And I love him, faults and all. I'm not going anywhere."

Sammy smiles and looks between the two of us, a flicker of hope blooming in his little eyes. "Really?"

I nod. "Really."

He jumps up to kiss me and hugs Julian. "Where's your ring?" Julian asks.

I dig it out of my pocket and hand it to him. He slides it onto my finger as the children watch on in awe.

Julian kisses me softly. "Now you're really stuck with the three of us."

I giggle and pull the three of them into a group hug. "Where are we going to celebrate?" I ask.

"I don't know, but can I have some champagne?" Willow asks as she pulls out of the hug. "It *is* a celebration."

"Definitely not," Julian grumbles. "You're only—"

Willow cuts him off. "Yeah, yeah. I get it, Dad. I'm only sixteen."

The children are in bed, asleep. Julian and I are downstairs in the living room, lying on the sofa in each other's arms. I brought my essentials back for the weekend today and put them in my old room.

"Let's go to bed," Julian says with a tender kiss to my lips.

"Okay." I smile, stand, and go to walk to my room.

"Where are you going?"

"To my bedroom."

Julian shakes his head and his dark eyes hold mine. "Your bedroom is upstairs."

Time stands still.

He takes my hand and softly kisses the back of it before he leads me up the stairs at a torturously slow pace. We finally make it to his beautiful, luxurious suite.

He opens the walk-in robe. "This is your wardrobe."

I look in and smile because it's already cleared out and empty.

He takes me into the bathroom and opens up the bathroom cabinet—the one I got caught snooping through at the beginning of this whole story. "I've cleared your side out."

I smile cheekily. "Am I allowed to look in here now, Mr. Masters?" I tease.

Who knew all those months ago that this story would turn out like this? I certainly didn't.

He smiles and stands behind me, his lips dropping to my neck in reverence. I watch us in the mirror. Julian towers over me and is wrapped around me like a blanket.

He adores me. I can feel his love seeping through his touch.

"You can do whatever you want now, baby. This is your house, and we are your family."

I smile as my eyes tear up, and I turn to him. "Then I would like to go to bed and make love to my fiancé."

He kisses me softly. "Not for long." I frown.

"You have six weeks to organize the wedding."

I frown as our lips meet. "That's not enough time!"

"I'm not waiting any longer. I want you as my wife."

28

Julian

ALINA MASTERS

1984 – 2013

Wife and beloved mother.

In God's hands, we trust.

I stand at my wife's grave for the last time.

Spencer and Sebastian are by my side, and we're dressed in our black dinner suits.

It's my wedding day.

The guilt I feel is heavy. After today, Alina won't be my wife anymore.

Brielle will.

I lean down and brush the dust from her name. I rearrange the pink lilies I've just placed in the vase. I touch her face in the small oval photo as she stares back at me, unblinking.

I step back, put my hands in the pockets of my suit, and stare at her.

"You ready to go?" Spence asks.

"Yeah," I murmur, distracted. "Give me a minute, will you?"

They both turn and walk back to the car, leaving me, and I swallow the lump in my throat as I stare at the headstone.

"I'm getting married today, Alina," I whisper through tears.

"I'm sorry that you didn't get to find your true love." I lift my gaze to look at the surrounding graves. "I'm sorry I couldn't love you the way you deserved to be loved." I close my eyes. "I've been punishing myself for it for years. You deserved so much better than who I am." I frown. "Was," I correct myself.

"I was so angry at you for killing yourself. For leaving the children."

I smile. "They're beautiful. You should see how much they're flourishing. You'd be so proud of the young people they have become."

I drop my chin to my chest and frown. "I've been seeing a therapist who's helped me see the error of my ways in all of this. It was never your fault." I wince like I'm in physical pain as I push the words past my lips.

"I can't live in the dark anymore, Alina," I whisper. "She's my light, my love, my soul mate. Her name is Brielle, and I knew from the moment I met her that she was the one. You'd like her, I know you would. She loves the children as if they were her own."

I clench my jaw.

"But they're your children, you're their mother. You will always be their mother."

I sniff as I stare at her photo. She stares back at me, void of emotion, just...like she always did.

"They miss you."

Tears fill my eyes again.

"I'm going to bring them to see you soon, I just haven't been strong enough to do it yet." I toe the dirt with my shoe. I regret so many things that I haven't done to honor her memory.

"Thank you for giving me my children." I screw up my face in pain and swallow harshly, feeling the sting of it in my throat.

I turn to see Seb and Spence leaning on my car, waiting for me.

And I know I have to do it, I have to say goodbye to my wife for the last time. Tomorrow, she will be the children's mother. Brielle will be my wife.

I bend and brush my finger over her image, and then I kiss the cold, hard stone.

"Goodbye, Alina. Rest in peace, angel."

Brielle

Julian rocks forward onto his toes in anticipation and I smirk. We are holding hands and facing each other as the priest reads our marriage vows. He can hardly wait until this ceremony is over, and his eyes dance with mischief.

Who knew that Julian Masters would be so excited about getting married?

I know I certainly didn't.

He gives me a slow, sexy smile promising me carnal things, and I blush... I know that look. For goodness' sake, Julian, don't look at me like that in the house of God.

Willow and Emerson are beside me and Sebastian and Spencer and Samuel are beside him. We stand before all of our united family and friends, and the church is filled with love.

This is a happy day for all of us.

"I will." Julian smiles as he slides the gold wedding ring onto my finger.

He rocks forward onto his toes again as if happy with himself, and I giggle.

"By the powers vested in me, I now pronounce you man and wife. You may kiss your bride." The priest smiles.

In slow motion, Julian lifts my veil back and folds it over. This is it, our whole story is coming to a beautiful climax, right here right now.

My eyes fill with tears at just how intimate this moment is.

With his beautiful big brown eyes locked on mine, he slowly leans in, holds my face in his hands, and kisses me tenderly. It's the most perfect kiss he's ever gifted me, and my feet lift off the ground.

"I love you," he whispers.

I giggle against his lips, and the crowd all laugh and cheer.

I turn to see my mother sitting in the front row. She's so happy and smiling with her hand over her heart, and I smile right back through my tears. She told me all along that the love of my life was waiting somewhere for me.

And she was right.

He was.

EPILOGUE

Brielle

Eighteen Months Later.

"THIS WAY."

Julian leads me through the crowd, out onto the terrace. We're at a wedding with Sebastian and Spencer, and I am thirty-six weeks pregnant with our first child. The dinner and speeches are over and the dancing has begun. I'm wearing a grey strapless evening dress with silver strappy stilettos. My long dark hair is down and set in Hollywood curls. My makeup is natural, like always. Luckily, I have a husband who is digging the whole pregnancy thing. I've never felt sexier.

He can't get enough of me.

This is a high society wedding. Everyone who's anyone is here. The groom is a childhood snooty school friend of Julian's, as well as the boys.

Life's good—better than good. Willow and Sammy are doing great. They're so excited for our baby to arrive. Julian dotes on me hand and foot too.

"Do you want a drink, sweetheart?" he asks, his hand automatically dropping to my stomach. His eyes search mine. "You okay?"

I widen my eyes. "I'm fine, Julian. Will you stop worrying?"

He didn't want to come tonight because he thought it would be too much for me. He literally cannot talk to me anymore without having his hand on my stomach.

"Can I have a lemonade, please?" I ask.

"Of course." He points at his two friends as he walks off. "Don't leave her alone for one minute," he demands.

"Yeah, yeah." Spence rolls his eyes and turns his attention to me as Julian walks away. "God, Bree, you must be sick to death of him. He's like a fucking rash."

I giggle. "He's pretty full on."

Spencer and Sebastian have turned out to be special friends. They've welcomed me with open arms, and their lifelong group of three men has turned into a posse of three men and one woman. We laugh and joke all the time, and I feel totally at ease with the two of them. We do a lot together and they spend a great deal of time at our house with us. I think they're just so thrilled that Julian is finally happy, my pregnancy is now special to all three of them. Or it could simply be the fact that all of them are pushing forty now, and this is the first baby where they've had a friendship with the mother.

Either way, I now have three doting men around me.

Julian reappears through the crowd with my glass of lemonade.

He hands it over.

"Here, babe."

I blow him a kiss as I take it.

Spencer frowns and glances across the room. "Who in God's name is that?" He gasps.

Our eyes roam to where he's looking. We see a beautiful blonde woman wearing an ice-pink dress. She's throwing her head back as she's laughing. Her natural blonde hair cascades down her back, and she has the most beautiful set of dimples I have ever seen. She's absolutely stunning.

"That's Lady Charlotte," Julian tells him.

"Lady?" I frown. "She has a title?"

"Her father is the Earl of Nottingham."

"Really?" Spencer whispers, fascinated.

"Don't bother pursuing that one. She is well and truly out of your league, old boy." Julian takes a sip of his beer. "Her blood is too blue, even for you."

Spencer smiles and raises his eyebrows at Seb, totally accepting the silent challenge.

Julian kisses me on the lips and puts his hands around my waist. "Let's go, Mrs. Masters."

I smile up at him. "Okay."

"Why do you want to go?" Spence interrupts. "Stay here with us."

"Because the prospect of taking my beautiful wife home and doing unspeakable things to her body is a lot more appealing than staying here with you two," Julian says flatly. His sexy eyes hold mine, and I get a flutter of excitement in my heart.

I cup his cheek and give him a quick kiss.

"Lucky prick." Spencer frowns, keeping his eyes firmly on Lady Charlotte. "I need to get me some of this pregnant sex you keep going on about, Masters."

"Hmm." Julian smiles against my lips. "You'll need a woman to investigate that further, Spence."

Spencer purses his lips as he stares at the beautiful woman in the pink dress. "I do love a challenge. Maybe Lady Charlotte is dying to be impregnated tonight."

I giggle and Julian rolls his eyes.

"Or simply dying to get away from you," Seb mutters, taking a swift sip of his beer.

Spencer smiles mischievously. "I'll bet you two hundred pounds, Seb, that I have a date with her by this time next week."

Julian chuckles and shakes his hand. "Double it. Four hundred. You don't have a chance in hell with her."

"You're on." Seb smiles, shaking Spencer's hand.

Spencer's eyes dance with delight. "Deal."

Spencer kisses me on the cheek, his hands dropping to my stomach. "Goodbye, darling. Enjoy your unspeakable things." With his eyes firmly on Lady Charlotte, he disappears across the room, heading straight in her direction.

I kiss Seb and he rubs my stomach. "Goodbye, Breezer."

I smile. I have become very fond of this man.

"See you, Seb."

Julian shakes his hand and then leads me towards the door. "Time to go."

We walk out of the function centre and over to Julian's Porsche. He has a new one now. It's navy blue, and of course, it's the latest model.

He opens my door and helps me in.

Always a gentleman.

He pulls out onto the road and his eyes flash over to me as if he's waiting for something.

"Drive it like you stole it." I smile.

Without showing any emotion, he puts it into gear and hits top speed in five seconds flat. I laugh out loud as I'm thrown back into my seat.

I love the adrenaline rush it gives me.

Every time he does that, I'm reminded of the very first time I met Julian—the naughty man I love.

One Hour Later.

Julian hisses softly. "That's it, baby," he murmurs against my neck.

I'm on my side. Julian is nestled in behind me and has my top leg lifted over his forearm. His thick body is sliding in and out of mine. His hand rests protectively over my large stomach, and his lips roam from my jaw to my mouth.

Sex with him at the moment is gentle and tender, and the expression on his face as he tries to hold himself back from being rough is simply priceless.

He looks like he's in pain, sitting somewhere between ecstasy and hell. His hips start to pick up the pace and he holds me in position. I feel the burn of his cock and close my eyes, letting the pleasure take over.

"Oh, yeah," he groans against my neck. "That's it," he pants.

My body starts to shudder and he grips me tight.

"Don't come yet, babe," he begs. "Please."

When I come while pregnant, my body contracts so tightly that his body just climaxes instantly. He has no control. None. For the first time ever, he has absolutely no control, and it turns him inside out.

Maybe that's why he's so obsessed with pregnancy sex.

His thrusts get deeper and faster, and I close my eyes to try and hold it off. My breasts bounce as he grips me tight. It feels too good.

I throw my head back onto his shoulder and cry out as my body shudders, contracting hard. Julian jerks forward and comes deep inside my body.

He hisses as he slowly slides in and out to continue emptying himself, his lips making sure to find mine.

"I love you," he breathes against my open mouth.

I run my hand through his stubble. "I love you too."

Three Years Later.

ALINA MASTERS
1984 – 2013
Wife and beloved mother.
In God's hands, we trust.

I stand at the end of the grave with Henry on my hip. I'm now six months pregnant with our second child.

424

Willow has her arm linked through mine while Sammy is helping his father. I watch on as Julian leans down, brushes the dust from her name, and rearranges the pink lilies that Sammy has just placed in the vase. He touches her face in the small oval photo, and she stares back at all of us.

He steps away and puts his hands into the pockets of his suit, staring at her.

Things have changed. We have photos of Alina in the house now, and I encourage the children to speak of her openly and honestly. Willow has had some grief counselling, along with Julian. Sammy doesn't seem to need it. He was too young to have ever felt any connection or loss. I'm his mother now, and sometimes he slips up and calls me mum when we are alone.

Sammy takes my hand and smiles up at me. He is the light of my life.

We come to the cemetery often with the children, and I know Julian still comes alone sometimes too. He has never forgotten Alina. I know he says he never loved her, but on some level he did. She gave him his two greatest gifts, and he will be forever grateful that she went through with those pregnancies.

Henry struggles to get out of my arms, so I put him down and watch as he takes off across the cemetery.

"Henry," Julian calls. "Come back here, please."

"No!" Henry yells as he runs as fast as he can in the other direction.

Julian's eyes meet mine and I giggle. This child will be the death of him.

Henry is as wild as they come.

"Don't make me come and get you," Julian calls.

Henry keeps running, squealing with laughter.

Willow and I laugh as Julian shakes his head and takes off after him. We watch on as Julian scoops Henry up on the run, scolding him as he struggles to break free.

"I never thought I'd see the day when I was the good child." Willow smirks.

I kiss her temple and wrap my arm around her. "Pumpkin, that child would make the devil look well-behaved."

Two Years Later.

Julian is sprawled on the sofa, watching television with a four-month-old baby sleeping on his chest. We have five children now. Willow is twenty-one and blossoming. She is working for the Masters Group, as well as doing business and commerce at university. She's dated a few girls, but of course, none of them are good enough for Julian. She's hinted a few times that she may move out, but I won't let her yet. I want her close for a few more years. Julian has finally given in to my nagging, and we are building her an apartment above the garage. I can keep her close forever.

Sammy is thirteen and still the light of my life, even though he has gone completely girl crazy. Julian goes Hulk every now and then, throwing his PlayStation in the bin because he's been on it too much, but Sammy and I sneak it out when he goes to work the next day. Henry is five, and oh my God, this child was put on Earth to test us. He's silly, like me, but strong like Julian. He's the spitting image of his father, and even putting his shoes on can end up in World War III–like arguments. Things have to be done his way and *only* his way. Julian and he lock horns at least twice a day. Aaron, our angel baby, is nearly two. He's upstairs asleep and he is the absolute image of Sammy. Both in nature and looks. He has dark hair, a big smile, and he always wants to keep everyone happy.

And then we have baby Alexander. Another boy. High-maintenance and wants to be held all the time. It's rare if Julian doesn't have him in his arms.

The outside world knows Julian as the serious cranky judge.

But the children and I know better. He's a beautiful father and husband who adores and dotes on us all.

He's the glue that holds our family together. And we love him.

Julian Masters
Requests the company of :Bree Johnston
Occasion: Situation Inspection
Date: Thursday
Time: 7 p.m.
Place: Room 612, Rosewood London
Dress code: Bondage

I smile and knock on the hotel room's door. I still get my invitations for our Thursday nights every week. Julian isn't about to let that side of himself go.

When we are here, we aren't Mum and Dad with responsibilities.

He is Mr. Masters and I am his high-end call girl, and I fucking love it.

He makes me feel so alive in this room.

The door opens in a rush and he stands before me. Trademark navy suit, just-fucked hair with a wave in the top, and dominance oozing from every perfect pore.

His dark eyes hold mine and his tongue slides over his bottom lip in anticipation. My stomach still flutters every time.

He's just so... Perfect.

I'm wearing leather lingerie and an oversized coat. I have thigh-high black leather boots on, and my hair is set in a high ponytail. My red glossy lips finish the whole look. I really take my role-playing seriously these days. I know how much it means to both of us.

"Come in." He gestures to the room and I walk past him, stepping inside. I notice the whip and the baby oil on the bedside table instantly.

A thrill runs through me.

"Where would you like me, sir?" I ask as I take off my jacket. Our eyes meet.

He unzips his suit pants. "On your knees."

. . .

Read on for an excerpt of Mr Spencer...

MR SPENCER - EXCERPT
FULL BOOK AVAILABLE NOW

Chapter 1

Charlotte

Same fake people. Same stupid crowd. Same uninteresting men that I've known all my life.

"Isn't it?" a voice says.

Huh?

I drag my eyes back to the man standing in front of me. For the life of me, I can't remember his name, although I'm quite sure I should know it. He always tries his very best to impress me every time I run into him at one of these family events.

Which is often.

"I'm sorry, I didn't quite hear you. What did you say?"

"I said it's great to get to know you better." He smiles and tries to turn on his charm.

I smile awkwardly. "Yes. Yes, it is." My eyes roam up and down him. He's nice enough, I suppose. Tall, dark, handsome, and has all the factors that should excite me...but don't.

I'm so utterly bored, as if I'm a stranger standing on the outskirts, looking in at all the beautiful people around me. And I know I shouldn't feel that way, because according to society, I'm one of those beautiful people.

"And then I went to Harvard to study Law and graduated with honours, of course," the dull voice drones on.

I smile on cue and gaze around the room, doing anything to escape this boring conversation. I exhale heavily as my mind wanders. The wedding reception is beautiful—straight out of a story book. It's in an exotic location, there are fairy lights everywhere, lots of stunning fashion to admire, and anyone who is anyone is here.

Why doesn't this guy interest me? Nobody seems to anymore, and I've no idea what's wrong with me.

I widen my eyes at my friend, who is standing at the other side of the hall, silently calling for help. Thankfully, she takes the hint and walks over immediately.

"Charlotte." She smiles as she kisses my cheeks. "I've been looking all over for you." She turns her smile over to the poor man in front of me. "Can I steal her for a moment, please?"

His face falls and he purses his lips, nodding begrudgingly. "Of course."

I give him a small wave and link my arm through my friend's. We walk towards the hall.

"Thank God for that," I mutter under my breath.

"One of these days I'm not going to save you. He was all kinds of cute." She tuts as she grabs two glasses of champagne from a passing tray. I smile and take my glass from her, and then we stand just out of view of the man we escaped.

Lara is one of my closest friends. Our fathers have been best friends since childhood, so we kind of inherited each other by default. She's like a sister to me. Our families mix in the same social circles and we're at a lot of functions together. I don't get to see her as much as I would like to, as she lives in Cambridge now.

Then we have Elizabeth, our other friend. Elizabeth is the complete opposite of us. We met her at school, where she attended through a scholarship. Her parents don't have money, but boy, does Elizabeth know how to have fun without it. She's wild, carefree, and has grown up without the social restraints that Lara and I have. She can date whoever she wants, nobody is after her money, and nobody judges her. To be honest, I'm not sure that anybody judges Lara or me either, but our fathers are both very wealthy men, and with that privilege comes the responsibility of upholding the family's name and reputation. Both Lara and I would give our right arm to live the life Elizabeth has. Elizabeth—or Beth, as we call her—lives in London and is hopelessly in love with the idea of being in love. Although she can't seem to find the right man, she's having a whale of a time looking.

Me, however... Well, I've never really been interested in love. After my mother died unexpectedly in a car accident when I was eighteen, grief took over. My father and two brothers suffocated me in the name of protection. I went to school, hung with my girls, and regrouped for a few years. Somehow, time slipped away so quickly, and now here I am at the ripe old age of twenty-four and I've had hardly any experience with men at all.

"Oh, he's lovely," Lara whispers from behind her wineglass.

I look over and see a tall man with dark hair standing in the corner. "Aren't you seeing someone?" I ask Lara.

"He's lovely for you, I mean. Somebody around here has to look at the men on your behalf."

I roll my eyes.

"Surely someone here interests you?"

I look around the room that is alive with chatter, then over to the dance floor that is full. "Not really." I sigh.

Lara falls into a conversation with a woman next to us, effectively dismissing me, and I look around the decadent ballroom. I look up to the ceiling and the beautiful crystal chandeliers.

I love chandeliers. In fact, I love ceilings in general. If a room has a beautiful ceiling, I'm done for. As Lara continues to talk to the lady beside her, I glance through the crowd of people, and then I freeze instantly. On the top level is a man. He's talking to another two men and a heavily pregnant woman. He's wearing a perfectly fitting navy suit and a white shirt.

I watch him for a moment as he laughs freely, and I smile to myself. He looks like fun. Devilishly handsome and clearly older than me, he has fair hair that is slightly longer on the top. His jaw is square, and his cheeks are creased with dimples.

I wonder who he is.

I continue to look around the room, but my eyes keep coming back to him. He's telling a story and being all animated, using his hands to enhance his tale, and the three people he is with are all laughing loudly. A man walks past him, slaps him on the back and says something, and then they all laugh again. I sip my champagne, lost in thought.

Hmm.

I look over to the door and then glance at my watch. It's 10:40 p.m. I can't go home yet; it's too early. Honestly, I would rather have my teeth pulled than come to these events.

My eyes drift back to the interesting man, only this time I see that he's looking down my way. I snap my eyes away guiltily. I don't want him to know that I noticed him. I sip my champagne and stare back out over the crowd again, pretending to be busy.

Lara finishes her conversation and eventually turns back to me. "Who is that man over there?" I ask.

She frowns as she looks around. "Who?"

"The guy on the top level." I glance over and see he is still staring down my way. "Don't look now, because he is looking right at us," I whisper.

"Where?"

"He's up on the top level, talking to the pregnant woman."

"Oh." She smiles her sneaky smile. "That's Julian Masters. He's a judge. Damn fine specimen, isn't he? He was widowed once."

I glance up in time to see one man placing his hand on the woman's pregnant stomach before he kisses her on the cheek as she smiles lovingly up at him.

"That must be his new wife," Lara mutters, curling her lip in disgust. "Lucky bitch."

"I'm not talking about that guy. I mean the blonde man," I tell her.

She glances back up and her face falls. "Oh. That's..." She narrows her eyes and she thinks for a moment. "Yeah, that's Mr Spencer. Don't even bother looking at him."

"Why not?" I frown.

"Most eligible bachelor in London. An appalling rake." She raises an eyebrow. "He's loaded, from what I hear, and I don't mean his wallet is loaded."

My eyes widen. "Oh." I bite my bottom lip as my eyes find him across the crowd again. "How do you know that?" I whisper, my eyes unable to leave him.

"Page two of the gossip pages, and he's on the tip of every single woman's tongue in London. I do mean literally." She links her arm through mine. "He's a look-but-don't-touch kind of man. Don't even think about it."

"Of course," I whisper, distracted. "I wouldn't."

"He's probably seeing ten women at the moment. He dates power types. CEOs, fashion designers, models, women like that."

"Oh, I..." I shrug. "He's very good-looking, that's the only reason I asked. I'm not interested in him or anything."

"Good, because he's heartbreak dressed in a hot suit." She inhales sharply as she visually drinks him in. "He's most definitely fucking delicious, though, isn't he?"

I glance his way again and smile. Why are all the hot ones always players?

"Yep." I sigh as I drain my glass. "He sure is."

"Let's go back and talk to that nice guy. The poor man has been chasing you for months."

I glance back over at the guy and wince. "Let's not." I grab another champagne from a passing tray. "What the hell is his name, anyway?"

Spencer

"Do you want a drink, sweetheart?" he asks as he drops his hand to her pregnant stomach. "Are you okay?" he asks softly, thinking we can't hear.

Bree widens her eyes at my best friend. "I'm fine, Julian. Will you stop worrying?"

Sebastian and I exchange looks with a roll of our eyes. Good God, what has she done with my best friend, and who is this imposter standing in his place?

"I'll have a lemonade, please." Bree smiles.

"Don't leave her alone for a minute." Julian points to Seb and me before walking off through the crowd.

I roll my eyes. "Yeah, yeah. God, Bree, you must be sick to death of him. He's like a fucking rash."

Bree giggles. "He's pretty full on."

I smile at the wonderful woman in front of me. She has transformed my best friend Julian Masters' world, and I adore her for it. Julian reappears through the crowd with the drinks, and I glance down and see a woman in a pink dress. I've never seen her before.

"Who in God's name is that?" I ask as I study the perfect specimen.

"That's Lady Charlotte," Julian answers.

"Lady?" I frown. "She has a title?"

"Her father is the Earl of Nottingham."

"Really?" I reply, fascinated.

"Don't bother pursuing that one. She is well and truly out of your league, old boy." Julian takes a sip of his beer. "Her blood is too blue, even for you."

I watch the gorgeous creature talking and laughing with her friend.

"Let's go after these drinks, Mrs Masters," Julian says to his wife.

"Okay." She smiles.

I look over to my friends, annoyed. "Why do you want to go? Stay here with us."

"Because the prospect of taking my beautiful wife home and doing unspeakable things to her body is a lot more appealing than staying here with you."

I smirk at Masters. "Lucky prick." My eyes fall back to Lady Charlotte. "I need to get me some of this pregnant sex you keep talking about, Masters," I mutter.

"You'll need a willing woman for that, Spence," he replies.

My eyes go back down to the woman in the pink dress. "I do love a challenge. Maybe Lady Charlotte is dying to be impregnated tonight," I reply.

Julian rolls his eyes.

"Or simply dying to get away from you," Sebastian mutters.

I glance over to my dear friend. "I'll bet you two hundred pounds that I have a date with her by this time next week."

"Double it. Four hundred," snaps Masters. "You don't have a chance with her."

"Deal." I smile. My hands drop to Bree's pregnant stomach and I kiss her softly on the cheek. "Goodbye, darling. Enjoy your unspeakable things." I turn and head towards the woman in pink.

"Spencer!" I hear a woman call from behind me. I turn and see a brunette in a tight black dress. Sure, she's very attractive, but she's got nothing on Lady Charlotte.

"Hello." I smile.

She holds out her hand to mine. "I'm Linda." She hesitates. "We met at a Christmas party last year."

I fake a smile as I try to remember this woman. Nope, I've got nothing. "Yes, I remember," I lie. "How have you been?"

She beams instantly. "Great, although I do have a problem."

"What's that?" I frown.

"The plumbing in my room seems to have an issue."

"Really?" I smirk. There are hotel rooms at this resort, and she's obviously staying here.

"Really. I was wondering if you could come up and have a look at it after the wedding finishes."

I chuckle. Wow. That's the oldest trick in the book. "I am very good at unblocking pipes," I tease.

"I imagine you are." She giggles on cue and passes me a key. "Room 282." She smirks.

I smile down at her and stuff the key into my pocket. "If you'll excuse me, I have to see someone."

"Okay. I'll see you later." She grins.

Good grief.

I walk around the dance floor with my eyes glued to the woman in the pink dress. She's petite and curvy with the most perfect face I have ever seen. She's now talking to two men, with one on either side of her. One is older, while the other is close to my age. I sip my beer as I watch her move.

Hmm, she's fucking gorgeous and innately feminine.

She's also very different to my usual taste in women. She has a gentle air about her. I roll my lips as I watch her, and Brendan, an old school friend of mine, comes to stand next to me.

"Hey, Spence." He slaps me on the back.

"Who is that woman?" I ask, completely distracted.

He frowns. "Which one?"

"Pink dress. Charlotte."

His eyes widen, and he chuckles. "Stay away from that one, old boy. She's out of your league."

"And why would you say that?"

"Every man in the county is after her, and she won't give any of them the time of day."

I feel my skin prickle at the challenge. "Really?"

"Yes. And then you have to get past her father and brothers even if she is interested at all."

I frown. "What do you mean?"

"That's her father on the right. If I stand correct, he is the third wealthiest man in the country. He owns casinos around the world and has connections everywhere. On the left of her is her older brother Edward. Complete and utter bastard, that one."

I narrow my eyes as I watch him. "What does Edward do for a coin?"

"Guard Charlotte, from what I hear. He doesn't let her out of his sight. It's a full-time fucking job."

I raise my glass to him in a silent toast.

He shakes his head. "Not her, Spencer. She really is off-limits. Way too pure for you."

Excitement rolls over me. "The thrill of the chase is alive and well, my friend."

He chuckles. "Or the thrill of a death wish. You fuck around with her and her father will murder you without a second thought."

I smile as I turn to watch Charlotte talk to the two men. "Challenge accepted, old boy."

He laughs into his beer and shakes his head. "Next time I see you, it may be your funeral."

My eyes dance with delight. "Give me a good wrap in the eulogy, hey? I'm sure it will be worth it."

He chuckles, and with another shake of his head, he disappears through the crowd.

I stand on my own, simply watching her. She is the most beautiful thing I have seen in a very long time. At once, she glances up and her eyes fall on me, holding my gaze. I smile and raise my beer to her in a silent toast. She immediately looks away and fidgets with her hands in front of her.

I smile to myself as I watch her. Run along, boys.

I want her alone.

Charlotte

Mr Spencer smiles sexily and raises his glass in my direction. I bite my bottom lip nervously. Is he really doing that to me? He's standing alone in the crowd, a beer in one hand, his other hand tucked away in his expensive suit pocket. I snap my eyes away as my stomach flips with excitement.

Stop it! He's probably not even aiming it at me.

"Charlotte, I have someone I want you to meet," my father says.

"Dad, not now. I don't want to meet any of your boring friends." I sigh.

He rolls his eyes, and I glance back over at Mr Spencer still staring at me. I glance back up to my father. "What is it?" I ask with a huff.

"His name is Evan. I know his family, and he happens to be a lawyer."

I cringe. "Father, please," I moan. "Stop. I'm not dating one of your boring friends' sons."

My brother Edward looks at my father and scowls. "Yes, please stop. The thought makes me murderous."

I roll my eyes at my overbearing brother. "You too."

My father and Edward fall into conversation, leaving me to glance back over at Mr Spencer. As soon as our eyes connect, he crooks his finger and gestures for me to go to him.

Me?

I frown, look around, and point to my chest.

He nods with a sexy smile. I look around, instantly filled with some kind of guilt, and I subtly shake my head.

Oh my God. My stomach flips over.

He crooks his finger again, and I find myself biting my bottom lip and dropping my head to hide my smile.

"Would you like a drink, Charlotte?" my brother asks.

"Please." I smile as I concentrate on not looking Mr Spencer's way again.

My father falls into conversation with a man who walks past, and I glance around nervously. I'm not sure whether to go and talk to Mr Spencer or not. No, that's a bad idea. Perhaps I'll go and get some fresh air instead.

"I'm heading to the ladies'," I whisper to my father.

"All right, love." He smiles as I put my hand on his shoulder. I walk through the ballroom and out onto the back terrace and down the steps. Fairy lights are strewn across the garden, giving it a romantic feel. Waiters are circling the garden with trays of fancy cocktails and champagne. This wedding has been amazing, and the attention to detail has been impeccable. Every detail is perfect. I walk along the pathway down to the outdoor bathrooms. Once there, I head inside and close the door behind me.

Peace at last.

I can hear the music in the distance as I stare at my reflection in the mirror and reapply my fuchsia lipstick. My thick, shoulder-length blonde hair is down and pulled back on one side behind my ear. My pink strapless dress fits perfectly and clings to my curves. I roll my lips as I stare at my reflection. Eventually, I exhale heavily and snap my lipstick back into my silver clutch.

Most eligible bachelor in London, an appalling rake.

Great. The first man I've been attracted to in forever and he's a womaniser. Typical.

For once, I would like to meet an honourable man who is actually appealing.

Why does it have to be one or the other? Who made this godforsaken rule that any man who is a tad interesting must be a player? And why are all the good men boring as hell? God must definitely be a man.

With one last look at myself, I head back out into the garden and make my way up the path towards the party.

"Charlotte," a deep voice calls from behind me. I turn and falter, taken aback. It's him.

It's Mr Spencer.

He smiles sexily and his eyes hold mine.

"Hello." My heart rate spikes.

"H-hi." I smile nervously.

He steps towards me and takes my hand in his, and I inhale sharply. He holds my hand up in the air and nods, as if bowing.

"Forgive me for following you, but I had to come and meet the most beautiful woman in the room tonight." He kisses the back of my hand tenderly, and I raise my brows. "My name is Spencer." He smiles against my skin.

Oh, he's really quite...

I pull my hand away sharply. "I know who you are, Mr Spencer."

He smirks harder, and his mischievous eyes hold mine.

"You do?" he asks smoothly with a raise of his brow.

I clasp my hands nervously in front of me. "Your reputation precedes you."

His smirk breaks out into a broad smile. "Ah, you can't believe everything you hear, now, can you?"

His voice is deep and permeating. It somehow sinks into my bones when he speaks.

"Can I help you with something?" I ask. What the hell does he want?

"I hope so." He smiles and picks up my hand again. "Would you do me the honour of dancing with me?"

I swallow nervously, and he smiles and drops his lips to the back of my hand to kiss me softly. His sexy eyes stay fixed on mine.

Okay, hell...he's good. Really good.

"I..." I stop talking because I really can't concentrate when he's touching me.

He's so forward.

"Charlotte?" he repeats, pulling me out of my thoughts.

I shake my head in a fluster. "I don't think that's a good idea."

He turns my hand over to gently kiss the inside of my wrist. I feel his touch deep inside my stomach.

"Why not?" He gently licks my wrist, and my knees nearly buckle out from underneath me.

Oh, for the love of God!

"My father and brother..." I frown as my voice trails off. How in the hell am I supposed to string two words together when he's doing that to me?

He steps forward and takes me into his arms. "We'll dance here, then."

What?

He pulls me close to him, takes one of my hands in his, and smiles down at me as he begins to sway to the music.

"You're a wonderful dancer, Lady Charlotte." He smiles mischievously.

I smirk at his sheer audacity. "Does this routine work on every woman you meet?"

He smiles his first genuine smile, and I feel the effects of it hit me deep in my stomach. "Please don't talk about other women. I'm in the courting zone, concentrating on you and only you." He spins me around, and we both chuckle at his ridiculousness.

He lets me go and holds one hand up, and then he spins me in his arms and pulls me back to his body at force until we come face-to-face.

I stare up at him, my heart skipping a beat. "I have to go," I whisper.

"Why?" His intoxicating breath washes over my face.

"My father will be looking for me."

"How old are you, Lady Charlotte?"

"Too young for you, Mr Spencer."

He smiles softly. "I have no doubt." He bends down and softly kisses my lips.

My chest constricts.

He kisses me again, soft and tenderly, hovering his lips over mine. Unable to help it, I smile, and that's when he kisses me again but this time more urgently, his arms curling around my waist and bringing me to his body.

I've never been kissed like this.

His tongue sweeps through my open mouth and our tongues dance together.

For three whole minutes, I drink him in as we kiss like teenagers.

"Jesus fucking Christ, Charlotte," he gasps as he kisses me again.

I lose control and my hands go to his hair, and then I feel something hard up against my stomach.

Is that...?

I instantly pull out of the kiss and step back, panting for breath. He reaches for me again, but I step back farther. "Don't touch me!" I whisper sharply, holding my hand up in defence.

"What? Why?"

I shake my head. "I'm not the kind of girl you are used to, Mr Spencer."

He scowls hard. "And what kind of girl is that?"

"I'm not one of those high society sluts. Y-you should go back inside and find someone else to...entertain you," I stammer.

"I don't want anyone else!" he snaps. "If I overstepped the line, I apologise. I never... I mean..."

He's tripping over his words, confusing me.

I step back again, creating more distance. "You stepped over the line...by a lot." I glance up and I can see my father is out on the terrace, looking for me. "I have to go." I brush past Mr Spencer, walk up the path and up the stairs. My father smiles the second he sees me.

"Are you ready to leave, Charlotte?"

"Please," I say quietly. My eyes fall back down to the garden where Mr Spencer stands.

My father puts his arm around me and we walk around to the front of the house to get into the back of his Bentley. His driver shuts the door, and I peer out just in time to see Mr Spencer appearing from the shadows next to the house, watching me leave.

He smiles softly and blows me a kiss, and I drop my head at once, gripping my clutch on my lap.

"That was a great night, wasn't it?" My father smiles as the car slowly pulls out.

"It was." I force a smile. My fingertips rise to brush my lips, which still tingle from Mr Spencer's touch. I smile to myself softly.

No wonder he's the most eligible bachelor in London. He's perfect.

And he's trouble.

* To continue reading the paperback version of Mr. Spencer, find it in your favorite bookstores from September 2024.

AFTERWORD

**Thank you so much for reading and for your ongoing support.
I have the most beautiful readers in the whole world!**

Keep up to date with all the latest news and online discussions
by joining the Swan Squad VIP Facebook group and
discuss your favourite books with other readers.
@tlswanauthor

Visit my website for updates and new release information.
www.tlswanauthor.com

ABOUT THE AUTHOR

T L Swan is a Wall Street Journal and #1 Amazon Best Selling author. With millions of books sold, her titles are currently translated in twenty languages and have hit #1 on Amazon in the USA, UK, Canada, Australia and Germany. Tee resides on the South Coast of NSW, Australia with her husband and their three children where she is living her own happy ever after with her first true love.